VAMPIRE LEAGUE

Book I

Leap in the Dark

VAMPIRE LEAGUE

Book I

Leap in the Dark

by Luiza Dobrzynska

ALL MATERIAL CONTAINED HEREIN IS

COPYRIGHT © LUIZA DOBRZYNSKA 2020 ALL RIGHTS RESERVED.

***

TRANSLATED AND PUBLISHED IN ENGLISH WITH PERMISSION.

***

PAPERBACK ISBN: 978-1-7353456-4-2

EPUB ISBN: 978-1-3937802-5-0

***

WRITTEN BY LUIZA DOBRZYNSKA

PUBLISHED BY ROYAL HAWAIIAN PRESS

COVER ART BY TYRONE ROSHANTHA

TRANSLATED BY WIESLAWA MENTZEN

PUBLISHING ASSISTANCE: DOROTA RESZKE

***

FOR MORE WORKS BY THIS AUTHOR, PLEASE VISIT:

WWW.ROYALHAWAIIANPRESS.COM

***

VERSION NUMBER 1.00

PART 1
The Dance Macabre

"You will not find a happy one among the people of this land, until the death ends his life."

Gerard Phil read the sentence twice, then underlined it and put the copy of "The Trojan Women" on the table by the bed. He felt tired. In fact, he had felt worse since the surgery, even though the doctors assured him that everything was all right, and Anne repeated these words after them. He should believe them, he was in no pain after all, but he felt that they were not telling him something, and that his condition was not as good as they claimed. Sometimes he wanted to shake his wife hard and shout:

"What is it you are not telling me, Anne?! What are you silent about so stubbornly?! Why do you cry when you think I can't see you, and look at me so sadly when you think I'm asleep?!"

He did not even know whether he already knew the answer to these questions, or whether he was afraid to hear it, and most of all whether he was afraid to hear it from Anne, whom he had trusted absolutely so far. Everyone was surprised when he married her. He, the idol of women from all over the world, the movie beau with, as it was said, the beauty of an angel, he married just her, a tiny and unattractive divorcee with a small child, who was in addition three years older than him and not important in the world. And he knew why he did it: he simply loved her. She also loved him, they had belonged to each other since the beginning of the world. She was smart, sensitive and tender, with a deeply rooted sense of righteousness. They once swore that they would always tell each other the truth, no matter what it would be, and they never lied to each other... until now. Now everything changed, something separated them, he felt it and he was helpless.

Through the ajar door of his room, he could see the room in which she was sleeping, he saw her slim figure huddled on the bed, curled up in a fetal position, and he was overcome by a desperate desire to get up, go to her and explain what was unspoken once and for all. He knew full well that he would not do it, because he could no longer stand on his feet, so he only reached his hand to the lamp switch, but froze in the middle of the gesture.

It was Him sitting on the windowsill. He hadn't called any other way this strange person who had been haunting him since his stay in the clinic, a young man with sinister eyes and volcanic black hair, falling on his back and shoulders. He thought he was a delusion, born of painkillers he received, so he said nothing to anyone, but He appeared again and again, persistent like a thought, and stared at the actor with those eyes that were oblong like leaves and in the color of a gold tinfoil. For a delusion, he was terrifyingly real, and Gerard was starting to be afraid of him.

"What do you want from me?" He asked in a choked voice, against all logic, because talking to delusions makes no sense. "Why are you bothering me like this?"

The stranger moved and unexpectedly answered, thus providing the proof of his undeniable existence:

"I don't torment you, I just can't decide whether to make my offer to you or give up."

"What offer again? Why don't you let me go to sleep in peace?" Against his will, Gerard let himself get involved in the conversation, although he did not yet fully believe in the reality of the guest.

"You will fall asleep forever soon," He said with deep, piercing sadness. His voice was melodic and velvety, cool and hot at the same time.

"Your wife has deceived you," he continued. "Perhaps she thought she was doing you a favor, I don't know, anyway the doctors advised her so. She probably doesn't want you to suffer, so she prefers that death takes you unaware that you have to die."

"I have to?" Gerard asked in a choked whisper. He had suspected so, but confirming these guesses was a terrible experience, all the more terrible because it simultaneously made him aware of his wife's dishonesty. He didn't know what was worse for him.

"It's cancer, my poor Fanfan, and the most malignant one, adenoma. Nothing can help you, not in the current state of medicine. Today or tomorrow your exhausted body will finally give up. Ah, what a pity," the uninvited guest pulled his left knee up to his chin, and began to rock freely his other foot, hanging from the windowsill. "You won't ask why I am here?"

"So far, to torment me. I don't even know who is this person making fun of my agony," the actor answered him hatefully. Now that he knew the truth, he could clearly feel the cold breath of death at the nape of his neck, and fear he had never known before gripped his throat.

"Not at all, my little," said his guest with a benevolent smile. "I haven't even thought about it, what an idea. I am here to offer you a proposition, no big deal, a simple choice between the life and death. But to make this choice, you must first know who I am."

"Who? A demon? The devil himself?" the actor asked, scanning his black-dressed figure with a look that was not as much curious as it was terrified. He was beginning to guess, and although his suppositions were absurd, he shivered all over his body. A captivatingly beautiful, narrow face with a small nose, almost hook-like bent at the top, a surprisingly gentle line of lips with predatory features and those cat eyes, glistening from under angular eyebrows, did not have any humanity in it, though it was less ghostly than it could have been expected from someone making similar proposals.

"My name is Sinclair Radhjaleah," the newcomer narrowed his eyes. "But everybody calls me Never."

"Is it from English *'jamais'*?" Gerard interrupted him.

"No, from *nefferdin*, which means son of the devil in one of Arabic dialects," answered the guest. "I was called so in the East when I was still very young and I did not know how to, well, show restraint."

He smiled, showing white teeth, sharp as in a shark, much more numerous and narrower than human, with slightly longer, but not exaggerated fangs. They made his smile terrifying.

"Vampire," Gerard whispered. "I should have guessed right away. Why do you want to save my life, or rather make me be like you?"

Never jumped off the windowsill and straightened his entire black figure, excessively thin, but at the same time, with quite broad shoulders.

"I've been to all your films and plays," he said. "You are a great actor, boy, really great. In addition, you have a cute smiley face and beautiful green eyes, and this is my favorite color. Don't look at me like this, I don't have unusual tendencies, but of course it's a pity about all this, don't you think? I have followed your career and liked you, and this does not happen to me every day, so I'm asking: do you want to live?"

"Do you know anyone who would say no in my place?" Gerard asked despairingly.

"You may be surprised, but there are people like this," the uninvited guest leaned over him. "I want you to know that I will respect your decision, whatever it may be, although I will mourn you. I do not blame you for the distorted views on vampires, in the end you drew your knowledge from books and movies, and we have been slandered in them from the very beginning. Not everything is as you think, I can only tell you that, because there is no time for more detailed explanation. You are dying, my poor. What do you need that for? You will leave, to go who knows where. In a few days, your body will start to break down. This is the cruelty of nature that we elude, which is why people hate us so much that they would attribute any possible crime to us. And we are not bad, well, in any case not worse than the entire human tribe. Think, I am giving you a chance and death will not give you any. She is a cruel lady and nothing moves her. Make a choice."

"You're a real bastard," the actor whispered after a moment's silence. "Do you want me to die in suffering? Now I know why Anne didn't tell me anything."

He fell silent, trying to imagine what her life was like in these last days since she learned the truth. How did she live, day after day, hour after hour, smiling cheerfully, talking to him, editing hundreds of letters and answering the journalists' questions. And the children? He had not seen them since the surgery. She probably didn't want the two little elves to look at his death, and she was probably right. Suddenly, he missed them so much that it hurt.

Never did not take his golden eyes off him.

"I don't want you to suffer," he said gently. "I want you to make up your mind. What do you choose?"

Gerard closed his eyes, ran his hand over his forehead, and made a decision.

"I choose life," he said quietly and shook with a shiver, which he couldn't control. Never stroked his face with his fingers, slowly sliding them down to his neck, where an artery pulsed under the skin.

"Don't be afraid," he whispered tenderly. "It won't hurt. I'll just give you a little bit of my blood and you will get in a lethargy. They'll put you in a coffin and bury you, and I'll watch the cemetery in order to open your grave at the right time and free you from there. Remember, you won't be alone for a moment."

He leaned forward and Gerard felt a sharp prick on his neck. The pain was negligible, peculiarly pleasant, and the dying man's heart shrunk in despair at the thought that all his plans and hopes must end in such a way. He felt upset, not about Never, who was just taking away this pathetic remnant of his life that was still smoldering in him, but about his inexorable fate. The vampire carefully sucked a few drops of blood, tasting it with obvious pleasure, then dug his teeth into his own wrist.

"Drink," he commanded, putting his hand to Gerard's lips. The actor felt the salty, hot liquid fill his mouth, and the world dissolved before his eyes into the empty and dark silence.

* * * * *

He opened his eyes suddenly, like someone awakened by a jerk of the arm, or a violent shot above his head. There was silence all around, it smelled of wood, freshly dug earth and wilting flowers, the darkness was impenetrable. The sense of confinement made him realize that he was lying in a casket. He was overwhelmed by a feeling of growing panic, choking, his heart was pounding so hard that its beating sounded like a snare drum. At the same time, as if from a distance came a sound resembling a rasp, and then the murmur of the soil shoveled away. Shortly afterwards, an incredibly strong jerk tore off the lid of the casket, and Gerard saw Never's face above him.

He took a sharp breath from the space opened above him, and used all his willpower to control his trembling nerves. Never's strong hands helped him get out of the grave and stand on compacted ground between the rows of tombstones. The world around him was silent, except for the usual night noises, the stars blinked high above, occasionally obscured by small clouds, the darkness was transparent like a crystal to the vampire's eyes, so he could easily count the leaves on a nearby poplar. Somewhere nearby, a hunting owl roared, but otherwise it was soothingly quiet. Never tidied up the tomb with quick moves, putting the marble slab into its place and arranging in perfect order the bouquets of flowers, candles and wreaths, tied with three-colored ribbons.

"Well, that would be enough," he said finally, rising from his knees. "How are you feeling, kid?"

"I'm terribly hungry," Gerard confessed after a moment's hesitation.

The description he used was not entirely accurate. What he felt was a state between hunger, thirst and something like burning desire, and it could neither be completely defined nor described in words. For a novice like him, it was not easy to master.

"Yes, I know," Never said sympathetically. "I am sorry, you have to suffer a little longer. First of all, we have to get to Paris, and besides, we will have to get some clothes for you, because I guess you are not going to walk the streets like that?"

Only now did the actor notice how he was dressed.

"Oh my, this is my Cyd costume," he groaned. "I played Don Rodrigo in it. They must have dressed me in this rag for the casket. What a shame..."

Never laughed, amused at his face.

"They didn't think you'd get up again," he said with gruesome humor. "And if I predicted that they would put you to eternal sleep in these glittering clothes, I would bring you something to change into. And like this, I only have spare pants in my trunk. Well, we will manage somehow."

He unfastened a bowie knife, hidden in his sleeve, from his left forearm, and cut the puffy sleeves of the costume with it.

"Normal pants on the bottom and it can do. Come on," he said urgently.

Gerard followed him obediently, trying to somehow control the hunger that was tormenting him with terrible strength, which was however a futile effort. As soon as the night watchman with a flashlight appeared in his sight, the faint thread of reason broke under the pressure of a primal instinct, shuttering any moral objections he might have. He instantly jumped right next to the poor man and stunned him with a blow to the neck, inflicted with a force he never expected from himself. He knelt by the lying man, looking chaotically for something sharp, his teeth were still too short and blunt to use.

Unable to find anything, he hit the flashlight, which fell out of the guard's hand, against a stone, and slashed his neck with a piece of glass. Blood spurted on his hands. Trembling with impatience, he put his mouth to the cut artery, drinking in huge gulps the liquid nectar, for which he was so thirsty. The blood had a refreshing, wonderful taste of fresh strawberry juice, which should surprise him, but he didn't think about it. It was only when the flame consuming him from within began to dim, that he sobered and was terrified by what he had done. He raised his head. Never stood above him and looked at him with pity.

"Well, if you do things in this way somewhere in the city..." he said. "Now finish this pleasure, we have a long way to go and rather little time."

"And him?" Gerard asked, wiping his mouth with guilt. The older vampire shrugged.

"What about him? You bled him to death," he said. "You must learn to tame your appetite, because if you keep killing like this, you won't get far. Leave him and come."

The actor followed him obediently, oppressed by terrible remorse. Physically, he felt great, like a young god. He had not felt so good in a long time, after all, he had been feeling bad for some time already, even very bad, and in Mexico, where he was filming his last movie, and he could barely stand. In spite of the overwhelming feeling of health and strength, he felt terrible now. Here he was guilty of the death of an innocent man, and he barely rose from his grave, so what will be next? He didn't want to be a killer, and that aspect somehow escaped his attention when he accepted the vampire's offer.

"Don't worry," Never said, apparently guessing his thoughts. "I will teach you how to be full and not to leave behind a trail of corpses. We are in the twentieth century, if you remember. Get in the back seat, you have a bottle of water and a towel there, clean up in case the cops stop us."

He tossed him trousers from the trunk and sat behind the wheel of an elegant Royce, parked discreetly at the cemetery gate. Gerard pulled on the pants meekly, then wiped his face and hands with a wet towel, looking at himself in the mirror on the back of the chair.

"Hurry up," he murmured after a moment. "As far as I know, we should take refuge somewhere before the sunrise. It can kill us, can't it?"

"Don't worry, it's going to be a rainy day, and such days are safe for us," Never replied, driving quickly but with good feel. "The sun does not kill us, at least not immediately. Cloudy days are safe, and the rainy ones even more, it is all related to the level of melanin in the skin, or something equally moronic. I don't know exactly, Gusto takes care of these things, I've never had a head for science."

"Does it mean that the thing with aspen stakes is also nonsense?" Gerard asked after a moment, deciding that he was more or less clean, although his sweatshirt could not be completely cleaned of blood.

"Yes and no," Never shook his head reluctantly. "You see, many rumors about us are bullshit, total bullshit, but there is a grain of truth in some of them. You noticed yourself that you are reflecting in the mirror completely normally, I can also assure you that we do not grow bat-like snouts, we are not afraid of flowing water and we do not turn into dust like dried leaves after death. As for the stakes, certain kinds of wood resins are poisonous to us and the stakes made of these trees, embedded in the heart so that the blade passes exactly through the Sino atrial node, do kill. However, it is not the aspen that is the most dangerous for us, but rather the black alder, then the alder, and the aspen is only in the third place. Of course, it is important whether the wood is fresh or old and dry. For example, Tygier was already pegged twice, and he survived. The first time the Hunters made a 1 cm mistake in the calculations, and the second time he came across complete amateurs, they used oak, can you imagine, kid, oak! It's as if..."

He didn't finish and stepped on the brake pedal with all his might making the Royce jolt. In spite of this, they heard that something big hit the mask violently and was thrown aside. Never cursed and jumped out to the side of the road.

"Have you lost your mind, Fronda?!" He screamed, helping someone to get up. "You couldn't think of anything more idiotic?! You got bored or what?!"

He shoved a tall, shapely young man in the most fashionable cut of jeans and a navy blue shirt into the car. He sat back next to Gerard and smiled at him, brushing aside his way too long fringe. He had a nice, slightly square face with very delicate features, straight nose and beautifully outlined lips. His brows made for a more brutal accent, lying with heavy arches over wide-set oval eyes, in which cheerful sparks glowed. Despite this, their expression aroused the vague certainty that they were the eyes of a really young man a very long ago. And yet he looked like he was twenty something, no more.

"Don't be angry, Rajah, I'm not crazy," he said in a conciliatory tone. "Someone had to warn you about the ambush. You have to change the route and drive through Saint Germain Des Pres, and only Shadow and I had the courage to look for you. And Shadow wouldn't stop you."

"True," Never agreed.

Fronda looked at Gerard.

"Well, well, you managed to capture this comedian after all," he said. "I am happy. The idea was good, the implementation too, as I can see, but the time may not be the best. Wild hunt threatens us, and this one here is completely green."

"So what? I couldn't wait any longer, you know it better than I do, and you are the one having an affair with this nurse" the Indian grunted.

"I know, I know," Fronda waved a hand casually and turned to the actor. "I am an admirer of your talent. I've been to all your movies, to every play. Nobody can move every string in me like you. When, as Octave in The Moods of Marianne [1], you shouted, "Empty is my place on earth!" I cried, I swear.

Never burst out with laughter.

"Right. Don't believe his single word," he said. "He was a medieval knight, he may have cried at his birth, and even that is not sure."

"A medieval knight?" Gerard repeated, frowning at some memory.

Fronda nodded in agreement. The memory suddenly became clearer: an old trip to Chateauroux, a museum in an old castle, and a blackened portrait before which he stopped for a moment. The portrait depicted a young knight whose position could be determined only by a knight's belt with a sword, and a silver plate on a chain made of large, decorative links, because he was dressed in a simple sleeveless caftan, laced with a thin leather strap at the front. Gerard remembered that he had been looking for long at his face, beautiful even despite the medieval manner in the drawing, smoothly shaved, surrounded by black hair, falling on the forehead and covering the ears almost completely, which was not a fashionable hairstyle among knights at the time.

[1] The Moods of Marianne - play by Alfred de Musset

"Who is this?" he asked the curator.

"It's an uncatalogued painting," said the elderly man. "He lived in the fourteenth century, only that much is known about him, but there is a legend about this man among the inhabitants of this area. During the Hundred Years War, he was said to be someone like Robin Hood. They called him Messier la Fronde, from the slingshot he was supposed to use extremely skillfully. I don't know how much truth is there to it."

Encouraged by a flash of interest in the eyes of the famous actor, he told him several of these legends, while Gerard studied the portrait with fascination. So would it mean...? Something flashed under the shirt collar of this young man next to him. Gerard couldn't help himself. He reached and pulled out from under his shirt a medallion on a flat chain with decorative links, connected pivotally, exactly the same as in the portrait.

"I was right," he whispered, looking at the silver plate, though he didn't know why the cold metal was stinging his fingers unpleasantly. "It was you on the portrait in Chateauroux. French Robin Hood from the Hundred Years' War, Messier la Fronde from a folk legend."

Fronda laughed with delight.

"How astute... Fortunately, few people pay attention to this daub, although I admit that it is close to the original. My real name was Dideric. Call me Theo, like everyone else."

"Gee, you must be six hundred years old," Gerard sighed.

"Six hundred twenty-seven," Theo corrected him. "But it's not hard, you just need to wait. There are people older than me and no one is surprised."

He smiled warmly, revealing girl-like dimples. He was insanely handsome in this boyish way that women of all ages like, but most of all, teenagers. In addition, he had some capricious charm that made him likeable from the first moment.

"A knight, so probably a Christian... and how did you become a vampire? Never made you one?" Gerard asked incredulously.

"That would be a feat given that he is more than two hundred years younger than me," Fronda laughed. "No, my little, my master was someone else. A woman."

"Mademoiselle Pas de Chance," Never added.

"Pretty?" the actor asked after a while.

"It depends how you look at it, Fanfan," said Theo. "A bit strange, but definitely attractive. She was called the Black Lady of Sologne and considered slightly crazy because she walked at night rather than during the day, but her real name was Catherine. My banner was stationed near her castle, so we met... of course, it was after I was already pardoned, only to join the army anyway. Do you want me to tell you this story?"

"Sure," Gerard answered enthusiastically.

He loved such stories, although he never even dreamed that he would hear something like this "first hand". His curiosity apparently flattered the older vampire, who gave him a pleased look and began to talk:

"You see, I knew very well that I should not get involved in a relationship with Catherine in any way, but that is exactly why such a relationship was attractive to me. We were in war, and war flirts do not require long chases, so I took the opportunity without thinking about tomorrow. Before that, I had been hiding in the woods for four years, hunted like an animal, my life was one big fight. The possibility of being the knight of my king again made me dizzy and made me forget what hurt, as if it were not there at all. This was a mistake, because that is why I did not pay attention to how strangely Catherine was behaving, especially towards me. I think she chose me then already, but the battle that later took place near her castle, thwarted her plans. It was a fierce battle between our knights and the Black Prince troops. Without going into details, I will say that I was unlucky and my comrades-in-arms left me on the battlefield thinking I was dead. These were different times, there were no sanitary services or field hospitals, so I was just lying in the company of corpses and the dying, waiting for death, and it was a terrible waiting. When the sun set, she came."

"And she bit you?" Gerard risked.

He didn't yet know which topics were taboo among vampires, but this one apparently wasn't, because Fronda just shook his head.

"No," he replied. "I lost too much blood for her to risk the traditional procedure, so she just forced me to swallow her blood, and then she took me to a safe place. There, I licked my wounds for a long time, because the English cut me almost into slices, like a herring, but I recovered. And that's how it was. Oh, I almost forgot."

He knelt in the back seat and reached across the driver's seat into the glove box under the dashboard.

"Sit down properly," Never scolded him. "We are almost there, I would not like to attract the cops."

Theo returned to his seat and showed Gerard what he had reached for: a very old dagger with the same crest engraved on it, as on the plate.

"I found it recently at the museum," he said proudly. "It cost me half an hour of fear and an overnight chase down the streets to get it. I barely managed to lose the cops, I probably wouldn't be able to convince anyone that I just took something that belonged to me."

"You'll always get into something." Never turned across St. Germain Boulevard and drove into an alley. "Sometimes I have serious doubts about your mental health. To risk a life for some rusty shiv, one really has to be you."

"It's not just any rusty shiv, but the misericord I received from my father the day I was knighted," Theo looked at the dagger with nostalgia bordering on emotion.

"I've warned you before, don't get attached to objects. We get off here," said the Indian, stopping the Royce at the back of a small pub.

He looked around alertly.

"Nobody. We can come in", he opened the door with the key taken out of his pocket, and brought his friends somewhere down the winding stairs, through several floors separated from each other.

As it turned out, there was a kind of bedroom arranged at the very bottom - a spacious room with several beds, separated by curtains and screens. Most were already taken.

Theo went to the screen in the corner and pulled a curtain aside, revealing a low bed covered with animal skins.

"Hello, my cot," he said affectionately. "Did you miss me a lot? I am here now, dear cot..."

He lay down on the skins and closed the curtain.

"Gee," Gerard muttered.

"Don't get discouraged easily," Never consoled him. "Fronda is a freak, but what to expect from someone from the

Middle Ages? Meet others. This is Tygier, the one who reads "Nuclear Physics" is Gusto Vanderbelt, here lies Jyan Min, called Velvet, the one in leopard jacket is Jackie the Liar, and this is Saladin ibn Hakim. Others are sleeping anyway. And this, my friends, is our new companion, Gerard Phil, who is still too young to have a nickname.

"Glad to meet you", the introduced muttered without interest.

Gerard noticed that there were only men here, all without exception dark-haired, as if no other color of hair was present in this clan. He was too tired for other observations. Following Never's example, he found a free couch for himself and closed the screen behind him. Falling asleep, he managed to think that this all turned out strange, and then he fell into a light, restless sleep.

* * * * *

When he woke up, many of the hideout's guests had already gone out for their night escapade, and those who stayed, stretched lazily and yawned. Never handed Gerard a tall glass filled with dark red, cloudy liquid. Gerard tried it suspiciously and looked at him, not hiding his surprise.

"It's conserved blood," the older vampire explained to him. "We have our suppliers at every blood donation station. How else could we cope in these complicated times?"

Gerard nodded.

"I understand that," he said. "But tell me why I can clearly taste a strawberry?"

"Depending on your blood type, Rh factor and the donor's diet, you'll taste different flavors," said a vampire named Gusto, lifting himself on his elbow. "Your body has already started to adapt. Rajah, fill one for me, too."

Having received a full glass, he sat up and began to drink with gusto. He was not very tall, but built like a wrestler, with a long face of the cowboy from Marlboro ad, and curly hair, rather dark brown than black. He spoke with a clear German accent.

"Why are you rubbing your fingers like that?" he asked after a moment.

"They hurt as if they were burned," the actor confessed with some embarrassment. "I don't know what happened."

Gusto shrugged.

"You probably touched Fronda's medallion," he said. "It's silver, you must have gotten burned. Out of all of us, only Fronda is immune to this metal."

"But why?" Gerard asked curiously.

Gusto lost his confidence for a moment.

"I don't know," he confessed after a moment and stood up.

"Some scientist," came a malicious snort from the couch occupied by Tygier. "He became immune because he is damn stubborn and did not want to take this sheet off his neck for anything in this world. Wait, Gusto, I'm coming with you!"

Theo pushed back the curtain.

"Stubborn, my ass. This plate is my family heritage and the fact that I became a vampire, and in addition, against my will, is not a reason for me to part with it," he said rebelliously.

He took the bottle given to him and drank its contents, not bothering to pour the thick liquid into a glass.

"Do you always sleep here?" Gerard asked after a moment, following without interest the vampires leaving the hideout.

Never smiled.

"Not at all," he replied. "This is just one of the emergency points. We use them when the Hunters from Van Helsing

Institute... he is the vampire hunter from Dracula, they took his name for the logo of their institution... when they get active. Recently they tracked us down here, burned one of Gusto's studios and seriously threatened us all. It was an unfortunate coincidence with your initiation, but I had no choice. Fronda knew I was going to perpetuate you, so he followed me to warn us in time. After all, it was announced far and wide where you would be buried, so only a hopeless moron could confuse the way. I'm glad that we managed to get past the Hunters."

"Not quite, to be exact," Theo said lightly. "A Diana Huntress, an overzealous kid with a crossbow, caught me when I was leaving Erzika."

"Did you manage to warn Erzika's group?" the Hindu vampire was worried.

"Sure I did," his friend replied, uncapping another bottle. "And I gave Diana an anise kiss."

"I'm going crazy. Why anise?" groaned Gerard.

The knight in jeans took a sip and explained to him:

"That's the saying. This is because with the traditional blood donation, your victim feels the taste of anise, and with the usual kiss, of mint. It's a fun side effect." He chuckled as if it was something very funny.

"Strange," Gerard whispered.

"Strange indeed, but don't ask me what the mechanism of this phenomenon is. When you are in a romantic mood, you feel a taste of chocolate... like me right now. Dammit, I'll take a shower and go to Agnes, I am turned on."

He threw the empty bottle into the trash, smirked and walked behind the door, from where, after a while, came the sound of running water.

"Fronda is Mr. Squeaky Clean," Never said, listening to the sounds. "Others rarely wash themselves, taking advantage of the fact that our body does not emit any unpleasant odors regardless of the circumstances, and he just loves splashing in the water. When we once went to the sea, he was so happy he almost turned into a seal."

"Do you know each other well?" the actor asked after a while.

Never frowned slightly.

"Pretty well," he replied. "We're what Americans like Jack the Liar call 'sidekicks'. We've been together since the Napoleonic Wars and we've really gone through a lot. All right, get ready, we have to take care of you, Theo can do on his own."

"What do you mean, take care of me?" the actor asked, standing up obediently.

"Oh yes. We must give you a complete change of the so-called image" said Never. "You can't walk the streets with this outfit and hair, because that would be an overt provocation. Well, let's get to the apartment first, then I will think what can be done."

He looked at him critically. Gerard understood what he meant. He usually wore light or dark dress pants and a carefully ironed-on shirt in a matching color, sometimes a jacket, and a light trench coat on cooler days. Everyone knew him in this outfit, from Gibraltar to the Ural. The experienced vampire from distant India had already dealt with similar cases and knew well what a haircut and a properly selected outfit can do to change a man in the eyes of others. He stopped the car in front of a clothes store on their way, and after a while, left with a large package under his arm.

Then he took his younger friend to a large apartment, located in an old, half-ruined tenement, bearing the sign "A historic building, not to be demolished."

"They didn't get here," he said contentedly. "Otherwise, they would smash everything, you know, they are very careful in what they do. They destroy and burn everything with exemplary accuracy."

The apartment did not show any signs of an unexpected visit. It was arranged rather strangely, although in a way that did not lack a certain taste. The whole apartment was decorated in the shades of subdued navy blue and light purple, not overloaded with unnecessary furniture. The sleeping area was marked by a carved screen, a crystal chandelier of a peculiar shape hung from the ceiling - a kind of a multi-armed star, casting colorful flashes. In one corner there was a huge cabinet, full of books, in the other, an old-fashioned clavichord, and several large pillows lay on the dark purple carpet, replacing chairs in the eastern-like custom.

"The bathroom is there," Never said, pointing to the decorative door in one of the walls.

Gerard nodded and went there, taking on his way the towel and shaving kit, passed to him by Never. He did not want to see himself in the mirror, which showed him with brutal clarity a bony body, half-translucent skin with veins showing on the temples, bloodless lips and the thin face in which only the emerald green eyes shone as in the old times. How could he not have noticed before that he was in really bad condition? Maybe he didn't want to see it? His wife saw it for sure, so he couldn't understand why she was silent, letting him die unaware. After all, they had once promised that they would always be honest with each other, regardless of the circumstances.

"I wonder since when I look like a ghost," he thought bitterly, unwrapping the soap from its packaging. He shouldn't really care, but on the bottom of his heart, he had a secret attachment to his looks, and wanted to preserve it. After all, it was his face, not a great talent, which won him crowds of admirers of both sexes, he was well aware of this, and accepted it a long time ago. Few viewers, both cinema and theater, are able to really recognize the talent of acting, in fact only directors and a handful of those critics who really know their job can appreciate it. The overwhelming majority of people just need a pretty face, a shapely figure and an engaging way of playing. And if such an actor has enough sense to choose those from among the numerous offers that really hide good opportunities, he was assured of success regardless of the presence or lack of a bigger talent. This, of course, was only true for the film, because a stage hates dilettantes and immediately exposes them. However, also there hardly any viewers can distinguish between a decent actor and an excellent one.

Gerard washed thoroughly with soap with a faint jasmine scent, shaved and combed his definitely too long hair, after which he decided not to think about what had been anymore, but to focus only on what is or will be. That was the most reasonable thing to do. When he left the bathroom, he found new clothes hung next to the door - a cherry T-shirt, fastened with three buttons in the front, narrow jeans, shiny shoes with elongated pointed front, and a leather biker jacket.

"A fashion show," he said loudly, wiping the water off his hair with a towel. "If my friends and industry colleagues saw me like that, I would probably have to leave the country secretly."

Never came out from behind the screen.

"Don't whine," he said. "Sit down, I'll cut your hair and make some masking hairstyle. You need to have a more neutral look, because the whole thing can end up with a total flop before we count to three."

* * * * *

"Have you ever seen your Black Lady again?" Gerard asked as he and Theo played another chess game. The medieval knight liked this game, although he learned it relatively recently, only about a hundred years ago. Never rarely wanted to play with him, especially since he did not play well and did not like to lose. In the past, Theo had a good partner, a certain Sven Bergstrand, a Norwegian, supposedly an excellent companion and a chess champion, but it did not last long. Sven was killed in a clash with Hunters, and this because of his own stupid mistake. Fronda did not like to talk about it, just as he did not want to mention any of his friends lost in similar circumstances. However, he could talk for hours on many topics, even without being asked to.

"Never," the knight replied, unconsciously playing with one of the pawns. "I ran away from her as soon as I could stand up, and hid in a forest where she couldn't find me. The Sologne woods were dense and extensive at the time, and one could be hiding there until the end of the world. You have to understand me, son, I was firmly convinced that Catherine condemned me to eternal damnation and I was more afraid than ever before. I was crazy with terror and loneliness, so I hid from people, until I finally joined a pack of wolves."

"You kidding me, brother," the actor looked at him in amazement.

"As I live and breathe" Theo hit his fist on his chest. "I'm not kidding, kid. I spent many years running with wolves. They accepted me easily, and in addition my help was often useful to them."

"Horror," Gerard sighed, shaking his head in disbelief.

"Better watch your queen," his friend advised maliciously. "Why horror? I did nothing wrong. I played with the wolf pups, cared for wounded paws of the adults, and in the spring I howled at the moon. Don't stare at me like that, my wolf companions simply went ape crazy then, so what, was I supposed to be different? It wasn't such a bad life after all. But the years went by and nothing happened, and one day I realized that no devil would come for my immortal soul, at least as long as I live. Then I left the woods. But the world around me had changed, my friends were dead, and the Black Lady disappeared without a trace. Suddenly I realized that I was alone, completely alone, and that I had to learn to live again: to eat but not kill, and to hide from people that I was different.

Then, for the first time, I began to feel sorry for homosexuals, whom I had condemned for years, like my contemporaries did, and whom I watched indifferently as they were burned at the stake. I understood what it meant to be different and hide it, trembling so that it would not get out. I had to learn it without anyone's help, because at that time I could not use psych location yet, and use it to find people like me, and still a big question remained whether they would like to help me. In those days, each of us existed on our own and nobody trusted anyone. There were only some bonds between a student and a master, and those I rejected voluntarily. Fortunately, I immediately knew with some sixth sense that the blood of animals can hurt me, and I did not touch it, but other matters... Do you know what all this was like for a man of faith? One big nightmare. I am still not sure I will not face hell after death (eventually it will come)."

"For now, you are facing something completely different, my French Robin Hood," said Gerard. "Check, my dear. And mate."

Theo's eyes widened and he was speechless as he stared at the board.

"Damn you, you sneaked up on me," he said finally with admiration. "Lapinsky castling, well, well, I didn't suspect you knew this move. Never mind, I'll show you how it's done in a minute."

He collected the figures from the board and put them up again. A door slammed in the corridor, and Never marched into the apartment with a bundle of daily newspapers.

"The sun is high and you are still at chess?" He asked. "Well, maybe I exaggerated, not high, but it rises. Leave this fun for tomorrow and go to sleep."

Fronda stretched, casually swept the chess pieces into the box and went to the bathroom. He always took a shower before going to bed and after getting out of it. He loved it.

"In his day, to take a bath, you had to plunge into a river or a lake, unless someone lived by chance in a city where there was a bathhouse," Never once said to Gerard. "And in the winter it was not possible at all. Theo says sometimes that people don't even know these days how comfortable they are. He himself has always been fairly clean, and when the showers came into mass production, he almost went crazy with happiness."

Gerard waited patiently for his turn, then bathed and went behind the screen. Never was sleeping already, curled up under a blanket, making up for the last week, when he lived very intensely. He could go amazingly long without sleep, and also now you could bet two or three hours would be enough for him. Theo read Technical Review by the night lamp. He bought all publications of these kinds, not because he was madly interested in the latest scientific achievements. He had simply understood a long time ago what his survival in the world, hostile to beings like him, depends on. Making every effort, he kept pace with the development of science, and despite the lack of basic education, he had a superficial knowledge of everything.

Gerard lay down on his bed and hugged his cheek to the cool pillow, but somehow he could not get to sleep, although it was dark and pleasantly chilly here, behind the screen. Finally he raised himself on his elbow.

"Fronda, can I ask you a private question?" he asked shyly.

Theo lowered the magazine and gave him a friendly look.

"Shoot," he agreed. He always tried to use the dialect of youth, only when he was very upset, he archaized the pronunciation and syntax slightly.

"See," the actor began. "We've known each other for some time now and I'm beginning to wonder why you're actually with Never. He's definitely a cool guy, but I'd rather imagine you in the company of a pretty girl. Are the things not working out with girls?"

Fronda winced slightly.

"It's a complicated matter," he said reluctantly. "Things are working with girls and, working well! It's just that there is a strict intersex division between us vampires. Us on one side, ladies on the other. For example, the group of Erzika Szabo lives nearby and if you want we can visit them. But to stay in the same place, live together..."

He shook his head.

"Why not, actually?" Gerard was surprised.

The older vampire rubbed his left eye with his finger.

"Think about it," he said. "Think, why are women with us, actually? Because they love us? Not at all. A woman is with her man a) for social reasons, b) for a sense of stability, c) for passing the genes and raising the offspring, d) for status, e) for money. There is probably a feeling somewhere in all this, but it is of secondary importance, because you don't need to change your name in order to go with your beloved to the cinema or, say, to bed. When a woman transforms into a vampire, those issues cease to exist. By necessity, she becomes independent, the superstitions and social restrictions disappear, the family no longer counts, and she will not have children anymore, so why would she need a life companion in the common sense? Let's say you meet a girl, a sweet, beautiful one. You start an affair, after some time you confess to her who you are, or, which is more often, she discovers it herself (you can believe me, they are not stupid at all). At first she is slightly frightened, and then delighted with you being different. However, time goes by relentlessly and one day she begins to beg you for blood. You give in and, if it is possible (because it not always is), you perpetuate her. And this is the end of the affair. Your Dulcinea is with you another month, two, three, but she always leaves before the end of the year. Our brotherhoods are necessarily same-sex and you can't do anything about it."

"It's very sad," Gerard whispered.

"Not as much as you think. Better sleep now, kid, it's not worth worrying about all this."

Theo winked at him comfortingly, then put down his magazine and turned off the lamp.

Gerard settled down to sleep obediently, but could not sleep for a long time. Despite Fronda's several centuries of experience, he couldn't be right about everything, Gerard couldn't believe it, but his words were not very optimistic for the male sex as a whole. In addition, it sounded incredible to him that Anne was with him for one of the reasons mentioned by his friend. He deeply believed in their mutual love, which, however, could not matter to anyone now, since he was long dead in the world's opinion. When he finally fell into sleep, it was short and not restful. Still, he slept through the dawn, judging by the fact that his two companions were already dressed and arguing lively.

"Wow, did I oversleep? I'll be ready in a minute!" he called, jumping out of bed. Never handed him a glass.

"Drink it, its leftovers," he said. "We ran out of the canned food, we must go to town. It's not that bad actually, we can have fun after dinner."

"Okay, where are we going today?" the actor asked eagerly, pulling on his pants.

"Maybe to Erzika's place? We could watch the nude beauties" suggested the Indian.

"I would go to the zoo. I haven't been there for an awfully long time," Theo sighed, combing his black mane in front of the mirror.

"We can, although I don't like seeing cages," Gerard said reluctantly.

Theo glanced at him and combed his hair to the side with a long stroke.

"You are looking for problems where there are none," he said. "These animals are the nth generation born in captivity, and they are not harmed here. I personally remember the former menageries, which were more like concentration camps. When I visited such a place for the first time, I was sick for a week. I absolutely cannot see anything wrong in today's zoologists."

He put the comb back on the shelf and looked at himself with satisfaction. He was a bit vain, although not enough for it to be a major problem.

"Fine. We will eat in the city, and then we will go to the zoo," Never agreed with him, his voice far from being enthusiastic.

He did not like seeing animals in a cage either, especially since he himself had some animal features and none of his friends would be surprised if he suddenly stood on all fours and roared. He had in himself something of a black leopard, raven and bat at the same time, and he was surrounded by an aura of incredibleness. Gerard had already learned his story, so he was not as surprised by this all as at the beginning of their acquaintance. He already knew that little Sinclair was raised in the temple of the goddess Kali when he and his mother were banished from the town of Dwarka, where the beautiful Sita had a home. It was her beauty that tempted the English aristocrat, of whom Never hardly knew anything, except that he was supposedly extremely terrifying, ruthless and at the same time extremely attractive, even for a vampire. His mother spoke of him reluctantly, which was hardly surprising - after all he became the cause of her shame and misfortune.

Vampires are generally sterile, but there are some specific exceptions to this rule, and Neville Poe of Widmore was probably such exception, since his night visit to Sita brought about such fruit. At first, the boy was not much different from the other children of Dwarka, except for the cat-like eyes, he even ate the same things as others, however, he aroused some incomprehensible fear in people even then. Over time, more and more inhabitants of the town were hostile to him, and when they also realized that the boy somehow managed to escape the ambushes (they attempted to kill him several times), he and his mother had to flee to the woods.

The priests of the goddess Kali took them in quite willingly, and they spent the next few years among strange, gloomy rituals in honor of the goddess of death. Sinclair was already twelve when his mother met a local landowner near the temple, Nathoo Radjhaleah, and he fell in love with her so much that he officially married her, adopting her son at the same time. Such protection was very useful to the boy, when he slowly lost the ability to eat normal food and the bloodthirsty inclinations began to arise in him. His foster father hid him then in his private menagerie, located in a huge park, until the boy learned to control his instincts and mask the nature of the vampire.

Never was probably the only specimen of his kind and one had to get used to him to be able to find pleasure in his company. True, he could blend in with the crowd when he wanted to, but since it required some effort from him, he did not bother when he did not have to. At night, like right now, it was less important, because the friends kept rather to the side streets, less well-lit (no vampire likes bright light, even one like Never, who moved around during the day without too much pain). Anyway, it was easy to hunt a meal on the side streets, near dingy pubs. A few drunken guys were enough for the vampire to eat without harming anyone.

Contrary to the popular belief, a vampire does not need too much blood to satisfy his appetite for hemoglobin, which is why his victims are usually difficult to detect. Except for temporary anemia and bruising on the back of the neck, there are no other symptoms, and no alcoholic will consider this a serious thing, even an experienced doctor will not pay much attention to it. This is one of the reasons why vampires like best to hunt near pubs and taverns. The second reason is that the blood mixed with cheap alcohol has a great taste for them. Gerard was very surprised when he found a clear note of asparagus soup, halva or melba with pineapple and even caviar in the liquid drank straight from "the source".

"It depends on the blood type, and also on what such a person has eaten or drunk before," Never told him. "A vampire's taste buds simply read blood that way. Gusto Vanderbelt calls this a flavor conditional reflex, but it probably doesn't matter why this mechanism works in this or the other way. It is nice. Isn't it?"

"Yes, indeed" Gerard agreed.

Having satisfied their appetites, the friends decided to devote the rest of the night to entertainment and, as Fronda suggested earlier, went to the ZOO. The gate was already closed at this time, but this was no obstacle for athletic Fronda or for Never, nimble as a cat. They both climbed the fence without any effort. After a moment's hesitation, Gerard followed their example, convinced that he would fall and break his neck, but for some reason his sense of balance was now much better now, and his body seemed lighter, more agile. True, in the past, Gerard used to not need a double in filming shots requiring almost circus-like performances, but he had never climbed so high without any protection before.

"Don't touch the wires, they are live," Never warned him, throwing his jacket on the wires. "We're not as sensitive as people are, but the right voltage will give you a good jolt. Better avoid it."

They rappelled to the ground along a rope thrown down from the fence. The lack of artificial lighting did not bother them, as the vampire's eyes are more sensitive than human ones. Sometimes they develop this sensitivity to the extent that they achieve so-called adaptive micro-ability: they see in the dark with great precision, at the expense of losing the ability to extract small details from a larger plane at the same time. This is very troublesome, because it means a loss of the ability to read print, but it doesn't happen often.

Generally, vampires have very sharp eyesight, though oversensitive, just like the three friends wandering around the dormant ZOO and looking into the cages with curiosity. The animals, hairless, hairy, covered with scales or feathers, sometimes raised their heads at the sound of their footsteps, curled slightly under the touch of the hands inserted into the cages, flashed their semi-sleepy eyes in the dark, sometimes murmured quietly. It was strange to visit the garden at night, in silence, broken only by the voices of night birds or the distant hum of cars passing through the streets of the city.

"Go ahead," Theo said, seeing that his younger colleague was afraid to get closer to the cages of larger specimens. "Animals like us. Don't forget that I used to live among wolves and somehow they didn't eat me. Gusto says it's the pheromones that inform most animals 'calm down, I'm harmless and not good for food'. I don't know exactly what a pheromone is, but I believe Gust. His head is a real encyclopedia and works like a digital machine.

He took the lock pick from his wallet and opened one of the cages with it. Inside was a magnificent black panther, and her golden eyes glowed in the dark like Never's eyes. Gerard scooted back, but Theo entered the cage without fear and knelt beside the huge cat.

"Don't be afraid, Fanfan," he said, placing his hand on the panther's head. "She's really friendly."

He gently scratched the animal behind the ears and on the dewlap the cat turned to him. The panther gave in to his caresses, striking her tail nervously against the bottom of the cage and rubbing her mouth against Fronda's hand whenever he stopped scratching her. Gerard watched the idyll from a safe distance, not daring to come closer, because he did not trust the predator, even born and raised behind bars. He became a vampire too recently to learn to benefit from his new status, and one of those benefits was undoubtedly this relative safety against animal attacks. Not that Gerard did not like them - although he was afraid of some of them, he definitely found reptiles repulsive, but he liked dogs, horses, birds... He preferred to be careful though...

"Do you come here often?" he asked, watching his friend.

"To her? To her yes, often," said Theo, hugging his cheek against the panther's head.

"Crazy," the actor murmured with an involuntary shiver.

"Believe me, no animal will attack you if you do not tease it," Never cried, trying to wake the eagle, sleeping in his aviary nearby. The eagle finally woke up, squawked and pecked his hand. Never, amused, pulled his wing lightly, and ruffled the feathers around his neck.

"Let's go to the pavilion for exotic birds," Gerard suggested after a moment. "I'd like to see them up close."

In fact, he wanted Fronda to finally get out of the panther's cage and lock it well. He even preferred the company of venomous snakes, motionless and lethargic at night, though they made him shake with disgust. Neither Never, familiar with snakes because of his Hindu blood, nor Fronda, who was not afraid of any creature, had such reservations. Gerard, by comparison, was a typical product of the twentieth century civilization and secretly breathed with relief when all three left the menagerie.

It was still a middle of a night, so there was no one in the park next to the zoo. They liked to come there on rainy days and at night, because usually too many people were walking around the park to feel safe there, even when it was cloudy. Pedestrians on the streets were not a threat, they hurried to their own business and did not have time to look at people, but the park was different. A park is a place to relax and have fun, it's too easy to be exposed there. Only during heavy rain and deep night were they safe, just as they were now. The trees rustled steadily, sometimes a night bird cried or a cat mewed in the bushes, couples in love whispered somewhere, hiding from the whole world.

"Have you noticed the sweet taste of the night air?" Never sighed lyrically, breathing deeply. "In India it is hot and humid as in a Turkish bath, and here in France it is like a fresh fruit."

"Funny. I never thought about it that way," Gerard muttered.

In his life he had too many interests and things to take care of to think about the night air. First there was war, then studying, a fight for a position in the world of art, movies, traveling stage, activity in the actors' union, marriage and children... Where is the time to enjoy the night air in such a world?

"In Fronda's time the air was probably not so toxic, but now..." he said uncertainly. Theo laughed softly.

"It was clean in the woods, but it smelled of manure, smoke and carrion in the villages, and it was even worse in the cities," he said cheerfully. "After all, no one dreamed about the sewage system, the buildings were crammed densely, and the smoke from hundreds of chimneys also did their job. And if you also lived next to a tannery or near a slaughterhouse..."

He waved his hand in discouragement and then they heard a thin, desperate scream from afar.

"What is it?" Never stopped, surprised. Theo looked at his watch.

"Almost three," he replied. "Someone seems to have had a long nightmare."

The scream sounded again, a scream of a young, clearly terrified girl.

"What kind of girl wanders around the park at this hour?" Never ran in the direction the voice was coming from, but Fronda easily outran him. Gerard was the last. Despite the apparent recovery, he still had little strength and got tired easily, even though his agility and reflexes clearly improved.

"It will get better," Never comforted him, and he was probably right, but for a moment Gerard felt like an adopted, helpless child in his friends' care, which distressed him a lot.

The sight that appeared before his eyes was unexpected to say the least; a few men, armed with sticks, tried to beat with them a skinny girl in a colorful dress, held by the hair by one of the attackers. The girl struggled and tried to get away, so that it was difficult for them to hit her.

"What is going on here?!" screamed Never indignantly.

"We mind our own business. Go your way, and you will not be hurt" - said one of the men aggressively.

Theo shook his head.

"Can't do it," he said. "I may be a weirdo, but I don't like it when four or five muscle guys attack one skinny girl. Let her go, and do it now, or I'll get angry."

"You don't know what you are talking about. She is a witch" the one who was holding the girl tried to explain, but it only made the vampire angry.

"Witch! What else will you come up with?!" He shouted. "What century are we in, the fifteenth?! Let this girl go, you bastard!"

One of the men rushed at him with a stick raised menacingly, but Fronda dodged, grabbed the stick from him with an ironic smile, broke it on his knee and sent his attacker down with a blow to his chin. The other man jumped at Never, but he received him with such a blow with the backhand that the attacker literally turned in the air and collapsed, spitting blood from his broken lips. Without waiting for what would happen next, Theo went at the remaining others, tearing throat of one with his sharp teeth, and breaking the other's arm with a skilled grip.

The fight was short, though fierce. Gerard did not participate in it, uncertain of his strength and skills, he limited himself only to helping the girl get up and pulling her away to a safe place. He still didn't understand why she had been attacked and what she was doing in the park at this hour. She didn't look like a prostitute. Slender and small, rather not pretty, dressed in a simple knee-length dress, completely devoid of makeup and jewelry, she could not be the representative of the oldest profession in the world. She hugged him, trembling and panting.

It was only when Theo and Never brushed off their hands and came closer, having chased away her tormentors for good, which she dared to release the actor's arm and step out into the circle of the dim light of the lantern.

"Thank you," she said softly. "They surprised me, I didn't manage to escape."

"You'd better be careful with this night-walking, miss," Theo looked at her kindly. "Do you want us to walk you home?"

The girl shook her head.

"Thank you, I can handle it now," she said, and dove quickly in the bushes, as if afraid that they might follow her.

"Strange creature," Never murmured, looking after her. "Well, let's get out of here, it will be dawn soon."

Gerard shuffled behind his friends who were talking lively about something alien to him, but near rue Madeleine he turned into another street. He wanted to be alone for a moment, and think about what was happening to him. Not so long ago, he didn't believe in the existence of vampires at all, and if someone would have told him that he would become one of them, he would laugh at him. And for some time now, he had been drinking blood, sleeping through the days, and wandering at night in the company of two other freaks. He didn't like it at all. He liked demonic Never, he liked the medieval knight with a violent and capricious temperament, and well, he himself did not want to die, but he still did not like what happened to his life.

He had the impression that he had been fooled, although he knew that it was just the opposite, because he was the one who had fooled his destiny and escaped the inevitable death. If Never were not fascinated with him, he would be long dead. He stopped mechanically in front of the window of a small bookstore and for a moment looked indifferently at the volumes exhibited there.

Suddenly, he flinched. His eyes were attracted by a small book in a modest cover, placed casually in the corner. The author, according to what was written on the cover, was... his wife, Anne-Marie Phil. Before he thought about what he was doing, he grabbed a piece of a chipped brick lying on the sidewalk and hit it against the glass, which shattered to pieces. He hid the hastily grabbed book under his jacket and quickly walked away towards their house. It was high time to hide somewhere, because the sky was starting to turn dangerously gray.

They were the only people that lived in this old tenement house. It was dark, damp and half-ruined, it would have been demolished long ago had it not been entered in the register of historic monuments. The fact that people did not want to live there was very convenient for the three vampires, for they could feel at ease there. Their apartment, safely hidden on the third floor, became their refuge and it was all they needed for happiness. The black screen, forming a dome above their beds, gave them a sense of invisibility in case someone wanted to look into the window.

Nobody would see them anyway. Due to the clever arrangement of the mirrors, only brick walls and shabby wallpapers, carefully preserved on a fragment of one of the walls, could be seen from the outside. The illusion created in this way was the work of Never, gifted manually and technically. The screen was an additional protection, both against people and against the sun, which could break in here with them. Inside, each of the apartment's residents had a bedside lamp, especially useful for Never, who suffered from chronic insomnia. Fronda also liked to read before bed, but he fell asleep quickly, so quickly that he usually did not have time to turn his lamp off and it was necessary to do it for him.

Gerard undressed and slipped under the blanket into his bed, ignoring the Indian's questioning look. He turned on the lamp and opened the stolen book on the first page, where the publisher placed a photograph of him and Anne in the background of the gathered crowd, next to a pompous quote from Spinoza. He did not remember who and when took this picture, not very good one, as he judged. On the next page, however, there was something much more important - words, undoubtedly written by his wife's hand:

"I wake up early, it's still night...The consciousness never gives up, a memory chases a memory, and here I see your dead face on the pillow again, your open eyes, the calm, absent expression, soft arrangement of hands, the sight of which ensured me you felt no pain or worry... Death separated us for the whole eternity."[2]

Tears clouded the letters and he couldn't read any more. Wiping his eyes, he looked at the black wall of the screen for a moment, wondering if he should continue exploring this short diary, for it suddenly seemed a kind of sacrilege to him. Anne probably hoped that hundreds of thousands of people would read these words, but in her wildest predictions she couldn't sense that they would be read by him, the one she wrote about, the one she mourned.

He had not thought before about the pain she must have experienced, it was only from the chaotic notes in this booklet that he began to learn about her suffering, the struggle for her husband, her lover, her prince from the fairy tale to die peacefully, without spiritual torture, which would certainly become his experience if she would have told him the truth. And yet in their relationship the truth had always been the most important thing, they built their small world on it. God, those walks among the trees in the summer, and in the winter, snowflakes swirling around them, the soft darkness covering their physical closeness...

How cruelly fleeting all this was, so short, so incredibly easy to destroy by... by what exactly? By one abnormal cell, which

---

[2] "A moment of sigh" - Anne-Marie Philipe

began to grow in his unaware body, to slowly destroy it. And if Never got interested in him, where would he be now?

No longer in control of himself, Gerard yanked the arm of soundly sleeping Fronda.

"My sword and shield," Theo demanded unconsciously, sitting up on the bed and immediately falling back on the pillow without even opening his eyes.

"Fronda, tell me, is there such a thing as life after death?" the actor called out right into his ear.

"Go to the priest with that," Theo groaned, trying to hide his head under the pillow. "How am I supposed to know? I guess there is. I believe it. You found a hell of a time for your theological deliberations..."

Gerard waved a hand at him dismissively and went back to reading, cursing his weakness, which made him back away cowardly from each subsequent sentence, and in fear of it, read the previous ones a few times. Suddenly, he desperately missed his children. He saw them for the last time before going to surgery, later Anne took them to her friends and did not bring them home on the pretext that the convalescent needed peace. Perhaps she thought these two fragile creatures were too delicate to be exposed to the sight of the dying father?

He realized with horror that during those twenty days from the day of the surgery till his "death", he did not think of them even once, and now... it was too late now. He belonged to another world, as different as if it were on a distant planet. Why should he think of them in this wonderful one-on-one with his beloved woman? He didn't know that these were his last days, it was hidden from him so well, so thoroughly...

He did not know whether to condemn Anne for her deception, or to admire the determination with which she fought for his right to happiness. No, he couldn't blame Anne for what she did to him. She was probably deeply convinced that she was doing the right thing, she fought like a wounded lioness so that not even the slightest shadow would appear in his sky.

"I wonder what she would say if she woke up last night and saw that rascal Never by my bed," he thought, turning the page over. "That would be something to write about for her."

He thought back to that dreary, rainy November night. Why exactly did this Hindu demon wait so long before he made him his final offer? After all, it was close to being too late. If you consider it well, he didn't even leave him time to think about all this, and now he remembered well how carefully Never sucked those few drops of blood from his neck. He was already on the brink of life and death. And in general... how did he find out about everything?

"It wasn't me," said the Indian from his bed. "Fronda was having an affair with a nurse who assisted in your surgery and told him what she saw. And then he told me everything because he knew how much I admired you."

"Do you read minds?" Gerard was worried.

"Not at all. But my hearing is devilishly good, and you mumbled instead of just thinking. Sleep now."

"Just a minute," he promised, not taking his eyes off the printed pages.

"On the day of your funeral, when I left the cemetery, I knew I would come here often..." he read and tried to imagine what Anne felt like when she was leaving the old cemetery.

Of course, even she had to realize that this was pointless, because the deceased can be everywhere, except in the cemetery, where his body is left like old clothes, no longer needed by anyone. However, it is hard to blame the devastated woman for clinging to the shadows of memories. And yet he lived, he lived thanks to the little whim of the age-old vampire, who decided to perpetuate him, even (he felt it now) against his will. Anne, however, did not know about it, and all that was left to her was the cool, shady cemetery in Ramatouelle. She lived for her children, she had to be strong because of these two little human beings, the souvenirs of their love.

And yet their life will be painfully short from a vampire's point of view. How many years were ahead of these children, sixty, eighty? How many among them will really be worth living? He felt a sudden shame. He was given an eternity with which he had nothing to do, which he could not share with his loved ones, and although he had no say in it, he felt guilty.

He put down the book and turned off the light. Fronda, sleeping on the nearby bed, was breathing peacefully in his sleep, sometimes muttering something. Gerard stared at his smooth face, almost boyish, even though it belonged to a vampire over six hundred years old, and tried to imagine what he felt when the Black Lady turned him into a bloodsucker, a damned one by contemporary beliefs. Before that, he survived the death of his wife and son, and maybe he hoped that when he would fall, he would meet them in heaven?

The Black Lady took this opportunity from him, it must have been really terrible for him. He couldn't think about it for a long time, his eyes were closing on their own, after all it was almost the middle of the day, the time of the lowest activity for vampires. Before he finally fell asleep, he realized that he would rather lie here than in the grave. When he finally got into a sound sleep, he was sleeping so deeply that nothing could wake him up, he only got up from bed when Never accidentally dropped the radio on the floor.

"Oh boy, I overslept again!" He called, jumping out from behind the screen. "What time is it?"

"Almost midnight," Never told him. "That's what happens if you play at night. Fronda has run to Agnes or another one of his madwomen long ago. He was actually a little angry, he said that the next time you ask him abstract questions when he wants to sleep, he'll beat you blue."

Gerard shook his head slightly.

"Who was I supposed to ask? These are tough issues," he sighed. "Listen, is he really religious?"

The Indian smiled cat-like.

"Sure," he said. "He even goes to church on Sundays and holidays. This requires a lot of determination, because a vampire feels among such an accumulation of people with attention focused in the same way, more or less as if ants got all over him. Most vampires are too sensitive to sit in any temple, but Fronda is a damn stubborn man. He withstood the emanation of silver, until he was able to become resistant, so he will withstand everything and a bit more. Dress faster, you've wasted enough of the night."

The actor reached for his shirt.

"How does he reconcile all this?" he murmured quietly.

He couldn't understand it all, though he admitted that something that was incompatible for him, could be perfectly consistent with logic for a medieval knight. After all, he was not a child of the same era as Gerard, and in his time, religion significantly affected all areas of life. He regretted very much that he did not have Fronda's faith, it would be easier for him, but he was not able to believe like him.

For him, the world was material and cognizable, only now he was beginning to understand what was hidden beyond the things specified by science, like a strange panopticon of peculiarities that people did not realize. It all made him feel confused like he had never been before. In vampires, mood has a special impact on physical well-being, much stronger than in humans, and much more brutal, and his mood was now as nasty as ever.

Never seemed to perceive it well, and although he was not inherently sympathetic, he decided to help him.

"Let's go to 'La Lontananza'," he suggested. "They have fantastic strippers there, and the waitresses aren't bad either. It will lighten everyone's mood. A little fun has not hurt anyone yet, and it looks like you really need it."

"OK," Gerard agreed without enthusiasm.

He had heard a lot about the strip club, run by the Erzika Szabo's group of vampires, but he had not visited it yet. He did not like striptease shows. Treating a woman like a toy, serving the excitement of the senses, was in conflict with his innate sense of decency and respect for the dignity of others. He also knew a lot about Erzika, mainly from Fronda, who was her lover once and had not forgotten about her till now. So far, however, he had met neither her nor any other vampire woman, perhaps because in this artificially created nation, both sexes indeed avoided each other. In general, he associated the term "vampire" with a predatory, ruthless creature with protruding fangs and red eyes. So he discovered with pleasant amazement that the girls working in the club looked like nice, charming, and gentle creatures. The vampires of horror films could have nothing in common with them.

"Bloody Mary No. 13, two times," Never stopped one of the waitresses, an ethereal blonde in a translucent black tulle dress, and gave her his business card. After a while, the girl brought two tall glasses, filled to a height of three-quarters with an opaque ruby liquid.

"Drink it, don't worry, it's a cocktail especially for us, with the addition of tomato juice and gin," Never took one of the glasses and drank with visible delight. "For special guests there is everything here, but you must have an ID, as you saw. Conspiracy above all. The ladies have enjoyed it for a long time, and nobody has caught their tracks yet."

Gerard listened to him absentmindedly, unhappy even more than before, because the sight of these beautiful girls, unrestrained in their cheerfulness, reminded him of Anne, the nicest gray mouse, modest and inconspicuous. He felt more and more that such immortality, deprived of the loved ones and forcing to hide from the world, was not worth much.

"Could I perpetuate someone?" he asked carefully, trying not to reveal his thoughts to Never.

"Yes, some time in the future. In a few dozen years maybe..." the Indian answered indifferently.

"Why so late?" Gerard couldn't hide the disappointment that his friend didn't seem to notice.

"Why? You might as well ask why a five-year-old girl cannot give birth," he said. "Your blood is not mature enough yet. And it's a good thing. You can't recognize for now who is right for that and who isn't, and believe me, it's not an easy matter."

The actor hung his head.

"Is it just me that can't stop thinking about what was once and will not come back?" he asked bitterly.

"Drink," Never advised him. "You have to get through it all like through a chickenpox. A little alcohol helps wonderfully to get over such attacks. I'm serious: I chewed hash to bear myself when I realized the change, but I do not recommend it to you or anyone else."

"Did the change come spontaneously for you?" Gerard asked, obediently taking a few sips from his glass. The drink had a pleasant, slightly salty taste and undoubtedly contained a lot of gin, enough to get stunned with it.

"Yes, when the growth hormone secreted by the pituitary gland stopped working," said Never. "It is this hormone that does not allow us, for example, perpetuate children or drink their blood. Remember it well, never attack a child, even if you are dying of hunger, because you will hurt yourself, and it can be serious."

"I wouldn't do that anyway. And animal blood?" Gerard gratefully took another drink from the pretty waitress and sipped it slowly, savoring the taste, which was unlike anything.

Never shook his head.

"It's out of the question," he said firmly. "You risk taking over animal traits and even mental illness. Do not get your knowledge from horror movies, there is usually not a word of truth there, which is probably why Fronda likes them so much. He says they are relaxing to him."

"How did he manage to keep his mental balance? After all, he was born in the deep Middle Ages, how he can feel well in the twentieth century?" the actor sighed.

He still couldn't understand living through so many centuries.

The Indian shrugged.

"Don't exaggerate, after all, he did not land here straight from the Hundred Years' War, but remained active all this time. He witnessed all the changes. Of course, he also had to have a more flexible mind than the average person to be able to adapt, it is not so simple after all. You'll find out for yourself, if you live long enough."

"I may not?" Gerard looked with moderate interest at the stage, where a fiery brunette was dancing "the dance of the seven veils." She was really beautiful and he wondered if she was this famous Erzika.

"A lot depends on you. Among us, the main commandment is the eleventh one: lie low," Never said, almost harshly.

The conversation broke off because Gusto Vanderbelt sat down at their table and began to speak in a low voice. His words were obviously very interesting to Never. Gerard felt worse and worse in this playful company, as if he did not belong to it at all, and he was more and sadder even though he was on his third drink already.

"I want to go home," he said finally.

Never looked at him with some concern, but after a moment he took the Royce keys from his pocket and tossed them to him across the table.

"Just drive carefully," he admonished him just for the record. "You've been drinking."

"Yes, yes..." Gerard got up and started for the door, happy that he could leave this cheerful, loud place filled with sensuality, which somehow caused him more distress than bad words would.

Outside, he was greeted by rain. The whole sky was covered with leaden clouds, the air was saturated with moisture, and the rain was falling on wet streets in large, lazy drops. Gerard thought that the day that would soon get up, would probably be dark and devoid of sunshine, and he did not know himself when the decision got ripe in him. Perhaps the reason was that he suddenly realized what day it was; the anniversary of his "death", which is celebrated as a birthday among vampires. Never and Fronda did not do it - Never did not "die" and Fronda had long forgotten what was the date of the battle in which he almost died. Gerard did not intend to change this tradition and did not remind them of his own anniversary, but he decided to celebrate this day in his own way.

He sat behind the car wheel and headed down the road to Ramatouelle, to "his" cemetery.

A sentence from his wife's diary was trashing under his skull:

"I knew that I would come here often... Ten minutes, no more, and then let all the worst happen, death, torture, if only I could see you... For the first time in my life I want the impossible."

He wiped the tears running down his face with the back of his hand. Impossibility! Nothing is impossible in the world, Fronda said, and he was already leaning toward it, and though he had no hope that Anne would be there at that hour, he somehow wanted to get there. He did not think at this moment what would happen if, despite all forecasts, the day was sunny, but fortunately the dawn was muffled by the low hanging clouds and a fog, although it stopped raining already. He was driving the Royce as fast as he could, and even though he was getting closer to Ramatouelle, his longing became ever greater, even more desperate.

Suddenly he was overwhelmed by the idiotic conviction that if he could touch the cemetery ground with his feet, everything would turn back, that he would be able to become the same as before again. Maybe it was the result of the alcohol he had drunk, but this hope clung to him and on his part, he did not want to give up on it. What he was really counting on, rushing along the path of the lost happiness, he did not know too well himself.

After braking near the cemetery, he got off and started looking between the tombstones. On such an ugly day there were no people here, the graves stood haughty and silent, glistening with wet surfaces. Flowers in stone vases hung their heads sadly, trees shook showers of dirty drops on paths. It was not without difficulty that Gerard found the right alley, but he stopped without entering it.

A thin, small figure in a gray coat and a scarf on her head stood motionlessly next to the stone plate full of fresh bouquets. She didn't cry, but her whole body radiated suffering. Gerard stared at her, not sure what he should do, and whether he had the right to do anything at all, since he now belonged to a completely different world, which neither Anne nor the children could enter. Her sight, however, attracted him irresistibly.

Slowly, in uncertain steps, he walked over and stopped near Anne. He wanted to say something, anything, but the words got stuck in his throat and each of them seemed hopelessly trivial. He hesitated, until Anne, as if feeling that someone was looking at her, turned suddenly and looked him straight in the face. They stared at each other for a moment in complete stillness and silence, then Gerard reached out with his hand, trying to touch his wife's shoulder.

Anne jumped back, raising her arms in a defensive gesture.

"Who are you?!" She shouted hysterically. "Don't come near me! Don't touch me!"

She backed away, between the tombstones, without taking her terrified eyes off him. Gerard suddenly understood that they were separated by an impassable barrier, and that even if they shouted to each other from both banks of this black river, they would not understand each other anymore. It hurt him so much that he lost his breath for a moment.

Before he could make any decision, Fronda jumped out from behind the cemetery trees, grabbed his arm with an iron grip and pulled him after himself. He was really angry. He had not seen him like this.

"What are you thinking about?" He hissed, pushing the actor into the car. "What did you actually want to do? You could even kill her, you idiot! If she starts telling now that she met her deceased husband at the cemetery, she could end up in the lunatics' asylum and then what? Is that what you want? Even if this psychiatrist is not associated with VHI, we may be in hell of a trouble."

He sat behind the wheel and kicked the gas pedal angrily.

"I don't even have a driving license. If we have problems with the traffic cops, it will be your fault!" he said over his shoulder, steering the car onto the highway.

"Do psychiatrists cooperate with VHI?" the actor asked in a choked voice.

"What do you think? Who do you think a man attacked by a vampire, a strigoi or a demon will go to today?" Theo drove, clutching the steering wheel in both hands as if it were a weapon. "In your opinion, she probably will go to a police officer and say: "Respectable gendarmes, please, pardon me, but in the blink of an eye ago, a strigoi tried to attack me." right?"[3]

Gerard curled up in the back seat. He understood now that he had made a terrible mess, but he still felt the desperate regret and longing that had brought him here.

---

[3] Fronda uses medieval language here. [t.n.]

"Don't be angry, Fronda," he muttered. "I wanted to... Oh, you won't get it anyway. Or maybe you could help me? Would you perpetuate Anne?"

Fronda stepped on the brake so abruptly that the Royce skidded. In the rearview mirror, Gerard could only see his eyes, but their expression was enough to know that Theo was boiling with anger like a volcano.

"Get it out of your head," he said emphatically. "Women who have children are not good for it at all. They must not be perpetuated, do you understand? This can lead to unbelievable complications for everyone."

He turned his boyish face and large eyes, very angry now, at Gerard.

"For everyone, do you understand?" He repeated. "It's one of the main principles of our lives: don't do anything that would endanger the clan. You have to learn it."

He stepped on the accelerator again, but this time he drove more calmly.

"You've heard about VHI from Never," he continued. "But you don't know the details. What you did was a typical mistake that could draw their attention. You shouldn't have come here. Look at me: there was a time when I wore an iron armor, rode better than today's stuntmen, and knelt only before the king. At the same time, I firmly believed that the Earth is flat, the stars are holes in the dome that surrounds it, and if a bat flies over a cow, its will take its milk away. I didn't have time for school because of the war. I had no idea about the antipodes, well, I didn't even know what the outhouse was, because they were simply not there yet at the time, and almost everyone was dealing with these matters in the fresh air. And now I listen to The Beatles, I wear jeans, I read science magazines and I am passionate about football, and you know why? Because if I couldn't adapt, I wouldn't be in this world anymore. You have to know how to do it, kid. You can't let the world overtake you in development."

"How did you guess where my legs took me?" Gerard asked after a moment.

Theo shrugged.

"You think it was difficult? My difficulties were to catch up with you on time, for this purpose I stole a police car. The poor car is now parked by the cemetery," he answered angrily.

He was really infuriated, and for the rest of the way Gerard wondered helplessly whether if Theo was that angry, then Never would simply tear him to pieces.

At home, it turned out however, that the Indian was not going to lose his usual cool.

"Go to sleep," he said after hearing the report. "You've got a good lesson and I hope it taught you something."

* * * * *

"Hello, boys," Never rushed into the apartment like a bomb, as was his custom, brandishing a bundle of magazines. "Here is your press: for Fronda "Chess Quarterly", "Horizons of Technology" and "Scientific Review", and for Gerard "Theater Guide" and "Le Cinema". In addition, daily newspapers, of course. It's always worth knowing what's going on in the world. Hey, Fanfan, look at page eighteen of "Le Cinema", you'll see something very interesting there."

Intrigued, Gerard turned several pages.

"Indeed!" He called out. "Fronda, they are making a TV series about you!"

"Seriously? Show me," Theo snatched the magazine from his hand and began to read greedily.

"Oh, man!" He called after a moment. "I told Agnes too much, and she told everything to the director who's going to shoot it. He wrote the script, as he claims, under the influence of the Froissard's chronicle... Like hell he did! Look at the picture, maybe you know this youngster?"

The actor looked closely at the black and white photography.

"Like a skin torn off you," he said.

"Don't use this comparison with someone from the Middle Ages," Never looked over his shoulder. "But it's an amazing resemblance, indeed. Do you know him?"

Gerard shook his head.

"He's some Belgian," he said. "He just appeared in this business, so I didn't get to meet him. In my opinion, the perfect match, only his hair is shorter and probably a little brighter than Fronda's... although it may be the lighting, and you can make it darker anyway. I used to dye my hair a neon carrot color for the part in 'Carousel', and it was OK too, as far as I remember. Wait a minute! That girl next to the director... isn't that Agnes Varden, my photographer?"

"It's rather my own Agnes," Theo carefully studied the picture, not very clear. "Yes, it's her. We've been having an affair for years."

"The famous Agnes Varden and a vampire from the Hundred Years War..." the actor shook his head in disbelief.

Never drew the screen curtain tighter. It was daytime already and the stray rays of the sun were coming in through the crack. They didn't like it - vampires, for understandable reasons, hate the sun, even when they are partially resistant to it.

"I'll be famous," Fronda sighed, stretching on bed and putting his hands under his head.

"You could apply to be a consultant for the filming. After all, probably no one today knows more about the Hundred Years War than you do," at that moment, Never had the face that he always put on when it was not clear if he was serious.

"All I know is that it lasted a hundred years," the friend answered, opening the "Chess Quarterly."

"That's probably not enough," protested Gerard.

"A hundred years is not enough for you?" Never snorted sarcastically.

"Understand, I only knew my piece of this war. It's really not much," Theo explained cheerfully. "I saw the world from the position of a single province, and even a single forest in which I hid with my team. These were not the times when you could buy a newspaper at the corner and know everything, or turn on the radio and the announcer would read the news.

Most of us had only a vague idea of what was happening in the next village. Some gossip, spread by vagabonds and traveling circus troupes, sometimes a herald or a messenger stopped in the tavern, and said something. I wouldn't be able to help them."

This conversation awakened in Gerard the longing for his former life again, and it was so intense that he lost any will to read. He lay down and pulled the blanket over his head. Since he was a vampire, he slept well usually, but he had unpleasant dreams and one of them was that night, but after waking up, he didn't remember anything about it.

Theo was just taking a shower, and Never was cutting his hair to a reasonable length in front of the mirror. His hair was no less a mystery than he was: long and shiny, it seemed to live its own life, and grew at an incredible pace. He cut it, braided it, tied it with elastics, but in spite of this, he never controlled it completely.

Theo jumped out of the bathroom, wiping himself with a hairy towel.

"Where are we going today?" he asked cheerfully.

"Let's take a walk down Inkermann Boulevard," Gerard suggested. "I used to live there, I would like to visit the old neighborhood. I promise I won't cause any trouble."

Since the unfortunate trip to Ramatouelle, he smartened up a little bit and knew how dangerous all recklessness was. Any ill-considered step could endanger not only the three of them. The hunters were tracking their brethren all over Paris with such ferocity that they had to be on double guard, and many vampires, unable to withstand such tension, moved somewhere into the province, removing their traces as carefully as they could. Those who remained, because of their age and experience, were able to take on appropriate "protective colors". And besides, they enjoyed playing with fire.

"All right, why not," Fronda agreed. "And you know what? We'll go to the theater. Today they play 'Cinna[4]'. Are you coming, Nev?"

"I have something to take care of, have fun today," answered the Indian.

He had his own life, about which he did not confide in others, unlike talkative Fronda. Never's friends respected his privacy, although sometimes they were curious where he disappeared, sometimes for a few days. Theo and Gerard liked his company, but the two of them also felt good. It sometimes happens that vampires cannot stand the company of their own species, but it wasn't the case with them - they felt like brothers and so they behaved.

"Come on, get dressed," Theo urged his younger colleague. "Put on something warmer, it is quite cold today."

Gerard winced slightly. Vampires are only minimally sensitive to adverse temperatures, but he was still too young to develop the proper indifference. It was more of a mental discomfort rather than a real inconvenience. In spite of Fronda's ironic glance, he put on an extra sweater and a jacket.

---

[4] Cinna – a tragedy by Pierre Corneille

They took the bus, not wanting to take Royce from Never, who apparently had something to do. Theater tickets on Inkermann Boulevard were already sold out, but Fronda, charming as usual, spoke to the cashier so sweetly that she let them in through the side door. It was always his signature move, like that he could wrap every woman around his finger. Gerard cautiously kept a little behind and slipped the cap deep over his eyes, because his enlarged photo hung in the hall, with a black velvet ribbon across it.

He felt more at ease in the dark aula and could drown with all his heart in the spectacle he knew almost by heart. The young, enthusiastic acting team did their best, although Gerard was of the opinion that a few tips from an old hand like him could improve their skills a bit. He felt his heart twist at the thought that he would never be able to give this advice, nor would he ever stand on stage again, uttering words that had been written by someone centuries ago. It was really painful.

Even during the break, he could not think of anything else and hardly paid any attention to his companion, gossiping as usual. After the break, they returned to the audience like everyone else, and apparently everything was fine, but as they left the theater, Fronda suddenly squeezed Gerard's shoulder and whispered in his ear:

"Don't look back, Fanfan. They're following us, probably Hunters."

"Did I give us away with something?" Gerard worried, feeling his heart rise to his throat.

"Not at all! It's my fault, kid, we shouldn't have come here," Theo looked around secretly and added. "We're separating. I will engage them to follow me, and you will come back home, but carefully. Check if they follow you."

"Will you be all right?" Gerard looked at him anxiously, but Fronda only smiled.

"I was already leading the hunters astray when your grandparents weren't even planned yet," he said and pushed his friend. "Now!"

Gerard jumped into a side street and, zigzagging along little alleys, ran till his strength left him. He still didn't regain it fully - he got tired quite easily. When his breathing calmed down, he surveyed the surroundings the way Never had taught him and, assuming he had lost the pursuit, went to rue Madelaine. Never was not there yet, and for the first time Gerard was alone in the apartment.

The tenement had thick walls, the sounds of the outside world hardly reached inside, and the silence that was almost as heavy as a pile of snow, was unbearable despite the radio being turned on. This silence and loneliness were unbearable. Contrary to the popular belief, a vampire-loner is something that practically does not happen, because in reality, the undead are not afraid of anything as much as of a lonely existence, and are always looking for the company of other individuals of their species. Even Never hated being alone, and yet he was a rather unusual bloodsucker who spent his early youth in the jungle.

It seemed to Gerard that centuries had passed before the Hindu finally returned home.

"Don't worry," he said after hearing his account. "Fronda generally knows what he's doing. He'll probably be home before you wake up. Go to sleep, you are barely standing up."

"What if he doesn't come back?" he asked anxiously.

The older colleague patted him on the shoulder.

"Have more faith. If Theo weren't as good as he is, he wouldn't be alive today," he said comfortingly.

The actor, still not fully convinced, went to bed, sure that he would not fall asleep with worry, but the sleep did not let him wait long. When he finally opened his eyes, it turned out that not only did Theo not return, but Never also disappeared, and worse, Gerard realized that the Indian had locked him in without asking for his opinion. Angry at his unceremoniousness, he dressed quickly, then slid down the gutter to the house's yard. He was skilled in such exploits, after all, during the shooting of one of the movies, he played the scene of escaping from a prison himself, without the help of a stuntman. And it consisted of sliding down the rope from the tower thirty meters high.

Once he was down, Gerard wondered what to do next. He didn't know where to look for Fronda. He could be literally everywhere, and most likely at one of his numerous girlfriends, of whom the actor did not know a single one, except for Agnes Varden. However, he knew from the press that Agnes had left for Meudon and she was not currently in Paris. He was at a loss what to do until he thought of Erzika Szabo. Theo was still infatuated with her and visiting her often, so the beautiful

Hungarian could know something about him - if not where he was, at least where he could be. He slid the cap over his forehead and ran out into the street.

"To 'La Lontananza'," he instructed the taxi driver who stopped at his sign. The driver started as he was told, without bothering to look at the passenger. When he got there, Gerard jumped out of the car, tossed a few coins to the taxi driver and knocked on the back door.

A pretty, tall girl with the shape of a wrestler opened for him.

"What do you want? This is an entrance for staff only," she growled unfriendly.

"I need to see your boss," Gerard said. "I'm from Never's group."

She thought about it, then pulled him inside and closed the door. Gerard followed her down a dark and narrow corridor to the small dressing room, where Erzika Szabo was preparing for the show.

"What is it, Gina?" she asked.

"Someone from Never to you," the girl replied briefly.

Erzika looked back.

"Ah, it's you, Fanfan," she said with moderate cordiality. "Fronda told me about you. Come in, please. What happened?"

"Fronda is missing. We split up to escape the Hunters from the Van Helsing Institute and I got home and he didn't."

Gerard made his statement as short as possible and tried not to look at the undressed dancer. She was really beautiful, but she belonged to the type of women he always avoided: with aggressive makeup and conscious of their beauty, treating all men as an easy prey. The cat's face with slanted eyes, slightly prominent cheekbones and tiny lips, framed by waves of black hair, made a rather unpleasant impression on him.

"He didn't come to me," she said, reaching for the powder. "Maybe he went to...? Although, if you think about it, he wouldn't hide with any one of his flames for a day. He doesn't trust them enough. They are lovers, not friends."

"Friends..." Gerard repeated thoughtlessly and suddenly it got clear in his head. "Can I borrow your car?"

Erzika took keys with a pearl gray key ring from the drawer of the dressing table.

"Look for a Chevrolet in that color in the parking lot," she said. "Just don't crash it for me please."

"I will be careful." The actor promised her and hurried out, grabbing the keys thrown at him.

He had no idea if what he thought of had any sense, but he was ready to try everything. He did not know that he had become so attached to Fronda, crazy and reckless, but endowed with extraordinary grace and always unconditionally loyal. Now, when it was not known what was happening to him, Gerard felt fear choking his throat and knew that he would not get peace until he would find his friend.

He rode the Chevrolet up to the wall of the Zoological Garden, parked by some bushes and climbed the wall. He was suddenly certain that he was not wrong. This strong feeling became like a direction indicator, leading straight to the rear of the black panther range. The door with a massive padlock seemed to be untouched, but on closer inspection, Gerard saw that the padlock rests on only one of the metal wheels, and he jerked the door desperately.

It was dark inside the cage. After a while, the sensitive eyes of the vampire saw the massive silhouette of the big cat and the second shape, curled at his side. The panther's golden eyes glowed like blades in the dark. The powerful animal murmured restlessly, licking its huge paws, but Gerard did not pay attention to it any more, absorbed by something else. On the straw next to the wild cat lay Fronda, curled up in an unnatural position, motionless as if dead.

"Theo, what's going on with you?" groaned Gerard, dropping to his knees next to his friend. "Don't die..."

Fronda moved.

"What a nonsense," he said with an effort. "I'll be fine, but you have to get me out of here. A guy shot me..."

Gerard noticed that there was a short, wooden bolt under his friend's right ribcage side - like a crossbow. Theo touched the dark, hardened stain on his shirt with his hand and groaned quietly:

"Help me..."

The panther watched them, tapping her tail nervously on the cage floor, but she did not try to attack.

Gerard led his friend outside, then closed the cage and involuntarily breathed a sigh of relief.

"Can you cross the wall" he asked.

"Are you crazy, in this state? I have a lockpick in my pocket, you have to open one of the side gates. It's not difficult, you just have to set all the latches" Theo answered him, leaning on his shoulder with all his weight.

The actor could barely hold him and by the time they reached the gate, he was at the end of his strength. Following the instructions of his friend, he opened the lock and after a while, the pearl-gray Chevrolet was rushing back to "La Lontananza" with insane speed. Gerard felt somehow that the wounded knight would receive the best care at Erzika's. After he got to the club through the back door, Gerard placed his friend on the sofa in a tiny wardrobe and looked at him, worried.

In the light of the ceiling lamp, it was clear that Theo was in bad condition, maybe very bad. He was pale with that porcelain, translucent whiteness of the alabaster statue, so eagerly attributed to vampires, and the actor no longer knew if his friend really was not breathing or it just appeared so. He barely managed to refrain from pulling the wooden arrow out of his body immediately. He sensed that it could have fatal consequences, but he felt that he was going to go crazy in a moment if he would not do anything.

Fortunately, Erzika ended her performance with a storm of applause, and returned to her wardrobe, covered casually with a lace and feather peignoir on her shoulders.

"Shot with a crossbow," the actor answered her questioning look.

The girl clapped her hands and called out something incomprehensible. The next second, Gerard jumped abruptly to the side, completely unprepared for what happened. Right next to him, something of human height materialized, like a thick darkness, with sparks of yellow light spurting out of it at the height of the eyes.

"Shadow, bring Gusto here, and fast," Erzika instructed him as calmly as if she were dealing with an ordinary piccolo.

"On it," Shadow whistled and floated out through the crack under the door.

"What... what is this?" asked her guest in a shaky voice.

Erzika sat in front of the mirror and began to wash off her makeup.

"It's Shadow," she said. "Sometimes he's useful. People are terribly afraid of him, I don't know why, and yet he not only does not bite, but can't even touch anyone."

Gerard shook slightly and looked at Fronda again.

"Isn't it already... too late?" he whispered.

"You are talking nonsense," the dancer snorted angrily. "As you see, his hair hasn't changed color, so he must live."

"What? Have mercy, I was only recently perpetuated" Gerard looked at her helplessly.

"Oh, right," Erzika turned toward him. "Vampires' hair whiten when they die. We don't crumble to dust as in the

70

trashy movies that Fronda likes so much, but we get gray because of shock. It's hard to kill a vampire, so death is far more shocking for us than for humans."

She knelt by the sofa and stroked Theo's hair with her fingers.

"I like him very much, you know?" she whispered.

"Don't you love him?" Gerard asked a little mischievously.

Erzika shook her head, laughing.

"No. Relations between us are like brother and sister," she said. "He was my master."

"Oh, and you left him?" now the actor understood what Theo once told him.

Erzika shrugged.

"Someday you will know what it is like. It is impossible to resurrect what united us... although I would like it very much," she finished quietly.

A sound of quick footsteps came from nearby, the door slammed, and Gusto burst into the dressing room in the company of the inseparable Tygier. The long-haired Pole was not only his assistant, but also his closest friend. The tiny room became at once impossibly cramped.

"Get out of here," Gusto unceremoniously pushed both Gerard and Erzika away. "Tygier, give me lancet number 5."

Skillfully using the narrow blade, he drew the dart from Fronda's body and examined it carefully.

"It's black alder, fresh wood," he said. "He was poisoned. It will take some time for him to recover, but then he will be like new. Tygier, serum."

"I'll take care of him," said the Hungarian firmly when the man finished his medical treatment. "You go home, and say hello to Rajah."

"Thank you," Gerard said affectionately.

The girl shrugged.

"For what?"

Gerard left the club feeling terribly confused. He was happy that Theo was already safe. He liked him more than Never, even though it was Never who was his master and guardian, but so peculiar one, that the actor was a bit afraid of him in spite of all. Theo, on the other hand, was a quite ordinary, cheerful man, except a very handsome one, with a charming disposition, though one must admit that he was somewhat reckless and crazy.

"A bit of a meshuga[5]," as Jackie Liar used to say about him.

This American did not look like a vampire at all at first glance. In fact, none of the vampires Gerard knew so far looked like a diabolical bloodsucker from books and movies, and Jackie the least of them. Jackie, a former Navy SEAL, had a stocky figure and a round face of a good-natured cheerful guy, and he didn't have sharp fangs. As Fronda said, even during the

[5] Meshuga - a madman in Yiddish

Hundred Years' War, the custom of biting victims in the neck was already going out of fashion, vampires used small blades to pierce the arteries rather than their own teeth. As a result, the adaptations in shape of abnormally long fangs and jaw deformation, formerly characteristic of vampires, were less frequent. Fronda's teeth were indeed a bit sharp, but if you didn't look too closely, you couldn't get suspicious. Vampires older than him did not come to Paris, and there were not many of them, probably only a few, scattered all over the world.

"A man is always at risk in this trade," claimed Gusto Vanderbelt, whose workshop had already been burned several times by the Hunters, together with everything that was in it. Despite these occasional losses, he was still conducting his research, and if anyone was able to help a vampire to whom something really bad happened, it was him. Theo was safe in his hands.

When he returned to the apartment at rue Madelaine a few days later, his friends gave him a warm ovation, like for a hero, which he liked very much.

"All right, all right" he said with false modesty. "It's not the first time I've ever run into the hunters. I'm at the very top of their blacklist."

"So it's not because of me?" Gerard made sure. He was still tormented by a sense of guilt for what had happened. Theo shook his head with a smile.

"Probably one of their spies spotted me during the intermission," he explained. "It was an ordinary coincidence, the most powerful thing in the world. The most important things happen by accident.

He rubbed lightly the shot wound with his hand and frowned. He was still in pain, although the wound was already almost scarred. Never gave them both a little mischievous look.

"All right, my monsters," he said. "I am going to Danielle, and I'd appreciate if you two are reasonable. If you feel like some art, I advise you from the bottom of my soul, choose a cinema. There are no intermissions there. I will try to find out something about the Institute's activities on my way, because there is something fishy about the way you were attacked. Perhaps we are dealing with a wider action here."

Theo waved a dismissive hand.

"Vampires have always been hunted and will continue to be hunted," he noted lightly. "Don't get weird, there is no reason to worry about a few mortals."

"You're worse than Achilles, because he only had one weak heel, and you have several. One of them is overconfidence," Never said and left. After a while, a faint roar of a starting motor could be heard from the yard.

Theo chuckled.

"His Danielle is a pretty blonde, a lovely girl," he said. "Okay, where are we going today?"

"Shouldn't you rest?" Gerard asked anxiously.

"I am rested already, now I want to have fun and hunt," Fronda replied firmly and grabbed the newspaper. "Oh, I'm going to the Louvre and then to the carousel."

"Will we have enough time? The Louvre is big." Gerard looked at him doubtfully.

"It was smaller in my day, but it was my king who began to expand it," Fronda got dreamy, as he always did when he remembered his time. "Well, we'll see."

He always spoke about the medieval achievements with a bit of pride, although at the same time he admitted that compared to the 20th century, these were terrible times. He was wonderfully illogical with all this, and it was a part of his charm.

Wandering around the Louvre indeed took the friends a lot of time, so they decided to go home by a night bus. Theo liked night public transport.

"Not many people and mostly drunk. No danger," he used to say. Gerard would have preferred a taxi, but didn't want to argue with his friend.

"I'll get off two stops early," he only said. "I forgot to give back the keys to Erzika, it is surprising that she has not asked for them so far."

"She probably has spare ones," Fronda comforted him. "Okay, go, but remember to come back before dawn, otherwise you'll have to go to Gusta for a sunburn ointment."

Gerard nodded and, having found the right stop, jumped off the bus to the sidewalk. He got to like the night streets where there was almost no danger, he even began to find some pleasure in the life he now lived. It had its charm, though he understood now why vampires formed fraternity groups. Loneliness that no mortal has any idea about, bothered him sometimes too, though on the other hand there were also pros - his body was not very sensitive to pain or temperature changes, and regenerated easily even from very serious injuries. Not only this. If he were to say what attracted him most to his present existence, he would probably answer that the wonderful awareness that you don't have to hurry anywhere, that whatever would happen, the world would wait for you.

"Yes, it has its good sides..." he thought, turning around the corner, and at that moment he felt as if a boulder fell on his head, and everything just disappeared. It was as if he ceased to exist.

* * * * *

His consciousness returned only after some time. He was lying on a flat surface, his arms and legs tied up. It was only after a long time that he realized that this surface was the roof of a building, not very high, because the crowns of trees reached above it, partially obscuring the evening sky.

"Evening already?" He said aloud, surprised. "Have I been here all day?"

"If that were the case, you would look like a medium-rare beef steak," a contemptuous voice answered.

Overcoming the weight of his sore head, Gerard looked around. On the roof, besides him, there were a dozen people of both sexes, of different ages, all armed with crossbows, knives and old-fashioned pistols, no doubt shooting silver bullets. A tall man, about fifty years old, leaned over Gerard and checked his bonds.

"No doubt it's him," he said to the red-haired girl, watching the prisoner with some greedy curiosity. "Stig was right, as usual. He's been tracking Fronda for some time already. What now, star of the stage, the screen and the blood receiving? Wasn't it better to die properly, as befits a man?

"None of your business," Gerard snapped.

"Now, Olgart?" the redhead asked, looking at the older man. He nodded.

"See, Kyra," he said. "Vampires are highly sensitive. By killing this individual here after dusk, we will certainly bring his buddies, including Fronda. It could fail during the day, but now..."

He took a sharpened wooden peg and a kind of a hammer with a very wide, flattened head from the haversack over his shoulder. Kyra looked at it all with excitement, it was probably the first time she was to witness this gloomy ceremony. Gerard shuddered, but suddenly felt something like a gentle brush in the heart - a joyful certainty that his friends were already nearby.

Indeed. In the crown of one of the trees, Never and Fronda watched what was happening on the roof, not daring to move so as not to reveal their presence.

"Lots of them," Theo muttered, biting his lower lip slightly.

"And placed strategically," Never added. "Look at all this weapon. Haven't they shot at us enough yet? Should I fire at Olgart or in the air as a scare, what do you think?"

"They've got Kevlar vests," Fronda said, unrolling the leather strip he had hidden in his hand.

"What vests?" Never did not understand.

"Kevlar. It's a bulletproof material," his friend explained impatiently. "You could read "Horizons of Technology" sometimes, or at least American comic books, like me. Anyway, you shoot like an old woman. A chimpanzee shoots coconuts better than you."

"And of course you'll get right at the aim with this toy," Never bit back.

"This toy was a recognized weapon back in the days when your ancestors were still jumping in the trees."

Theo took a lead rod weight out of his pocket and, grasping a branch with his right hand, turned slingshot with his left hand. Olgart, who had already put the sharp end of the stake to Gerard's chest and raised the hammer, fell as if hit with a thunderbolt when a lead bullet hit him on the temple. Kyra screamed nervously. Out of the corner of his eye, Gerard caught two familiar figures that jumped down on the roof, and he called out desperately, tugging at his bonds:

"Watch out, it's a trap!"

"Get down!" Never shouted to Fronda, who reacted immediately, thanks to which the arrows with silver arrowheads missed the target.

The hunters grabbed the guns, dropping the crossbows, already unnecessary.

"Never!" Theo shouted in resentment.

"OK, OK" answered the Indian angrily. "I'm sorry, Fanfan."

"For what?" Gerard wanted to ask, but he soon understood everything. Never let out a long scream, so terrible that the whole building seemed to tremble.

It was not an ordinary scream, but a prolonged howling, cutting under the skull like a power saw, and taking away the ability to think autonomously. The hunters let go of their weapons, falling to the roof in convulsions, as if struck by some neurotoxin. Gerard, less sensitive than them, but unable to plug his ears like Theo did, twisted in his bonds with a plea for mercy, inaudible in that roar, when suddenly the terrifying sound broke to a thin groan. Never dropped to his knees, clutching his head with his hands. Blood was flowing from his left temple. Kyra took a swing to strike again.

"She is deaf!" Gerard called, for whom everything suddenly became clear. "She reads lips!"

"And you are telling us this now?" Theo jumped up, but Kyra was already holding guns, ready to shoot, in both hands.

"Don't move, it will hurt less," she warned in a threatening voice. Olgart, who had just regained consciousness, stood up unsteadily.

"Well done, girl," he said. "Now they..."

He did not finish, because suddenly something completely unexpected happened. An Alsatian shepherd appeared out of nowhere, enormous even for this breed, and jumped at Olgart with a low growl. Surprised, the hunter stepped back and fell on his back, shielding his face with his hands. The big dog struggled with him and Kyra, while Theo cut the ropes that Gerard was bound with.

"Where did this dog come from?" the actor moaned, rubbing his numb wrists. There was still ringing in his ears from Never's shrieks, and his stubborn limbs wouldn't listen to him.

"I have no idea," Fronda confessed. "But if it wasn't for him, we would say goodbye to this world, sure as there's carts to horses."

Never, who had already recovered, skillfully tied down Kyra, Olgart and their companions, who were still not fully conscious. The dog watched it, wagging its tail friendly. The Indian scratched his ears, examining the fur around his neck. The sheepdog whined softly and licked his hand.

"He doesn't wear a collar and probably never had it," Never said. "He seems to be a stray dog."

"Let's take him with us, then," Fronda suggested cheerfully.

"Exactly," Gerard joined him. Never waved his hand.

"Well, he deserves at least a good dinner from us," he agreed with them. A police siren wailed from afar.

"Let's scoot," Fronda whispered.

Friends reached the outer ladder that led from the roof straight to the ground. Theo grabbed the big dog under his arm, as if he were a little puppy, and came down from the roof with him. Friends followed his example. All three got to the royce parked behind the trees. Pushed unceremoniously inside, the dog curled up in the back seat and followed them with shiny eyes, quietly whining from time to time.

"I wonder why he helped us," Never wondered as he started the engine.

"Maybe he's not stray at all. Maybe it's a laboratory dog, and the Hunters made some experiments on it," Gerard suggested.

Fronda's black eyes flashed with indignation.

"If that's true, I'm not surprised he bit them," he said angrily.

Never drove, trying not to go too fast so as not to attract the attention of the traffic cops.

"Well, we have Hunters off our backs," he said after a moment. "They'll have to explain this noise, and if they start talking to the gendarmes about vampires, they'll definitely end up in a nuthouse. And as for the dog, we have to get some meat for him."

"The butcher will be closed at this time," Gerard said, stroking the animal's neck. The dog kept its muzzle confidently on his lap and flicked his ears lively, as if he knew what they talked about.

"No, it's not closed," Never said, braking next to the butcher's shop. He picked the door lock to the back room, went inside, and after a moment left, holding a large package under his arm.

"And now, home," he commanded cheerfully, sitting behind the wheel again.

The hunters apparently did not know the location of the apartment, because it was intact. The friends left the car in the garage and went to their apartment with the dog on their heels. "Full blood for everyone, I guess?" Never headed to the kitchen, from where he brought bottles with contents that was almost black in artificial lighting, and unwrapped a large bone, generously covered with meat, from the wrapping paper. The dog grabbed the meal and laid down with it on the rug, grunting with joy.

"How did you find me?" Gerard asked, having satisfied his strongest thirst.

"It wasn't that hard," Never explained to him. "Fronda, the old jailbird, knew where the Van Helsing Institute branch was located near Paris, and realized that they had taken you there as soon as we had looked through the streets around Erzika. While the psycholocation is not difficult for any of us, he is even more sensitive than an average vampire."

There was a crack of a bone crushed in huge teeth, coming from the rug area, and Fronda shook his head admiringly.

"I'm really curious why he helped us," he murmured. Everyone liked the dog. He was a beautiful specimen of his breed, though thin and neglected, but large, hairy, with a powerful chest, wolf-like color and gorgeous, dark brown eyes.

"Okay, but what will happen to him next?" Said Never after a moment. "With our lifestyle... a dog?"

There was a moment's silence, then Gerard whispered half-heartedly:

"A shelter?"

Fronda's eyes glared unexpectedly, his lips trembling as if he were about to cry.

"A shelter?" He repeated. "But why? He's not done anything."

He knelt on the rug and embraced the dog by the neck.

"Rajah, be a human for once," he asked in a suspiciously hoarse voice. Gerard suddenly understood something that should have been clear to him from the beginning: although younger by two hundred years, it was Never who made all the decisions. Fronda was probably just like people in his days - impulsive, brave and rather irresponsible, so the role of a leader had to be given to Never.

Still, Gerard took his side without hesitation.

"I can walk him," he offered.

"We will take him with us, it's a great camouflage," Theo added hopefully.

"And when we all get attached to him, then bang! The dog will die of old age," Never finished, grimly. "I have already been there, Fanfan, when you were not even in the world yet. Fronda was hysterical for two weeks, I thought I'd go crazy because of him. Anyway, do as you want, I'm washing my hands."

"Wash the glasses too, once you are at it," the actor advised mischievously, while Theo gave a shout of joy and hugged the dog biting on the remains of the meal, as if he were one of his former wolf friends. Never huffed like a cat and went into the kitchen, and Gerard joined him after a while.

"Why do you tease him so much?" He asked quietly. "After all, you like him a lot."

Never turned the tap on.

"Fronda is a ridiculous fool," he said grimly. "He always has some wild ideas that later come back to haunt both of us. When I met him, he wore a headband and a black burnous because he was trying to get a kidnapped beauty out of the harem. I don't even know if he succeeded, but I would bet yes. He saved my life and I, a moron, instead of saying "Thank you" and running as far as possible, began to roam with him and soon it was difficult for me to live without his company. Perhaps I have some unfulfilled fatherly feelings towards him, although I am so much younger than him."

"Or maybe he knows better what he should do? Maybe you shouldn't treat him as if he were weak-minded?" the actor asked.

The Hindu looked at him with pity and returned to the room.

"Tomorrow, early dusk, we will have to take the animal to the vet, vaccinate him, get rid of flees, buy a leash and a muzzle," he said sternly. "You are responsible for it, Monsieur de Joinville."

"Your order, General." Overjoyed, Theo kissed the dog on the mouth, then stood up and took his chessboard out of the drawer.

"Feel like playing?" he asked Gerard.

"You know what? With great pleasure," the actor agreed. "I can use some relaxation."

Never tuned the radio on and threw himself on the chair, opening the new Newsweek. Both friends stared at the chessboard, absorbed in problems of a strategic nature. It was always like that when they started playing a game.

"The situation in Vietnam is getting worse again," said the Indian after a long moment. "I don't like it. And in the US, anti-war demonstrations of hippies are increasing."

"They should try their luck to demonstrate like this in France, for example in 1369," Theo snorted, not taking his eyes off the board. "I'm not sure if any of them would save his life. Americans lack discipline, and no wonder, what kind of nation is this? They are not a nation at all. It's a pathetic motley crew with a criminal history, and it's no wonder they don't have the slightest bit of a real patriotism."

"And still, this is the cradle of democracy," Gerard remarked, wondering at the same time whether to move the bishop or the tower.

"Democracy is a bullshit. How can you let the fate of the country be influenced not only be the wise and educated, but also by an illiterate moron?" - Theo moved his queen and glanced at his friend. "And what will you do now, smarty pants?"

Gerard scratched his head.

"I don't know," he admitted. "Maybe I'll just pull the tablecloth?"

They both laughed, but an unexpected sound interrupted them. The dog rose slowly from the carpet, growling strangely, then suddenly shook violently. The black, brown and tan fur flew in all directions. A thin, curled up, completely naked girl, whom they probably already knew, was kneeling on the carpet. She was definitely not pretty, but her eyes retained the almond shape and warm color of the dog's eyes, and the thick head of black hair, reddish at the ends, fell on her forehead and neck.

"What are you staring at?" she murmured reluctantly.

"There is enough to look at. Where do you have your dress, our Sylph from the park?" Theo took off his shirt and tossed it to the girl. A silver plate flashed dully on his hairy chest.

"I lost it," said the girl, dressing quickly.

She was short and thin, Fronda's shirt almost reached her knees.

"You are the one from the park? Now I understand why these guys wanted to beat you up." Gerard leaned his head on his hands. "But there is something false in it. Why a dog, not a wolf?"

"All werewolves are shepherds," Never instructed him. "It's logical, you know? What does the wolf have in common with a man? Nothing and nothing again. And a dog has been accompanying a man for tens of thousands of years, so it is not surprising that when genes got mixed due to some sort of cataclysm... Well, young lady, say now, who you are, actually."

The girl sat on one of the pillows.

"My name is Augusta Monteloupi, Oggy for friends," she said with a sigh. "Although I don't have any friends now anymore. I was born in Palermo. It happened to me when I was adult already. I was going to study archeology, I was in love with a handsome boy from the neighborhood... Suddenly, one day, my ancestors' heritage awakened in me and everything collapsed. It is so in my family that a werewolf is born about once in a hundred years and there is nothing anyone can do about it. Everyone, thankfully, was too busy at the time with what Hitler said in the newspapers to notice that I was changing..."

"Wait a minute," Gerard interrupted her. "So, how old are you?"

In his opinion, the girl could not be older than twenty.

"More than you think," she said. "Werewolves do get older, but very slowly. About five years per century, no more, that is, if they live so long, which, as you probably guessed, can be problematic. When I found out that the family curse reached me, I began to hide, not wanting my otherness to hurt my relatives. I slowly got used to being alone and hiding from people, although this is not always pleasant.

"Why did you help us?" asked Never.

The girl smiled weakly.

"You helped me too," she reminded him. "From then on, I stayed close to you, though you didn't know it, and when I realized what was happening, I couldn't remain indifferent. The difficult part was to climb the ladder to the roof as a dog. I would disappear right after the action, but when you promised me a dinner, I decided to go with you. I haven't eaten anything in two days."

She buttoned the shirt carefully and turned her warm brown eyes on Fronda.

"How can you wear silver?" She asked, wrinkling her nose.

"I'm used to it. A question of self-discipline," Theo answered her, for a moment coming back in his thoughts to those days, when he was paying with an endless nightmare for the possibility of keeping the only souvenir of the past.

"Well, baby," Never said slowly. "As you can see, living alone is not very safe for you. Join us. You will have friends, a protection and food always provided, because judging by your looks, you have not eaten enough for a long time.

Oggy licked her lips slightly.

"That's true," she admitted reluctantly. "I think it used to be easier for me to hunt or snatch something, now I must fast for most of the time indeed. I eat only raw meat actually, so I have problems with it. But I would not like to bother anyone with my problems... I made a mess here, sorry."

"Don't worry. We run a bachelor household here and we are not overly pedantic," Theo comforted her. "But seriously, Oggy, stay with us. I know what it means to be lonely and hunted. You deserve a better fate."

He sat in his place, folded his hands on the bare torso and looked at the girl kindly. She smiled shyly.

"You know you're the first person to tell me that?" she whispered gratefully.

"Don't overestimate it, he just knows how to talk to women," Never said, a little jealously. "But he's right, stay. You bought your way into our brotherhood with a tribute of blood, so to speak. Now tell me what to buy you: a dress, underwear, cosmetics?"

"Just a dress. I don't wear underwear. Can you imagine me as a dog in panties?" Oggy chuckled.

She looked slightly better, though her elongated, thin face with bloodless lips resembled a bit more a dog's mouth than an average girl's face. They could not see the shape of her ears, they were covered by untidy strands of hair, dull, and reddened at the ends, but her teeth were definitely dog-like, with large fangs, although slightly smaller than that of a sheepdog. When she kept her mouth closed, they were not visible.

"I dream of a bath," she said, wrapping tighter Fronda's shirt, too big on her. "Where's the bathroom?"

She marched in the indicated direction cheerfully, as if she had lived in this house for centuries.

"There were already four of us once," Never said quietly, resting his pointed chin on his hand. "Even more. We must guard this little one well, Hunters would not forgive her."

"Don't you worry about that," Theo turned away and turned the radio knob. Sports news was being broadcast, and he never missed it, especially in the summer months, when most meetings were held.

* * * * *

Gerard woke up in the middle of the day, feeling a real confusion in his head. He dreamed of something so strange that he could not put it in words, but finally, from a flood of overlapping images, he caught one: the image of Anne, sitting on the porch of their house in Ramatouelle, supported by elbows on a table with ceramic tiles, covering her face with hands in silent despair. She was silent, so silent that this silence rang louder than the loudest lament.

"Oh, Anne..." Gerard whispered. The longing overwhelmed him so much that he felt like crying, taking advantage of the fact that no one could hear him.

Never was sleeping on his bed, which he rarely did, because he needed much less sleep than others, Fronda was also asleep, apparently dreaming of something not very pleasant, because he clenched his hand in a defensive gesture. Oggy murmured in her sleep on his quilt, curled up like a dog she partly was. She had been sleeping like this from the beginning. She explained to Theo that she would feel safer this way, and Fronda agreed without hesitation, chivalrous as always. This girl quickly proved to be an extremely valuable acquisition for all of them.

Being able to move around easily on the sunniest day, she ran many errands for them, though she had to be very careful not to turn into a dog at the least appropriate moment. Never quickly discovered that it was easier for her to control these transformations when she had eaten well and was satisfied with her life, and he carried out relaxation exercises with her every day, which proved to be very helpful. However, Oggy and Fronda understood each other best, which was easy to predict, since his chivalry and handsomeness had always been a kind of lure for the fair sex.

He smiled despite his troubles. He knew well that hardly any man could compete with his medieval friend, and that, contrary to appearances, it wasn't just a matter of beauty. Fronda was tender, polite and gentle, he had unusual charm, he treated every woman, even the Huntswoman from VHI, like a lady, but naturally his pretty face and diamond-like eyes also did their job. No wonder his spell worked on Oggy as well. Suddenly, the actor flinched. His sensitive hearing caught a strange sound coming from the staircase. Someone was going from door to door, trying to walk as quietly as possible, which in itself was suspicious. Nobody lived in this tenement except their brotherhood, so such creeping along the corridor did not bode well.

Gerard got up quietly and shook Fronda.

"Get off me, or I'll do you a plastic surgery," Theo murmured indistinctly, hiding his head under the pillow.

"Get up, someone is walking around the house," Gerard whispered in his ear.

"Then kill him," Theo mumbled, but when yanked again, he finally sat up. "I hope it is something important, otherwise I'll really beat you up for waking me in the middle of the day."

Oggy woke up and snarled like a dog. Even as a human, she retained a lot of dog qualities. Never also came to his senses in a second and started to listen carefully.

"Hush, guys," he said after a moment. "There is a whole liquidation group in the building. Dress quietly and take what you care about most in your handbags. We have to run. Oggy, close the porters, there is nothing to conspire now anymore."

"In the middle of the day, right? Rare pleasure," Frond growled in dissatisfaction, quickly pulling on his jeans.

"There are ten of them," Oggy muttered, drawing the black curtains quickly.

"Maybe it's just a construction committee?" Gerard asked with a weak hope.

"The construction commission does not sneak. And doesn't wear military boots" Never opens the masked additional door to the corridor.

Friends sneaked out to the old kitchen stairs, of which the intruders apparently did not know.

"The gate below is walled up, and the lower floors are still cluttered with debris from the time of war," Theo said quietly, trying to avoid the light falling through the dirty windows.

"And that's why we have to escape through the window," Never decided.

"In this sun?" Fronda stared at him.

"Do you prefer a stake in the heart? Well, then it's your choice."

The Indian opened the window with a sharp jerk.

"Maybe it doesn't shine that much," Theo consoled himself uncertainly, looking out into the yard. It was a kind of well and despite the strongly operating sun, it remained almost completely shaded.

"In that case follow me, fearless knight," following Never's example, Gerard slid down the gutter into the yard and caught the Rolls-Royce in two leaps. Right behind him, Fronda slipped inside, followed by Oggy. Never started the engine and took off for the streets of Paris at the fastest speed allowed.

"What's happening?" Oggy asked tearfully, hugging Fronda's shoulder.

"What's happening is that for now we are without a roof over our heads," Never answered her, braking a bit to yield to a group of preschoolers under the care of a teacher. "And we don't know for whom the bell tolls."

"No, don't ask for whom the bell tolls. It always tolls for you," Gerard recited with emphasis.

"Then we must know if it is a single initiative or an entire crusade."

"Aah, crusades..." Theo sighed with nostalgia.

"Are you crazy? What was so appealing about them?" the actor asked, appalled.

"A weapon for one, our green-eyed treasure," the knight explained to him. "There is no finesse in today's arm. Any cowardly scrub can pull the trigger or plant a bomb. Melee weapons were something else. It required courage, dexterity, strength, finesse..."

"Finesse, comtesse. These times are gone, you relics of knighthood. And now shut up, because I need to focus" his friend interrupted with disgust.

His training in the Kali temple taught him to use everything he would have at hand in a fight, so he did not worship the melee weapon as much as Fronda. Anyway, the type of weapon was not important now. Never felt that something very bad was happening, something he had already experienced, and his golden eyes, visible in the rearview mirror, were full of anxiety. He had already lost friends before, and did not want it to happen again, especially since he felt responsible for them. He should be able to protect them. His intelligence quotient, measured in tests at a research institute in Florida, was an incredible 250 points, and broke all previous records. Even so, he was losing to people more than twice more stupid, and losing badly, unable to save his friends from death at their hands. It was really difficult to understand.

The Indian drove through the streets for some time to lose a possible chase, finally parked the car in a guarded parking lot and turned to his friends.

"Me and Oggy will go see what's going on," he said firmly. "Stay here until we come back. You are safe in the car, but just in case, lie on the floor and cover with a rug. I don't want a living soul to see you both. We will come for you after dusk."

"Great, there will be time to sleep," Fronda yawned.

"Could you sleep at such a moment?" Gerard was indignant.

"I slept even the night before my execution," Theo said dismissively, laying on the floor.

Reluctantly, the actor lay down next to him and covered them both with a patterned cover from the car seat.

"Don't worry so much," his friend comforted him. "It could be a false alarm."

"I hope so," Gerard muttered, unconvinced. "Ouch, take this plate away from me! It stings like nettle."

"Sorry," Theo hid the plate under his shirt. "Colorful dreams."

He laid his head on his bent shoulder and after a moment, a steady breathing announced that he was sleeping the sound sleep of the just. Gerard couldn't sleep. The unusual situation, the stuffy interior, the smell of dust from the cover, it was all too irritating to let him sleep as if nothing had happened. Theo had several centuries of experience behind him, so he could not worry about anything, but the actor was still a very young vampire and did not manage to get used to certain things. He suffered for some time, listening to his friend's steady breathing, until he finally fell into sleep, even though a shallow and nervous one. He was woken by Never, opening the car door.

"Get up, sleepy heads," he commanded. "It's dark already. Our flat is gone, as well as most emergency points, so it is a crusade. The danger is so real that it stinks, and don't laugh at it, because the matter is damn serious. We must warn whomever we can."

"Who's laughing?" Theo took a small comb from under the car seat and put some order to his disheveled hair. Whatever was happening, he always took care of his appearance, which was not surprising, as he was somewhat vain. Oggy watched him sadly, tired and apathetic. She was also worried about her friends who gave her the first sense of security in many years and showed so much affection. Fronda noticed this and patted her comfortingly on the shoulder.

"Head up, baby, we've gotten through worse problems," he said with a dismissive smile.

"Speak for yourself," Gerard muttered sourly and turned to Never. "Where shall we go now?"

"To everyone, in turn," answered the Indian.

He took three shiny revolvers from the haversack, keeping one of them, and giving the other two to his friends.

"Yuck, this is supposed to be a weapon for a knight?" Fronda took the black-and-brown browning with two fingers and looked at it in disgust before putting it in his back pocket.

"What did you expect, a sword? What would it look like by a wranglers belt? Don't be whiny in such a moment" Never rebuked him sharply.

He had the same problem with him for many decades. In the fourteenth century, there was practically no firearm yet, the first clumsy guns were just created, and Theo was still trying to ignore its existence. He believed, like most knights, that this is not a noble weapon, although it must be admitted that when the need arose, he shot really accurately. Oggy didn't want a gun. She was of a rather peaceful nature, and she was reluctant to fight even as a dog, and now she accompanied men only because she was afraid to be alone in the car. The first place they went to was the night library, which had long been a convenient contact point. However, they found no one there, and the usually quiet reading room looked as if a hurricane had passed through it. Next up was the underground of the metro, where Gusto Vanderbelt temporarily moved his laboratory, but they were not even allowed in there - firefighters and security guards were fighting with a spreading fire.

"I don't like it. Looks as if they had damn good bearing," Never said when they returned to the car and continued their trip.

Theo paled and grabbed his arm.

"La Lontananza! Now!" He shouted in a worried voice. "I have bad feelings."

"Okay, but don't catch me like that when I'm driving because there'll be an accident," muttered the Indian and stepped on gas.

Until now, he did not really believe in the existence of vampires - renegades, but rarely did Hunters strike with such flawless precision. This seemingly unlikely possibility had to be considered. On the way to the club, they checked one more place, but there were only signs that it was left in a great hurry there. Someone hurriedly carved the words, "Save yourselves." And that alone was alarmingly supportive of that grim concept. Finally, they arrived at "La Lontananza". The club was not locked, and the damaged interior clearly indicated that they had arrived too late.

"Look for some clues. Maybe the girls left a message, like the other group," Never recommended to his friends. So they separated, searching everything scrupulously: the aula, the pantry, the storeroom, wardrobes and the basement. Despite the haste, everything had to be searched very carefully, so they looked under every curtain and every overturned piece of furniture.

"We haven't searched the office," Never reminded them.

Gerard, who was nearest, headed for the administrative rooms and opened the office door, masked with artificial ivy. He felt as if he was losing air, he staggered, grabbing the door frame with both hands. For a moment he felt so weak that he got nauseous.

"Don't come here, Fronda!" he screamed desperately, seeing that his friend was heading towards him.

Too late. A violent blow threw him sideways, all the way to the wall. Never grabbed him just in time, not letting him fall, and they both looked without a world at the silent, grief-stricken Fronda, kneeling over Erzika Szabo's body. A wooden peg was stuck in the girl's chest, her hair, eyebrows and even eyelashes had the ghostly color of translucent snow, informing that this attack was effective. Oggy squeezed Gerard's arm nervously, stifling a sob, on the other side Never was clenching his fingers on his wrist and gasping for air.

"Too late," Theo finally whispered. "Its all my fault."

"No, not yours. Don't talk yourself into such things" the Indian scolded him sharply.

"Mine!" Fronda shouted. "If I didn't perpetuate her then...!"

"She would have died anyway, and as an old toothless witch," Never cut in. "You gave her over a century of a wonderful life. Thanks to you she was really happy."

Theo lowered his head and for a moment it seemed he would cry, but it was only an illusion.

After a dozen seconds he got up, took Erzika's body in his arms and headed for the exit. Friends followed him in silence. They buried their murdered friend in a botanical garden, among the flowers she always loved.

"Now we must leave from here," Never said quietly after a long moment, when they stood silent, unable to find words to say goodbye to Erzika. "We can't stay in Paris anymore, it looks like a big manhunt. We must disappear from here immediately."

Theo looked at him with eyes that were burning in the dark.

"No," he said dully. "If they want war with me, they've come to the right address. Now I will dance with them."

"What do you want to do, crazy?!" the Indian shouted, but his friend was already walking toward the exit, and Oggy followed him, as inseparable as a shadow.

"Is he... is he going to do what I think?" Gerard asked as he followed Never.

Theo was already behind the wheel of the Royce when they caught up with him.

"Are you getting in or staying?" he asked grimly.

"Alright we get in, sure," the Indian pushed Gerard into the back seat. "Whatever you do, we can't leave you alone, can we? Where now?"

"To the zoo," said Theo briefly.

"Did you love this girl?" Oggy asked quietly, trembling all over her body from the hurricane of emotions.

"I loved her. That's why I circled around the club like a moth, although I knew it would be better to leave Paris..." Fronda clenched his fingers on the steering wheel and said nothing more.

His silence was hard for everyone, like lead, especially since his mouth usually wouldn't shut. Gerard squeezed into the back of the seat. It was the first time he saw a victim of the Vampire Hunters, and he was still feeling sick from this sight. He couldn't understand why such people were portrayed in books and movies as positive characters - their mode of action was disgusting and horrifying. For him, they were not heroes or saviors of the tormented humanity, but ordinary, unscrupulous murderers, hunting for what they did not even try to understand.

"Why are they doing this?" he whispered.

"Mainly because of jealousy," Never answered seriously. "And also for sport. Some like to kill, hence the success of organized hunting. And the Hunters know that they are not in danger for killing the vampire, and they are basking in the splendor of their own heroism. It's very human."

"There are no vampires like those in the movies, right?" the actor still couldn't shake off the impression, and it moved him to such an extent that he began to chatter his teeth involuntarily.

The Indian adjusted in his seat.

"True and not true," he replied. "There may also be a madman or a psychopath among vampires, and then it gets dangerous. But it never looks exactly like in the movies, don't worry. We're not so bad."

The car stopped at the wall of the sleeping zoo. Theo disappeared for a moment among the buildings, then returned, carrying an apparently heavy bag on his shoulder.

"What do you have there?" Never worried.

"Explosives," Fronda replied. "I still have it from guerrilla times. I went to railroads just like the others, and I know how to plant and how to set off."

"You have been a guerrilla?" Gerard wondered thoughtlessly.

Theo gave him a side look, starting the engine again.

"Why does it surprise you so much?" He growled. "I've always been a good Frenchman, regardless if I wore a metal shirt or a trunk and a black beret. Anyway, you also took part in the war, I remember you. You were a liaison officer in the group that captured the Paris City Hall."

Gerard sighed.

"It seemed to us we were such heroes," he said bitterly. "And when I was in Poland, I was shown a film from the Warsaw Uprising. I couldn't sleep for a few nights. Horror. And this fate was given to people by people."

"Yes, but vampires are the quintessence of global evil," Never said ironically. Frondie, where are you taking us? You can tell me, we're buddies."

"To VHI. Time to stop running," Theo replied briefly.

Never cursed powerlessly in Hindi, then shrugged.

"Maybe you are right," he said. "I'm with you."

"Me too," Oggy joined him.

"And me too, what the hell," Gerard didn't know where he got the courage that filled him right now, but he tried not to think about it.

The murder of the beautiful dancer, although he was not associated with her in any way, shocked him far more than it did for Never or Fronda, who had already seen many such cases. As a vampire, he was still maturing, and his emotions were new to him. It was certain that he had never felt such instincts before, and it even frightened him a little, it was so far contrary to his current pacifist worldview, but he did not think to fight it. Like never before he wanted not just justice, but a revenge on Hunters, and he was not surprised that Fronda took explosives with him. Since he knew the location of the Institute, it was the most logical solution, more logical than others.

He somehow didn't care who might die in the process, and that was already truly alarming. Former Gerard Phil would have thought quite differently. However, he did not have time to ponder it, because the car stood in front of a large, dark building, hidden between the trees of a secluded park.

"Careful now," Never whispered, getting out of the car. He didn't have to say anything more, there was a certain emotional bond between the vampires that made them understand each other after half of a word, and often without words. Oggy followed them, unsuccessfully trying to take on her dog-like form, which would be much more useful now. Gerard had already noticed that she had serious problems with it - she hardly controlled her transformations at all. Never started teaching her how to do it, but he admitted it was going to take time.

The VHI building seemed to be asleep, but it felt like apparent peace. Never spotted a dark box, almost indistinguishable from the wall, opened it and began to manipulate the thin wires filling it. He worked quickly and skillfully. Finally, he stood up and beckoned to his friends, signaling that he had taken care of the alarm without problems. He loved all apparatus, especially microprocessors. He was unrivaled in this, which often came in handy, as Fronda was a technical anti-talent, and when facing electronics, he would be helpless like a two-year-old child. All he could do was to set up detonators, which was going to be useful right now. Never touched the lock and hissed softly.

"Chemically pure silver," he whispered. "Fronda, let's do it."

Theo knelt down and moved one of his lockpicks in the lock. After a moment the door opened with a quiet creak. The Hindu came in first.

"The hunters are sleeping," he said quietly after a moment of straining his sensitive senses. "But..."

Oggy sniffed suspiciously, turning her head like a hunting dog, then pointed to the floor with her finger. Never nodded. He quickly found the stairs leading to the basement and ran down them somewhere. Gerard, who walked down last, noticed the switch on the wall. The pale light of a light bulb suspended from the ceiling flooded the basement, revealing something like a cell, whose grille glistened with a bright glow of chemically pure silver. A dozen or so prisoners crowded behind the bars, including Lambdon Tygier, Jackie The Liar, and several half-naked dancers from "La lontananza". Never put a finger on his lips in a warning and beckoned to Fronda. Theo opened the lock with some difficulty - his fingers, already burned at the front door lock, were getting numb. He was less sensitive to chemically pure silver than others, but a long contact had to take its toll on him. Finally the grille was opened.

"Take everyone you find to the park," Theo ordered. "But be quiet. No murmur."

The prisoners scattered obediently around the institute, while Fronda, assisted by his friends, began to methodically place explosives across the entire ground floor. He was silent as a stone, and he spoke only once, when the phone shattering the night silence, ringing in the watchtower, from which the bound and gagged guard had already been taken. He picked up the phone, listened without a word for a moment, then hissed:

"Too late, Stig. They'll die before you get here."

He set the last load calmly and went out into the park, where the released vampires surrounded in a tight circle the terrified and semi-conscious Hunters, dragged out of their beds. The vampires helped themselves generously; each of them drank even more than they should have. They all knew already that they had to leave the city they loved, that most of their friends were murdered, and they survived only because they were supposed to serve the Institute as guinea pigs. Hatred of the Hunters burned everyone, but they waited for Fronda's order, whom they silently acknowledged as the leader. Theo rolled his cold eyes along the staggering people.

"Which one of you is it? Who is responsible for the death of Erzebeth Szabo?" he asked ominously.

Everyone was silent, terrified both by his gaze and the tone of his voice. Oggy tugged her friend shyly by the sleeve.

"None of them," she said. "Not this smell."

Fronda pursed his lips for a moment.

"You are lucky," he said after a moment, as long as eternity. "I advise you from my heart, change your profession, because if I catch you with this job a second time, there will be nothing left to pick up. Remember it well, I'm not kidding."

He turned and walked deeper into the park. His friends followed him, confused. Gerard had calmed down a bit already and was relieved that the massacre had not taken place. Theo was walking without looking back, but at one point he must have pressed the radio detonator button, because there was a terrible bang. The Paris branch of the Van Helsing Institute ceased to exist.

* * * * *

Gerard stared sadly at the city lights flashing in the calm water.

"You were right," he said. " It is just a bluff that killing supposedly isn't acceptable these days. A hypocrisy that no one believes anymore. Human fate, human life, man as an individual, it doesn't matter now anymore. In your time, certainly very difficult, at least there were no such absurdities as pitying a criminal who was justly punished for his actions, and forgetting about his victims at the same time. Indeed, now they are even blamed for causing trouble for the poor bandit."

Fronda shrugged slightly.

"My times... The Middle Ages are still alive in me," he said. "I am the Middle Ages, despite the fact that I am trying to catch up with the present times in every possible way. I can't run away from myself after all... You will understand this in a little while, kid."

Gerard moved his eyes to his smooth, almost boyish face, examined his deep eyes with elongated shape, the square jaws, the clean line of lips, always giving the impression that they were to smile any moment, mischievous dimples in the cheeks, then the entire flexible, tall silhouette of the knight. It was hard to believe that all this was over six hundred years old. He nodded.

"You should be considered a Living National Treasure," he said. "This is how people in Japan with some extremely rare skill are described."

"Japan," Theo repeated thoughtfully. "I was there, back in the samurai era. A beautiful country, but strange people. You can't communicate with them. Did you know that when the atomic bomb was dropped on Hiroshima, at first I thought they got what they asked for?"

"Of all war criminals, only Japanese were never punished... but nevertheless it was a terrible way to end the war" the actor shuddered at the thought.

"Terrible," Fronda agreed and threw a flat stone into the water. "But the Japanese had only themselves to blame. Whoever starts a war, has moral responsibility for all its consequences, including those that hit him. And contrary to the popular belief, the second war was not started by Germany, but by Japan, who attacked China and seized Manchuria."

Putting things in this way was new to Gerard. He could not deny the cold logic in Fronda's reasoning, though his own pure heart could not accept it. He belonged to those people who think with the heart, not with the head, so this centuries-old wisdom that Theo expressed bluntly, like any other of his views, did not quite convince him.

"So you think Americans had the right to drop this shit?" he asked carefully.

Theo looked at him sadly.

"Right or not right," he replied. "It wasn't their fault that other arguments did not get through to the descendants of the samurai. Thanks to these bombs, the war could finally end, although I admit that the effects of this move were extremely cruel, and their aftermath will be present for a long time. But now the Japanese play a victim, and America apologizes. Nobody reminds Japan of the Nanjing massacre, for example. I will tell you something: If they had the nuke, my little one, they would drop it in New York and then they would pose as heroes. It wouldn't occur to Japs to apologize to anyone. To date, they believe that everything was and is allowed to them, and that it is the one who defends themselves against their aggression that is guilty."

He paused for a moment.

"But don't be fooled, I also think Oppenheimer and others like him are criminals against humanity," he continued after a moment. "This bomb should never be created."

"The Americans had to have it. The Germans almost produced theirs," Gerard reminded him.

"If that happened, there would probably be no one left to give or receive the apology," Theo threw a stone in the water again. "And do you know that the Nazi scientists found asylum in the US? They lived comfortably, worked and earned lots of money. For me it is even more disgusting than using this damn bomb, whose real effects no one could ultimately predict yet in 1945."

A big black van stopped near them with the screech of the tires, and Never jumped out of it, extremely pleased.

"I swapped the royce!" He called out. "I had to pay a lot extra, but it's worth it. A racing engine, armored glass in the windows, double sheet metal and cast rubber tires."

"And it takes corners as easily as a tank, I suppose" Fronda finished for him.

"Come on, we won't be using this car in the Paris Dakkar race," Never opened the side door. "Look how much space there is. We also have a broadband radio, sliding window blinds, even a tourist fridge. Don't complain, just jump in."

Oggy was asleep in the van's kennel, rolled up under a blanket, and next to her stood a well-stuffed bag.

"We'll be taking turns driving," Never said. "Oggy and I by day, you two by night." Before leaving France, we must stop by Saint Tropez. A brilliant forger of documents lives there, we will give him a good price and we will get everything we want on spot."

"Let him also make a vaccination book for Oggy," Theo looked worriedly at the sleeping girl. "You never know when her wolf nature will take over, it's better to be prepared."

"Good point," the Hindu praised him and started the engine. Gerard looked at the window and his eyes welled up at the thought of seeing Paris for perhaps the last time. Theo felt in similar way, but he was more hardened.

"Eh, Fronda," Never sighed pityfully, watching his friends in the rearview mirror. "I'll tell you something: crying is not unmanly at all."

Theo laughed bitterly.

"Who told you that nonsense?" He asked. "You've probably listened to radio shows for women. There is no more pathetic sight in this world than a crying man. Don't expect this from me."

"A male chauvinist," Oggy said from her bed.

She had been awake for several minutes and stared at her friends with her warm dog eyes.

"Go ahead, I can even be a male chauvinist pig," a friend encouraged her kindly, unconsciously archaizing the syntax, as always in times of agitation. "Women never know what they want. They complain that men are getting effeminate, that they are soft, and they have been trying for years to redo them in their own fashion. Nobody will make a half-woman from me. I can wash myself, but no force in the world will make me use a moisturizer or a hairspray. I will not clean, wash or cook, and I will certainly not whine when I get a splinter under my fingernail. What kind of a man needs to be held by the hand at the dentist or faints when he sees blood.

"There is something to it, indeed" the girl agreed.

The van rushed through the night streets of Paris, then left the city and accelerated. They didn't even travel twenty kilometers on the highway, when they noticed a car stopped by the side of the road, and in the light of its headlights, a young woman leaning on the bonnet.

"Stop," Theo asked, touching Never's shoulder.

"What for again? Oh, knight, these women will do you in," the Indian shook his head in dissatisfaction, but he stepped on the brake obediently.

"It's Agnes," Gerard whispered in amazement.

"Theo, you made a mess again. We will die because of your arbitrariness" Never snarled, but Fronda jumped out of the car without listening to him, and embraced the girl.

"Ah, that's her he called," Oggy guessed.

"Why not the Hunters headquarters, too, while he was at that," Never hit the steering wheel helplessly with his open hand, and then lowered the window. As usual, Theo did whatever he wanted, against his instructions and even common sense, so it was better to keep an eye on him.

"You will not forget?" Agnes asked tearfully.

"Never," Fronda assured her affectionately. "It's good that you made it, though I feel guilty that I dragged you to such a desolated place at night. Someone could have attacked you..."

"Oh, what attack," she said. "You are more in danger. In Meudon, where the crew is filming the show, a Swede found me. He watched everything and then asked me about the main actor, why I chose him. Hell knows how he knew that I had a hand in it, I am not officially a part of the team. We filmed the interiors at night, fortunately he caught us at dinner in a restaurant, because he would definitely end up going at this poor man with a stake. Although I would never confuse you, and Jean Claude is a puppy anyway, he is twenty-three years old."

Agnes threw her arms around his neck and clung greedily to his lips. Oggy watched it jealously from inside the car.

"Love doves, five centimes a piece, damn it," Never murmured furiously and honked the horn urgently.

"Forgive me, baby," Theo sighed, sad to break the kiss. "Hunters are chasing us. Watch out for them and watch over that kid, so that they don't hurt him by mistake."

"You got it," Agnes promised him sadly.

He lifted her chin with three fingers.

"Keep your head up," he ordered playfully. "Crying is strictly forbidden. We are left with memories, and you will admit that they are wonderful. Wait, say goodbye to someone else."

He looked meaningfully at the car. Gerard, feeling unbelievably stupid, got out and entered the spotlight beam.

Agnes's eyes widened in surprise.

"Gerard!" She called out. "So you are alive? Oh God, I'm so happy. And how are you feeling now?"

"Pretty good, although I have rather little strength and it probably won't be much better. You know, this damn illness has really gotten to me," answered the actor, kissing her heartily on the cheek.

"Stick with Theo, and you'll live long," Agnes advised him. "And since you're leaving, stop at Ramatouelle on your way. Anne is there, you better say goodbye to her, because you will regret the missed opportunity for centuries."

"I tried to talk to her once and it only scared her," Gerard thought of the day at the cemetery with sorrow. However, his old friend shook her head.

"Try again," she said emphatically.

"Damn you, are you asleep?!" Screamed Never. "To the car, idiots!"

"Forgive me, our boss is impatient," Theo kissed Agnes again and pushed Gerard in front of him to the van.

Through the rear window they saw Agnes Varda get into her car and drive onto the road.

"She was right," Gerard said after a moment. "Rajah, I have to see Anne."

Never muttered a curse.

"Okay," he said grimly. "But on one condition: you must be absolutely obedient. When I give a sign to retreat, you will comply immediately. And don't blame me if she attacks you or rejects you with contempt."

"All right," Gerard replied hastily.

Theo looked at him with sympathy and admiration in his dark eyes.

"Two peas in a pod, clowns," Never growled through his teeth, steering the car towards Ramatouelle.

He knew the road well, and he had traveled it several times during those twenty days after Gerard left the clinic. Twenty sad, bad, November days, during which he weighed the decision whether to save the dying life of a great actor or let him leave for the unknown. Did he regret this decision? No, not even for a moment, even when he was in trouble because of Gerard.

Oggy wanted to say something, but she just barked and got out of her dress, embarrassed. She shook like a dog. Gerard scratched her mechanically between the ears and on the neck, wondering if he liked her more as a girl or as a dog, especially since both characters were the same Oggy, friendly and cheerful. Fortunately, by the time they arrived, she assumed her human form again. Never stopped the van in a comfortable shade, right next to the house, at the sight of which Gerard's heart went up his throat.

"Get out," the Indian grunted. "Of course we will go with you, but we will remain hidden so as not to disturb you."

Gerard nodded, went around the house, and entered through the side gate into the garden. His wife was sitting on the porch, lit by a dim light bulb, resting her elbows on a ceramic tile table, and her head on her hands. The actor stood for a moment, trying to even his breath, then overcame his fear and entered the circle of light.

"Anne..." he whispered. Anne jerked her head up, showing a gray, aged face.

"You came back..." she sighed in disbelief.

The next moment he was hugging her in his arms, he felt her convulsive tremor with his whole body, and he did not know if what was filling him at the moment was a tremendous pain or unspeakable happiness.

"I believed I'd see you again," Anne whispered, stifling a sob. "I wanted to believe it. They told me that you became a monster, the creature of the night, they wanted me to help them capture you... I called the gendarmerie and reported that psychopaths were harassing me. The gendarmes chased them away. I searched the area for many days to make sure they really disappeared from here. I was worried about you and I wanted you so much to come back..."

Gerard hugged her tighter and suddenly wished he could just take her with him. Everything would be much simpler.

"They were right, Anne," he said softly. "I'm someone terrible now. I drink blood to live, and I have the life of the cemetery guard on my conscience."

"No, you don't," Anne interrupted him almost angrily. "The man you are talking about survived your attack and was taken to prison straight from the hospital. He had been robbing graves for years, as it turned out in the investigation. And you felt guilty because of such trash?"

"One can't take another person's life, trash or not. I am glad that this guard survived," Gerard was surprised how much he felt relieved. The event in the cemetery lay with a weight of a stone on his heart, he didn't even realize how much. Anne looked at him with her gray eyes with pain and happiness at the same time, her lips trembling slightly.

"Do you want to see the children?" she asked quietly.

Gerard shook his head regretfully.

"Better not," he replied. "I could not find enough strength in myself to leave, and I have to flee France. Those who harassed you are really dangerous."

"I hope you... you're not lonely," Anne's voice trembled despite her will. Her husband hugged her tighter.

"I have friends," he said.

The tiny woman in his arms clenched her teeth so as not to cry. She hated herself for not being honest with him when she learned that he would die. She lied to him, following the advice of doctors, she wanted to spare him spiritual suffering, but now she was sure it was a mistake.

"Forgive me if you can," she said hoarsely. "I wasn't honest with you, but I paid dearly for it. You don't even know how much I suffered before we met there, in the cemetery. I know I acted like an idiot, but when I calmed down and considered what happened, I felt so much joy... I don't care about your transformation at all. Now that I know you are alive, the pain filling my life will be much easier to bear. Knowing that you lead your mysterious night life somewhere out there, I will be able to get through everything."

"Oh, Anne..." Gerard buried his lips in her hair and wished that moment would last forever. However, it had to end painfully quickly, because not far from them, hidden safely in the bushes, waited two unusual men and a skinny, not pretty girl with dog eyes. They were waiting for him, letting him say goodbye, though they were being chased by the danger from which they had to flee the country as soon as possible. He belonged to another world now.

"Maybe someday..." he began, but Anne interrupted him again:

"Don't say anything. I have to atone for my guilt towards you and our love, based on mutual trust, on the truth... However, when it gets very hard for me, I will always be able to think that somewhere in the world there is a man whom I love. Kiss me now as you used to, and go to your friends. Let's not prolong this moment anymore, otherwise I will finally cling to your legs and start howling for you to stay or take me with you. Let me keep the last of my dignity."

* * * * *

"Indeed, brilliantly counterfeited," Oggy looked at the documents smelling of new print, provided by the counterfeiter. "Paper, watermarks, stamps, everything agrees perfectly."

"Sure. If you have that many years to get better in your profession, then your skills must improve," Never took the papers from her and put them in the glove compartment under the dashboard, together with a few dirty socks. "Like this they will lose the smell of novelty, just a trick. Fanfan, change your facial expression please. My eyes hurt from looking at your sour face."

Gerard, stuck behind the wheel of the van since dusk, murmured something unintelligible in response. He felt bad, very bad, and could not improve his mood despite the attempts he made. Theo sat beside him with a radio to his ear, and cheered on Notre Dame team, whose match with Bayer Leverkusen was broadcast by one of the stations. Finally, he regretfully turned the radio off, because as they approached the border, the reception became worse.

"Don't be mad, Gerard," he said. "But I thought your wife would shed a few tears over your forever damned little soul, and here - nothing."

"We're atheists," the actor growled reluctantly.

Theo hummed some psalm and then said:

"The unbelievers are real hell-raisers. They have no one to turn to in an extreme situation and they lose their heads. Do you know what Jackie Liar once told me? That over there, in America, people like you two have the words curved on the tombstone: 'Here lies an atheist. He is all dressed up, and he has nowhere to go.' At least we believed in something."

"It didn't stop you from committing the worst crimes at all," Gerard turned the steering wheel so angrily that it threw everyone sideways.

"Yes," Fronda agreed. "Think, however, how much worse we would be without our faith."

"Anyway, we're going to Spain." Never unfolded the map and began to study it diligently. "A very old and very powerful vampire lives there, he'll help us decide what to do next. If there really is a vampire renegade in the ranks of the Hunters, everyone is in danger, not just us."

"Treason is the most powerful weapon I know, and believe me, I know many of them," Theo said sadly. Oggy put her head on his shoulder and rubbed her cheek on his neck. Fronda stroked her head tenderly. He liked this girl like a little sister, and she clearly favored him.

"Turn, Fanfan, there is a border crossing there. We must get to Spain as soon as possible and warn everyone," Never said, straining his cat's eyes into the dark.

"Don't worry, we'll warn them if it's necessary," the actor murmured without much interest.

"Goodbye then, sweet France," Theo sighed regretfully. "Who knows if we'll see you again?"

"Don't get too emotional," the Indian rebuked him. "Only what's ahead of you counts, you taught me this yourself, didn't you?"

Theo poked Gerard friendly in the shoulder.

"Keep your chin up," he comforted him. "History does not want us anymore, so we will create our own. And believe me, it has its unusual charm."

"If you say so," Gerard was not at all convinced, but Fronda's cheerful talk, as usual, dispelled his sorrows, let him look at the future with brighter eyes. He stared at the road rushing by outside the window, and somewhat against himself, he felt the first faint surge of hope.

PART 2
The Mystery of Stonehenge

"She didn't tell you anything specific?" Gerard asked, frowning.

For several days, the four friends had been sitting in an old house near Paris, and watching everything on TV, for lack of something better to do. They should actually be heading to England now, but Fronda, to whom it occurred out of blue to call his old friend, insisted on helping her, even though she hadn't even explained to him on the phone what it was about.

"Nothing at all," he replied, stretching lazily in his chair. "Only that someone needs my help and that he is her special friend. She made me say that I would do nothing to him, unless he agreed. That's all."

"That's not much. Let this unlucky person contact us quickly, because we are sitting here pointlessly, while a well-paid job awaits us in England," Never murmured.

The new documents, a "house on wheels" type car, and a several-month travel around Europe consumed almost all the friends' savings. They had a choice to either steal or find a way to earn their living. The idea was given to them, quite by accident, by the eccentric vampire from Spain, Octavio di

Mauro. Like Gusto Vanderbelt, he was involved in scientific research and even had a well-organized laboratory located in an underground bunker. It was built back during the time of General Franco, and equipped well. Octavio, along with several of his fellows, adapted it and equipped for his purposes. Mainly small inventions came out of this laboratory, making it easier for vampires to live in the modern world, but they also worked on more serious problems.

"Think for yourself how hard it is to be a scholar in the modern world," he said. "Anyway, not only in modern times, it has always been this way. You study, work, you get some results, and here boom! a dementia, and goodbye, beautiful mind. Or you die in a stupid accident like Pierre Curie. We don't have these problems."

"Yeah, but you can't be famous for your discoveries either," Oggy said. "You can't publish under your names."

Octavio winced slightly.

"It seems so, but a real scholar works not for himself, but for the happiness of humanity. Besides, it's not like we get absolutely nothing out of our inventions. We sell them. You would be surprised, my dear, how many inventions were patented by people who did not even have a finger in their creation. They got all the results from us, of course not for free."

"That's disgusting!"

"Yes, but practiced for centuries. Edison also bought inventions of real science artists. He bought or appropriated them, because such things happened too. And for a long, long time he was considered a genius, although this title suited him just like a Hasidic hat to a pig."

They liked Di Mauro very much. Despite his age, he was as enthusiastic as a young man. Together with similar enthusiasts, he ran a truly thriving scientific institution, which even had a section called the "Department of matters deemed supernatural". It explored everything from legends and myths to the real adventures of people who came across something inexplicable. Theo, a true believer in ghosts, witchcraft and aliens, immediately found a common language with the employees of this department. He promised them solemnly that he would write about all such manifestations he would come across.

They stayed at the institute for some time before returning to France to see how the "big hunt" ended. Examining all the evidence, they were convinced that the hunters at the Van Helsing Institute had help - and that it was someone from their own circle. It was a nasty news that was difficult for them to digest. A traitor vampire was a rare thing, but it would not be the first such case. Reluctantly, they had to consider this possibility too.

It was Octavio who offered them to set up what could be called a mobile detective agency.

"Unlike many of us, you do not have problems with moving around," he explained. "Over time, most of the perpetuated get hysteria attacks at the very thought of traveling farther than the nearest tolls. Hell knows why this is happening, some kind of mental blockade or something... And even those who can force themselves to change their place of residence, find it hard. You are not like that, so you could, so to speak, serve the community. And earn handsomely at the same time."

"Can we do it?" Gerard asked dubiously.

"Why not? You are an actor, you can play the role of any character, and pretend whatever you want, a dream case for a detective. Fronda knows how to seduce women and fight, Oggy's sense of smell will find everything and everyone, and Never has his high IQ. In my opinion, it's sin not to take advantage of it."

"And what, we buy a newspaper ad that we provide non-standard services for 'the children of the night'?" Theo snorted.

"What stands in your way?" Octavio was unfazed. "After all, we have our language code, nobody but one of us will understand what this announcement is all about."

He was so enthusiastic about the idea that he was the first to write an advertisement that could not arouse suspicion in the uninitiated, and put it in several international magazines at his own expense. This brought a quick result - they solved a few small puzzles, and they were contacted by Theo's acquaintance, asking them to come to London and help her solve a case. They would probably have been there already, were it not for Fronda's phone call to his former friend, and as a result they found themselves here, in the middle of nowhere, in an old crumbling house, waiting for no one knew what.

The Indian turned on the television and began to switch channels.

"Theo, look!" He exclaimed after a moment. "It's you."

"Hell, indeed! I forgot they filmed my apotheosis," Fronda was happy.

For a moment, everyone followed the adventures of the screen hero with interest.

"Well done beating up this rascal!" Oggy cried with delight. "You really fought like this?"

" Even better. Don't forget that the actor does not want to hurt his colleague from the set, and I wished to do just that," her friend answered proudly.

"And you really wore such a sexy outfit?" Gerard asked with interest.

"Not quite the same, but similar. What was I supposed to wear in those days? Wranglers or a suit from Armagni?"

"Very flattering," Oggy smiled, turning her warm, doggy eyes toward him.

"Mmm, not sure," The actor grimaced. "Just get a whip and you can apply for work at your nearest sex shop."

"Get off me, many used to wear things like that at the time," Fronda felt resentful and wanted to add something else, but the doorbell rang.

"I'll open it," the girl volunteered, getting up from the couch and running into the hallway.

She did not like it when her friends began to argue and she was happy that something was happening that would distract them away from the subject of the dispute. She quickly traversed the long, winding corridor (indeed, this old house was simply made for the seat of the vampires), ran downstairs and unlocked the heavy door, not without a trouble, literally freezing at the sight of a young man who stood in the doorway with a worried expression.

"I'm very sorry," he said. "Agnes Varden sent me here. Are you the one who is supposed to help me?"

Oggy opened her mouth, then closed it, shook her head and struggled to get out her voice:

"No, I don't think it's me. Come inside, I think I'm starting to understand what your problem is."

She closed the door carefully, habitually checking through the infrared viewfinder whether anyone was watching the house, but all she saw was the lights of Agnes Varden's departing car. She led the guest upstairs.

At the end of the corridor they heard laughter and a loud shouting:

"You got so fooled! The guy put you to sleep like a baby! A man like an oak with a brain like a peanut! Why have you drunk this nasty stuff?"

"Get off me, how could I know? Besides, it wasn't like that at all..."

"Yeah, yeah, sure. Who can check now if you are telling the truth?"

The amused friends only fell silent at the sight of Oggy and the clearly frightened man who stood behind her.

"Holy crap!" Fronda yelled after a moment.

He did have a reason to be surprised. The visitor differed physically from him only in that he looked about a few years older, had shorter hair, and it could be seen from afar that he was dying of fear.

"This Agnes could have warned you at least," Gerard said, folding his arms on his chest.

"She could. But she did not. She probably thought it would be funnier this way," Never said.

He was always against his friend's affairs with ordinary women, because this usually resulted in problems.

"I'm..." the guest began.

"Jean-Claude Drouen, we know," Oggy interrupted. He nodded.

"I have a problem," he said. "I have a horrible problem."

"You probably didn't protect yourself," Fronda chuckled with amusement.

"And you didn't check who you hang out with," Gerard added maliciously.

"You didn't think when you did it, so now do as you think," Never joined his malice.

"Stop fooling around, guys," Oggy said, disgusted.

"All right, we shut up now. So what's the matter?"

The actor took a letter out of his pocket, with the inscription "Agnes Varden" on the envelope, and handed it to Theo without a word. He opened it and began reading aloud:

"Friend, listen to the owner of this letter and try to help him as much as you can, for the memory of what once united us. It is very important to me, and remember what you once promised me. Always yours, Agnes"

He looked at his guest with a mixture of amusement and surprise.

"What is this about?" He asked. "Should I improve your acting skills? That would be difficult, I've never been a comedian. Unless you want to learn how to fight properly, because I noticed that you are taking too big a swing, and if you support the strike with your shoulder, it will be much more effective."

The actor shook his head.

"The problem is..." he began. "I know who you are, Agnes told me. The thing is, I look very much like you, and that's what causes my trouble."

"Fronda is too handsome for this to pose a significant problem. You should rather be happy," Oggy interrupted him.

He looked at her helplessly. Up close, the similarity he complained about was becoming a little less obvious. His eyes were gentle and calm, unlike Theo's, which literally pierced a person throughout.

"Nothing to be happy about," he said. "The thing is, I'm really in trouble. It started with the feeling that I was being followed. Friends put it down to fatigue, stalking mania, and hell knows what else, but later it got even worse. I started to get anonyms with more or less the same content: *'I know who you are.'* At first, I didn't pay attention to it, but as it repeated, I began to get nervous. Finally, a few weeks ago, I received this."

He handed the vampire a crumpled piece of paper, on which someone wrote in capital letters:

'You are dead. The fact that you managed to reverse the process, will not save you from VH's revenge. You will pay for your crimes.' There was no signature.

"Reverse the process?" Fronda looked questioningly at Never. "Is it even reversible?"

"Theoretically, yes," answered the Indian. "Gusto Vanderbelt worked on this... Wait, Gusto?"

"Gusto is the traitor you are looking for?" Oggy asked in surprise.

Never looked at her somberly.

"Gusto or Tygier are the only possibilities, because only they know the results of the work on reversing the perpetuation process," he answered slowly. "We can safely rule out Lambdon, because the Hunters would have attacked Octavio's research station long ago. That leaves us with Gusto."

"Oh no," Fronda protested vehemently. "I don't want it to be Gusto. I don't agree to this."

Never approached him and took the piece of paper from him.

"You may disagree," he said. "But now everything fits into a logical whole. Anyway, we'll think about it later, now let's deal with the issue of your double. It can't be denied that you put him in this lousy situation by your confessions to Agnes. We have to figure out how to fix it."

He looked at the young Belgian who was still standing, clenching his hands and mouth involuntarily.

"Stop shaking," he scolded him sharply. "It is a shame to be such a coward, if only because of the similarity to Fronda. Sit down."

"Excuse me, can I smoke?" Jean-Claude asked quietly.

"Go ahead," Never waved his hand and started walking around the room.

"I can only think of two options, one is to make this boy one of us, and the other is to do something to make the Hunters see him and Fronda together," he said after a moment.

"The second idea is out of question," Oggy said firmly. "I don't agree, no way. It is not only extremely dangerous to Fronda, but also unreliable. They may still think these two have something in common, and that's all these fanatics need."

"Well, then the first option remains." Never shrugged and looked at the actor, who was sitting huddled in a chair, crumpling helplessly the empty Gauloise package in his fingers.

Without a word, Gerard reached out with his own package in his direction, the guest lit up with relief, thanked him quietly and probably only then he realized what Never said.

"Oh no," he protested vigorously. "This is not an option at all."

"Why not? It is nothing scary, it does not hurt, it is even quite nice" Gerard wondered kindly.

Jean-Claude shook his head emphatically.

"Out of question. Not if I have a say in it. I don't blame you, you were dying, but I really wonder at the two of you."

"I didn't have a choice, either," said Never.

"Me neither, I wasn't given it," Theo joined him.

"But I don't want it," Jean Claude almost shouted these words. "Understand, I have a wife, children. I want to enjoy life. To eat what I like, drink good wine, sunbathe on the beach on a clear day. Play in the theater, make movies and be stopped by teenagers on the street. I want to make love to my wife every evening. To watch my children grow up, go gray with worry at the sight of reprimands from their teachers, do homework, go to the movies and to Disneyland with them, then get mad when the son grows his hair floor-long and the daughter does not come back from her date until late night... Participate in all their sorrows and joys, wait for my grandchildren to be born... All this has been taken away from you. Seemingly you have more, but in fact you are poor, poor and without a soul. I would never want to share your way of life."

There was silence for a moment, then Fronda said:

"Wow, way to tell us off. I like this guy. There is something about him, no doubt about it."

"But we're in the tight spot now. How to help him if he rejects the only possibility?" asked Gerard, on whom his colleague's words made a very unpleasant impression.

"Dude, you don't know what you are saying," Never said to the guest. "You will have to pay dearly for all the pleasures you have listed. You will age, my dear. And the old age means you know what: hypertension, atherosclerosis, varicose veins, obesity..."

"You are visually impaired, hearing impaired, you are grumpy..." Fronda added.

"The stomach, kidneys, liver get bad, the hair falls out, not to mention the teeth..." Oggy joined.

"Diabetes, sclerosis, cataract, and a senile atrophy for dessert," Never finished. "All kind of sweet treats. Do you really need it?"

"Yes I do. Can't you understand that I just don't want to be a vampire? I only came to you because I am cornered and nobody else can help me."

Jean-Claude took another cigarette from the packet, but only turned it in his fingers without lighting it, and looked at Fronda with a mixture of fear, curiosity and fascination.

"Is that you..." he hesitated. "Was it your character that I was told to play?"

"What?" Theo looked at him thoughtlessly. "Ah, yes, at least it looks so. A lot of what I told Agnes ended up in the series, although not everything was like in the scriptwriter's dreamed, but never mind, his intentions were certainly good. You were also acceptable in it, but..."

"Fronda, stop babbling, will you. This guy has not come here for artistic consultations," Never interrupted him. "Since you promised to help Agnes, you should keep your word. What are you going to do?"

Theo smiled ironically.

"You know what?" He said. "Stay here and I will go with our guest to the point number three. As far as I know, it is now empty."

"I think so, but what are you up to?" Oggy looked at him suspiciously.

"I won't involve you in this, it's my problem and I can handle it myself. Wait for me and don't worry too much, " her friend replied.

"Yeah. You've probably come up with something moronic again," Never grunted.

"Don't worry, Rajah. My plan is flawless, idiot-proof. Come on, star from the sky, why are you sitting like this?" the last words were obviously directed at the actor.

"Remember what you promised to Agnes? Nothing against my will," reminded Drouen, who was clearly still impressed by the extraordinary company he was in.

"Oh, come on. I know my promise and I will keep it."

Theo grabbed his arm and pushed him out of the door unceremoniously.

"Somehow I don't like it," Oggy muttered, running over to the window and watching them both get into a black Opel, their guest's property.

"Does Fronda really know what he's doing?" Gerard asked, looking at Never, who grimaced reluctantly.

"He never knows what he's doing," he replied. "He always acts like the last idiot and always gets away with it somehow."

*****

A steel gray sedan drove up to an abandoned warehouse over a long closed open-pit mine. Several men and one girl got out of it, all dressed similarily in black military-style overalls.

"Are you sure it's here, Stig?" the girl asked softly.

"I have no idea," answered Stig. "This woman, who gave me the letter, drove away too quickly for me to ask her anything. It is good though that our word of mouth is starting to work effectively, as can be deduced from this. This woman was a hundred percent human, so the tip is rather legit. Just in case, everybody put on your silver, there can be more of them here. Kola and Pietro guard the back, Senta, check if there is a rear exit. Everyone stays in touch."

The Vampire Hunters obediently fastened wide chains around their necks and wrists, and activated the headphones hidden under the caps. Like any operational VH group, they were well equipped and ready for any eventuality.

"Testing, testing, one two three... Can everyone hear me? Be careful, Fronda and his buddies are dangerous," said the squad leader. "Prepare the explosives, if there is no other way, we'll blow up this warehouse, but nobody dares do it without my orders. We're coming in."

Carefully, he opened the door with a padlock hanging on it, cut long ago. The Hunters' eyes saw a dark corridor - airlock, ending with a door with a round porthole of thick glass, letting in a dim light. Holding on to the wall, they moved quietly to the end of the corridor, into a place from where they could look through the porthole, while invisible in the shade. In a small room, which was probably supposed to be something like a wheelhouse for compressors, and now furnished like a living room, a young man was sitting, resting his elbows on the table and covering his face with his hands. Thick, black hair fell on his hands, glistening matte in the light of a small light bulb, suspended from the ceiling. After a moment he raised his head.

"It's Fronda," Stig whispered to his people, barely suppressing excitement. "Prepare crossbows."

He wanted to give one more order, but fell silent with his mouth half open. The door on the opposite side of the room opened and the vampire, whom he had known so well and tracked around the world for years, entered in a light step. The man sitting at the table jumped up and ran to the wall as if in a senseless attempt to escape. He was almost identical to the newcomer, but deadly pale and visibly exhausted, both physically and mentally.

"Relax, why these nerves?" Fronda tossed the bag he had brought on the table. "I brought you some food while I remembered. Fruit, burgers and fries. Eat while it's hot, then we'll have fun."

A shiver shook his double.

"Let me out of here," he asked in a broken voice. "You promised not to hurt me... Water, give me water."

"I only promised you wouldn't serve as a meal for me if you don't let me, or make you like me against your will," Fronda interrupted cheerfully. "But you must admit that I have strong persuasion skills. I didn't have to use many arguments before you let me drink your blood."

He took a bottle of mineral water from his jacket pocket and threw it at the actor, who unscrewed the cap with trembling hands and began to drink eagerly. The hunters watched the scene unfold, holding their breath, not quite understanding what was happening.

"Why won't you let me out of here?" The prisoner asked, quenching his thirst. "I haven't done anything to you."

"Do I want to hurt you, Jean Claude? I just want to give you eternal life, deliverance from old age and death. The two of us can have a great laugh," Theo laughed, showing white fangs, slightly longer and sharper than those of a human.

He went to the radio on the dresser and began to spin the station finder.

"I don't want it," Drouen whispered.

"Gosh, aren't you stubborn..." The vampire glanced at him over his shoulder.

"I don't want to, understand?!" Jean Claude shouted desperately. "Don't touch me anymore! I won't give you one more drop of blood, monster! I hate you! You're even worse than I was told!"

Fronda stopped the knob at the country station and turned away. His eyes shone mockingly as he looked at his double from under the bangs carefully combed over his brow, drumming his fingers on the piece of furniture to the rhythm of the song on the radio "Ghost riders in the sky".

"Oh, I think I must remind you of what we were talking about," he said with an evil smile, sliding the drawer of the dresser and taking out a rolled whip with a varnished handle.

The actor stepped back into the corner, curling his whole tall figure up and covering his face with his shoulder.

"Please, don't hit me again," he groaned pleadingly. "You know I'm afraid of pain..."

"I know." Fronda approached him, striking his thigh with the rolled whip. "What kind of young people we have these days... I'll have to work hard on you before you are any good for anything."

He unfurled his whip and shot it in the air.

"This poor boy is not here of his own free will. We were wrong about him. We're coming in," Stig said into the phone, thinking it would be dangerous to wait any longer.

He lunged at the door, the rusted lock let go and the Hunters rushed inside. Fronda realized the situation in a split second and with a flash of a whip knocked the crossbows out of the Hunters' hands, forcing them to retreat.

"Surrender, bloodsucker..." Stig began.

"And it will hurt less," Fronda finished for him. "I've heard that before. You are so pompous. Only I'm not afraid of pain, and as for your 'surrender'... forgive me, but I don't even know the word."

With a nearly imperceptible movement of the whip, he snatched the browning from Pietro's hand and caught it in the air.

"I advise you to be careful now that I have a weapon," he said. "Silver bullets don't kill vampires only."

He ducked and using a judo move, sent Senta, creeping behind him, on the floor. He probably pretended not to hear her before.

"Sorry, sweetheart," he said sarcastically. "I know it's not the way to treat ladies, but I would prefer to stay in one piece."

"Go at him!" Stig commanded, but he was stopped by the sight of a Browning aimed at him, and he suddenly thought of something.

"How can you hold the silver handle?" he asked in amazement.

Fronda shifted the pistol to his right hand and showed him with a smile the inside of the left one, as if marked with a hot iron.

"If you have a warrior's heart, you can endure such a small thing" he replied "Learn, comedian."

Senta got herself up from the floor, walked over to the actor, squeezed into the corner, and embraced him protectively. Others followed her with their eyes, comparing in their mind the staggering man and a sneeringly smiling enemy standing in front of them. Now, up close, they could clearly see the bite marks on the neck and nape of the unfortunate prisoner, his pallor, characteristic for vampires' victims, and a mad terror in the eyes, like in someone driven crazy by something he cannot understand.

"Stig, he needs help," said the worried girl.

Without taking his eyes off them, Theo backed away slowly until finally he got behind the back door with a sudden jump and locked it with the outer bolt.

"Kola, Pietro, follow him, maybe you'll get him. Andre, he is running towards you!" Stig ordered, pressing the microphone to his larynx. "Let's take care of this one. It was close, we would have liquidated him and who knows, maybe it was us who led Fronda to his trail? I don't think someone like him is watching TV. Lothar, look for a phone and call an ambulance. Animal bite, heavy blood loss, general exhaustion."

The fair-haired Hunter nodded and ran out. Stig and Senta led the actor to the sofa and helped him sit down.

"Listen carefully," Senta said emphatically. "We'll call the ambulance and the gendarmes soon. Be careful what you tell them. You were attacked and bitten by a monkey that escaped from the circus. That won't be far from the truth. Don't mention vampires or anything like that, because they'll put you in for an observation in a madhouse. It's best to answer to all the uncomfortable questions that you don't remember."

"I understand," Jean-Claude whispered.

He made the impression that he had not realized yet that he had been released from the hands of a vampire and was now safe. Senta gently cleaned the wounds on his neck with hydrogen peroxide from a first aid kit, her commander checked the pulse and reflexes skillfully, revealing his medical education.

"Very poor general condition," he said finally. "He might need psychological help, but we cannot give it to him so as not to expose our activities. Hey, man, can you hear me? You need to get a grip. You must not lose it. Remember what we are telling you: it's best to stick to the version that your car broke down and you wanted to call for roadside assistance from here, and then a trained chimpanzee who was hiding here, attacked you. You don't remember anything else. They'll probably vaccinate you against rabies, but what can you do, it's still better than a madhouse."

A whining ambulance signal came from far away. The Hunters forced the actor to get up and led him outside, where the ambulance stopped after a while with a squeal of wheels. They helped him get inside.

"Take care of him," Stig said to the paramedics. "He's had a hard time and he's lost a lot of blood. His pressure is 90/60 and heart rate 120, he is in shock."

"Thank you," whispered Jean-Claude, squeezing his shoulder.

"Take care, man," said the Hunter heartily and slammed the ambulance door shut.

"Not a trail," Pietro reported, running up to him.

He waved a hand dismissively.

"We'll get him someday," he said, looking at the departing ambulance. "It's important that he's here and we know it. I hope this poor celebrity will quickly forget this nightmare. He is lucky that Fronda did not manage to force him to agree to a blood exchange, we could then only shorten his suffering... This wicked Fronda wanted to vampirize him, but he delayed it just to have fun, sadist."

Just in case, the Hunters planted the explosives under the warehouse and set them off remotely once they were at the safe distance. That was their model of operation - destroying the Undead's hideouts so that they would finally have nowhere to hide.

Meanwhile, Jean-Claude Drouen could not believe his luck when he got to the hospital, which now appeared to him as a safe haven, where no one like his tormentor could enter. Like most people, he too believed that a vampire could not enter where he would not be invited. This was obviously nonsense, as were most popular opinions about vampires. Examined by several doctors and surrounded by the most tender care of pretty nurses in snow-white aprons, he closed his eyes with relief, as soon as his sobbing wife fell asleep from fatigue by his bed.

He did not have time, however, to fall into a refreshing sleep, when he heard a murmur and after he opened his eyes, he saw to his horror Oggy, arranging a large bouquet of flowers in the vase. Paralyzed with terror, he didn't even think about reaching for the bell button and calling the nurse on duty, when Oggy turned her thin face towards him and smiled.

"These flowers are from all of us," she said. "Fronda preferred not to show up here, the hospital may be under the Hunters' observation, but he is sending you an apology. He couldn't handle it in another way. You are a good actor, but you would not be able to pretend such a terror to convince the Hunters. This had to be done with a proper realism. I'm sorry you had to go through all this, but believe me, that was the only way to make the Hunters leave you alone. Don't be mad at Fronda, he risked a lot. No one else would dare bring Hunters on his own neck."

"So it was all set up by your friend? Now I understand," the actor felt a huge wave of relief flow down his agitated mind. "I should probably thank you, but first I would have to get used to it somehow."

The girl narrowed her brown eyes in a smile.

"It's not easy for you, I know," she said tenderly. "Try to forget everything and enjoy life alongside your beautiful wife.

We are the dark side of the world that you may never meet again, and it's good that you won't. You are not resilient enough to share our lives with us, which can be really cruel and requires enormous spiritual strength."

"I noticed that," Jean Claude answered shyly at her smile. "I have no more regrets, I finally got what I wanted: you helped me, while risking your head, as you said. These Hunters..."

"They may still bother you, I warn you. They'll want to get some details out of you," she interrupted him.

The actor nodded.

"I thought so," he said. "They won't have a chance. I'm going back to Belgium with my family. It will be probably harder for me there, even here it is not easy for me to get a contract, everyone can only see me as a reflection of your friend from the Middle Ages, whom I believed to never really exist... but I will be fine."

"I'm convinced of that." Oggy leaned forward and put a sisterly kiss on his forehead.

Jean-Claude put his arms around her neck and gave her a gentle hug.

"You are very kind for a vampire," he said.

"Probably because I'm really a werewolf," the girl explained to him.

"In that case I change my opinion about werewolves," he promised her solemnly. "Give Fronda my greetings and tell him I have no more regrets that he has roughed me up a bit. I acknowledge that it was necessary and thus will forget what arguments he used. Say hello to Gerard as well, he was my idol once."

"Of course. Good luck. Someday you'll be a big star," the girl stroked his forearm with the drip needle in it, and left, closing the door quietly behind her.

*****

"I hate ships, I hate rocking. What a relief to have solid ground under my feet again," Never sighed, relieved to get off the deck of the ship.

"I agree," Gerard said weakly, barely able to stand upright.

"Weaklings," Theo laughed, not bothered by any shakings at all.

"Come on, boys, what feat is it to cross the English Channel? You'd better tell us where to go now." Oggy unfolded the map and began to study it diligently.

"For the time being, to a taxi stand, and we are to look out for the car with a heart on the glass of the driver's side door," Never said, pulling a crumpled letter from his pocket.

Friends headed towards a taxi stop, illuminated by a colorful neon. They felt insecure here in Dover, but no one seemed to know them. People passed them indifferently, busy with their own affairs. They were very late, but Theo thought that the matter Agnes Varden called him about, was more important than the matter of the newly constituted World Union of the Living. This is how the organization was ultimately called, in effort to avoid the words "vampire" or "undead." - WUL for short.

"WUL can wait, my ex girlfriend can't," he said firmly and no one tried to argue with him.

Now that they were finally here, they still didn't know what their task would be, they only had the address to which they had to go.

A young girl with short hair and lips covered with silver lipstick was sitting in a cab marked with a heart.

"The final stop?" she asked.

"Lenor," Theo told her.

The girl nodded.

"Get in, brothers," she said shortly, starting the engine.

"We apologize for making you wait here for us, but we took care of one rather special thing on our way," Never explained, taking the seat in the back.

"Am I asking something? My thing was to come here and wait," the taxi driver answered him indifferently. "I will take you to the assembly point now, and you will meet Lenor tomorrow. And I warn you, she is in charge here."

"So you have a coherent organization here?" asked Theo, surprised, sitting next to her.

"Yes. Here on the island it is necessary, on the mainland you can probably do without it" the girl pressed the gas pedal and skillfully directed the car to the highway.

"Not exactly. We already have our organization," he answered her. "The Van Helsing Institute has recently expanded its activity, and you know... What is your name, actually?"

She smiled slightly.

"Betsy," she said.

Before she could react, the Frenchman took her hand, lying on the steering wheel, and placed a courtly kiss on it.

"I am Theo," he said.

"Oh..." Betsy whispered, so surprised that she turned to the wrong lane.

"Hey, charmer! Please don't talk to the driver," Never tapped Fronda on the shoulder. "Hold back the spreading of your spell for a better moment. Betsy, don't you know why we were brought here?"

"Nobody said anything to me, but I bet it's about Stonehenge," anwered the girl, returning to the right lane. "What is going on there lately... Anyway, Lenor will explain everything to you, she always has her finger on the pulse."

"Stonehenge? I read something about this place," Oggy interrupted. "These are supposedly ruins of a druid temple or something..."

"Druid Temple, my ass. This pile of stones can be anything but it," Betsy snorted contemptuously.

"I really don't know how we can help here. If I'm not mistaken, many archaeologists have worked on solving Stonehenge's riddle, and they still know as much as we do, that is, nothing," Gerard remarked reluctantly.

The whole thing smelled to him of metaphysics, and he didn't like that at all. He definitely preferred simple and understandable things.

"You, the French, have always been terribly conceited," Betsy said venomously. "English science doesn't need your help, and if we can't solve a mystery, you surely won't be able to help us."

"Why don't you turn to Sherlock Holmes with your case then?" snapped Never, who as an Indian, had rather unfriendly feelings for the British, even though his father was an Englishman.

Betsy shrugged.

"Ask Lenor about that. She made the decision to bring your team here," she replied.

Theo got thoughtful, looking out the window.

"We're starting to be famous," he said after a moment. "I don't know if it's bad or good, but these few successful actions have brought us admirers. Until now, the vampire nation did not have an operational group, only now we filled this niche, and this means that they will be dragging us all over the world. Anyway, Octavio warned us about that."

"Don't whine, Fronda," Never interrupted him. "You complain too much. I don't know about you, but I got tired long ago with sitting in the same place like a stone. And since we are already roaming the world, we can also continue our fight. Have you already forgotten about Erzika?"

Theo paled and clenched his teeth until the muscles showed under the skin on his broad jaws.

"I didn't forget," he said dully. "And I won't forget."

"What Erzika?" Betsy asked, glancing at him sympathetically.

"Our friend. Hunters murdered her during Long Pegs Night," Never explained to her, seeing that Fronda was not going to answer. The vampire massacre in Paris had its name already.

"Fronda is tracking her killer," Gerard added. "And we're all with him, for good and for bad. We don't know who the bastard who killed this beautiful creature is, but we'll find out, and then woe to him."

He really thought so. His old human reasoning was replaced more and more by the thoughts of a vampire, for whom blood is a daily element, life is not life, and death is not death, and it is not any more scary than the drops of the autumn rain.

"Do you have any trail?" Betsy stopped the taxi in front of the dimly lit motel, with a gas station and a convenience store behind it.

"We have Oggy. She's a werewolf and remembers the smell these bastards have left," Never looked at the girl with some concern.

Despite the shortness of the journey, he was constantly worried that she would turn into a dog, for example during customs clearance, which would have fatal consequences, as she would be immediately taken to a quarantine. Now it was already less important, moreover, in the double bottom of one of the briefcases, there was an ID card, prepared especially for her by a professional counterfeiter, certifying that the German Shepherd had been adopted from the RSPCA shelter.

"Check in here," said the cab driver. "I'll be your liaison. They accept dogs in this motel, so it won't be a problem when your friend turns into a wolf. Don't make too much trouble, at least for now, and if you are hungry, call this number. The courier will deliver the goods to you within half an hour. Wait for me, I'll come here tonight."

She gave Never a small business card.

"Works good for me. We'll rest a bit before meeting Lenor. As far as I remember, you need to have nerves of steel for the conversations with her," Theo sighed, throwing the bag in which he usually kept all his handy assets over the shoulder.

Friends checked in with the yawning receptionist, giving her the currently used personal data, and then went to the indicated room, furnished with spartan simplicity, but clean and spacious enough.

"I am going to bed," declared Gerard, who was still dizzy after the sea voyage. "It's going to dawn soon."

"It doesn't matter, it has started to rain anyway," Fronda said, looking out the window. "I'm going to the market at the station, I have to buy new shaving supplies and a few more things. You need anything?"

"For me, a herbal shampoo and a good deodorant," Oggy asked.

"For me, film magazines," Gerard murmured sleepily.

"I don't need anything. Although, wait, if they have a liquor department there, a small bottle of cognac," Never said, checking the contents of his travel bag.

Theo nodded and left, whistling. He loved 24/7 stores at gas stations, and shopped mostly there when he remembered after an overnight hunt what he should do before returning home, or to the place currently replacing it. At the time he usually did it, there were few customers, and the service, tired and sleepy, paid no attention to him. This market was no different. Theo did the shopping quickly, threw some packaged beef for Oggy into the basket on his way through the meat department, paid at the checkout and left, bumping at the door into a big girl, laden with packets.

"I'm so sorry!" He called, collecting the scattered packages. "I should be more careful. I will help you, it's too much for such little hands."

The stranger laughed, helping him pick up things.

"No, it's me who is sorry," she said cheerfully. "I didn't look where I was going. Maybe it's indeed a bit too much stuff, but they stole everything at the airport, all our luggage. Fortunately, I had my money and travelers checks with me. You're from France, right?"

"My accent, isn't it? Yes. Theo Lebrigadon, at your service."

He refrained at the last moment from giving his real name, and used the one in his new documents.

"Carolyn O'Grady, from southern Scotland," the girl held out her hand to him. "Can you help me take this to the motel?"

"This motel? I live there too" Theo was happy, looking at her kindly. She seemed very pretty to him, though maybe a bit too tall.

"Then we'll see each other, at least until Colin and I find out what happened to our brother and what he got involved in here," Carolyn said friendly. "I always told him that he should have stayed in Yorkshire and not wander around hell knows where. Well, because a man should not tear himself away from his family, right? But it is pointless talking to him."

Her Scottish accent made the Frenchman hardly understand her, especially since his English left much to be desired.

"Maybe, but if everyone thought so, any global progress would be impossible," he told her.

"It's here," Carolyn paused in front of the door marked with a number seventeen. "Thank you for your help, Theo, you are very kind."

"Oh, you just don't know me," Fronda laughed defiantly and went to the room where his friends were waiting for him.

"What took you so long?" Never said severely.

"I met a nice babe." Theo replied, tossing beef to Oggy, who sunk her teeth in it with satisfaction.

"What? Theo, I think we talked about it. You are playing with fire, although you have burnt yourself several times before," the Indian looked at him with dissatisfaction.

"If I listened to you, I wouldn't take a step outside the apartment," Fronda laughed carelessly.

He unpacked his purchases, grabbed the soap and shaving accessories, then locked himself in the bathroom.

"Nut case," Never murmured.

He took the newspaper and began to browse it. There was a whole range of small announcements and gossip messages that were a kind of code that vampires around the world used to communicate with each other in really urgent situations. Now he also read and quietly translated the message: "Avoid Vienna,

Hindeburg, Dusserdorf." This indicated the activation of the Van Helsing Institute in these areas, maybe it was the result of some planned action, or maybe the Hunters participated in the annual training there. There was not a word about England, and anyway Never was not sure if the island-isolated vampires and hunters communities had any global affiliation. Maybe the Hunters did.

After a while, he folded the newspaper and stretched out on the couch. Gerard had been sleeping for a long time already, Oggy was finishing dinner and just licking her fingers (they could not make her unlearn the habit) when Fronda returned from the shower, wrapped in a large, hairy towel, which replaced his pajamas regardless of the season.

"Get some sleep," he ordered. "It is already dawn, and at dusk you will definitely have to go to meet Lenor, so we must be in shape. When you meet her, you'll understand why."

He threw himself on his couch so hard that the springs moaned.

"How's your hand?" Oggy asked him, curling up into a ball next to him, as was her custom.

"It is OK," Theo said shortly.

"How come you got burned? Your medallion is also made of silver and somehow it doesn't burn you." The girl looked at him questioningly.

"Usual silver is different from the chemically pure silver. Even I am not immune to this. Sleep, baby."

Theo reached out and tousled her hair. Her hair was dog-like not only in appearance, but also to the touch, but he was already used to this, as well as to other Oggy's anomalies, what's more, he became more attached to her every day. Never drew the curtains thoroughly, and just in case, he hung one of the room's blankets over them with a few safety pins, locked the door from the inside and went to bed as well. He needed the least sleep, but he decided to regenerate his strength in advance, because he had the rare ability to accumulate rest - after having slept through two days straight, he could go on without sleep for as long as a month.

When they started to wake up, the sun was just setting, so they had some time to prepare for the meeting with Lenor and eat something. They had a reserve supply of 'canned food', so they divided it fairly among themselves and drank it up to the last drop.

"We will need to replenish our reserves, but we can do it later. For now, this has to do for us," Never said, draining the last drops of blood from his glass and licking his lips with delight.

"No worries, Lenor will probably give us a drink," Theo sighed, rinsing his glass carefully and putting it back on the shelf. "You know, it's kind of weird for me to think I will see her again. We parted in anger so many years ago, I don't know how she will react to me now."

"She'll probably get an allergic rash," Gerard laughed, combing his hair away from his forehead in front of the mirror.

Unlike his friends, he cut his hair very short, leaving it a little longer only above his forehead, so that it could be combed back, which, in his opinion, was the only proper hair style for a man.

Someone knocked on the door. Oggy opened it and wanted to close at first, because the red-haired girl standing in the doorway was certainly not who she expected.

"Excuse me," the girl said. "Does Theo Lebrigadon live here?"

"Carolyn! Come in, please." Theo beamed so much that Oggy looked at him suspiciously. The girl shook her head.

"I just wanted to say that you took one of my parcels by mistake yesterday," she said shyly.

Fronda glanced at the table where he unpacked the shopping yesterday.

"Oh, indeed," he said, noticing an elegant package with women cosmetics among the things left there. "I'm sorry, Carolyn, I am distracted sometimes... Here you go."

He handed the package to the girl who gave him a nice smile, shook his hand and walked away, leaving behind the scent of Miss Dior perfume.

"Fronda, put out that stupid smile. Now is not the time for flirting," Never considered it appropriate to warn the friend in advance.

"It's always time for that," Theo sighed lyrically. "I'd invite her for a lunch..."

"You are nuts. What lunch can you invite her for? Control yourself for once" the Hindus hit him with the open hand on the back.

"But I don't want to control myself, I want to go for a lunch with Carolyn," Fronda insisted. "Or for a dinner."

"Is he always like that when a girl catches his eye?" Gerard asked, tying his tie in front of the mirror.

"They're all the same, his type," Oggy explained to him.

"Exactly," Never nodded. "I have known him since Napoleon's time and I assure you that he hasn't changed a bit in those years. I can't even tell you how much trouble this caused us, but the guy has learned nothing."

There was a knock again, but this time Betsy was standing in front of the door, chewing gum nonchalantly, her hands in the pockets of her suede jacket and the cap over her eyes.

"Ready?" She asked. "Come on, the boss doesn't like to wait."

The friends locked their room and got into the taxi they already knew, with the unpleasant feeling as if they were going to the matriculation examination. Betsy drove the car through the gloomy streets at maximum speed, and no one thought about how they could talk to her, so they were silent, preparing nervously for the meeting with the mysterious Lenor. They knew little about her, only as much as Fronda had said, and yet he did not confide in them about everything that connected him to this Englishwoman. Despite his apparent talkativeness, the medieval knight was able to protect well what he did not want to talk about. Finally, the taxi stopped in a rather unexpected place: in front of the huge office building on Piccadily Circus.

"Thirteenth floor, office number four," Betsy said briefly, parking at the taxi stand.

Not without certain fear, the friends attached to their clothes the identifiers to be used as passes, given to them by the taxi driver, and passed the guards, putting on brave faces.

"We have a problem," Never said as they got into the elevator. "There isn't a thirteenth floor here. There used to be no such numbers in public buildings in England. And what now?"

"Nothing," Fronda said. "I also know this superstition. We're going to the twelfth, and we'll continue on foot."

"On foot, but where?" Gerard murmured skeptically.

He also heard about the superstitions associated with the unlucky thirteen and he had already slept in hotels with no thirteenth room or thirteenth floor, but he considered it one big stupidity, devoid of any sense, because he could not quite understand how the change in numbering can affect the actual state, if there was one. However, it turned out that the builders of this office building bypassed the logical trap in a simple way - the building had a thirteenth floor, but it was unmarked and omitted in floor plans. Closed shut, it was supposed to be unused, but there were those who were not afraid of number thirteen.

The door leading out of the corridor seemed bricked up, but it was an illusion, they were simply carefully lined with bricks and painted the color of the surrounding walls. Currently, slightly ajar, they invited inside, showing a corridor lined with gray rubber flooring and illuminated with fluorescent lamps. As they walked, they heard murmurs of conversations and the sound of typewriters behind the offices' doors, as if lively work was going on everywhere. Office number four was rather a large conference room, not an office, lined with a carpet, gray just like the rubber flooring of the corridor, and decorated with several abstract paintings.

People were sitting at the table, several men in immaculate suits and a woman, at whose sight Theo involuntarily stopped at the door.

"Well, well," she said. "Terry, Terry, quite contrary... We haven't seen each other for a long time."

"Not long enough," Fronda said grimly, stepping inside with such a face as if he were entering a cage full of vipers and scorpions.

Lenor smiled with satisfaction at these words. To Oggy's surprise, she wasn't pretty and the girl couldn't understand what Theo had seen in her once. She had an elongated Egyptian profile, hair cut short like Betsy's, in the color of molasses, and a flat boyish shape, wrapped in a tasteful costume made of burgundy cloth. The sharp makeup emphasized the unpleasant impression she made.

"Sit down, brothers," she said. "I didn't call for help to argue about the break up from over a century ago that the poor knight's took so hard... Ah, Terry, seeing your sweet face so sulky is like pure honey. You have always been able to suffer perfectly, like a troubadour."

"And you always had sadistic tendencies. To the point, Lenor," Fronda admonished her, frowning in an angry grimace.

Lenor placed on the table top her manicured long-fingered hands, ending with sharp nails, painted the same color as her lips and costume.

"The matter is not simple," she said emphatically. "Our people are dying and we find their bodies in Stonehenge, as if they were some kind of a sacrifice made there by Druids. It makes no sense because this pile of stones was created hundreds of years before the first Druid appeared, but at the same time it has amazing effects: the bodies found are not changed in any way, even if they lay there a few days under strong sun. What's more, they have no traces of traditional staking, they are just dead."

She shook her head. Apparently, what was happening was beyond her comprehension. When she stopped smiling slyly, she became a little prettier, more kind, and feminine.

"Ogham sect?" Fronda asked after a moment.

"I don't know. I do not know anything. My people are afraid to investigate this matter, and anxiety psychosis has prevailed among all the confreres," she answered him seriously.

Oggy noticed, not without envy, that for a second their eyes met in silent agreement, a reflection of what had to connect this unseemly couple long ago.

"Maybe it's a branch of VH?" Gerard said.

Lenor frowned ironically.

"Who would be afraid of these clowns? Don't worry, we keep an eye on them, and we know what to expect from them. No, honey, it's not them."

"Still, they were the ones who made the massacre in Paris," Never noticed.

"No wonder. You were unorganized. We have an era of large corporations, the time when vampires could exist in isolation from each other is over," said Lenor. "I run a large import company and thanks to that, I can gather a large amount of brotherhood around me without raising suspicions. People like me occupy this entire floor. I'm their leader, but I wouldn't do much alone. It must be taken into account that agreement is constructive, so we cannot waste time on feuds or independent rummaging wherever we want. These times are gone. We have crazy progress, the world is cataloged and numbered, and we must protect our identity, so we must follow the progress and see the possible threats in advance. Here in the British Isles, we understand it better than you do on the mainland. We fortified ourselves so that VH is helpless against us, but there are other groups besides these imbeciles, at least two."

"Interesting," Theo muttered.

"More interesting than you think, Janville. They're so secretive that we can't reach them."

Lenor looked eloquently at one of the silent men accompanying her, who took out a red briefcase from a drawer hidden under the table.

"Here you have all the materials we have managed to obtain," he said. "It's not much, but maybe there will be somehow helpful for you."

"Maybe."

Never took the briefcase from his hands. This case looked interesting, but at the same time gloomy and menacing, and he felt that what they knew about it so far, was not even the proverbial tip of the iceberg.

"Where do we start the search from?" Fronda asked thoughtfully.

"From Stonehenge, of course," Lenor answered him. "Go there, Terry, and you'll find out that this place is even stranger than they say. You are very sensitive, even for a vampire, so you will probably feel it with double strength. Maybe it will even lead you to some trail."

Fronda nodded without saying anything. He knew Lenor well enough that he read between her lines how serious the situation was - this woman never asked for help, her independence once even frightened him, and her desire for power fascinated him, instead of repelling.

Meanwhile, Lenor turned to Never.

"Move out of the motel. Here are the keys to my summer home, you will be safe there. Betsy will take you away and stay with you as a liaison officer. She knows all the local connections, and there is no time to teach you this, there is no such need anyway, in the end you came only for this one action."

"If Theo doesn't want to stay with you," Oggy muttered maliciously.

Lenor looked at her pityingly.

"He won't, baby," she said. "Our romance is a thing of the past and it ended in very unpleasant circumstances: for him to leave me alone, I had to send my colleagues at him, and he had to lick his wounds for a long time. Only then did he realize that it was over."

"Did they beat you?" Oggy opened her eyes wide and looked at Fronda with pain.

He shrugged.

"In a way," he said reluctantly. "They tied me to the bridge span and whipped for a long time until I was out of it. If it wasn't for Rajah, I might not have survived it, because it was only an hour before sunrise."

"Don't exaggerate, you were watched. I didn't want your death, just to stop you from bothering me at last," Lenor explained to him with poisonous sweetness.

"And you want to help her...!" Oggy ran out of breath with indignation, she wanted to say something more, but only growled. Not warned about her phenomenon, the Londoners jumped up from their seats as the huge shepherd leaped out of the dress, and climbed with his paws on the table, baring his fangs in fury.

Theo put his hand on his neck, laughing.

"Relax, Oggy," he said. "It's been a long time, and besides it's not just about our lady Macbeth. I am sorry, but my knightly education does not allow me to take revenge on a woman, which means that I have to forget everything. Anyway, I was the one to blame, I couldn't understand the simple word 'no'."

He looked at the dog's eyes, caressingly scratching the rough fur on the animal's neck. Oggy whined and licked his face with a pink tongue, then jumped off the table and sat down, putting her head on her friend's lap.

"Wow," Lenor said after a long moment. "This girl is a werewolf, isn't she? I've never seen a lycanthrope, I thought they all went extinct a long time ago. I see that she likes you very much."

"Yes, a little," Theo admitted. "We shouldn't have told her about the past, she is still too young to understand that there is really nothing to talk about."

"Do you think it's wasting your breath talking about me?" asked the Englishwoman, squinting her cat's eyes.

He smiled.

"Let me put it this way: I felt as bad with you as with none other girl... but the pain you gave me was always of highest quality."

"Okay, enough of these confessions," Never interrupted. "We haven't come here to reheat the chops from the day before yesterday, let alone play Freud. The contract said that we get one hundred pounds a day per person from you plus costs, do you hold the offer? It's a lot of money."

"Of course I hold," Lenor winced dismissively. "My business brings a nice income, you don't have to hurry."

She looked at Fronda, who was sitting thoughtfully, still scratching Oggy absent-mindedly behind the ears. She had long since concluded that making the decision to part with this extraordinary man was the biggest mistake of her life, but too much time had passed since that day to try to tie the torn threads of that matter. They both had a different life now, too many bad words and bad deeds came between them to make fixing anything possible.

"Boys," she said after a moment. "I care about explaining this matter more than you think, not only because it constitutes our to be or not to be. The bodies found in Stonehenge and the real danger may not have anything to do with each other, because they are found only during the spring solstice, while vampires die all year round, except that usually we do not find bodies. Something really strange is going on here, and I hope you will explain it. Those of us who decided to tackle this problem, broke their teeth on it. To be honest I have already lost hope of solving this puzzle, but then Octavio called and recommended your group to me as the most operative among our population. If you can't handle this, I don't know what to do anymore."

Gerard tapped his fingers on the table top.

"We will do what we can," he promised on behalf of everyone. "I hope, however, that your food supply is working well, otherwise we will have to hunt, and this may interfere with our work."

"My villa is well stocked," Lenor ensured him.

She caught Fronda's eye and smiled secretly. She knew what he was thinking about now.

*****

"Are you sure it's here?" Carolyn looked incredulously at Colin, sitting next to her in the taxi. The huge factory complex somehow didn't fit her own brother, who never had any inclination to be a businessman. It was true though that they hadn't seen each other for ten years, and that is a long time.

"That's the address they gave me," Colin O'Grady said uncertainly. "What is this place?"

"Medlab," the taxi driver said indifferently. "Pharmaceutical company. That's the address you gave me."

Colin looked uncertainly at his sister.

"Well, let's check it, since we are already here. Maybe Johnny indeed works or worked here?"

"Three fifty," the taxi driver turned off the meter, rolled up the bill he received, and opened the door.

"We are here for John O'Grady," Carolyn said shyly, approaching the guard at the entrance gate.

He picked up the telephone receiver hanging in his booth and said to someone on the other side:

"Some people to see the boss."

After a moment he hung up the phone and pressed the button to release the gate lock.

"Block F, second floor, conference room," he said. "You're late, the meeting has already started."

Carolyn wanted to correct the mistake, but Colin squeezed her hand to stop her. If not everyone was admitted to see their brother, one should take the opportunity to get to him without unnecessary formalities.

"Boss? Is Johnny a big deal now? Why hasn't he written about it?" asked the girl as they walked along a row of metal and glass buildings.

"I have no idea," her brother answered. "We will find out. Something stinks in all this."

"It's those chemicals," Carolyn wrinkled her nose in disgust, looking around for Block F.

Indeed, the complex had a smell characteristic of chemical factories, and difficult to bear for people not associated with this industry. Finally, having found the right building, the siblings first had to be entered in the great record book at the watchtower, and only after they were thoroughly controlled by some peculiar device, did they receive plastic identifiers with the inscription "GUEST," and were allowed to proceed. They were more annoyed than surprised by these exaggerated precautions, and therefore, having arrived at the conference room, they passed the secretary trying to stop them and went inside without knocking.

John O'Grady, a redhead, just like his brother and sister, stopped the lecture he was giving mid-sentence and looked at the newcomers with immeasurable surprise. The table at which the conference participants were sitting was covered with papers, enlarged photos from the projector were displayed on the white screen, but they were not chemical formulas or anatomical graphics, but photos of young faces, as if Medlab was in the process of developing anti-wrinkle cream and was looking for models for ads.

"What are you doing here?" O'Grady asked sternly.

"What a nice way to greet your younger siblings," Colin snapped. "We know you didn't invite us, you don't have to say it, but we couldn't stay in Yorkshire. Tony Medlock conned us, ran with all the money, and left us with incredible debts and a ruined reputation. What were we supposed to do? You are our only family."

"You shouldn't have come here. You have no idea what's going on here." John looked at his colleagues, who looked no less worried than him.

Carolyn put her hands on the table.

"We have no idea, and you have no idea what our situation was like. Does that mean you won't help us? Where's your Scottish solidarity?" she asked sharply.

John sat down and sighed heavily.

"Forgive me, this surprise threw me off balance," he said. "Of course I will help you, but you shouldn't have come here, especially now that we have a conference. I will give you the keys to my house, you will go there and in the evening we will talk and think what to do next. "

"Why are you so mysterious, Johnny? Do you manufacture biological weapons here on the government's orders or what?" Colin snorted contemptuously while his sister studied with interest the pictures displayed on the screen.

"Oh, I know him," she said suddenly, pointing to one of them.

"What?" asked the gray-haired man next to John.

John looked at the girl alertly.

"Are you sure?" he asked, then rummaged in the slide stack and dropped one of them into the projector.

An enlarged photo of a young brunet with black eyes appeared on the screen, shown in a slightly different projection.

"Of course," Carolyn said cheerfully. "This is Theo Lebrigadon, he lives with his friends in the motel where we stayed. I met him at the night market, he's very nice."

The participants of the meeting exchanged gloomy looks.

"Fronda is here, Doctor," one of them murmured.

"Damn it. Sister, don't come anywhere near him, do you hear? When you see him on one side of the street, cross over to the other!" John O'Grady was clearly nervous, which surprised Carolyn very much.

"What do you have against him?" She asked. "He's a really nice young man."

"He's not a human at all, he's a monster. Stay away from him," the doctor dug a bunch of keys out of his pocket and tossed it to his sister. "Jim, Alice, Mike, take them to the motel, let them take their belongings and lodge with me. By the way, check if Fronda really lives there, because if so... Well, we'll talk later."

"Don't you suffer from some kind of paranoia, brother?" asked Colin suspiciously.

"Would we all suffer the same, and in a reputable pharmaceutical factory?" one of the men appointed by the boss took him confidentially by the arm. "I assure you, boy, each of us would like it to be just paranoia. Don't ask any more and you won't learn unnecessary things. "

Alice, a plain looking, brown haired woman with a physique of a wrestler, followed them in silence, the other man brought the company car marked with the factory logo.

"Man, I feel like a prisoner," Colin said, confused, getting into the back seat next to his sister.

"It's not that bad," the escort consoled him. "Mike, drive more carefully than the last time, it's not a race. You see, we're running a long-term action here, very dangerous one, and that's why Johnny is unhappy with your presence, but what is done, is done. I don't know if he will loop you in, but if he does, you'll understand everything."

"I think he just got into some suspicious business," Carolyn blurted out. "Drugs, weapons, illegal medical experiments?"

"You have watched too many American movies," Jim laughed kindly. Mike snorted like a horse, even grim Alice smiled slightly.

"We're not gangsters, miss," Mike said. "I have a PhD in microbiology, Jimmy is a chemist, and Alice recently did a master's degree in biochemistry. Medlab is our home, not just work, but it was John who created this company from the scratch. You have no idea how hard he worked, days and nights. You have a wonderful brother, respect him."

The car stopped in front of the motel. Jim came in first and asked the receptionist:

"Excuse me, does a young Frenchman, Theo Lebrigadon, live here?"

The receptionist flipped a few cards in the registration book and put his finger on one of the names.

"He and his friends checked out before dawn," he said. "They did not provide a contact address."

"Damn," Jim muttered, biting the fawn mustache. "What did his friends look like, baby?" he asked Carolyn, who breathed a sigh of relief that she didn't quite understand upon hearing the receptionist's words. She felt with some sixth sense that her brother's coworkers had bad intentions toward the handsome Frenchman, and she couldn't believe that he was really someone evil.

"Two guys and a girl," she said reluctantly. "Plain and with terrible hair. Are they on your blacklist too?"

"The less you know the better. Get your things and get going," Alice grumbled, clearly unhappy with the questioning.

"Okay, okay..." Colin shrugged, thinking that his older brother would indeed have a lot to explain to them.

*****

"A bit small, but one can live with that," Never appreciated the modern, even futuristically furnished villa, equipped with all possible security and alarm systems.

"A television in every room," Oggy said, jumping cheerfully. "I can watch what I want and not worry about Theo willing to see a match, or Gerard a spectacle. But there is nothing to eat, I mean, in my sense, there is only blood for you."

"Don't worry, I'm going out, I'll buy you something," Never said. "Hey, Fronda, when are you going to Stonehenge?"

"As soon as it gets dark," his friend replied, studying the gallery of abstract paintings on the walls with interest. "It will just be the spring solstice, I want to find out what is happening there then. I will take Oggy with me, her sense of smell may be useful. And for now I will sleep a bit."

He stretched with delight and went to his room.

"And we'll do the reconnaissance of the area at night, so you go to sleep too," Never told Gerard.

He nodded.

"Can I come with you, Rajah? I would like to go for a walk, to run around," Oggy asked, but the Indian shook his head.

"I'd have to take you on a leash. Better become a dog and run around the garden, you'll make use of some energy."

Oggy barked with delight, jumping gracefully out of her dress, and ran out the open door, swinging her tail. Her dog nature demanded exercise she had been recently deprived of for security reasons. The garden surrounding the Lenor's villa was, in fact, a large, grassy space, bordered with trees and shrubs, forming a kind of hedge, a perfect screen protecting against prying eyes. Lenor knew how to arrange her living space.

When Never returned from his escapade, Oggy was already after her bath and was lying in her room on a comfortable sofa, with her hands under her head.

"I bought you some steaks and dog biscuits," he said cheerfully, tossing her a bag.

The girl raised herself on the elbow, ripped open a pack of red meat with her teeth and bit into it with satisfaction. Her diet was typically canine, even more so because she did not eat anything that was cooked or baked. She was rarely persuaded to something other than meat for which she had uncontrollable appetite. Nevertheless, if it was necessary, she could fast for several days in a row, but when she had enough food, she could devour a huge amount of it.

Having satisfied her hunger, Oggy wrapped herself in a bathrobe that was too big for her, and closed her eyes. If she was to study Stonehenge at night with Theo, she had to get a good sleep, for it would probably take them all night, and there might be another thing to do during the day if some important results would come about. She liked her detective work, and with her dog instinct she was suited to it better than anyone else. Never, who by his very nature needed very little sleep, also decided to take a nap this time, after all the events of the last days were quite tiring and he had not even closed an eye for a week. After checking the alarm indicators for the whole house, just to be sure, he lay down in his assigned room, immediately falling into a watchful nap.

A rest in the safe place restored all four wonderfully, so that everyone woke up at dusk ready for any action.

"I don't know about you, but I haven't slept so well in a long time," said Gerard, mixing canned blood with guava juice and a little cognac. "Anybody for a drink?"

"Me for sure," said Theo. "I'm hungry like hell. Rajah, what about you?"

"Yeah, why not. When are you leaving?" Never looked at him questioningly.

"In a moment. I just have to make sure I have everything," Fronda put his bag on the table and began to browse its contents. "I have the camera, spare film reels, voice recorder, flashlight, caliper, Geiger counter, Octavio's sensor, mini-crossbow... Got everything."

"Why do you need a mini-crossbow?" Asked Gerard.

This term was used to describe the object of the length of the male forearm, which was a launcher of miniature arrows loaded with a sleeping agent. In the British Isles, it was better not to walk around with firearms, and the mini-crossbow could successfully pass for a hand-held telescope.

"You never know who you can come across, kid," Theo instructed him. "I live so long because I know how to be careful and I never trust my luck. Oggy, get ready!"

"Just a second," the girl answered him, putting on the black tracksuit.

Theo was also dressed in black, tight pants and a matching turtleneck, which was a suitable costume for an investigation in the dark of the night.

"Take also her dog ID, just in case," Never handed the friend a yellow book, made for Oggy by the forger friend.

The door opened and Betsy entered, nonchalant and cool as usual.

"Here," she said, throwing car keys to Oggy. "Just be careful, it's Lenor's private car, she will be furious if something happens to it. What about you?"

Never thought about it.

"We'll start reconnaissance with Soho," he said finally. "I once exchanged letters with Deidre Golden Locks, a perpetuated nymphomaniac, who made herself a nest there.

And it is widely known that prostitutes always know everything."

"No problem. I brought many horny clients to Soho, they know my taxi there," Betsy said calmly.

"Well, till dawn then," Theo swung his haversack over his shoulder and walked out whistling, following Oggy.

The investigation entrusted to them intrigued him much less than the opportunity to explore the ancient ruins, of which he had heard so much, and about which every scientific authority actually said something different. During his first stay in England, he did not even see them, busy with other matters.

"I drive," Oggy firmly took the place behind the wheel of a sports Ferrari. "I was living in London until the age of fifteen, left-hand traffic is a piece of cake for me. Listen, what if we come across this sect there?"

"You're right. We will park in hiding and we will be very careful, even if nobody is there," Theo agreed with her.

He did not want to run into Druids either, although despite the suggestions he made, he did not believe in their existence. He couldn't quite understand that someone might still be praying to the trees in the twentieth century, although he had seen stranger things. Oggy drove with a steady hand, glancing at the map from time to time.

"Oh, there," Fronda pointed at the dense clump of bushes. "Drive between two shrubs so that the branches cover the car from both sides. You maneuver perfectly, honey. And now hoods over heads and let's get to work."

He examined the car carefully and adjusted several branches.

"We have all night, take your time and watch out for any suspicious smell," he said.

Stonehenge's dark circle irresistibly fascinated him, but he forced himself to search the area thoroughly first. The grass, trodden by thousands of tourists visiting this place, did not contain any suspicious traces, but right next to the road on the other side, the detector surrounding Fronda's wristle began to squeak softly. Theo turned back and searched the area again.

At one point, he leaned down and using a tissue, picked up an unexpected object from the ground - something like an old-fashioned hairpin with pointed tips. The proximity of the chemically pure silver again activated the detector, so he turned it off impatiently, without stopping examining the pin. After a while he slipped it into his haversack and moved on. A lot of work awaited him. He had to examine each stone himself, measure the distances between the places that seemed "hotter" to his sensitive fingers, take samples. Archaeologists, historians and hobbyists of all sorts did it before him, but as a vampire, he paid attention to other things than they did, and could see more.

Oggy was poking around, sniffing carefully in every corner and listening diligently, but nothing suspicious was happening, the night was calm and quiet, as if the whole world had frozen. Suddenly, she caught a strange smell, barked a warning and leapt into the bushes. She knew that her friend, warned, would hide from the eyes of those who were approaching, whoever they were, and she was right.

Theo, warned by her bark, fell to the ground behind a small mound of boulders, pulling the hood deeper, and paused, listening intently to the growing singing. An eerie, ghostly procession was approaching the circle, the silhouettes in long white robes carried armfuls of herbs and flowers, their voices were growing, getting stronger, filling the circle with a Celtic song of incomprehensible words. The rite had some magical beauty, an eternal power, connecting a man with the whole world of nature, from which he tried to cut off for centuries.

Theo watched, enchanted, and listened until the Druids left, heading for the woods. He didn't even feel how long it all lasted, as if these strange people could force the time to serve them freely. As soon as the procession disappeared in the distance, Fronda came out of his hiding place and entered the stone circle, not without certain fear, cowering his arms as if waiting for a blow. But there was peace inside the circle, even larger than outside. He felt a faint tingle inside his hand. He took off his gloves and raised his hands, trying to sense the strange currents of unknown origin. Geiger counter in his bag was silent, so it wasn't radioactive radiation, and yet he had the impression that it was x-raying through him, making him transparent like a sheet of ice.

For all its strength, this thing was not violent. On the contrary, it gently took possession of him, embracing him with its current so gently, that he did not even think about defending himself, absorbing this extraordinary feeling with his whole body. Without thinking about what he was doing, he slowly took the hood off his head and faced the Heel Stone. It was there that a shy, pinkish glow was now rising, for the first time in centuries not arousing in him fear and the desire to immediately escape, but rather an overwhelming delight, so remarkable that he stared at it without noticing that his heart slows down its rhythm and his breathing becomes shallower. He didn't hear Oggy's desperate scream as she tugged at his clothes, yelling:

"Wake up! The sun is getting up! What's up with you?!"

The sun was rising above, flooding the stone circle with its glare, but the vampire staring at it felt nothing but the mild warmth caressing his pale skin, though usually a faint glow was enough to leave a burning streak on the exposed body. The deadly terrified girl, pushed to the last resort, concentrated all her will power and, having transformed into a dog, jumped on her friend's back, sinking her teeth in his nape. Growling furiously, she knocked him down on the grass and shook him like a terrier would do to a rat, until he screamed. Only then, with great effort, did she regain the human form again, and pulled on the tracksuit that had fallen on the ground during this struggle. She had never made two transformations in such a record-breaking short time before and it exhausted her like a marathon run.

"What's going on, why did you bite me?" Frond asked half-consciously, covering his neck with his hands.

"Stand up, Theo, we have to run," Oggy pulled the hood over his head with trembling hands. "Wait, I'll bring the car, because the sun will burn you when you leave the circle. Don't look at it, look at the ground."

"Oh boy, I don't remember anything..." Theo muttered, still rubbing his neck mechanically.

Oggy hurriedly brought the Ferrari out from under the bushes, and breaking the rules of the monuments conservator, drove it to the circle.

"Hurry!" she urged her friend.

Fronda staggered out of the circle and fell into the back seat of the car, feeling as if one of the boulders seen here lay on his chest and did not let him breathe freely

"Get me out of here..." he groaned.

Oggy pressed the accelerator and drove the ferrari to the road. She was trembling, trying to maintain the highest allowed speed and not to exceed it, so as not to alert the police, although she wanted with every nerve to squeeze out every possible force of the car to join the others as soon as possible. She saw her friend in such a state for the first time. He was always tough like a rock, he did not complain or whine, even then, when he got burned while pulling that boy from the fire...

It was on the way from Spain to France, they stopped at a burning house. The fire brigade was still too far away, the house was in danger of collapsing, the young couple, really too young for an eight-year-old child, tried in a panic to get to the house from which they had just run out, banished by flames. Fronda, strong and athletic, climbed a tree by the house and followed a branch to get through the window into the nursery. He made it at the last minute, burned both his hands, pulling the smoke-poisoned child from among the burning furniture, but yet he managed to do it in time. The young mother, looking like a girl herself, sobbed desperately, grabbing the boy in her arms, her husband tried to say something, but he cried so hard that he could not get out a word.

Hearing the siren of the fire engine and the ambulance signal, they quickly left to avoid the questions, it was only far away from this place that someone noticed how much Fronda had suffered in this action. They stopped somewhere by the side of the road, Never took care of the wounds on his hands and bandaged them expertly, but for a few weeks their friend was dependent on their help, because with all the vampires' resistance to injuries, their burns heal very badly and slowly. He did not complain even once during this time, although he must have suffered a lot, and none of the human painkillers works on vampires...

The girl looked back. Theo writhed in the back seat, pressing both hands to his chest and moaning in pain, making Oggy tremble at the steering wheel, trying to see the way through the tears coming to her eyes. After the time that seemed a century to her, she finally arrived at the villa and rushed into the house, where Never, Gerard and Lenor jumped from their places at the sight of her.

"Hurry," she said through her tears. "Theo fainted at Stonehenge, he is in bad condition. Help me, Rajah, I can't bring him here alone."

Never ran after her to the driveway and after a while they both led inside their friend, staggering on his feet.

Lenor helped them put him on the sofa.

"I'll bring something to drink," she said.

"It is not that. Heart rhythm extremely slow, clinical signs of a heart attack," Never said, examining the semi-conscious Fronda. "Oggy, bring a stethoscope from my bag."

"Are you a doctor?" Lenor asked.

"I don't like to talk about it," the Indian took off his friend's hood and turtleneck, briefly looked at the red marks on his hands, left by the sun's rays that brushed him outside the circle, and stopped at the wounds from the dog's teeth at the nape of his neck.

"Whose job is this?" he asked in surprise.

"Mine," Oggy, who had just returned, handed him a stethoscope. "I had to bite him to get him out of trance, because I wouldn't be able to pull him out of the circle. He's too heavy and too strong."

"You've really applied yourself," Never started to listen methodically to Fronda's lungs and heart.

"Not good," he murmured after a moment. "We will need heparin, equalizing fluid, calcium, glucose, solumedrol and ephedrine. Oggy, I have a prescription book and a stamp in my bag, a fake one but it doesn't matter, it's gonna take time before they realize it. Bring them."

The girl nodded and ran.

"What's all this for?" Lenor asked incredulously.

Never looked at her and thought that for an uninvolved person, her lips tremble too much when looking at his friend.

"I'm afraid there might be a blockage," he said. "In addition, we have pulmonary edema, which came out of nowhere, severe bradycardia and a blood pressure drop. Thanks, Oggy. Rush with this prescription to the nearest pharmacy immediately, say it is a matter of life or death, make them serve you first."

"I'm coming with you, I know the short cut," Lenor said firmly, taking dark glasses from her purse.

"It's full daylight," Gerard warned her.

The businesswoman gave him a hard look.

"I'll take the risk."

When both girls ran out, Never looked at Gerard and without wasting time on explanations, grabbed his wrist, pulling him to the sofa. The actor shouted in surprise when blood spurted from his cut vein.

"Shut up," muttered the Indian, forcibly pouring Gerard's blood into Fronda's mouth.

The actor looked at him in amazement.

"You have the same blood type," Never explained. "In his condition, tissue compliance is a key issue, my blood would kill him. When a vampire is dealing with a human, the matter is meaningless, but he can only accept blood from a tissue-compatible vampire. Yours will help keep Fronda alive now, until I can give him medicine."

"But what exactly happened to him?" Gerard asked when his friend finally released his hand.

"We don't know that. But I think we'll find out," Never answered, putting the stethoscope to Theo's chest again.

He wasn't really sure if his treatments would be effective, but the only alternative was to watch his friend die. When

Oggy and Lenor arrived, he took the medicine bag from them and quickly prepared the IV set.

"I need to give a shock dose right away," he said, breaking the necks of the ampoules hurriedly. "Drugs in a vampire's body are poorly absorbed and accumulate for weeks, so a one-time injection will suffice, provided it is a truly horse dose. We will give saline solution, calcium and glucose by drip infusion, it will put him back on his feet."

"You really are a doctor. Amazing." Lenor shook her head in awe.

"What's so amazing about that? I am a 'marten', not a 'moth', so I could study without hindrance. The things we do to pass the time."

Never deftly inserted the needle into the vein on Fronda's forearm, and released the stasis.

"What marten?" Oggy asked in a whisper.

"A marten is a vampire insensitive to sunlight," Lenor explained to her equally quietly. "There are only few of them, but they do exist."

"Rajah, are you sure you know what you are doing?" Gerard worried, seeing Fronda begin to tremble all over his body.

"I hope so," murmured the Indian, finishing the drug delivery and attaching the drip tube to the needle.

After an eternity-long moment, Theo opened his eyes and raised a hand to his chest.

"What was that?" he asked weakly.

He looked at the drip and frowned.

"Are you crazy, Rajah? What do you want to make of me, a fire hydrant?" he called indignantly.

"No, I want to save your life," Never said calmly. "Did something happen to you there at Stonehenge?"

"In Stonehenge?" Theo scanned his friends and stopped at Lenor. "There is indeed something there. I don't know what, but something weird. I felt its presence, I felt it draining life energy from me. These are not Druids or Hunters, they are completely different. Something much worse."

He took a deep breath.

"What is it in your opinion?" Lenor asked, handing him a cup of canned blood.

Fronda took a sip.

"I'd like to know myself," he said thoughtfully. "When I get better, I have to go back there and check it out. Could you get me an infrared camera and a thermal imager?"

"Did I hear it right, do you want to go back there?!" Gerard exclaimed in amazement.

Theo looked at him with a smile.

"Did you know that the word 'chevalier' comes from the word 'cheval[6]'?" He said. "And I'm a knight. And the rider always has to get back on the horse that threw him off. Knights do not give up in any situation, especially in one that poses a threat to others."

"Theo," Lenor leaned over him. "There are no more knights. Don't fool around."

Fronda touched her cheek with his fingers.

"I am," he whispered.

---

[6] (French) horse

When he sat in the armchair in front of the TV a few hours later, wrapped in a bath sheet, still shivering after a cold shower, he was already looking normal, and it would seem that the whole thing was some kind of delusion.

"I'm already feeling well, really, only in my head creaks terribly," he tried to convince Never, who was conducting a check-up.

"No wonder," the Indian meticulously checked the sphygmomanometer readings and unfastened the armband from his shoulder. "Your pressure is 190/110. It's the effect of steroids, but if I didn't give them to you, you wouldn't survive. Pulmonary edema can kill even a vampire. This pressure will persist for some time, then it will gradually fall to normal levels. You may have headaches, nausea and trouble sleeping, but you will live because of what I injected in you."

"What was wrong with me?" Fronda asked softly.

Never spread his hands.

"Clinically, it looked like pulmonary embolism, but not only like that," he replied. "Something like multi-organ shock. You have clearly been exposed to some unidentified, and very dangerous factor, and for my part, I advise you against further investigation of Stonehenge. Do you want to become a martyr on the altar of science?"

Theo looked at the door of the room where Oggy was sleeping, tired from the last night's incidents. Gerard also went to bed because the Soho tour was quite exhausting, considering the clash with a group of the drunk "teddyboys". Lenor drove her ferrari to the company's headquarters, despite the strongly operating sun.

"I don't care about any science," he said after a moment. "But what lies within Stonehenge is a threat to us, and perhaps not only us. Listen, Rajah, I don't know how to express it, but the force that nearly killed me, is almost certainly not from here, from Earth. It is a being, so different from us that we may not find words to describe it. Is it possible that Stonehenge is actually a temple, but built to provide the sinister deity with survival opportunity, while preventing it from escaping out? Rajah, this megalithic complex is already collapsing, and when it is further destroyed, IT can crawl out from there to the world."

Never folded his sphygmomanometer carefully.

"Have something to drink," he advised. "You have read too many stories by Lovecraft and Robert E. Howard, you are being carried away by imagination."

"I wish it were so," Fronda murmured, taking the mug he was given. "Are you saying that I invented my seizure too?"

His friend shrugged and sat down next to him, looking at the television screen, on which two teams of hockey players were just hitting each other with sticks. They were silent for a moment, then Theo looked at Never and asked:

"Why haven't you ever told me that you studied medicine?"

"Because there is nothing to brag about." Never shrugged. " I just used constructively those few years when you had an affair with Lenor. I had my purpose in it. You see, you often emphasize that you are different from everyone, because you were born before the Hundred Years' War and you were a knight, and it does not occur to you that I am also different. Tell me, don't I look somehow weird, even for a vampire?"

Theo looked at his supple figure, the hands with reed-long fingers, long face with slightly protruding chin and almond eyes, a clearly Egyptian skull.

"Well, a little," he admitted.

"Yes, you see it," the Indian sighed. "But you don't wonder why I look like this. I am sick, Fronda, just like my mother was. It's probably Marfan's syndrome, causing the destruction of connective tissue, if this expression is not too difficult for you, but at the same time giving such... aristocratic appearance to a person. I have all the symptoms. If the genes of my vampire father hadn't been activated at some point, I would have looked like a zombie and acted like a psycho. I'm a vampire, so I'm in control of the disease, but I'm aware of it, and sometimes when someone says how handsome and attractive I am, I wonder what he would say if he knew the truth. Because my appearance is the result of an illness, although it barely marked its presence."

"Barely?"

"Yes. If I were a human, I would look like a caricature... Because I'm not, I only have Marfan's discreet external features. Easy to overlook for a layman, probably not for a specialist. When we are in Egypt one day, look at Akhenaten's bust and compare him with me, you will surely see the resemblance, because this half-crazy pharaoh was also sick with it, just like his whole family. Now you understand why sometimes I behave strangely and why I decided to become a doctor? I am afraid that someday my disease will start to get worse as suddenly as it stopped."

Theo stared at him with darkened eyes.

"I didn't know," he whispered.

"How could you know? You yourself are indecently strong and healthy, maybe that's what attracted me so much to you at the beginning."

Never poured a portion of the plasma with rum from the bottle and stared at the screen again. Theo was silent. He knew very well how wrong the opinion was that the vampire's blood was a wonderful panacea for everything. Yes, it inhibited the development of every disease, cured many of them, but the damage they did, remained. Gerard, devastated by cancer, still looked like a skeleton covered with skin and had little more strength than the average twelve-year-old. Lambdon Tygier, a hemophilic, bled unbearably long after every slightest injury, and was bruised all the time. Lenor's hair never grew back after the typhus she was dying with, Fronda was one of the few who knew she was wearing a wig.

He himself really enjoyed excellent health throughout his short life, he practically did not know what it meant to be sick, and that is probably why he was such a beautiful specimen of a strong vampire. He had not realized this till now, many of his brethren, treated worse by nature, envied him this aura of flourishing health. He wrapped himself tighter with the sheet.

"Now I understand why you did it, although I wouldn't have enough patience regardless of the situation," he said. "Hell, I don't like the day if I can't sleep through it. Doctor, how about a sleep pill?"

Never laughed softly.

"No kidding, after what I've already given you? You better prepare for the fact that you won't be able to sleep for a few days in a row. And you better give up on Stonehenge, otherwise something really bad will happen to you."

His friend pondered.

"It certainly doesn't work on people like it does on us, but the mechanism is similar," he said finally. "It steals life energy, although it cannot be ruled out that it can only do it at sunrise, which is why Stonehenge's visitors have not complained about any massive ailments. After all, hardly anyone goes there at night."

"Maybe it is so," Never agreed. "Or maybe it just likes us more? Or this something steals energy only if it manages to establish psychic contact? With people, it is either more difficult or limited by a kind of emanation of 'blue stones'. Did you know that the only source from which they could have been delivered is three hundred and fifty kilometers from Stonehenge as the crow flies? And each of these stone monsters weighs many tons. At that time, no cranes or even block lifts were known. And yet some primitive tribe took the effort, unimaginable even today, to process, transport and set these colossi. The trilithons are perfectly balanced and placed with mathematical precision. Someone who commissioned and supervised this work knew exactly what he was doing, and it certainly wasn't just somebody's insane whim."

"See? And you said I read too many horror books," Theo poured himself another portion of whole blood. The Indian shook his head.

"Never mind what I said, Fronda," he said seriously. "You shouldn't go there. It's too dangerous. We will announce wherever possible that our people should stay away from the circle, and we should stop here."

A friend looked at him.

"I won't stop. I have to at least figure out if my theory is correct," he said and took a sip.

His head was still buzzing, blood was throbbing in his temples, his heart pounding painfully against his ribs. It was the result of hypertension, an unusual condition for vampires, whose standard pressure is 110\85 and very rarely deviates from these values by a few points. The force that almost killed him, in a strange way pulled him and called him into battle, what happened was like throwing down the gauntlet, and he never avoided such a challenge, even if it could cost him his life.

He was always extremely curious and inquisitive, which sometimes led to embarrassing situations. He felt that if he would not somehow confirm his suspicions, he would never sleep at night, and the easiest way to do it was to return to Stonehenge with the right equipment. Aware of what determines the survival in a constantly changing world, he studied scientific journals and even if he did not understand everything, he had a good general idea of the whole problem. He witnessed the birth of so many inventions and the confirmation of so many crazy theories, turning upside down the worldview established by centuries, that hardly anything could surprised him anymore. For the medieval knight, such adaptation to the dynamism of successive epochs was an unimaginable effort, but thanks to this, he managed well in this world without losing anything of his ideals.

Never threw his hands in the air many times and cursed his wild character without realizing that he liked him so much more because of that.

"Well, I think you know what you're doing, just don't overdo it. And be careful not to get hurt. I gave you heparin to avoid blockage, so you will bleed a lot before it stops working," he finally sighed, resigned. "If only we knew what really happened..."

"Is there any salt in this place? I haven't had such a strong desire for something salty in my life," Theo got up and started towards the kitchen.

"Salt? Right! How come I didn't think of it before," cried the Indian, rising from his chair. "Electrolytes, sodium and potassium! That's what you lacked in your body and hence the shock that almost killed you. This thing must have caused an outflow of electrolytes from your body, like some electrolytic vampire. No wonder you crave salt, but I don't know if Lenor uses it for anything."

Fronda thoroughly searched the kitchen and, to his satisfaction, found a bag of salt, which he then poured into a can of blood and mixed well. He drank the resulting mixture with visible delight, and slumped back in his chair with a sigh of satisfaction. He followed the hockey players on the screen for a moment, who were arguing with the referee for a change, then asked:

"Will you go there with me?"

Not receiving a reply, he looked at his friend in surprise. Never was sleeping, resting his head on the arm of the chair, so despite his earlier declarations he had to be very tired. The sudden solution of the puzzle bothering him had to cause a decrease in the nervous tension he had felt for many hours, and nature claimed its rights. Theo turned off the TV so as not to wake him up, and went quietly to his room.

Oggy was sleeping on his bed, curled up as usual - she liked best to fall asleep near him or at least in his room, then she felt safer, as she said. Without waking her, he dressed in his everyday clothes and looked critically at himself in the mirror. He looked like someone with a heavy hangover - heavy dark circles, pale lips, and an indescribable expression of weariness in his facial features. Whatever the dark power nestling in Stonehenge was, it really took its toll on him.

He took a silver pin from the bag and looked at it with concern. Vampire Hunters must have been to Stonehenge, perhaps chasing a vampire, so they were present in this region. An unfortunate circumstance.

Behind him, Oggy growled lightly, waking up from sleep, and stretched on the bed until her bones creaked.

"You awake already, kid?" Theo sat down next to her.

"I had enough sleep," the girl watched him closely and a little sadly with her brown eyes. "Do you really want to go back there? Aren't you afraid of death at all?"

He laughed softly...

"It won't be a threat to me," he assured her. "You can only get me by surprise, and now I know what to expect."

Oggy put her hands under her head.

"Were all the knights like you?" she asked.

"Everybody? I don't know. Some of them for sure," he answered her after some reflection. "As with any ideology, there are fanatics, activists, supporters, those who profess it for their own benefit and complete cynics, practicing believers, non-practicing believers, and of course practicing non-believers. They are better, worse and completely bad. For some, knightly ideals were just a cover, for people like me, they were the whole life. I was very young, and youth usually believes in ideals, only later one can see a monster behind the beautiful facade. I did not have time to see mine, these two lances saved me, which stabbed my chest and knocked me down from the mount right under the horse's hooves, the guisarme, which ripped my body, reaching under the armor. I still remember this paralyzing feeling when I realized it was over. In those days it was already a fight to kill, not to imprison and take the ransom, as it was fashionable earlier."

"Fun like any other. And how was your life in the woods?" Oggy looked at him curiously from under the black-red mane falling over her eyes.

"Before or after the perpetuation?"

"Before."

"I don't remember much," Theo admitted honestly. "And if anything, only in the proportion in which an adult remembers things that absorbed him in kindergarten. But I think it was good. I had friends, a goal in sight, I was young and healthy, people liked me... Many were hiding in the woods at the time, not just me. And it wasn't at all me who was the most famous, or in any way unique, after all there were lots of outlaw knights then. My team of brawlers was tiny, there were some that counted a few hundred men. If something was interesting in these relations, it was the fact that the villagers considered me, a knight, as one of their own. People fought separately then, the peasants did not accept nobles in their groups, and vice versa, but everyone accepted me. It's probably my charm," he finished playfully.

"Why was that" the girl asked in surprise, the lack of logic in this behavior boggling her mind.

He shrugged.

"Kid, learn some history," he advised her. "It all happened only a few years after Jacquerie, a cruel rebellion in which peasant and noble blood was pouring in streams. Any agreement was unfathomable for many years after that."

He sighed deeply.

"Everything was easier then than now," he added sadly.

"It was easier to end up on the scaffold too," Oggy reminded him.

He smiled pityingly.

"This too had its charm," he said. "It forced the convict to fight for his dignity to the end, and this diverted his thoughts from the fear of death. When he was busy posing as a hero, he forgot to be afraid."

"And the social costs of this event?" Oggy didn't seem convinced.

"Certainly much lower than today," he assured her. "On the one hand, it is much cheaper to send someone who deserves it, to scaffold, than to support him for years, on the other hand, it is more humane than execution after years on death row, or imprisonment for life, which is in fact a death in installments. Tigers and wolves that attack people are killed, although these poor animals do not act deliberately, but just follow their nature. Anyway, I think that every opponent of the death penalty deserves that a degenerate would murder his loved one in a cruel way. I wonder if he would still have the same humanistic views."

"Indeed, unlikely," the girl agreed with him.

Fronda's sense of justice was a native of his era, primitive and uncompromising, but logical to the point of pain. In these matters, he reasoned as coldly as a computer.

"In that case, you deserve to die, too," she said after deep reflection. "How many people do you have on your conscience?"

Theo laughed.

"I don't think I killed if I didn't have to," he said. "Of course, excluding the English. War is a time of justified killing, and I was a soldier. A vampire needs blood, but doesn't have to take anyone's life if he doesn't want to. Of course, there are degenerates among us, too, then the rest must get him and eliminate as soon as possible. The vampire killer threatens not only people. But we are not degenerates. If vampires murdered in the past, they did it because of hunger, like animals, not because of the lust to do evil, and never murdered because of the need for cruelty. Drinking blood is not too painful, almost not at all, the victim falls asleep to not wake up again. But you are right, we deserve to die according to my own views, especially me. Maybe someday I'll tell you why, but not today. This is a very painful memory."

The girl clung to him, sensing instinctively that he really needed it. From time to time, Theo took off the mask of a carefree happy-go-lucky, and for a few seconds the tragically sad face of a man who has lived through too much appeared under it. Vampirism is alien to human nature, the human psyche is not adapted to too long existence, to accumulating memories, and it requires a lot of effort to keep it in check. Oggy looked at the deceptively young, gentle face of her friend and sighed sadly. It was so easy to imagine him in a more romantic outfit and with a sword in his hand, especially now when she saw several episodes of the series about his adventures.

"How did you get that actor to let you drink his blood?" she asked, remembering their recent guest, a slightly older Fronda look-alike with gentle, non-aggressive eyes.

He waved a hand carelessly.

"Ah, that was easy. I caressed him with a whip a few times and it was enough. These are the effects of the present, soft upbringing, no one taught him to take pain like a man, in my age he would be dealt with in a different way. I also think that I just scared him, and almost to death, the poor man could not resist my argument, so that I could drink his blood without breaking my word."

"I think it was a dishonest act," Oggy said openly.

"Of course it's dishonest, but so effective," he laughed merrily.

He hugged her warmly and kissed her forehead. He knew very well that he behaved not quite fair... but he felt that if thanks to this, he achieved a difficult task, he was absolved of his behavior. Over the past centuries, he had come across the claim that "the goal justifies the means," believed by noble and generally honest personalities, that he could not blame himself for such a minor bending of rules. It wasn't the first time that he asked himself how he really felt about Oggy, this unattractive werewolf girl with warm eyes and faithful disposition, but he didn't find a convincing answer. Anyway, he was close to her, more than anyone else, maybe because he felt needed. Never or Gerard did not need him - they could do well alone, while she required care and tenderness, and this made him feel like a knight again. This in turn had the effect that he needed her as much as she needed him.

Weary, he closed his eyes without letting go of the warm shape that clung to his chest. This is how they were found by Lenor, who after dark appeared in the villa and entered his room without knocking.

"I sincerely hope I am disturbing you," she said with subtle viciousness. "I got an infrared camera, a thermal imager, and a fluorofilm for the camera. I also have this: be careful, Fronda, this is the latest type of scanner for geologists and I paid a lot of money to borrow it. When are you going to do the testing?"

Theo examined the devices brought to him with concentration.

"When? Today," he replied after a moment. "I hate things that drag on."

"Today? You're not strong enough yet," Oggy said, eyeing Lenor with a look of resentment.

"On the contrary, I feel great. Don't worry so much about me, kid, I recover quickly," he patted her back patronizingly and scooped all the equipment back into the big bag in which the Englishwoman brought the equipment.

Never peered into the room, finishing wiping himself with a large towel.

"Wait until I get dressed. I am coming with you," he said firmly.

"And I?" Oggy called.

"All right, we will go there together, it will go faster," Fronda agreed, not wanting to hurt his friend.

Lenor nodded.

"Take this too," she said, handing him something resembling a deodorant.

"What is it?" Theo asked.

"Be careful, don't press it. It is hydrogen cyanide spray, a very effective weapon, of course, provided that you do not breathe it yourself," she replied calmly.

"You use something like that?" Gerard, who appeared in the room a minute ago, made big eyes.

Lenor gave him a cold look.

"The fact that those from van Helsing don't matter here, shouldn't suggest to you that we don't have problems with Hunters," she said. "We've got them, except our Hunters are of a completely different caliber, and you'd better not come across them. But if you do come across them, don't hesitate to use gas, because these may be your last moments."

"Fiddle-faddle. I will certainly not treat anyone with hydrogen cyanide, I have seen enough people suffocated by gas during the first and second wars," Theo replied firmly, giving the container back to her with obvious disgust.

"Your choice, but you will have only yourselves to blame."

Lenor put the gas in her purse with a blank expression. She would love to go with them, but that night she had to be at the company's board meeting for an important holding, and she always adhered to the principle that work first and then pleasure.

"Are you sure you feel well already?" she asked, just for the record.

"Peachy," Fronda assured her and kissed her heartily on the cheek.

"And I still think you should wait a few days, but I know I might as well talk to the wall," Never said, putting on a black tracksuit similar to those his friends wore.

He had no illusions that his words would do anything. Theo was always impulsive and violent, carefulness and slow recovery were not his things, he acted in "all or nothing" mode.

Friends got into a slender Ferrari, which Lenor apparently gave them to use freely, which was a favorable circumstance, because they had to leave their van ashore.

"I wonder if they're paying us too little for such a risk," Never murmured as they approached Stonehenge.

Perhaps it was a suggestion, but everyone felt unpleasant chills on their skin and felt a little warmer. Oggy growled restlessly, though she still maintained human shape.

They stopped near the circle and got off.

"I take the scanner, Gerard the camera, Theo the thermal imager," the Indian ordered, distributing the equipment. "Oggy stays on guard. Watch the area and all of us, if one starts to behave abnormally, immediately alert the rest."

"And if you all start?" the girl asked not very clearly.

"Then do what you think is appropriate, just don't bite Fronda anymore, because heparin is still affecting him and he'll bleed like hell," he instructed her.

He saw that she was out of balance and could barely maintain her human form, but he deliberately did not let it show. She had to deal with this matter herself, someone's participation would only upset her unstable balance. Pretending not to see anything, he turned and started the scanner. The ultrasonic waves tickled him uncomfortably in the palm of his hand, the recorder squealed at high tones and at that moment Never received a powerful mental blow, as if it were some kind of intelligent force, indescribably different from everything he knew.

Surprised, he almost let the valuable device out of his hands. Something was indeed here, he had no doubt about it now, and he ran the scanner as thoroughly as he could, walking around the stone circle, and then stepped between the stones, ready to escape immediately in the event of any sensation.

After taking measurements, he immediately went outside and first of all checked his heart rate. It was accelerated and irregular, but not alarmingly bad, perhaps due to a short stay in the dangerous place.

"Watch out for the inside of the circle, go in there just for a moment and shorten it as much as possible!" he called to warn his friends.

They finished their work in a hurry improper for a scientific work, but justified by an unknown danger lurking in the dark. When they finally returned to the Ferrari, it turned out that, firstly, they had used much more time than they assumed, and secondly, that the car was guarded by the shepherd, putting his ears down in shame.

"Poor girl, could not bear it" Gerard nodded sympathetically, "Last night was too tiring. Well, hop into the car, baby, we're not going to spend the day here, are we?"

Theo picked up her tracksuit from the grass.

"Pity that there is no psychotherapist for werewolves, maybe he could help her control it?" he muttered to himself.

Recently, Oggy had more and more difficulties in controlling her wolf nature, and everything seemed to indicate that this was not going better.

"Will you drive?" Never asked, interrupting this thoughts.

Theo shook his head.

"I'm a bit weak," he admitted reluctantly. "Maybe one of you?"

A friend gave him a long look, then sat behind the wheel. They had to wait until the next evening with working on the results of the research carried out at Stonehenge - on the way they gave the collected materials to Lenor, stopping by the company's headquarters. They agreed that she would appear in the villa soon after dusk and they would discuss together what was seen on the kilometers of various types of recorded tapes. They had a whole quiet day ahead of them, and it came in handy for them, because even Theo, who was still bothered by the high blood pressure, yawned incessantly and fell asleep, barely putting his head to the pillow.

He slept like a stone, and so did others, so that it was only Lenor who woke them up by setting all the alarm clocks at home.

"Get up, sleepy heads!" She called as they ran out of their rooms half-unconsciously, convinced that this was the end of the world. "I have not seen anyone sleep so long in my whole life."

"Go to hell, rag businesswoman. I thought it was the trumpets for the Last Judgment," Theo sighed, sitting helplessly on the sofa and rubbing his temples.

"Fortunately for you, not yet. I wonder how you will excuse yourself there," Lenor took the projector from the bag and set it on the table. "If you are already sober enough, we can start."

"Wait, I'll bring something to swallow," Never brought a few bottles of blood from the kitchen, a few cans of various juices and a bottle of cognac. "Oggy, give me glasses."

"Can I?" Lenor asked politely, waiting for the Indian to mix drinks for everyone. "Look at the wall. This is a film from an infrared camera. Take a good look at them. Do you see the difference between the inside of a circle and what is outside it? And now the photos from the thermal imager, these blue areas are cooler, but inside the circle it is as if something was boiling underground, and compare it with the chart from the scanner. Look at the edges, see? This something is hotter than its environment, it clearly pulsates, and does it rhythmically, as if... it was breathing or what? This is not a blind force, not a ghost, it is something material, as real as we are, but completely unknown."

Never nodded and drank from his glass.

"I felt it," he said. "It thinks, but in such a different way from ours, that agreement is not possible. I'm afraid we don't have any reference points. I can understand people's thoughts, animal thoughts are not a mystery to me either, because they are in harmony with nature, but this is alien. It seems to me that if we had the opportunity to face this something eye to eye, assuming that it has eyes in our understanding, then what we would register with our five senses could lead us to a madhouse."

Lenor looked at the image from the projector, leaving no doubt as to the rightness of Fronda, who also looked at the slides thrown by the projector and sipped his cocktail, saying nothing.

"Terrible," Oggy whispered, trembling all over her body, and clang to his knees.

"There are things in heaven and earth that the vampires never dreamed of," Gerard, who was moved least among them, sighed philosophically. "When Never made my transformation,

I thought that nothing more unusual would happen to me, and here it is getting more and more strange. And what now?"

"Good question," Lenor poured herself some cognac and diluted it with blood. "It poses a threat to us, but maybe not only us. Now that we know the truth, what should we do? I am open for suggestions."

"The question is not what we should do, but should we do anything at all," Theo said seriously.

Friends looked at him, intrigued.

"What do you mean by that?" asked Never.

Theo slowly brushed aside the hair that fell all over his eyebrows, covering his eyes, and answered:

"I don't know if we have the right to do anything. It is living and, as you say yourselves, thinking, although we can not understand how. Perhaps we would pay with our lives for the attempt of direct contact and not gain anything, and one should probably ask this something about its reasons. I think that it has the same reasons as us anyway. To survive. It is a parasite, but so are we, just like all people, because in the end, man is the only inhabitant of this planet who gives nothing from himself, but instead takes things, and in a robbery way."

"As we can see here, not the only one," Lenor muttered grimly.

Fronda's reasoning could not be faulted and she searched in vain for arguments against his thesis.

"When you put it this way, it's hard to deny," Gerard admitted. "And I will add something from myself: I don't know if we would be able to do anything to harm it. After all, those who built Stonehenge also had their knowledge, and could not invent anything other than to isolate this creature. An interesting puzzle for biologists. My stepson, Allain, was crazy about the natural sciences and would probably jump to the ceiling for joy if he had the opportunity to study something like that. By the way, I would give a lot for knowing exactly what it is. Prehistoric intelligent jellyfish?

The question hung in the air for a moment.

"Something much worse, I think," Oggy finally murmured.

"So we're doing nothing?" Lenor asked.

"Why nothing? You have to announce that the circle is dangerous for vampires and give it a rest. If I'm not mistaken, this is not the only danger in this area," Fronda said and looked at Lenor.

The Englishwoman winced slightly.

"True," she admitted reluctantly. "Do you remember what I told you about the local Hunters? Well, we are rather guessing they are here. Those who probably saw them, disappear without a trace, as if they never existed. Certainly those from VH got to none of them, because their few victims are later found with a stake embedded in the heart, in agreement with the old tradition, during the last year it happened only twice, and we managed to save one of them. If you also find out where they disappear, you will really earn your fee honestly."

"Are you saying that we haven't worked honestly so far?" Never asked, frowning.

His correspondent friend from Soho also claimed that something bad was happening, because her Japanese friend,

Riha, who had an obsession of someone following her for several weeks, disappeared in unexplained circumstances, leaving all her belongings in their shared apartment. It was hard to blame the Stonehenge fright for it, the reason must have been completely different.

"Apparently a new kind of Hunters has appeared, especially for those who got bored with old ones," said Gerard.

He thought that the members of the Van Helsing Institute were enough trouble. Being a physically weaker and still inexperienced vampire, he was afraid of meeting them more than of anything else, though the days when he regretted his transformation had passed. The life he now lived was dark and fascinating, he got to like it, although it required him to give up what he passionately loved: acting. Those who forced him to make such sacrifice, also became close to him, almost like his family was once: demonically handsome Never with the disturbing eyes of the color of golden tinfoil and Theo, whose captivating beauty hid a steel character, were now like brothers to him. Sometimes he dreamed at night that he was standing on the stage, his face turned towards the audience, and hears the storm of applause, but he didn't think about it anymore after waking up. The old life was over, it ceased to matter, now there was only what was before him.

"An investigation needs to be done, but this time we can't guarantee that it will work," Never's voice broke brutally into his thoughts. "After all, you are not idiots either, and you haven't found anything yet. They certainly camouflage themselves very well, they know what they are doing, and we have a limited field of action. Well, let's try, what else to do?"

He thought about it, while his friends reviewed the results of their research again, while Theo made a note to Octavio di Mauro and argued in a whisper with Lenor which slides he could attach to his package. He took his work as an independent correspondent for the "Supernatural Affairs Department" very seriously.

"Oggy, get ready," said the Indian finally. "We're going to Deidre. Your sense of smell will be useful, maybe those who followed and then kidnapped Riha, left some scent trail in their apartment."

"There are probably quite a few scent trails," Lenor murmured sarcastically.

She did not like those of the vampire women, who used their preserved youth and beauty for erotic conquests, and there were quite a lot of them.

Never smiled mockingly.

"No, Deidre doesn't bring customers to the private apartment," he said in a well-informed tone.

He took Ferrari, together with Oggy, delighted with the prospect of a night trip to Soho, so Fronda and Gerard had to stay at home as deprived of transportation means. Lenor went to work - it would seem that nothing else existed for this woman, apart from the company and the activity for the union. Although she was not a "marten", she often worked well into the day on her affairs, probably using innovative protective creams, wearing a hat with a veil, huge mirror glasses and gloves. It might look old-fashioned, but it protected her to some extent from the sun's rays.

"How about some chess?" Suggested Gerard, finding that there was nothing interesting on television, and that Lenor's book collection was limited to businessman handbooks, statistical yearbooks and specialized magazines.

Theo shook his head.

"No thanks. You know what? I'll take a taxi and go to the motel. Maybe Carolyn still lives there? I would invite her for a dancing or to the cinema..."

"Are you serious?" Gerard looked at him almost in horror.

"Don't worry," the friend patted him on the back. "I will probably come back before Rajah and Oggy finish their investigation. Where's the phone here, damn it?"

He wanted to call the taxi company Betsy worked for, but on the second thought, he changed his mind. The bus stop was only two streets from the villa, and it was somehow awkward for him to mix the nice taxi driver into his heart affairs. He quickly took a shower, shaved, changed clothes and combed his hair, then ran out of the villa, chased by Gerard's worried look. The green-eyed actor did not feel he had enough strength to fight to keep him in a safe place, Fronda was stubborn and romance-prone at the same time, a fatal combination for a vampire on uncertain terrain.

He had made overnight trips many times before, in the company of a girl he met, or one of his former lady friends, whom he had not seen for twenty years, aged and in her own opinion unattractive. For him, these few extra wrinkles or kilograms were a meaningless detail, and for them of course, his interest and nice words after so many years were a great pleasure. In general, women liked him, and he knew how to use it. Perhaps the secret to his success was that he knew that women like to be conquered, so he always conquered, although he could save himself the trouble in many cases, where all he would need was to whistle.

Gerard shrugged resignedly and sat down in front of the TV, following the fate of the heroes of some tearful drama without interest. He wouldn't have kept his friend at home anyway, there was no point in trying, and yet he felt as if he failed to guard something.

Meanwhile, unaware of his dilemmas, Theo caught a passing taxi before he even reached the stop. Happy with his good luck, he ordered to be taken to a motel whose address he fortunately remembered. He usually had trouble remembering street names, especially in foreign cities.

"Is Carolyn O'Grady still living in the same room?" he asked the slumbering receptionist as soon as he got in the dimly lit hallway.

The older man looked up abruptly.

"What?" He asked, disoriented, and looked into the book. "Oh, no, she checked out two days ago. She didn't leave the address."

Theo grunted an old French curse and bit his lips. He did not like such surprises, maybe because the success of the fair sex spoiled him a little - he was not used to being "stood up", as Oggy put it, using the colorful language of social lows.

"Oh well, thank you," he said with disappointment he couldn't conceal, and left.

The cab was already gone. Initially, he wanted to go to a taxi stop, but after some reflection he decided to have a walk. Maybe this night could still be rescued? He liked to be alone sometimes, to observe the city's nightlife from a distance, climb trees and roofs in the footsteps of semi-wild cats, who were afraid of him a little, but allowed him to assist their night chants and occasionally rubbed their smooth heads on his hands, always ready to scoot back.

Sometimes, he watched with some unhealthy fascination the prostitutes bargaining with clients on street corners, or drunks arguing about something in front of dingy pubs. Or he admired a dressed-up company, heading towards the luminously lit S-class premises, with a row of shiny limousines in front, and he almost always managed to pick out a bored woman in an evening outfit and jewelry worth a fortune. He claimed that the blood of a great lady always has a better taste than the blood of a simple woman who eats anything and anyhow.

He hid among the trees growing on the edge of the highway. A convenient shortcut to the suburbs of London ran through there, and for someone who could see at night as well as during the day, the darkness that lay there was no obstacle. He knew how to move equally well in any terrain, even the most adverse. He was thus very surprised when he suddenly tripped over a protruding root, and fell on the soft moss, without having managed to extend his hands in a defensive gesture, although usually his coordination did not fail him. It wasn't until a moment later, when he tried to get up sluggishly, that he noticed a strange object stuck in his arm. It must have been very sharp because he hardly felt a prick. He took it for a falling piece of a dry branch or a young cone, knocked over by a night bird.

"What is it?" he asked aloud, realizing with concern that he couldn't get up.

Several people emerged from among the trees, flashlights in their hands, one of the men holding a kind of single-barreled shotgun of a type unknown to the vampire.

"Calm down, Fronda," he said, kneeling beside him. "It's a charge used to put animals to sleep at a distance."

"Oh. Right. You know me, it means you know who I am," said Theo calmly. "You will probably want to put a stake in my heart now?"

The man smiled in a vaguely familiar manner.

"We have the second half of the twentieth century, who is using pins now? It's retro way," he said kindly, taking a box from the bag slung over his shoulder. "I don't care about you suffering, besides, I need a body in good condition, with intact organs, for my research."

He opened the box and, tearing apart the sleeve of Fronda's shirt, tied his arm with stasis.

"Crazy. Ever since I arrived in England, people keep pricking me," said the vampire wryly, watching his manipulations. "What is that supposed to be?"

"A humane death." The Hunter deftly inserted a thin needle into a blood vessel underneath the skin. "Brietal, to stun you, propranolol to lower your blood pressure, pavulon, to relax your muscles and stop your breathing, and finally potassium chloride that will finish the work."

"Sweet," Theo muttered with resignation.

"I will inject slowly," the Hunter promised, breaking the necks of the ampoules one by one. "It won't hurt you."

"I guess I would rather deal with the nutcases from Van Helsing," Fronda thought, feeling the darkness and sweet nonexistence overwhelm him.

*****

A large, lysol-smelling autopsy room was already prepared when two laboratory technicians carried in a naked body and secured it with safety straps to a slightly sloping table, covered with plastic. Doctor O'Grady, surrounded by his assistants, a chemistry specialist, a biophysicist, two nurses and a second doctor, checked the zero on the scale, and the tray with tools, then raised a voice recorder to his mouth.

"Caucasian man," he began in an even, calm voice. "Perpetuation age between twenty and thirty years. Height 198 cm, weight 79 kg, asthenic body build, burn scars on both forearms and left shoulder. Blue pale skin, no signs of rigor mortis. We are starting the autopsy."

He put the voice recorder in his breast pocket and took the scalpel passed to him by the assistant, feeling the uncomfortable squeeze in his chest. He was not heartless. This was not the first time he was standing over the vampire he had murdered, and making a dispassionate, scientific autopsy, and every time he felt the same thing: regret and lack of internal agreement to what had happened. Here was another, young and beautiful body, which he had to cut and carefully examine, so that he could someday realize his biggest dream and find a way to reverse this process, which in his opinion turned young people into monsters without a soul.

He wished with all his heart that this would happen as soon as possible, so that instead of injecting the captured vampires with a lethal mix of drugs, he could give them an antidote and watch them become humans again. He hoped that he would also be able to isolate this mysterious healing factor that could save thousands, if not hundreds of thousands of human lives - naturally after eliminating the threat of the known side effect. That was the purpose of his life, nothing else mattered.

He put the blade to the skin and twitched. There was an unexpected noise outside the door, and Colin burst in, followed by a senior lab technician.

"I told him he wasn't allowed in," she excused herself, spreading her hands.

The young boy was clearly shaken and desperate.

"Police lost track!" He shouted in a choked voice. "They were outmaneuvered! Oh John, what now?!"

Dr. O'Grady turned around and the scalpel fell out of his hand.

"How come?" He whispered. "The inspector swore that everything would go smoothly."

"I told you from the beginning not to get the police involved," muttered one of his assistants, a broad-shouldered blond with a crumpled face and a bitter expression of the lips, hidden under a dangling mustache.

"Shut up, Raglan."

John O'Grady looked at his brother with concern and moistened his dry lips with his tongue. It was obvious that he was trying to think hard.

"If they kill Carolyn, I won't survive it," Colin buried his face in his hands and leaned back helplessly against the wall.

"They'll definitely kill her," Raglan said ruthlessly. "They got cut newspapers instead of ransom, and the police chased them. I don't think they'll try again. I warned you that they are dangerous people."

"You know full well that we have the money invested! Even if I wanted to pay them, I wouldn't get that amount within twenty-four hours," the doctor accidentally put his hand on Fronda's still body and jumped back with a slight cry of surprise.

"What happened?" the assistant asked.

"He's still warm," he muttered in amazement. "An opportunity... That's what we need. Don't you understand? Vampires use psycholocation, and Fronda knows Carolyn, he talked to her, he liked her so much that he was looking for her..."

"John, get a grip, it's a corpse. You gave him a golden shot yourself," the assistant tried to calm him down, but John did not listen to him.

"Quick, maybe we can bring him back to the world of the living. Samantha, intracardiac adrenaline! Martha, give me bicarbonate and let Ebenezer prepare the defibrillator immediately! We have to get him back. Yvonne, what are you looking at?! The monitor!" cried O'Grady, agitated by a desperate hope.

He grabbed the long-needle syringe Samantha had given him, while Raglan, stunned, attached the monitor electrodes to the lying man's chest.

"Samantha, ambu! Ventilate him!" The doctor glanced at the monitor screen, where the cursors was drawing two straight lines, and snatched the ends of the defibrillator from the hands of the second assistant.

"Three hundred and twenty for the start!" He commanded. "Clear!"

A short shock shook the body tied to the autopsy table.

"Atropine tracheally! Four hundred!" - the doctor put the electrodes against the lying man's breast again.

"V-fib!" Martha shouted, looking at the monitor.

"Again. Martha, fifteen liters of oxygen through the mask!"

John looked at the dial of the potentiometer and Yvonne increased the voltage indicator, obedient to his beckoning. Another shock merged with Raglan's involuntary shout:

"Normal QRS! We got him back!"

Theo opened his eyes and pulled on the straps that restrained him with an inhuman force, breaking them like thin ribbons.

"Are you nuts?!" He shouted. "What is this game?!"

O'Grady lowered his hands with a sigh of tremendous relief.

"Welcome to the living," he said, not even thinking about how stupid his words sounded now.

The vampire didn't pay any attention to them anyway.

"If your injections failed, then take a stake and let's get it over with," he demanded, rubbing his chest with his hand and trying to even his breathing.

"Amazing. The first one to survive. How did you do it?" the assistant named Samantha shook her head in amazement.

He looked at her, and suddenly he realized the situation he was in. He blushed, grabbed a green serviette from the table with a spare set of tools, and hurriedly covered himself with it, knocking the tools down on the floor. The men around him retreated against the walls, grabbing whatever might serve as a weapon along the way.

"How could you strip me naked like this?" Theo cried indignantly. "In front of the ladies?!"

"The fact that we wanted to cut him open, although he wasn't quite ready for it, does not bother him, but being naked does. A Frenchman, and so shy?" Ebenezer chuckled.

"What exactly do you want?" Fronda rolled his eyes suspiciously around the group.

"Carolyn was kidnapped," said O'Grady without introduction, "a huge ransom was demanded, and because I didn't have the money, I turned to Scontland Yard."

"Scotland Yard? They can't catch as much as a flu," the vampire interrupted him ironically. "Let me guess: they screwed it up?"

"You are our only hope. These kidnappers have already killed two people for whom no ransom was paid," Raglan interjected, seeing that his supervisor had lost his train of thought. "We know you like this girl, since you tried to date her. Will you be able to find her?"

"I suppose so, but you have to give me my clothes back, especially my plate," said Theo.

He jumped to the floor and staggered.

"Oh, we seem to have a problem" he muttered, grabbing the edge of the table so as not to fall.

"How are you feeling?" O'Grady worried.

"How am I supposed to feel after all the stuff you put me on? A stupid question. I feel like crap."

Theo took a deep breath, trying to control his dizziness.

"Martha, prepare also some caffeine. Damn it, pressure drop after propranolol..." John quickly put the needle on the syringe and grabbed the ampoules he was given.

"Mother of God, I have more chemicals in me now than a factory wastewater," Fronda moaned, feeling a prick in his shoulder. "First, Rajah stuffed me with all kind of foul stuff, now you, I wonder what will happen next..."

However, caffeine worked well for him - the dizziness stopped and he felt his strength returning. The vampire's body can do without oxygen much longer than any other, which is very useful sometimes, so that the cessation of breathing harmed him much less than might be expected. A second assistant, Yvonne, brought his clothes from the back room.

"Thank you," Theo smiled embarrassedly at her and hid behind the autopsy table so that he could dress in peace.

He really felt embarrassed and humiliated. The matter was further complicated by the fact that he liked the girls very much: petite, dark-haired Martha with a chubby baby face, Yvonne, a fiery brunette with a very Spanish appearance, and even Samantha, a blonde, not very young, but with full shapes of Juno and similar statuesque beauty. He was embarrassed by the fact that he was lying on the table, stripped of any garment, in the presence of these attractive women. This embarrassment was not obscured by the obvious truth that all three watched his naked body like an anatomical preparation, with a purely scientific approach.

Colin looked at his brother, wringing his hands in despair. It had only been twenty-four hours since he came to believe that he was indeed a Vampire Hunter, and not a dangerous madman, but he still could not process it. It just boggled his mind. Now, however, when their sister's life was in danger, he felt that he did not care who would save her: a vampire, a policeman, or a manic killer - as long as she could get out of it safe and sound.

"Take me where the police lost track," Fronda said, as if guessing his thoughts. He put the plate on his neck and slipped it under his shirt. "If poor Carolyn is still alive, I should sense her."

He came out from behind the table, adjusting the collar of his shirt, calm and relaxed, as if the fact that they had tried to murder him, and resurrected him from clinical death only so that he could find his executioner's sister, was the most ordinary thing in the world.

"We're both going with you," Dr. O'Grady said categorically.

He took off the white coat and left, bringing two revolvers after a while, and handed one of them to his brother.

"As you wish, but I'm in charge. And don't blame me if you get hurt, because there are no jokes with these people," Fronda warned them indifferently.

Raglan held his boss by the elbow.

"Are you sure you know what you are doing?" He asked quietly, pointing his eyes at the vampire. "I don't think he can be trusted."

O'Grady looked at him glumly.

"I have no choice," he replied equally quietly, and walked to the door behind his brother and Theo, who was still walking a little uncertainly, like someone a bit tipsy.

In front of the door, the doctor put a hand on his shoulder, hit by a sudden thought.

"It's daytime," he said. "Does it bother you?"

"What's the weather like?" Fronda asked.

"It's been raining since dawn."

"All well then. Are we going or talking?"

Theo smiled slightly, turning to him his eyes, glistening like polished anthracite. Under this gaze, O'Grady felt suddenly guilty and embarrassed, so much that he fell silent. He had never before tried to talk to those he killed when the opportunity arose, their way of thinking was unknown to him, so he did not know if this charming young man was speaking honestly, or maybe he was playing some game of his own.

Only when they left the city streets, did he speak again:

"Are you sure you can find Carolyn?"

"If she's still alive, and this could be questionable," the vampire answered calmly. "But it's worth a try."

He touched his plate affectionately.

"How can you wear silver?" John could not refrain from this question, although the situation was not conducive to scientific considerations.

"It's not very pure, and it's a matter of adaptation. If you want something very much, you can do a lot," answered Theo.

"It's here," said Colin, stopping the car. "Here the policemen lost sight of them. They headed in the direction of Salisbury."

Fronda looked around. The intersection looked normal, like any other at this time of day - it was full of cars, people crowded the streets, hurrying to their matters, and the vampire's keen eyes saw a red painted telephone booth.

"Do you have any change for the phone?" he asked his companions.

"What are you trying to do?" said O'Grady, frowning.

"Do you want to find your sister or not? If so, give me change and shut your mouth."

The doctor fell silent and reluctantly handed him a few coins. Theo got out and ran through the rain to the booth. Fortunately, he remembered the number of the taxi corporation to which Betsy belonged, and the side number of her cab, otherwise he would be in trouble, trying to find her at random. The conversation had to be short - he hoped Betsy was as intelligent as he believed, because there was no time for long arguments.

"Let's go," he said, returning to the car. "Either I have hallucinations after your Molotov cocktail, or we should really look in that direction. Go on, Colin."

John shook his head.

"How can you recognize one psychic emanation in such a crowd?" he asked.

"I don't know. I never thought about it," Theo answered him absentmindedly. "After some time, the ability of psycholocation becomes as natural as breathing, you stop thinking about it, how or why... And we learn to isolate the familiar signal from the background like we learn archery or riding a bike."

A gray Ford left the city and rushed down the road to Salisbury, driven by Colin's hand. Despite his worry, the redhead Scot was driving following the rules, and never took his eyes off the road, as if nothing unusual was happening, calm and silent now. His resemblance to his sister was now almost twin-like.

Halfway down the road, Theo patted his shoulder.

"Stop here," he said.

He got off on the shoulder and looked around. The gentle but decisive emanation seemed to be more intense, but he did not know if he could trust his senses, dulled by medications. He hoped so. He calculated the direction in his mind and became worried. It seemed Carolyn was somewhere near the sinister Stonehenge.

"Hell, I hope they don't keep her inside the circle," he thought. "I have to take the risk. Worse thing is, it stops raining. If it clears up and the sun gets out, I will be in trouble."

He got back into the car.

"Straight ahead and to the left," he commanded. "Keep the course southeast."

"Are you sure?" John couldn't help himself from asking this question.

Theo glanced at him briefly.

"Which sounds better: "yes" or "I hope so"?" he answered the question with a question.

He was silent for a moment, then asked, without looking at the doctor:

"Why do you kill vampires?"

"We've all lost someone because of your kinsmen," the doctor said grimly. "For me it was my wife, for Samantha - father... and so on. Call it a war if you want."

"I've had bigger wars on my neck. I understand you and respect you. You are putting things honestly, you fight fair and you don't try to add metaphysical ideology to what you do. I appreciate it. However, you must know that if I survive, I will turn you in, as the saying goes in gangster movies," said Theo calmly. "Oh, I know you want me to free Carolyn and then to kill me... you'll try anyway. It's your right, try it, but know that I won't make your job easier. Do you know how old I am?"

"Biologically?" John was not much embarrassed that the vampire had seen through his intentions, but he was worried by his insight and calmness.

"In real years. Six hundred and thirty-four. Exactly. I survived so long because I can take care of myself. You surprised me once because I wasn't expecting you at the motel, but I doubt you will be able to pull the same trick a second time."

Out of the corner of his eye, he watched the doctor's face, which did not change its expression. Even though also a redhead like his younger siblings, he did not look like them, he had much narrower jaws, a darker complexion, and a flattened nose of a boxer. Only his eyes, gray and piercing, looked like his sister's.

"I've heard a lot about you. You are a knight," said the doctor after a moment. "Nowadays, this word is an empty sound, we associate knights with don Quichote rather than anyone else, but for you, of course, their ideals must be still alive. That's why you're trying to save Carolyn in spite of everything. I'll tell you something: I'm working on a vaccine to restore those like you to humanity. Maybe soon the killing of vampires won't be necessary."

Fronda shook his head with a bitter laughter he couldn't stop.

"You haven't yet cut a vampire as long-lived as me, although you were close to having the opportunity," he said.

"Probably you were dealing with relatively young individuals, maybe very young, and hence your mistake. Already a 50-year-old vampire, dear doctor, has practically no intestines, kidneys, liver and pancreas are in atrophy. Gusto Vanderbelt called this process the body's self resorption, where the ordinary connective tissue fills up the free spaces. You won't change that with any vaccine."

John opened his eyes wide, looking at him in astonishment.

"You know such things? How come?" He asked. "According to my research, once perpetuated, a vampire cannot learn anything that goes beyond the worldview of his era, because the folding of the cerebral cortex is stopped. And you are proving the opposite to me."

"Fortunately, this is not punishable yet. Those of us who are unable to adapt to the changeability of epochs are quickly dying, and I preferred to survive. Stop here."

He opened the Ford's door. John and Colin got out after him. They were among the relatively dense buildings of typical English single-family houses, creating a monotonous, serene scene.

"Here," he said after a moment. "She is here. She is afraid. We must go... in this direction."

A scooter approaching at dangerous speed stopped right next to them.

Betsy jumped down onto the grass without wasting time for explanations.

"The police are coming here already," she said, ignoring the horrified glances. "Show us the way, handsome."

Theo went first, as if following a trail marked by invisible signs, until he reached a seemingly indistinguishable single-family house.

"Carolyn is in this building," he said firmly. "But there are at least six people there besides her, so we have to split up. Betsy is coming with me. You two have weapons, so you will distract these thugs, we'll find and free Carolyn. You have to act quickly and decisively to make it before the police arrive. As a side note: wipe the revolvers well and hold them through a cloth, and throw them to the ground before the police break in, otherwise you'll both be going to jail, regardless of the circumstances, and the girl will be alone."

John nodded in resignation.

"We're going from the front, we will distract them," he said, unlocking his gun.

Theo pulled Betsy with him and circled the house. Now that he was so close, he ceased to strain his sixth sense, and focused rather on the other five, trying to guess where the kidnappers could have locked their victim. Among the background of the voices of a few or even a dozen men, his sensitive hearing caught the quiet crying of some helpless and terrified creature.

"In the basement," he whispered to Betsy.

"It's this window," the girl whispered back, pointing to a small boarded up window, just above the ground. "I know this type of houses, it can't be anything else."

Theo knelt down and ripped the board off with one firm move. The crack noise merged with a scream inside the house and a gunshot. Colin and John, who thought there were three or maybe four kidnappers, burst inside like two gunmen from a bad western. The number of people present in the house surprised them, so that they barely managed to hide behind a wardrobe.

The one who seemed to be the boss, called something in a language they did not understand, and immediately a good half of the bandits ran out. A couple of John's shots could not stop them, and the situation would have become deadly if the sharp signal of the police car had not come from afar. The boss of the kidnappers cursed and shouted something to his people again. Taking advantage of the temporary distraction of the criminals, the brothers wanted to sneak out of the building, but the heavy fire forced them to seek shelter behind the heavy furniture again. Things got really dangerous.

Meanwhile, those who were supposed to run to the basement for the hostage, ran out of the house and, seeing the three escapees in the distance, started to chase them. Theo, whose hearing made it possible to distinguish between slight differences in sound intensity, realized immediately what was happening upstairs, and although Carolyn was on the verge of psychophysical endurance, he decided to flee immediately.

He did not know if John and his brother were still alive, and he preferred not to determine it, so he would not have to keep a good face in front of the deadly terrified, exhausted girl. To move faster, he almost carried her. She was heavy, but a few thugs chasing them, certainly armed, looked threatening enough to mobilize him to even the greatest effort. He knew well that it would be better not to risk fighting on such terms.

"There's an underground entrance not far from here," Betsy panted, running just behind him. "Hardly anyone knows about it, and I grew up here... Run after me."

They turned together behind a small hill, the girl pushed away a tangle of some thickets, and disappeared. Theo barely squeezed through the rocky hole, the brown-green veil fell behind him, thoroughly hiding the place, whose existence he would not have suspected. A narrow isthmus led to something like a pitch dark mine corridor.

Betsy turned on the flashlight she had prudently taken with herself.

"These dungeons stretch for kilometers," she said. "But only a short part can still be used. Others create a real tangle and all entrances to them have been barred long ago. Apparently, several people disappeared here without a trace."

"So what are we doing here?" asked Theo, supporting shivering Carolyn.

"We're waiting."

She seemed to listen, shining a flashlight down the corridor walls at the same time. Somewhere on the surface, police whistles sounded.

"They are chasing them," Carolyn whispered, clutching her whole body to the side of the Frenchman, who was still holding his arm protectively around her.

The taxi driver looked at him.

"Now the two of us can do it," she said emphatically. "I'll wait until the turmoil above is over and lead her to a safe place, that is to the police car, which will not leave without her anyway. Trust me, you shouldn't talk to the police. Anyway, it doesn't rain anymore, the sun will come out soon, and the sun light is not good for you."

"What about you?" Fronda asked with concern.

"I'm a human," Betsy said calmly. "You are not. If you go out in the sun, you will get burnt. Can you find the way in the maze?"

"Better than a trained rat. I don't get lost anywhere," he answered her, a little confused by her sudden confession.

He wasn't sure what to think about it, but there wasn't time to explain it.

"You shouldn't come back because of this pretty one's brothers," the taxi driver continued. "These few words of yours have explained the situation to me, and I know what bastards these two are. They will kill you anyway. You have to hide and hide well. You saw where I hid the scooter, right? Here you have the keys. And now the most important thing: this place will be searched by the police, because I will have to say where we hid, so you must disappear. Will you be able to open the grille? The locks are rusted, I think that with your strength you will be able to break them, just close it well behind you. Go to the exit on the opposite side, because detectives will be sniffing here for a long time, then make a circle and return to the road so that it looks like you are going from the opposite side. Don't tell you saw anything, because they'll take you to the police and won't let you out quickly, which can be fatal."

Carolyn sobbed violently, throwing her arms around the vampire's neck.

"I can't believe you are evil," she sobbed. "John must be wrong..."

Theo embraced and hugged her. He was eager to bury his face in her hair and pause for a minute to be able to fully enjoy the closeness of this sweet young body, but it was not the time or place for it.

"Dear child, in a way, your older brother was right," he whispered. "You'd better stay away from people like me, unless you want to waste your life, which ultimately nobody can forbid you."

The noise on the surface intensified, there was a scream and the sounds of a struggle, which soon ceased, giving way to calls.

"They're cops. They are looking for you," the Frenchman gently pushed the girl away from himself and stroked her cheek. "Betsy will take care of you for now. I must hide both from the police and your brothers. It must be like this. We belong to different worlds, baby..."

"Even if you like long goodbyes, make it quick and get the hell out of here," Betsy interrupted him vigorously. "If the police see you with us, you are finished. It's not France, our detectives take their work damn seriously. Now, go! This corridor will take you to the first grate, and remember what I told you."

"Yes, ma'am."

Theo saluted, kissed Carolyn's forehead goodbye and disappeared into the corridor indicated by the Englishwoman. When he reached the grille, he found out that it was very sturdy, so he did not try to break the lock, and reached instead for his lockpick set, which he did not part with. Fortunately, Dr. O'Grady and his men didn't search his pockets and gave everything back to him intact. After short manipulations, he opened the grille and plunged into the black corridor. He could not see anything - the tiny flashlight at the key ring could not help here, but after a few steps, the darkness seemed to light up a bit.

Soon, Theo understood why this happened. There were hyphae on the corridor walls, something like mycelium or moss, giving very little light, but it was enough for the vampire's eyes to see. The corridors really formed an unusual maze and it was easy to understand why these dungeons had been closed so long ago that hardly anyone remembered them. He was walking in the direction Betsy had pointed him out, infallibly choosing the right turning direction every time, as if he had walked this way many times before.

He had to mobilize all his strength to keep up the pace. It was stuffy underground, and he was still feeling the effects of the lethal mixture injected by Dr. O'Grady in his bloodstream. A chemical storm was still going on in his body, because the medications given by Never could circulate the body for weeks to come. Added to this were the chemicals the Hunter gave him by the motel, and then at their headquarters. No human would survive such a mixture of poisons, but the vampire's body absorbs chemicals extremely slowly. Hence, it is easier to neutralize or remove them on time.

"I need an exchange transfusion," Theo thought confusedly, wondering how much he remembered from medical radio programs. "The sooner I get to Never, the better, he'll know what to do about it."

He felt worse and worse as the surge of strength brought about by the excitement faded away. He put it down to the recent experiences and it took some time before he realized that the growing anxiety was not related to himself, but to something completely different. He paused and looked around alertly. There was silence all around, but now that he was alert, he clearly picked up something like a threat signal. From the depth of the corridors came a suffocating, humid breeze with an unspeakably disgusting smell, although not associated with anything known, but at the same time bringing some maybe telepathic, incomprehensible reception, slow and blunt like the silent impact of a wooden hammer directly into the brain.

"What the hell...?" he murmured and suddenly realized where he was.

These corridors led straight to the Stonehenge complex. It was strange that he had not yet realized how close to the hated circle he was, it was strange that when he got out of the car, he completely forgot about it. It could have been the result of medication that his thoughts only ran one way, to Carolyn awaiting the rescue, for only now he vaguely remembered that a stone complex flashed in the distance.

Other sensations were now joined by a sound coming from somewhere on the side, sounding as if some heavy, slimy mass was pushing through these corridors towards him. He started running away before he could even formulate the thought that it would be the wisest way out. He did not know and could not know what he was trapped with here, underground, but all his senses warned him about this something. He did not want to specify what was chasing him, he did not even try to look behind himself, the suffocating smell was enough, as well as the babble of other people's thoughts, resounding somewhere - neither in the brain, nor in the subconscious mind - so terribly alien in pronunciation, emotions and all points of reference, that he didn't even try to understand them. He had the feeling that something was breaking into his mind, into his body, is controlling his will and slowing his heart, just like the other time, but this time he was aware of what was happening, and was fighting with all his strength not to succumb to what wanted to enslave him.

He had never been afraid of death enough that he would not face it without fear, but now he did not even think of fighting. He didn't want to guess what weapon he should use against what followed him along the winding corridors of the underground labyrinth, but one thing he was certain was that it had not been invented yet. So he rushed forward until his body hit something cold and hard. A grate blocked his way, the same as the one he opened to get here.

He quickly found the lock with his trembling hand and reached for the lockpick. He had literally seconds to open it, but luckily he managed to set all the latches at the first attempt and the lock gave in with a creak. He rushed outside the grate, tearing the veil from branches of wild raspberries growing on this place for years, disregarding the sun looking from behind the clouds. He ran a good few dozen meters in the open space before he sobered up enough to seek shelter.

By some luck, he managed to find an abandoned hut, made of branches, which he could squeeze into with some effort, and only here he allowed himself to breathe a bit. His heart was still pounding with spasmodic contractions, he could hardly catch the air with unbearably dry lips, he felt painful sunburn on his hands and neck, but he got out of the circle and that was the most important thing.

Stonehenge stood not far away from him, menacing and majestic, he looked at it with horror he had not experienced before - the first time around he did not know what was happening, and now he was fully aware of it. He fought the irresistible urge to jump out of this hut and run blindly ahead, but he had enough sense not to do it while the sun was shining. Fortunately, black clouds were gathering again and it looked like it would be raining again. He looked hopefully at the sky through the gaps between the branches, forcing himself to patiently wait for the clouds to completely cover it, so he would be able to safely leave his imperfect shelter.

The sudden movement of the ground opposite the entrance to the hut distracted him from the clouds. Something large was clearly raising the forest litter up. Theo pulled his legs to his body, not taking his eyes off the growing bulge, from which something finally popped out, which looked more like an earth-clotted octopus tentacle than anything else. At the end of the leathery protrusion, a kind of mouth opened with four back bent teeth arranged in rosette, surrounded by a mass bulging like a waving collar. Fronda felt his strength and will leave him, and the world darkening around him.

In a last glimpse of consciousness, he jumped from the ground and fled before this something, swaying in front of his face, could reach him. He ran ahead, ignoring the branches hitting him, overwhelmed by panic fear. He didn't care anymore whether the cops were still searching the area around the kidnappers' house, whether the sun was still shining, or whether the Hunters were waiting for him. Everything was better than the nightmare lurking under the stone circle. Despite the huge stress, he managed to find the right path and a scooter hidden under bushes, the keys to which he squeezed nervously in his left hand.

He shouted and gave a blow blindly when someone grabbed his arm.

"Stop it, it's me!" Never's voice sounded above his ear. "Betsy called me and told me everything. Are you out of your mind to make deals with Hunters?"

"Never mind, Rajah, get me out of here, fast."

Theo was so relieved that he staggered and almost fell. Never pulled him into the car, threw the scooter into the trunk and sat behind the wheel.

"Betsy said you helped free that redhead," he said, shifting into third gear. "You've probably warned her that her brothers are a new type of Hunters, but that's no reason for you to look like that."

"They stuffed me with poisons, and then probably some antidotes, since I'm alive. Plus all the stuff you injected me with. I need a transfusion, and fast," Fronda replied weakly.

"I'm a doctor here, have you forgotten? Tell me everything as accurately as possible," Never demanded.

He listened without interrupting or commenting, although it was obvious that what he heard made a great impression on him, despite all his coolness. Two hours later, while Theo was lying in Lenor's villa, connected to the drip, Lenor, along with Betsy and Never, sat down by his bed, watching him with concern. Fronda looked better now. Never removed as much blood from his body as he could, replacing it with a new one, quickly taken from Gerard and mixed with canned plasma, but that didn't quite do the trick. He was still weak and had impaired consciousness, and he could feel the intense chemical taste in his mouth. For some time he fell asleep or maybe fainted. When he regained consciousness, Oggy and Gerard, who now clearly took over the role of "caretakers of the sick", were sitting beside him, talking quietly so as not to wake him.

However, Theo was awake already, though his eyes were closed. He opened them only when he heard the voices of Lenor and Never, returning from the city. Lenor, in a white shirt and dark blue pants, looked even more elegant than usual, but her makeup was much softer and maybe that's why it could be seen that she was worried about something.

"Speak, Terry," she said, sitting down next to the bed. "What is this new type of Hunters you mentioned to Betsy?"

Fronda shrugged.

"The new type is a new type," he said reluctantly. "Their leader is a John O'Grady, M.D., a completely crazy guy. He doesn't hunt with a stake, but with a shotgun for syringes that veterinarians use to put animals to sleep at a distance. He injects a vampire with a lethal mixture of medications, then conducts some scientific experiments on the corpse. That's why you don't find the bodies. He is possessed by the idea of inventing a vaccine that would reverse the perpetuation process. It has nothing to do with VHI. If you ask me for my opinion, then indeed those from Van Helsing are piece of cake next to him and his people."

Lenor nodded.

"I'll check this doctor," she said. "Funny, but say what you want, you owe your life to those kidnappers who grabbed his sister. If it wasn't for them, you would now swim in formalin like a frog or an embryo with four heads. Well, you've done a great job. In one fell swoop, you solved the puzzle of the Hunters, freed the girl, and helped put the gang terrorizing London to jail for two years. Ah, and the Stonehenge. They imprisoned the girl near the circle, did his proximity somehow affect your effectiveness?"

"He was deadly terrified when I found him," Never said. "I've never seen him like this. What have you seen, Fronda?"

Theo closed his eyes again.

"Betsy told me to run underground," he said quietly after a moment. "She didn't know anything, you didn't tell her. The catacombs led beneath the circle. I... I didn't see anything. I mean, I don't know, I can't be sure if I've seen anything or whether I was delusional after what I was injected. I will never know, because nothing in the world will make me ever go back there. The fear I experienced running away from this Unknown cannot be compared to anything. Next to it, every other fear I have experienced is a child's play, something like a slightly sore throat next to encephalitis. I can't describe it, so don't ask."

"Were you more afraid than when you stood on the scaffold?" Oggy asked.

"I've never stood on a scaffold, it's the invention of the writers of that stupid series," he replied impatiently. "I was released while leaving the tower. But I don't think I could feel on the scaffold the pale shadow of what I felt at Stonehenge. I want to leave England and never come back here."

Lenor put a hand on his shoulder.

"Do you still think we have no right to destroy this creature?" she asked quietly.

He looked at her.

"I don't think we can as much as scratch it," he said, equally softly. "And when Stonehenge finally falls..."

He paused. A thrill shook Gerard, who hadn't said a word yet. Theo, the medieval knight, was known for not being afraid of anything, he even considered fear a dishonor and a ridicule, so his words made even bigger impression.

"There are circles like Stonehenge around the world," he said hoarsely. "Do you think something like this is trapped under each of them?"

"Who can know that?" Never murmured.

His friend's words gave him food for thought, though he didn't know what was worse in them: the threat from the Hunters or this something from Stonehenge. Certainly neither was good news. His friend almost died, and although he managed to survive, who could predict the long-term effect of the chemical battle in his body? Anyway, the Indian knew well that the killer mixture given by O'Grady did not work only because a horse dose of ephedra was still circulating in his friend's veins, which did not allow a lethal drop in pressure, and because of the heparin, which prevented an embolism. To him too, as to Fronda, these chemical killers seemed far more monstrous than those from the VH labeled groups. Their cold scientific approach caused a shiver of terror.

Betsy entered the room.

"What's happening?" she asked.

"Our brave boy wants to mommy," informed her boss ironically.

"If you are so brave, go there yourself. Then we'll talk." Theo looked at her in resentment and looked away.

The taxi driver handed several densely written pages to Lenor.

"It's a report of the whole case," she said. "O'Grady kept asking me about Fronda and I barely managed to lose him. I gave false personal information to the police, so he won't learn anything from them, although on the other hand he doesn't seem to have snitches in the police."

"No Hunter has them," Never murmured.

Lenor stood up and pulled a bolero over her shoulders.

"Come with me, Rajah," she said. "You will help me prepare the final results of our investigation. Betsy, are you coming? "

"No, let her stay a while longer," Fronda asked.

Lenor's eyebrows rose slightly.

"As you wish, but don't keep her for long, we need her" she said with obvious dissatisfaction and left, swaying on the high heels of her fashionable shoes.

Oggy growled shortly from her corner. She couldn't stand Lenor, still unable to forgive her what she had done to Fronda.

"We're going for a walk, Oggy," Gerard said categorically. "It's already dark, so we can go together."

"OK."

The girl stood up reluctantly, gave Betsy an evil look, and followed the actor. She wasn't jealous of his friend's girlfriends, but sometimes she felt a little sad that she couldn't be one of them.

Gerard put his arm around her.

"Try sometime," he said warmly, guessing her thoughts. "Fronda likes you very much."

Oggy shook her head.

"I could turn into a beast and tear him apart," she said. "Werewolves do it sometimes, I won't risk it. Not with him."

Meanwhile, Theo was thinking about something completely different than these two.

"Betsy, you told me something in Salisbury," he said quietly. "Is it true you're a human, not a vampire like me or Lenor?"

The cab driver sat down next to him on the bed.

"Yes, I am," she answered calmly. "My brother became a vampire when I was still a little girl. He was terminally ill with his heart and he is still not fully functional, but he is alive. He works for Lenor as a programmer. You know, I've always thought that it is rather a strong and healthy person like you that is selected to be a vampire."

"Well, usually it was like this. But the way of understanding the world has changed. Now something else is important besides a healthy and beautiful body," he explained to her reluctantly.

The girl fell silent for a moment, then continued the topic:

"You must know that I love him very much, and when I was a child I didn't see the world outside him. Our parents died in a plane crash when I was two years old, Humphrey brought me up as best he could, that is, like a boy, because he didn't know otherwise. When I learned that he could die at any moment, I became an adult, although I was only twelve years old, and therefore I accepted his transformation with relief rather than with horror. I don't want to be a vampire myself, not yet anyway. But I help them, and you have to know that people's help is really useful for such a large organization."

Theo touched her hand.

"I understand," he whispered with a smile.

He had encountered such cases before, though they were rare. It always impressed him, for he knew all too well how frightened people were of what went beyond their orderly world.

Betsy patted the back of his hand.

"A life is a life. You won't understand everything. Get well and don't strain your brain," she said, then left, closing the door behind her.

He glanced at the falling level of plasma in the drip, then closed his eyes and gave in to a mild wave of drowsiness that fell upon him unnoticed. He no longer had the strength to think about what had happened in Salisbury, what he saw or thought he had seen, because come to think about it, such thing could not exist. Something that tried to kill him, however, had to be real, otherwise it would not be so dangerous, but this realism was as if from another world. Only now, after so many centuries, did he feel that he and his kinsmen were only humans after all, and beyond the human world, there was an unimaginable space full of the unknown, which was better not to be touched.

"No more orders bordering on the supernatural," he thought before he fell into a calm sleep.

*****

"All parameters are normal," Never said, relieved, having completed the examination of his friend.

It seemed that Fronda, with his usual luck, came out unscathed from the troubles that had fallen on him.

"What are we doing now?" Gerard asked, watching his friends from the armchair in front of the TV.

Never put away his stethoscope.

"We've done everything we were supposed to do here," he said. "We are coming back to the mainland, we will rest a bit and we will probably take the next order. Money will be useful, won't it?"

"Right, one has to live on something," Oggy agreed.

Gerard stood up and stretched.

"You know what?" He said. "I do not mean to underestimate the merits of Rajah and Oggy, but I think that if it wasn't for Fronda's romantic tendencies, we would have been investigating this matter for a long time. Though on the other hand, it was close, and we would have another one: the strange riddle of the vampire's disappearance. What is Lenor going to do about our doctor?"

The Hindu pursed his lips slightly.

"Well, she already knows a little about him," he answered reluctantly. "He is a co-founder and main shareholder of the pharmaceutical company Medlab, a rich and very influential man. Fighting with him will be rather difficult, because you understand, such a person can not be simply removed, there would be an investigation. But this is a problem for Lenor and her group. We have done our part, we have collected a check and this is where our role ends. I suggest we leave this week, preferably tomorrow."

"I'm for leaving, two hundred and fifty percent." said Theo, buttoning his shirt and checking at the same time if the marks from the punctures on his forearms have already healed.

His body somehow coped with what it had to accept, but it came back to normality relatively slowly, which made the impulsive vampire impatient, as he was accustomed to living in strength and health. Gerard looked at him ironically.

"Interesting, you keep pointing out that you hate everything English, and at the same time you had an affair with Lenor and you picked up Carolyn," he said with a hint of teasing in his voice.

"What these have to do with each other? Anyway, better let's pack now," said Theo indifferently.

"It's not like we have ten trunks to pack," Oggy muttered.

"I'm going to get the ferry tickets," Never said and left.

Gerard started picking his stuff up, and Theo went out into the garden. He did not even have time to look around it well, busy with the task assigned to them. Lenor gave him the copies of photos and reports, he had enough material to send to the Institute's correspondence address, but somehow he did not enjoy it. He was Octavio's correspondent not because he believed in science, but because he liked adventures, and this one left behind an unpleasant settlement, and he would like to forget about it as soon as possible.

He didn't even notice when Betsy approached him.

"Don't think so much, it's dangerous," she said quietly. "I have to tell you something, Terry. I saw Carolyn. Her younger brother, Colin, was seriously wounded during the operation in Salisbury. Carolyn stays with him in the hospital day and night. I thought maybe you would like to know that."

"And John?"

"He's in custody. He accidentally wounded a policeman, it will take some time before he gets himself out of it. This is a serious accusation. If he were at large, I wouldn't say anything to you," said the girl.

"Take me to the hospital." asked Theo, looking at her with the eyes glowing in the dark.

She smiled.

"I knew you'd say that. Come on," she said a little warmer than usual.

They got into the taxi parked in front of the gate. Fronda could not resist the feeling that Betsy knew him much better than she should, she knew that he always acts in accordance with what his heart dictates, and he does not think about the price when he is about to act the way he would centuries ago, when he was a young knight, just knighted. And she shouldn't know him so well, they'd never met before. He sensed that he could get to like her.

The girl was driving the cab with a steady hand, glancing from time to time in the rearview mirror and whistling the "Heartbreak Hotel" through the teeth, as if she were carrying an ordinary, everyday passenger, not a hundreds-year-old vampire. She had lived on the border of the worlds for years and she was doing very well, apparently. He thought he would like to talk to her, just like an ordinary young man with a girl he likes, but somehow he couldn't find the right words. Betsy did not encourage him anyway, she remained silent and stared straight ahead as if driving a taxi required total concentration.

She didn't speak until they arrived in front of the hospital.

"Trauma surgery, second floor," she said. "I'll wait."

"Thank you," Theo got out and ran into the hospital as if he was responding in a hurry to a call.

The experience of hundreds of years had taught him that this is the easiest way to bypass all guard, and it had not failed now either. Once on the ward, he looked around. Despite the night there was a lot of movement here, everyone hurried somewhere and no one paid attention to him. He preferred not to ask for anything so that it would not come out that he had no right to be here, so he began to look for the red-haired Scot on his own. Looking around, he saw her finally, huddled against the window, face hidden in her hands. He came over and took her in his arms. She looked at him and silently clung her face, wet with tears, to his chest, shaken by a silent sob. He understood right away.

"When?" He asked.

"A couple of minutes ago."

Carolyn hugged him tightly and cried louder, helplessly like a small child. Theo hugged her and stroked her tousled hair without saying anything for a long time.

"Be strong," he said finally. "Colin gave his life for you, so now make sure his sacrifice is not in vain. That's the only thing you can do."

The girl nodded and moved away from him, wiping away her tears.

"I know," she whispered. "I know, Theo. After all, I still have another brother, right?"

She stroked his face with his hand.

"You are so..." she paused for a moment, looking for words. "So warm. You have such a good, gentle, beautiful face, it's hard to believe who you are."

"Does it bother you so much?" asked Theo gently, taking her hands in his.

Carolyn didn't listen to him.

"And your eyes are so pretty too," she continued. "Many of you are like that, aren't they? Not only you. Oh, forgive me, Theo... I've made my decision. I'll join John in his work. You have to live with someone, right? And he is all I have."

The Frenchman smiled sadly and kissed her cheek. He understood what this girl was going through now, and wished he could help her in any way. The death of a loved one is an experience that cannot be shared with anyone, everyone is alone in the face of this great pain and this cannot be changed. He knew it well.

"Everyone chooses their own way of life," he said. "But remember not to judge anyone too lightly. Contrary to what your brother thinks about us, we are human. Sometimes even better than others."

Carolyn embraced him and they stayed like that for a moment without saying anything. Finally, Theo pushed her away and said firmly:

"Come, I'll take you home. A taxi awaits me in the driveway."

She agreed without a word. She looked deadly exhausted, and as she walked, she leaned on Fronda's shoulder with almost all her weight. For a moment Theo thought that maybe he should not take her to Betsy's taxi, especially after her earlier declaration, but these fears were premature - Carolyn did not even pay attention to who was behind the wheel, she just dropped into the back seat and closed her eyes. Betsy didn't say a word either, so the situation was unexpectedly safe.

The taxi driver took the matter calmly. She just slid the cap deeper over her forehead, and when Carolyn gave her brother's home address, she took the cab out of the driveway and headed for the right lane. It seem that nothing would upset this girl - although, considering the complex world she lived in, and the choices she had to make, it became less strange. Theo hugged Carolyn. He wanted to stay with her and help her in this difficult moment with all his knightly heart, but he knew it was impossible. Dr. O'Grady could leave the detention center at any time, and Theo might pay with his life for meeting him again, while not gaining anything.

After arriving at the address indicated, he helped the girl get off and made sure, out of habit, that it was safe before escorting her to the door. Before Carolyn took the keys out of her purse, she looked up at him guiltily.

"I know you saved my life," she whispered. "And I'm your enemy's sister and I want to cooperate with him... It's not fair, I know. Try to understand anyway."

"I understand," he leaned down and kissed her lips, not as hot as he would like, but ardently enough for her to give herself in to it for a moment.

She stood with her eyes closed for a few seconds, then shook her head slightly.

"No," she said sadly. "I don't want to."

She opened the lock and entered the house, closing the door behind her.

Fronda returned to the taxi and sat in the seat next to the driver.

"Sad, isn't it?" Betsy released the brake. "What do you think when you see someone like her?"

"I think how fragile the life is. How valuable and fugacious every living being is. How quickly what is beautiful and good, passes. Sometimes, however, I think that immortality in the form in which I received it, is not such a great gift, since the price for it is the awareness of all this," he answered her, combing his black hair with an unconscious movement of his fingers.

"Well, you can't have everything. If you weren't perpetuated, your body would rot in one of the battlefields of the Hundred Years' War, and where your soul would be, we don't know anyway," Betsy said.

He patted her lightly on the shoulder.

"I don't think about it," he said. "What would be, would be, and what is on the other side... After the experience at Stonehenge, I don't even want to know. I will find out when the time comes."

"And you are not afraid of the eternal damnation?" asked the girl defiantly.

"After what I've seen in these hundreds of years? You're kidding me. I can say without exaggeration that I have already been to Hell and I am not scared of it at all."

He closed his eyes and tilted his head back a little. The meeting with Carolyn upset him much more than he wanted to show, because he liked this little Scot and he felt sorry that they were standing on the opposite sides of the barricade, and who knows if she would not be the one to inflict him a fatal blow next time.

"No, no," he muttered unknowingly. "She wouldn't be able to do it."

The taxi driver smiled at the corner of her mouth but did not comment. Despite hundreds of years lived, Theo could be as naive as a child, and it was easy to get to know this side of him.

Their friends were waiting for them nervously at home.

"Have you lost your mind? You are just going out for an all night long trip, without telling anything to anyone?!" Never yelled sharply as soon as he entered the villa.

"We were dying of worry," Oggy added reproachfully.

"First of all, I was out for only half a night, and secondly, since when do I have to explain my every step to anyone? You are exaggerating with this concern for my humble person," Fronda replied coldly and at that moment he decided not to confide in his friends about where and why he went. They might not understand it.

"We have the tickets already, we are packed, it will be a dawn soon. Let's go to bed since we're leaving tomorrow," Gerard suggested, barely suppressing yawning. "Lenor probably won't mind if we sleep here again."

"You're right, Fanfan," Never agreed, glancing at the window, outside of which it was already graying.

"Sleep then, for now. And tomorrow - goodbye England, may it be for good." Theo sighed, putting his arm around Oggy.

She rubbed her cheek on the back of his hand and smiled, already calmed down. For her, the most important thing was that everything was fine, that she would be able to fall asleep curled up on his quilt again, listening to his calm breath. Whatever tomorrow would bring, this adventure could already be considered definitively completed, which in itself was a reward, regardless of the money earned.

PART 3
The Empty Wings

He had no idea how long he had been walking. An incredible longing drove him forward, not allowing him to rest, not letting him give up, although he had long forgotten what he was looking for. Sometimes, the painful question resurfaced, as if from the bottom of the lake: "Fronda, Fronda, where are you?", but he no longer knew where the pain was coming from. Sometimes, in his dream, yellow-orange flames loomed, devouring buildings with a hellish giggle, and he heard his own scream, but he wouldn't be able to answer now what it all meant.

Sometimes in his dreams the heads of his friends bent over him, he saw their eyes, narrowed and full of pain, he heard them saying something, but he could not understand a word of it. He was seeing people in uniforms, others in white aprons, rooms threatening in their sterility and the technological advancement of the equipment that filled them, but he did not know how to combine this image with his own fate. He walked ahead, hiding in the dark alleys and basements, sometimes in the canals, sleeping through the days in places he would not have even come near before. He stopped taking care of himself, he became ghost-like, dirty, unkempt, barely covered with scraps of rags. He didn't even know how long he wandered like that - weeks, months or maybe years? He didn't care. It didn't matter. He was slowly forgetting everything, sometimes he didn't even remember who he was. The world was becoming a chaos of gray-black spots, flourishing with rare blood-red - when hunger became unbearable and he had to satisfy it.

*****

They surrounded him suddenly, shelled him from the darkness with the strong light of halogen flashlights, encircled him, cutting off every possible escape route. There were six of them: two girls, three young boys and one older man, all dressed in black leather, studded with chemically pure silver. He felt its bad emanation as they came from all sides, hiding behind the lights of their flashlights as if behind shields. He knew who they were, but he wasn't afraid of them, on the contrary, he felt something like understanding of their intentions, a strange split of a personality, one of which was silent, and the other agreed to everything, perhaps because he suddenly felt unspeakable fatigue.

They attacked at the same time, knocking him down onto the pavement, holding his hands and legs firmly, and an older man put a sharpened stake to his chest. The first blow from the hammer shook Gerard's body, though to his surprise it wasn't painful. The grinding of the pierced bone coincided with the second blow. He was being killed. He still felt no pain, only a strange relief that everything was finally over, and his tormented mind would be able to sink into the colorless nothingness he had strived for for a long time.

"You aim too high," he wanted to say, but he choked on blood. He awaited a third blow with resignation, when someone else appeared - tall, slim and fair-haired, in ecru colored pants and shirt. He said nothing, just stood and watched. A gentle calmness emanated from him. The Hunters froze in their spots first, then automatically got up and left in unison, leaving their prey behind. The mysterious savior bent over the vampire, lying stretched out on the pavement, and touched the stake stuck in his chest. Only then did Gerard's world dissolve into all-encompassing non-existence.

*****

He awoke with the feeling that he had wasted a long time and that something terrible had happened. He slowly remembered the events of the last night, though what had been before it, he could only remember as one misty chaos. He flinched and touched the scarring wound on his chest with his hand. Then he ran his fingers over his neck and cheeks. Someone bathed and shaved him, cut his hair and put him in clean sheets, taking advantage of the fact that he was unconscious, the same someone put a few bottles of blood on the table next to the bed. So he knew well who he was dealing with.

The bottles were made not of glass, but of thin plastic that Gerard had not seen before. Seeing them made him think that he must have been wandering the world for years in a state of mental eclipse. What could have been happening during this time? Now he was too hungry to think about it. He reached for one of the bottles, and having bitten through the thin plastic, greedily drank its contents all the way to the bottom.

Taking a deep breath after that meal, he looked around. The apartment he was in, was economically and functionally furnished: the most-necessary equipment, a soft carpet and a TV set, the largest he had ever seen before. Everything shining with cleanness, kept in the same bright and warm ecru tone as the clothing of the mysterious savior. He remembered him well. Who could he be? The Hunters probably did not know him, their behavior indicated that he somehow overwhelmed them with his willpower. He wouldn't probably have to do it if he were somehow familiar to them.

He had to know well whom he was saving, otherwise he wouldn't put that blood on the table. Was he one of them after all? No, Gerard felt that he wasn't. He took a deep breath and reached for another bottle. He drank it in one gulp, and then his memories hit him like a hammer blow.

Their mission to penetrate the military factory, the fire, the scream, Never's strong arms holding him on the ground. It was the last thing he remembered clearly, then he probably set out to the world, after waiting for Never and the weeping Oggy to fall asleep. He was the only one that could not believe that Fronda was killed in the explosion that destroyed this damn factory. He couldn't wrap his head around the fact that he could die in such a stupid way, but now he felt despair rising in him again, because everything seemed to indicate that. Fronda could not have survived the explosion that destroyed the buildings of concrete and two-inch steel reinforcements, melted everything into a shapeless lump, covered with gray ash.

"He couldn't, but maybe he did survive," said a soft, gentle voice.

Busy with bitter thoughts, Gerard didn't even notice his savior come in and stand by the bed. He looked the same way he remembered him from the night events: tall and slim like a cane, fair-haired. He could not see his eyes, they were obscured by black glasses, but the sharp vampire's eyes immediately saw that he was not dealing with a human. The hair of the stranger looked more like feathers of a cassowary than normal hair, and the face, glowing with a kind beauty, was too smooth, empty, devoid of any irregularities, wrinkles or even expression lines. It resembled a face of an idealized statue rather than a living man.

"How do you know what I was thinking?" Gerard asked hoarsely. He had difficulty formulating sounds, his throat responded with pain to every word. He must have not been talking for a long time.

"You spoke a few words out loud," the stranger answered, then pushed the dressing away and examined his wound carefully.

"Who are you? Not a human and rather not a vampire..." Gerard could not resist the feeling of some strange numbness when he felt the touch of cool, velvet fingers on his skin.

"It's healing well," the blond man muttered. "And if you want to know, my name is Vandis. Vandis Winger."

His voice was mildly melodic, without any sharper tones.

"You are not human," Gerard repeated firmly. "Who then? Or what?"

The man straightened and removed his glasses. His eyes were uniformly black, with no trace of iris or cornea, glistening with flickering light.

"People call those like me Angels, if it changes anything," he said without emphasis, rather sadly.

"Really?" the actor was surprised and added immediately in disbelief. "Impossible. If you are an Angel, where are your wings, huh?"

"None of us needs them. People have a vivid imagination, you should know something about it. And they often multiply entities beyond the need."

Gerard sat up on the bed. He still felt weak, though his mind was much clearer and calmer now.

"Go easy on yourself," Vandis warned him. "You've gone through a nasty adventure and you certainly haven't recovered yet."

"Stop it. Don't be so good to me. I'm a vampire," Gerard muttered, feeling very uncomfortable under his gaze, devoid of any anger, and warm like the sun rays despite its blackness. "Do you know what a vampire is? I drink blood to live. You set up all these containers here, so you probably understood it yourself. Why did you help me? I'm the bad one after all."

Vandis put his narrow, cold hand on his head.

"There are the hunchbacked, the deaf, the paralyzed or the mentally ill in this world. Those with schizophrenia, paranoia, autism. There are criminals and people who are socially maladjusted, and so on," he said calmly. "There are also vampires. I do not judge, I help."

"Why?" Gerard felt his will to live come back under the stranger's cool touch.

"What else should I do? I can only do that."

Vandis sat down in front of him, folding his hands in his lap. The actor looked at him, feeling a strange sweetness in his heart, because here he had in front of himself an impeccably good being, the existence of which he had never even suspected.

"You must have many friends," he whispered after a moment.

Vandis shook his head sadly.

"It's difficult to be friends with someone like me," he said. "There is no creature in this world more lonely than an Angel. Because why would anyone want to be friends with one? With an Angel, you won't watch a match, go for a drink, or talk about girls or politics... I'm just boring, and in addition I don't have a sense of humor, and it is difficult to exist among people without it. People come for help and then leave. That's why I became a private investigator. One who is looking for missing people. Sometimes animals. I help those who need it, whether they can pay me or not. Yes, I need money like everyone else, but not as much as everyone else. I hardly eat, I am not interested in entertainment, so I need only enough to pay rent, taxes and new clothes from time to time."

"A detective... Maybe you could help me find Fronda?" Gerard asked with newly born hope.

"You called for him in delirium. Who is he?" the amazing eyes of his interlocutor looked at him with little interest.

"A friend," he answered with some effort. "The best one possible. He... I don't remember much, it's as if behind a fog... SETI hired us, we were to examine the famous Zone 51. We discovered a military factory there, or maybe rather a laboratory in which they experimented with new types of pathogenic viruses."

He paused for a moment. Memories slowly began to fit together, forming a whole.

"Fronda lost his wife and child in 1369 or so, during the epidemic of pulmonary plague," he took up. "And the very thought that someone could deliberately kindle such an epidemic... In short, he planted an explosive charge in the factory, but because he had experience only with those set off by hand, he did something wrong. Never claimed that he must have died."

"Must have died, or did die?"

"I don't know, there was a giant fire."

"Have you searched the fire site?"

"Of course, but we didn't find anything that could be associated with Fronda."

"Then there is hope."

"I don't know if there is. I tell you, nothing was left there, even the ash had melted. Never and Oggy repeated that no one could escape such hell. But I didn't believe it, so I ran away to look for him and... I don't remember anything more."

Vandis leaned his back against the wall and touched his fingertips together.

"What happened to you, is expertly called 'a vampire insanity'," he began. "It's a serious nervous disease that about half of you suffer from at some point in your life. It usually passes by itself if the affected vampire lives long enough, which is quite problematic. Judging by some of the signs, it could have even lasted a quarter of a century for you."

"That's impossible," Gerard opened his mouth in surprise. "Never and Oggy would definitely be looking for me!"

"You vampires use psycholocation," Vandis explained. "For an insane individual, psycholocation is useless and his actions are irrational. They could even search until the end of the world and not recognize you, even if they would step on you."

"And now what? Am I cured yet?" asked Gerard, who was terrified by this mysterious disease. He did not know how long he was wandering in a state of mental eclipse and what happened during that time, and in addition he felt uncomfortable under the warm look of the "Angel". Who was he really?

According to his worldview, such creatures did not exist, were a figment of fantasy, and here he saw one no further than a meter in front of him. Maybe it was normal? The biblical Angels were also real beings after all, not guardian spirits for polite children. Indeed, not only real, but even dangerous ones, who did not shun violence.

"Are you from God?" he asked, wanting to settle the question once and for all.

"We all are," Vandis replied with simplicity. "Of course, if we believe in His existence, it is easier to understand this. You don't believe it, I can see it on your face."

"Tell me about Him," he asked quietly.

He didn't know how it came to his mind. He was indeed an atheist, although after what had happened to him, he began to hesitate.

Vandis shook his head.

"I can't," he said. "These matters are too complicated for you to comprehend with a human mind. It is a secret that people will not penetrate, because for people, the key to learning secrets is a dictionary of articulated sounds. And this is far too limited to express the Inconceivable."

"If God exists, why does he allow so much misery?" Gerard whispered after a moment.

The mysterious man put a hand on his forearm.

"People demand too much of Him," he said seriously. "The key to understanding this issue, which is not only your concern, is free will. People got it as a gift, but they use it wrongly and, in addition, they blame the Creator for their own mistakes. They don't want him to rule them, but they want him to help them unconditionally. It's illogical, you'll probably admit it yourself. And yet... if people could just obey the simple ten commandments, the world would become a paradise."

"I'm not sure..."

"If you tell someone not to ski on a given day because there is a threat of an avalanche, and he will go against your advice and die, can you be blamed for his death? You warned him, and he used his freedom of choice in the wrong way. For example, if God said, "Do not kill," and people act against this commandment, how can they blame Him for the effects of their disobedience?"

This gentle reasoning dumbfounded Gerard, especially since it contained irresistible arguments. He sought counterarguments for a moment, then gave up.

"It reminds me of something," he said after a moment. "In 'Gone with the Wind' some slaves prefer to go back to their recent masters than to decide for themselves..."

"A long shot, but there is something to it," Vandis agreed. "When you get out from someone's dominance, you not only free yourself of its annoyance. You can't count anymore on its positive side, that is, a protection and lack of personal responsibility, either."

"When you release a working horse, he will no longer be forced to work hard, but he will not have a roof over his head, oats in winter or protection against wolves. Well, but it will be free and will rather not come back to the stable out of his own will," the actor nodded with understanding.

He considered what he heard for a moment. This strange individual was a skilful rhetoric, but it did not determine his origin. Who was he really?

He glanced at the hand on his forearm and got speechless. Earlier, he could clearly see a normal human hand, now he could distinguish four nail-less fingers, almost equal in length. After he blinked, everything went back to normal.

"An illusion," Vandis explained to him in a tired voice. "I can influence the perception to some extent, the rest is done by the unbelief, typical for humans. No one like me was recognized as a different being if he didn't want to. And I have a request for you. Don't talk to me about theology again. OK?"

"A different being," the actor repeated thoughtfully. "How different? Where do you come from?"

"I don't remember," he admitted with embarrassment. "In general, we have very weak internal memory, which means that events about others are remembered much better than those about ourselves. But enough about me, now the most important beings are you and the one you were looking for, even when you were in a state of insanity. Maybe you can find him now? Or maybe he will find you?"

Gerard smiled weakly.

"As far as I know Fronda, if he is alive, he has not given up his search," he said. "He's amazing, one of a kind. A kind of a fairy knight. He went through this insanity that you talked about at the very beginning of his path. He lived with a wolf pack in the woods then, until that madness went away. He doesn't know himself how many years it was, he suspects that at least twenty, if not twice as many."

Vandis nodded.

"Get well first, then we'll look for your friends," he said and touched Gerard's forehead with his fingers. They were cool, silky to the touch and caused the actor to fall to an all-encompassing, gentle, but irresistible sleep. Whoever or whatever his new friend was, he certainly had extraordinary skills and was able to use them properly.

*****

The good sleep fortified Gerard - he awoke from it almost at full strength. Vampire wounds usually heal very quickly, but there was obviously some other force acting here, and it was easy to guess who it came from.

It was dark in the apartment. Gerard got up, turned on the light and sought the bathroom. A cold shower was what he was dreaming about now, and as he was drying his scrawny body with a rough towel, he suddenly remembered the whole nightmare from which he had escaped into insanity. And if his friends failed to dodge the persecutors then? Somehow he could not imagine that they could not find him for so many years... actually, how many years were there?

He searched the apartment, but could not find any calendar. After some time, however, he found an abandoned newspaper and got speechless: it was 1987.

"So many..." he whispered in horror and his heart felt an icy cold. Now he was sure that his friends must have been killed, otherwise he would not be able to hide from them for that many years.

Gerard slowly folded the newspaper. He tried to force his mind to do a calm, dispassionate thinking, but he felt a despair growing against his will. He was still not ready to live alone, and such a possibility aroused a feeling dangerously close to panic in him. He mechanically put on the clothes prepared for him on the chair, and drank blood from one of the bottles he found in the fridge. He was struck by the fact that apart from the plastic containers of blood, there was nothing at all there - not because he wanted something else, of course. As a rule, vampires eat nothing but blood and mixtures containing small amounts of juice or alcohol.

He smiled sadly to himself. Only Fronda had the courage to try "something real" sometimes. For example, he liked ice cream, cotton candy and chocolate, although all this was clearly bad for him. Without him, the world will certainly be worse off. However, he did not think about it when he opened the fridge. Did the peculiar creature who saved him not need anything? You could really get such an impression when looking at the perfectly empty, shiny interior, because he probably did not drink blood, the containers of which filled the bottom drawer. So what did he eat if he ate at all?

The actor shrugged in resignation, concluding that he would not solve this puzzle now. The silence in the apartment was suddenly interrupted by the buzzing sound of a telephone bell. Gerard hesitated, not sure if he should answer the phone calls, certainly not addressed to him, but the phone rang so persistently that he finally picked up the receiver.

"Yes?" he said neutrally.

"Gerard, it's me," Vandis's quiet voice sounded in the phone. "I know that this may not be the best time for such questions, but haven't your missing friend's adventures ever been filmed for a youth series?"

"Yes, it happened. I didn't watch it all the way to the end, only a few episodes, but it's not bad at all. Why do you ask?"

"Well, because if they chose the main actor well, it means your Fronda is here," said Vandis. "Listen carefully: there is a taxi stand by the building, and the money is in the box on the TV. The address: 18a Clinton Street, Amado Night Club. Will you remember?"

"Sure, I'm on my way," Gerard threw the phone receiver down on the cradle, grabbed a few bills from the box, and jumped out the door, not thinking that he was not at full strength yet.

The detective's words gave him hope. It might be illusory, but he clung to it with all his might. He did not even wonder what the name of the city was, the streets of which the taxi driver, happy with the order, was taking him through, but he did not recognize it, although he probably spent the recent years here. The streets and buildings he passed were new to him and in other circumstances he would surely watch them curiously, but now he barely paid attention to them.

The taxi braked in front of the premises with an entrance lit by a neon sign. Gerard gave a banknote to the cab driver and jumped out, almost bumping into Vandis, who came out of nowhere.

"You were serious?" he asked almost breathlessly.

"Yes," the man replied calmly. "There is someone in the club that is deceptively similar to this actor and... I think he is not human, judging by the aura. I have to warn you: he's probably under the influence of drugs."

"Fronda would never..." Gerard began in a raised voice and paused. "Well, who knows? He has always been crazy. Let's go inside... And by the way, how come you are here at this hour?"

"I'm a private investigator, did you forget? I was here working on the order," Vandis passed the broad-shouldered bodyguard at the entrance and got inside the club.

In the flashing, multicolored light, Gerard could hardly distinguish the couples dancing wildly on the dance floor - his companion must have had much better eyesight than he if he could recognize anyone in this ghostly lighting. He looked around helplessly until Vandis tapped his shoulder and pointed at one of the couples. They came closer, squeezing in among the dancing people.

Despite the flickering of colored spots and streaks, Gerard understood, not without a squeeze in his throat, that this young man, jumping to the rhythm of rock-and-roll with his partner, is undoubtedly Fronda. He wanted to grab his arm, but at the moment someone knocked him aside.

"Theo, we're leaving!" A well-known voice sounded, cutting over the super-loud music without much effort. "You should be ashamed, you know?!"

"I don't know!" Fronda shouted cheerfully. "Don't be such a party spoiler!"

"I'll give you a party..." Never grabbed him and while struggling with him, pulled him outside, with Gerard's help.

Only outside did the Indian look at his helper and he was stunned.

"It's you!" He said after a moment and unexpectedly hugged him. "Fanfan, Gerard, our movie star! How come you are here? Where have you been for so many years? Anyway, it doesn't matter now, help me."

The two of them dragged their friend to the van, guarded by a great Alsatian. Seeing his friends, he got up and started wagging his tail enthusiastically, then jumped after them into the car.

"Aren't you ashamed, knight? What state you got yourself into..." Never shook his friend hard.

"Emily is a daughter of a plastic surgeon, she promised me a discount," Fronda chuckled. "I will look like Eroll Flynn... The Hunters will finally leave me alone."

He rested his head on Gerard's shoulder, laughing hysterically.

"He drank the blood of a girl who decided to overdose," the Indian said in an explanatory tone. "He saved her, but got himself stoned. We've been following him like this since dusk, me and Oggy. What can we do, he must digest this stuff. But you... Where have you been all this time?"

Oggy listened to them, wagging her tail vigorously. She did not assume human form, which did not draw much of Gerard's attention for now.

"I'd like someone to tell me that myself," he sighed. "Vandis says I suffered from some kind of insanity and I am willing to agree with him."

"Vandis? Vandis Winger?" Never cut in, astonished.

"Yes, that one. He saved me from the Hunters squad, so I guess he's okay," the actor said a little uncertainly. After all, he knew almost nothing about his rescuer.

"Winger is a living legend," the Hindu said slowly, brushing his hair away from his face. "One could hear about him from time immemorial, I was told about him from Sixto, who probably came from ancient Rome and swore that even his master did not know where this guy came from. If there are beings called Angels at all on Earth, he is one of them... no matter what these creatures really are."

"Yes, it is beyond doubt," Gerard admitted. "I wonder if there are others like him?" he finally glanced at Oggy, panting with her tongue out, and asked cautiously. "Is our girl all right?"

Never shrugged slightly.

"Well, let's face it, she's got a lot worse lately," he said reluctantly. "She becomes a dog after dusk already and cannot take human form until morning. During the day it varies too..."

He leaned over the semi-conscious Fronda and began to examine his pupils with the help of a small flashlight.

"Poor old rascal," he muttered. "He'll have a giant hangover tomorrow. Vampires react terribly to drugs, but you know how it is with our Fronda. Knight's blood awakened in him and he rushed to save the virgin in danger. True, she was not a virgin but rather a minor drug addict, but let it be his way."

"He has always been like that." Gerard looked at his friend's head, resting on his shoulder.

He still had his now-out-of-fashion hairstyle, a bit too long bangs combed to the side, an asymmetrical parting and frayed strands at ear height. Even if fashion went crazy, he always did his hair in the same way, although, for example, Never was happy to change the hairdo, although it was always for a short time. His hair seemed to live its own life and grew at indecent speed, destroying the efforts of hairdressers.

"Has he ever had any contact with drugs?" he asked.

Never frowned.

"Once or twice," he replied. "You know how crazy he is. He once licked hashish pulp and probably did a similar folly once again, not to experience different states of consciousness, you understand, but out of curiosity what it tastes like. As far as I remember, he didn't even get high then, after all a vampire needs a horse's dose to feel anything. He got knocked out like this for the first time, and I will make sure it is the last."

"What about the girl?" Gerard asked after a moment, when Never started the engine and got the van moving.

"An ambulance took her. She'll survive unless the next golden shot does her in," he replied curtly, steering the vehicle through the brightly lit streets.

Oggy put her head on Gerard's lap and squealed quietly, as if trying to say something.

"Ah, I don't know what was going on with me," the actor said absently, as if answering the silent question contained in her gaze. "But why didn't you start looking for me right away? I wouldn't be able to go too far."

"We couldn't," Never explained to him. "Fronda did run away from the factory just before the explosion, but he was too close and got caught in the shockwave. As a result of the shock, he lost his memory for some time, and we both had to follow him so that he wouldn't do anything stupid. In addition, we couldn't locate you, as if you evaporated without a trace. When Fronda finally regained his memory, he also cursed us for that big time."

"Yes, he can do that." Gerard shifted in the seat because he was uncomfortable, and besides, Fronda's head weighed on his shoulder like a stone.

Never drove fast until he left the town and stopped the car only at some large facility, reminiscent of an indoor swimming pool from the outside. Gerard helped him get their friend out of the car and together they led him to a room under the building, a well-protected bunker, furnished like the luxury apartments of a Hollywood star.

"There's a military depot above us," Never explained. "That's why we settled here. Peace and safety. Now tell us what happened to you."

"I wish I knew it! I was wandering here and there, but I don't remember anything," Gerard replied honestly. "All I know is that they wanted to pierce me with a stake and then Vandis appeared. It seems that he was the one who cured me of madness, because I don't think it was the Hunters with their stake."

Never nodded. From what he knew about the semi-legendary creatures related to Vandis, they had certain healing skills in the field of mental and also physical diseases. In any case, he heard that their presence accelerates blood coagulation and destroys the viruses' ability of reduplication. Who these beings were from a morphological point of view, he did not wonder, he had never met one before anyway, and hesitated whether to believe in their existence.

"Dear Fanfan, you are one of the very few lucky people who saw the Angel and remembered it," he said sadly.

"Does that mean that others forget about it?" Gerard asked, surprised.

Never sighed heavily.

"I don't know much about them," he said. "But you see, they are very puzzling creatures. If they don't want it, you won't even notice them, or you will take them for an ordinary guy. They are able to influence the human ability to perceive, they probably use phenomena that lead to the emergence of the so-called cortical blindness. This is sometimes unreliable, for example when they are dealing with children, which is why toddlers often rave that they saw an angel. Their brain is not mature enough to be influenced by these methods."

He threw himself on one of the beds and yawned loudly. He had to have skipped sleep for a few nights, because usually he was doing well without sleep.

"The vampire's mind is a bit different from the human one, so they have trouble with us," he went on drowsily. "But in the end we come across each other so rarely that it has no practical meaning. Vandis is not only an Angel, he is also a bit of an activist of his race, of which by the way, between you and me, I know very little. No one knows their history, culture or aspirations, neither man nor vampire. Anyway, people are so rarely interested in anything but themselves... They are so eager to accept that something that doesn't suit them, doesn't even exist... "

He put his hands under his head and stared at the ceiling.

Gerard stroked mechanically the head of Oggy, who was still staring at him like at a holy picture.

"I never believed in Angels, either," he admitted after a moment. "It wasn't until I met Vandis that I understood how little we really know about the world around us. If Angels exist, then maybe so do demons too? Devils with horns and goat's hooves?"

"I suppose so," Never said, quite indifferently. "But they walk among people in masks and just want to survive. No demon, even the most malicious, can match people's desire to destroy and hunger for cruelty." He looked at his friend with a smile and changed the subject. "I hope you stay with us now."

"Of course I will," answered the actor. "Pour us a drink, Rajah, we tell each other everything in detail. Or do you prefer to take a nap first?"

Fronda got up from the sofa, opened the bar in the corner and took a bottle of cognac from it. He poured himself half a glass.

"Leave it, damn!" Never jumped up. "Pure alcohol can kill you, and no alcohol can be mixed with heroin!"

"Shut up," Theo snapped, a gloomy glint in his eye. He drank his cognac in one gulp and tossed the empty glass into the corner. "Treat yourselves to a splash too. You are too sober. Or maybe you think I have a problem?"

"Go to bed. You've done enough stupid things for one day." The Hindu deftly avoided the sensitive topic, apparently not wanting to argue.

"What the hell do you know about it."

"I know you are starting to lose your temper. Pull yourself together or you won't live long. I won't always make it in time to get you out of trouble," Never said calmly, but a dangerous, crazy flame smoldered in his friend's eyes, and his pretty face was drawn in an unpleasant grimace.

"Don't bother. I was taking care of myself back when you weren't even planned yet," he said contemptuously, unconsciously archaizing the syntax, as always when he was in a state of nervous tension.

"We know, we know," Never came over and put his hands on his shoulders. "You were a hero of your time and you never..."

Before he could finish, Fronda pushed him away with wild force.

"You don't know anything about me!" he shouted, raising his voice to a level inaccessible to mankind.

"We know a bit, we've seen the series..." Gerard interjected.

"Series! And what did they show there?!" Theo shouted, turning to him. "Nothing and nothing again! Do you know that the English captured my castle by slaughtering everything that got in their way?! They had an order to only spare me, so they killed everyone else, men right away, and women..."

Never shook him hard.

"You did what you could!" he shouted, but Fronda didn't seem to hear him.

"I was defending myself," he continued, his voice beginning to tremble. "I was defending myself... I was blocking the way to my sister's room from them. She was only eleven and so pretty, so sweet, I loved her so much..."

"Stop it! That was over six hundred years ago!" Gerard shouted hysterically. He didn't want to hear what happened next, his heart was already up his throat.

"If so, why do I still feel Odette hug my legs?!" Theo shouted, his crazy eyes running from one friend to another. "Why do I still hear her voice: "Save me!"?! She clung to me in the most terrible terror, and I, instead of saving her, turned and stuck my sword into her heart!"

"Stop it! You had to do it!" Never again grabbed his shoulders and shook him with all his strength.

"I had to, and I should, because they would kill her anyway, but only AFTER! And then... I should point the sword blade at myself, but I didn't do it!" Fronda howled, as if he lost his senses. "I was a coward! I just chickened out! That's why I later jumped blindly in every danger, because I wanted to erase this shame, but all this in vain, in vain!"

He threw himself on the floor and stuck the fingers of both hands into his hair. Nobody noticed that it had to be already a morning outside, because Oggy had already taken on a human form, and after wrapping herself hurriedly in a large towel, pushed the friends away and knelt next to Fronda, embracing him by the neck.

"Calm down," she whispered tenderly. "You did what you had to do. You offered your sister the most precious gift under these conditions: a quick, pure death. And the fact that you did not want or did not manage to kill yourself... Think about what favors you gave your country by organizing the resistance movement in Sologne, how helpful you were for your king. Do you know how many lives you have saved, directly or indirectly? What hope did you give to people trampled by the boot of the war? You are a hero, whether you want to recognize it or not. Now sleep, and everything will pass, everything will work out. That blood had soaked into the earth a long time ago, other wars rolled over the world, one worse than the other, someone loses someone every day. You have risked your life many times so that there were as few tragedies like yours as possible, and I think it is good that your hand let you down at that crucial moment."

Theo raised his head and looked at her, as if slowly calming down. After a moment, he put his arms around her and pulled her close to himself.

"I love you, Oggy," he whispered and fell to the floor without letting her out of his arms.

After a moment, his breathing evened and slowed, letting his friends know that he had fallen asleep. Oggy gave them a gentle look.

"Go to the other room," she asked. "I'll stay here with him. He shouldn't be alone when he wakes up, and my eyes are getting heavy after the nightmares of this night, too."

Never nodded briefly, agreeing with her.

"She's right," he said. "We take a snack and go to the other room, we can talk there."

He took a bottle from the table, a few blood containers out of the small fridge, and pushed Gerard in front of him through the ajar door.

"This isn't his first outbreak," he said, mixing cognac with canned blood. "He is behaving more and more like a psycho recently. We are not able to deal with him, me and Oggy, especially since she has her own trouble now. I am afraid that this is the end of our Fronda. He doesn't have much time left. Soon he will be in such a bad state, that he will kill without hesitation and thus become a deadly threat not only to people, but also to us, and he will have to be eliminated. If I don't kill him in time, the Hunters will do it, except that I would be much more delicate and would not cause him unnecessary suffering."

"Is it that bad?" the actor was terrified.

Never handed him a glass.

"I've seen such cases before," he said sadly. "A vampire suddenly collapses under the weight of his past, and he can't cope with it. In the end, he goes crazy and begins to do various stupid things, until he finally falls victim to Hunters, who are just waiting for this. It's sad."

Gerard fixed his green eyes on the wall and sipped slowly, considering what he heard.

"We need to help him somehow," finally he said firmly.

The Indian shrugged.

"How?" He asked, sitting on the folding bed. "I've tried everything. Fronda is losing his mind and I can't stop it, as if he weren't himself, as if some malicious demon of self-destruction took control of him."

Gerard drank again and thought.

"I know," he said suddenly. "The solution here is Vandis. He can heal the spirit and the body, maybe he will find a remedy for what happened to our knight."

"Do you know where he lives?" Never asked with little hope in his voice.

"I don't know exactly, but I think I will remember the way to get there," said the actor. "I remember what the taxi driver was passing by on the way to the club. I'm sure I will be able to retrace this route."

He yawned involuntarily.

"Let's go to bed," the Indian suggested. "You won't do anything during the day anyway, and Theo must sleep off the yesterday's revel too, so he won't be acting up anymore. In the evening we will look for this Angel, or whoever he is."

"Right," Gerard finished his drink and stretched out on a felt blanket with relief. Even his worry over Fronda could not prevent him from falling asleep now, after all that had happened lately.

When he awoke, Never was already up and combing his long hair in front of the mirror.

"You have a snack on the table," he said, seeing that his friend was awake. "Hurry up. Fronda and Oggy are still sleeping, we won't have to explain to them where we are going and why."

The actor jumped off the bed, washed quickly under the tap and drank the blood prepared for him, almost choking in a hurry. They carefully walked through the other room, where their friends slept in exactly the same position in which their fell asleep - huddled and hugged.

"Do you think he really loves Oggy, or did he just say that?" Gerard asked, when they reached the surface in slowly falling dusk.

"I don't know that," Never said. "But I think so, Fronda doesn't lie in a drunken state. This is another unsolvable problem, because Oggy is a werewolf, and that means that during love making she can turn into a bear-like beast and tear her partner apart. Did you know that the Russian equivalent of a werewolf is a wurdalak, or a werebear, in a free translation?"

"Then if Fronda really loves Oggy, he'll be in trouble," Gerard added sadly.

"Perhaps," the Hindu started the engine. "The thing is that our medieval friend is a knight and he still understands the world in knight terms, regardless of the era, so our Oggy appears to him as an enchanted princess who needs to be freed from the curse. Preferably with a kiss. Or maybe I am wrong and he has only brotherly feelings for her? Who knows?"

"This all is so strange. Have you been in contact with Octavio during those years when I was away? Maybe he could help."

Never shook his head. He drove the van steadily through the crowded streets.

"You know what Fronda is like. He got bored of working for the Institute even faster than I thought, but we're sticking to it because we need money. However, we lost the common language with them and we don't want to confide everything in them. Well, here is the club. Where now."

Gerard looked around. The vampires' psycholocation abilities get better with age, and although he had not used his for a very long time, the more he now felt the weak directional signals somewhere in the subconscious.

"Straight ahead," he said, looking closely through the windows. "Right now. Straight... straight... right, now turn left and straight... This is the block."

"A nice apartment block." The Indian easily found a free space to park the car. He turned off the engine and got out. "Which floor?"

"Tenth."

The tower had two elevators, but they preferred to use the stairs. The actor felt a sudden emotion as they climbed higher and higher. This strange creature who had helped him, uninvited and not demanding a payback, made a deeper impression on him than he initially thought. He was glad to see him again, but the door to the apartment was shut.

"He probably went out somewhere. I'll wait for him, and you go back to those two. Theo must have someone with him now to stop him from doing stupid things," Gerard offered to Never after a moment's hesitation. "Just give me the address of your hideout, approximately. You know, when I get close enough..."

Never nodded in agreement.

"Good idea," he said. He scribbled a few words on a piece of paper torn out of his notebook. "Just be careful: if he doesn't come for a long time, take a taxi and come back to us. Don't let the sunrise surprise you."

"Don't worry," he reassured him, sitting down against the wall.

He wasn't going to get discouraged too quickly, especially since the life of a close friend depended on it. He was sure that Vandis, whoever he really was, would be able to help Fronda, and he was determined not to give up this possibility, even if he had to wait all night.

While waiting, he thought back to his friend. He did not know until now how difficult the experience was that he went through. He did not confide in anyone, and even when he told some events of his life, they were always cheerful. And yet there is no man whose life would only have joyful and pleasant moments. Theo posed for one all the time and was even quite credible in this role, and yet they should not have believed him.

No matter how you look at it, he was born and raised in dark times, full of cruelty and violence, times in which the way of thinking and acting was completely different than it is now. A medieval knight, lost in the twentieth century, forced to live on the border between sleep and waking, unable to forget about the past, and yet seemingly reconciled with the present. He had to finally break down, that was to be expected. Only why so suddenly? Was it related to the drug addict, whose life he had saved by drinking heroin dissolved in the blood from her body? Or maybe things had been wrong with him for a long time, but no one noticed it?

"I have been away for so many years, how would I know?" He whispered to himself. "And in the past he was strange sometimes, as if something was bothering him, and we underestimated it, because he usually laughed and joked as much as three men. I will probably have such breakdowns at his age too, although I have not lived through even a tenth of what he had before I was perpetuated... and I was older and also survived the war, even crueler than that one, according to historians... although what measure should be used to quantify the suffering of people and nations? The ideals Fronda fought for, were dead in his day already, though he does not believe it to this day."

He rested his forehead on his knees, brought high to his chest, and closed his eyes. He still felt weak, but the confusion in his mind was slowly beginning to subside and he remembered more and more of the details, blurred in the memory. He was glad that he had come back to life and no longer had to wander the world alone, without a purpose or plan.

He must have fallen asleep for a moment, because he was only awakened by a sudden touch.

"What are you doing here?" asked Vandis's voice.

Gerard jerked his head up, looking at him with unconscious eyes.

"Ah, it's you," he said after a moment. "We need your help. My friend, the one I told you about, is in a terrible shape, as if he was losing his temper. Various nasty things from his memory come back to him and he is reliving them, and Rajah says it is as serious as the insanity you healed me of. Will you help him?"

"I'll do my best," Vandis told him, without adding any of the typically human ornaments like "Actually I don't have time." or: "I don't really know if I can..."

Gerard got up and went with him to the elevator, and a moment later he was sitting on the rear seat of his motorcycle, wondering in the spirit that it went so easily. This strange detective, whoever he was, really wanted to help everyone. Maybe this was to him the sense, or even the condition, of existence? The actor, hugged to his back, felt a tremor of muscles, which seemed to be something that must have been equivalent to the excitement for this type of being. He thought that he didn't really know anything about them, he didn't even know if they were thinking and feeling like people, or maybe in some other way, the way that was unique for them, and whether this is not the borderline that prevents full understanding. After all, vampires do not differ from people in their way of thinking.

There was no denying that he was dealing with someone extremely different. The Vandis's hair, swept on Gerard's face, differed even to the touch from human - it was stiff, smooth and springy, smelling of smoked cedar and fresh pine needles. The skin on his arms, which he had accidentally touched through his parted shirt, did not resist his fingers, like a powdered plush. The eyes he remembered resembled the eyes of aliens from shoddy movies, except they were not slanted. Physical differences, however, were a minor matter compared to the psyche of Vandis. He felt that it was an unsolvable puzzle.

Gerard was so absorbed in thinking about the extraordinary nature of this man in flawless ecru clothing, clean and ironed despite the night spent in the detective investigation, that he missed something else. He didn't even notice how strange it was that Vandis knew when to turn, when to go straight and in what direction. More interestingly, Gerard knew that too. He had never used psycholocation on such a scale, but apparently his subconscious coped with it better than his mind.

A shepherd, spinning restlessly and squeaking, was waiting for them in front of the warehouse. Seeing them, he barked loudly, alarmingly, then turned and ran inside, disappearing into the dark interior behind the ajar door. They ran after him. The hatch in the floor, leading to their shelter, was open, so they went downstairs, closing it carefully behind them.

"You are here, wonderful," Never jumped towards them with visible relief. "Fronda has lost it completely. He speaks only Old French, I barely understand him, and asks me to kill him. I had to calm him down so that he wouldn't do something foolish."

"How did you calm him down? With an injection?" Gerard asked in surprise.

"What do you mean how? With fistopirin*, of course. As if you didn't know that this is the only way with him. Then I tied him up solidly, and you know that I can make strong knots," Never looked curiously at Vandis, unimpressed in his calm.

The detective did not return his gaze, focused on the task ahead.

"I'll go there," he said after a moment. Oggy howled. "No, you stay. Later I'll see what can be done for you."

He headed for the next room and carefully closed the door behind him.

At the sound of footsteps, the bound man raised his head, shaking his hair away from his forehead, and stared at him bluntly. Vandis came over, leaned over him and touched Theo's temples with his fingers, pressing lightly. He held his fingers for a moment, then straightened up, removed his dark glasses, and looked the vampire straight in the eye. It lasted maybe a second. Then he untied the ropes binding Fronda and stroked his head with a sad gesture of someone who feels hundreds of years older - as it was in his case anyway.

The door squeaked and Gerard peered inside.

"So?" he asked.

Fronda was silent, running his hands over his forehead and cheeks with the steady movement of a man stunned by a heavy blow.

"It's an ambiguous matter," said Vandis. "Heroin was only a catalyst here, there are traces of a substance called saturnin in his blood. This is a relatively new invention used to combat vampires, synthesized by Dr. Charles Kerry, a student of Professor O'Grady. While completely harmless to humans, it causes slow dementia in vampires, but fortunately for you it must be administered orally to work, and in addition, together with some plant-based carrier. It is almost out of the question for this to happen, so I'm not sure..."

"Fronda likes chocolate and fruit ice cream," Never interrupted him from the other side of the room. "It makes him sick, but he eats it anyway. So, here is your carrier. Is there any way to reverse this?"

"I tore the saturnin molecular structure apart," said the detective. "Your friend will recover in about two days."

He looked at them kindly from behind his glasses, mechanically scratching Oggy, who put her head under his four-fingered hand, behind her ears.

"I knew you are really excellent," Gerard said appreciatively.

"No. I just know how to do some things, that's all." Vandis smiled sadly. "What is my credit for this? None. I have already explained to you that help is the only thing I know how to do, I can't do anything else."

"And you haven't tried just living for yourself?" Never was surprised.

He was still devouring the strange visitor with his eyes, with the fascination that was unusual for this blazed bon-viveur, who was usually not surprised by anything or anyone.

"I don't know how to do that. I can live for others or not at all," Vandis told him.

"You don't know how to do that... Maybe we'll teach you? There is definitely a way. You must be terribly unhappy, you do not deserve it," the Hindu involuntarily assumed an almost begging tone.

Somehow, he began to care about helping this incredibly different, lonely being.

"I tried it once and I ended up slowly disappearing. It's useless. Don't bother with it. Everyone has their destiny."

There was a long moment of silence.

"Still, maybe there is something we could do for you?" Gerard asked finally.

The detective thought for a moment.

"Maybe you could help me, though not in the way you think," he said after a moment.

Oggy whined softly.

"Or maybe you could cure our friend since you are here?" Fronda said unexpectedly, in a completely normal voice. "Something is wrong with her. She has trouble controlling her wolf nature."

He was still rubbing his forehead and seemed not quite conscious, but his eyes were slowly regaining their former glow.

Vandis crouched down and looked Oggy in the eyes.

"I could, why not," he replied. "But it will require a lot of time. I have to teach her a few different meditation techniques, which will allow her to have a total control of her body, so it would be handy if you could take care of a particular, quite unpleasant matter for me."

"No problem," Never assured him. "Should we kill someone?"

Vandis did not get the joke, apparently the "Angels", whoever they really were, indeed did not have a sense of humor.

"Not at all, what an idea. You would just have to drive a little girl from the hospice outside the city to Bluewaters, a small workers town, quite far away from here," he explained seriously. "I used to conduct an investigation there and befriended Jeannie Meadows, the post office manager, and her husband, a local newspaper journalist. Very nice people. Currently, Henry Meadows is dead, he died in Rwanda, where he was photographing war damage, and their daughter Hope is dying of bone marrow cancer. Jeannie doesn't want to quit her job, which is the only therapy for her, helping her endure all this. So she asked me to pick up Hope from the hospice and bring her to Bluewaters. Maybe it would be wiser to leave the little one under the care of doctors and nurses, but she has maybe three weeks of life left anyway, and she wants to spend this time at home. I should actually do it myself, but I always feel as if I were dying myself in the company of terminally ill people."

"Couldn't you help her the way you helped us?" Gerard was surprised.

Vandis shook his head.

"I can only heal wounds, body and soul wounds," he replied. "Diseases, especially childhood ones, are beyond my abilities. Do you think I wouldn't help Hope if it was possible? I like her very much, apart from everything else."

The actor murmured something understandingly. He could sense the sadness in the Angel's voice perfectly well, and he knew how painful it had to be to know that he was powerless against such misery, despite all his extraordinary powers.

"It's not just about taking Hope home," the detective said after a moment. "It's also about staying with her a little bit. Can you do that?"

"Sure," Never said. "We have tons of time."

"How does Mrs. Meadows cope with all this?" Gerard asked, shuddering at the thought of being in a similar position.

"Not bad, considering what happens to her. First her husband, then the daughter... You need real strength to bear it."

Vandis's voice was full of sadness and regret.

Fronda put a hand on his shoulder hesitantly, as if he was afraid of offending him with excessive confidentiality.

"Don't worry," he said heartily. "We'll try to help Mrs. Meadows and her little girl."

"Just no vampire tricks, okay?" stipulated Vandis.

Never snorted, insulted.

"No worries. Children's blood is not suitable for our food, it contains too much monoblasts and too much developmental hormones. Our metabolism is too delicate to disturb it in this way."

"Oh, that's interesting. I didn't know that," Vandis looked at him curiously.

He had never been interested in vampires until now, although he had occasionally come across them, always on a pleasantly neutral foot. The news, drawn from books and television, had created a completely false image in his mind. He didn't believe that they were as bad as people claim though. His disposition made him seek good in every being, but he did not know that they could be so similar to people in feelings and reactions. While treating Gerard, he absorbed some kind of knowledge, though incomplete, and he knew now that vampires are just people like others, though a little atypical, and it was a nice news for him.

"Will you help then?" he asked just for the record.

"Of course. You don't have to worry about anything."

* * * * *

"What are you pondering on? Will you make a decision before Sunday?" Theo asked bitingly, tapping his fingernails on the chessboard.

Gerard touched the figures indecisively, switching between the rook and the bishop.

"I think I'm finished anyway," he said finally. "I see that the saturnin did not interfere with your chess skills. I can't believe someone added this nasty stuff to the sweets for children."

"I remember that the ice cream in Cincinaty had a weird taste. I have already let the institute know, they will deal with the manufacturer and his connections with Medlab" Theo was playing with the beaten pawn, without taking his eyes off the board. "Check to the king."

"Is Medlab still in business?"

"You don't know? Oh right, you have a big gap in your life. Yes, of course it is. Lenor took up the fight with this company, and lost. The rest of her group scattered around the world, I don't know if there was anyone left in the British Isles," Fronda put the figures back in the box. "And Medlab has already reached the continent with its tentacles, competing with the Van Helsing Institute. They don't like each other, weird, isn't it?"

"Speaking of Van Helsing, have you found Erzika's murderer?" Gerard asked after a while.

Theo shrugged reluctantly and brushed the hair from his forehead.

"We have," he answered reluctantly. "There is nothing to brag about, because it was an ugly story, and in addition, associated with something that I would rather forget about. Do you want me to tell you about it? Never will not be back for another hour."

"Tell me," the actor asked.

He still remembered that his medieval friend loved to tell various stories. Perhaps in this way, he was talking over what was stuck in his memory and could not be removed from there. Besides, he had a talent for telling interesting stories and people liked listening to him, even when the story itself was boring or banal. This time, however, the story itself was so extraordinary that the actor listened without taking his eyes off his friend.

In the year nineteen seventy-three, Never, Theo and Oggy went to Hong Kong, carrying out a small order for Octavio di Mauro. They did not know this city and they did not like it at all, especially since they received a warning about a group of Hunters operating there. This warning made them afraid to stay in one of the hotels, but luckily a good friend of Never, the actress Tang Pei, lived in Hong Kong. The Indian, usually cautious with this kind of contacts, was so enchanted that he promised to perpetuate her as soon as she would be ready.

Everyone liked the beautiful and smart girl with an interesting personality. The order turned out to be even easier than they thought, but the hospitality of the delicate Chinese woman was so pleasant that they decided to stay a few more days despite the danger. The second night, just as they were sitting by the mahjong, someone suddenly rang at the door. Miss Tang Pei looked in astonishment at the clock, showing midnight, but she stood up and went to open the door.

After a moment, she returned, bringing with her a beautifully built, young Asian with a long face and a hair falling over his eyes, almost like Fronda's. The knight, a regular visitor to the cinemas, recognized him immediately.

"Bruce Lao!" He called out. "I think I saw all your movies! You got the blow, man, you fight in fantastic way. I know a thing or two about fights, but when you do it..."

"Nice to be recognized by someone like you," the Chinese interrupted. "No beating around the bush: I know who you are, and I swear I'll bring Vampire Hunters on your back if you don't meet my demand. Or shorter: I will take care of you myself. You can be sure that I will manage to do that."

Never smiled contemptuously, not too terrified by this announcement. He had heard it too often to worry about it.

"What do you want then, master?" he asked casually.

Tang Pei looked at them, nervous and terrified by the situation. They paid no attention to her.

Bruce Lao raised his hand and rubbed his fingertips together.

"I am losing the ability to feel my fingers," he said. "The doctor warned me that it would happen. My spine will give in any day, I have recently fainted on the set and they are suspecting the beginnings of epilepsy, and that's not all."

"Well, human body was not meant to be pounded like a drum. It never occurred to you that you are not made of steel?" Never asked sarcastically.

Bruce looked at him and finished his statement:

"If I continue to lead such a life, I will become a cripple. If I don't - why should I live?"

"I feel you," Oggy said from her corner.

"Okay, me too, but what do we have to do with that? How can we help you?" Theo asked a little uncertainly.

"Give me your blood," Bruce Lao demanded. He gave them a wild look and added after a while. "I understand that there is nothing for free, but I don't come empty handed. I know you're looking for the murderer of Erzebeth Szabo, and it so happens that I know where to look for him. He's here in Hong Kong, and I'll give you his address if you help me."

"Wow! Slow down," Never raised his hands. "Don't think that this news is not worth its weight in gold for us, or rather in blood, but you must understand something: transformation is not a simple matter and it carries a big risk. You don't even know how big."

"I'll take that risk," the Chinese interrupted him decisively.

"Great. You'll risk it. But are we going to risk it? You have no idea what danger a vampire who should not have arisen, poses to everyone," the Indian looked at the silent Fronda. "Check him, knight."

Theo stood up and walked over to the oriental actor who was following him with his slanted eyes without moving from his place. He scratched his dark skin with a blade hidden under his shirt cuff. He scooped up the blood with his tongue and tasted it carefully.

"I sense traces of the PAS factor," he said after a moment. "But within the limits of the acceptable risk."

"What is the PAS factor?" Tang Pei got scared.

"It is the composition of amino acids, which, in combination with the fixing factor, leads to the physical deformations, changes in skin color and even the temperament," Never told her. "That's why we need to be very careful and not perpetuate whoever comes our way. Alright, in your case, we can really take the risk, but there is one more problem: the autopsy. If you die suddenly, they'll slice you like a salami, and no vampire can survive that. Your sudden disappearance is also out of the question, you are too recognizable, and we prefer not to alert the police, let alone the media, with our actions. You have to make a stipulation that you do not want an autopsy, but in any case it will be a damn risk."

Bruce Lao smiled coldly.

"I've already made that wish," he said. "My wife also knows what to do, you don't need to worry."

"Wife? You got your wife involved? I think I'm going to shoot myself," Theo sat heavily on the couch and propped his head with his hands.

"No kidding? With a slingshot?" Never looked at him with moderate curiosity.

"Go ahead, joke about it. Maybe it would be best if this yellow guy announced his glorious decision on the radio and television? Because they don't know about it in China yet," Fronda apparently stopped watching what he says.

Bruce Lao paled and pursed his lips.

"I'm sorry, sometimes I talk faster than I think," Theo understood that he had gone too far and he felt embarrassed. "Don't be angry, master, call me a frog eater and we will be even. The thing is that it is dangerous to involve third parties in the whole process. Even if your transformation goes smoothly, you'll be in danger because one person too many knows about the matter. You have children, as far as I know, and this is a powerful weapon in the hands of blackmailers. If your children were threatened, wouldn't you be able to hand over yourself and us to the Hunters?"

The actor lowered his eyes.

"Did you have children?" He asked a bit aggressively after a moment. "They didn't say that about you in the tv show."

"Oh, so you know the show and you think you know everything," snapped Oggy, who didn't like the Chinese one bit.

"The Hunters showed me one episode, I watched the rest myself. They wanted to recruit me then," Bruce Lao explained calmly.

Never whistled slightly through his teeth, but he refrained from commenting.

"Oh, I see. Well, I had a child, a son. But it's none of your business," said Theo sharply. "The Hunters wanted to recruit you, right? Indeed, they could use such a recruit. What guarantee do we have that you don't lead us into a trap?"

Never snorted.

"Don't be ridiculous, knight," he said. "He could have just brought them here, since he knew where we are. No, I think he's clean. The problem is what we are to do now. To agree?"

Theo got up and walked slowly towards the window. He breathed deeply with the night air, staring at the starry sky.

"I want to get Erzika's killer," he said after a moment, when he was sure he would control his voice.

He still couldn't forget the beautiful Hungarian woman with whom he was connected by much more than a simple romance. She was a lover, a friend and, in a way, a daughter to him. Despite the passage of time, the bond between them did not loosen, as was common in this type of relationships.

Bruce approached him.

"I will give you this man," he said shortly.

A truly Chinese cruelty now shone in his slanted Asian eyes - revenge was something that spoke exceptionally well to his eastern soul that was not touched by Western civilization, despite the appearances.

The Frenchman looked at him and forced a smile.

"I agree, but the final decision is up to Rajah," he said.

"As always, you put everything on me. I have no idea how someone who is over six hundred years old, can be so immature," Never grumbled reluctantly.

He wondered. He had never acted under such pressure before and would have refused in any other situation, but he somehow liked this determined young man.

"Let's say we agree," he said finally. "But you probably understand that it is better not to do it immediately. How much time do you need to close your affairs?"

"Two days at most," Bruce answered him briefly.

The Indian nodded.

"Perfect. So in two days, on July 20th, in the evening, in this apartment. Let's say at eight. We have enough time to prepare everything from the technical side, and believe me it is not that easy. So where is this Hunter?"

Bruce looked at him sharply.

"I'll give you his address. But don't think you can fool me. I wouldn't like to be in your skin if you as much as try."

He took a piece of paper from the table and with a few quick movements drew a kind of a small map, marking the way from Tang Pei's apartment to the house, whose exact address he wrote on the side in two languages.

"We'll see. Oggy, do you still remember that smell?" Theo asked, taking the sheet and looking at it critically.

"Sure," the girl said briefly.

"Then let's have some fun today, unless someone here sends us on a wild-goose chase," Fronda looked at the Chinese warningly, but he just shrugged and left, closing the door behind him.

"I'm terribly sorry," Tang Pei said, evidently embarrassed. "I really didn't invite him here, and I don't know how he learned about you."

Never waved a hand.

"Don't worry about it, sweetheart," he said. "I understand it's not your fault. Anyway, if we get Erzika's killer thanks to him, then the case is worth pursuing. We have been looking for him for sixteen years in every country. So what now, are we going?"

"Sure. Let's make hay while the sun shines," Theo was obviously determined not to let it go, even though it had been so many years since the Long Pegs Night, as the Paris massacre was commonly called. A lot had changed since then, but not his feelings, just as hot as ever.

The three friends went to the address indicated by the Chinese actor, although without any great hope that the message would prove to be true. With no intention of fooling them, Bruce could simply have been wrong, or himself deceived by someone. However, as they approached the inconspicuous house, Oggy snapped a warning.

"Is the smell the same?" Never asked quietly.

"Undoubtedly," Oggy shook slightly, apparently struggling to keep her human form.

Never pressed the doorbell button at the gate, and a sharp trill ripped through the night silence. He repeated it two more times before the cottage door creaked and an elderly man in dirty pajamas stood on the threshold. He was obviously angry that someone was disturbing his sleep.

"There is no doubt," Oggy whispered, as the host hurried toward the gate, accompanied by two big bandogs. Then she huffed and smoothly turned into a wolf.

The moment the retired Hunter opened the gate, trusting in his four-legged defenders, she pushed into the garden and lead the dogs behind herself to the back of the house, wagging her tail friendly.

Despite the poor lighting, the Hunter immediately knew who his guests were. He gave such a terrible scream of terror that he made tremble not only Fronda, who was vindictive, but not without human feelings, but even Never, who seemed to be completely devoid of such feelings. Then he suddenly went limp and fell on the path.

"What happened?" asked Oggy, who appeared next to them in her human form and was hastily pulling a dress over her head.

"Probably a major heart attack," Never said, touching the Hunter's neck. "It's too late now to kill him or to help him. He died of fear. People are so vulnerable sometimes..."

"In a sense, my revenge is complete," Theo whispered, surprised that he didn't feel the expected satisfaction. "If he got a heart attack at the sight of us, it means that the fear of our repay had been poisoning his life all these years and did not leave him for a moment. Let's go before somebody shows up here or the dogs come back. What did you do with them?" he turned to Oggy.

"Nothing special. I lured them to the shed and locked the door. When they start jumping on the door handle, they will open it themselves. You're right, let's scoot."

They later learned from a local newspaper that the coroner who arrived at the house had pronounced death due to natural causes, despite the fact that the neighbor who took care of the deceased's dogs, mentioned strange guests he saw leaving the gate on the night of death. The police closed the investigation.

Two days later, when the friends visited Tang Pei (for safety reasons they had already moved to a nearby hotel), Bruce Lao appeared in the apartment, gloomy and determined.

"I'm ready," he said. "I wish I could finish my film, but I can't wait. I understand that if I get paralyzed, which I am supposedly at risk of, you will not be able to help me anymore."

"Probably not. Permanent neurological changes can't be cured by being turned into a vampire," Never nodded.

"Exactly. I can't risk it. For now, I'm still fit, but even in a few hours there may be a stroke. Dr. Quang Duk warned that this could happen, and he is an outstanding specialist."

Bruce sat on the couch and rubbed his face with his hands. Theo shrugged.

"Lie down then, man," he said kindly. "Your story is over. When you wake up, you will be one of us, and may the Chinese deities look after us."

"And what happened next?" Asked Gerard.

He was sitting with the cheek supported on his hand, and stared at his friend with his lettuce-green eyes with eager curiosity. He tried to find some trace of cruelty on this beautiful face, which had to be hidden behind this mask of youth and strength, but could not see anything.

"Nothing," Theo answered him with some anger. "Imagine that we have worked our asses off to get the alleged corpse out of the crematorium in time, we almost got caught, but everything went smoothly... And he just ran away, as soon as he woke up. You know that if someone decides to subject a man to perpetuation, then he is responsible for him until he stands confidently on his own feet. You know well the procedure and its meaning. And our master of kung fu has just bailed on us, our help and care..."

"He did what?"

"I mean he ditched us, you might not understand the new jargon yet. He disappeared from our eyes so thoroughly that we could not find a trail, anyway, we had to get out of there quickly too. Crazy story."

He shook his head irritably.

"What about this Tang Pei?" Gerard continued.

"She joined us later for about a year. Rajah kept his word. She was a good friend, but Oggy didn't like her. We missed you, really."

The actor smiled sadly.

"I've wasted lots of time," he sighed. "So much has happened..."

"Indeed, you are right about that. Even a movie was made about you," Fronda said with a malicious glint in his eye. "A Roger Boisset was proving in it that you were homosexual."

Gerard stared at him and lost his breath.

"I?! Who could have thought of that?!" he exclaimed with a painful resentment.

"What do you mean who? He and others like him. You know, now the truth doesn't matter, it's what you can make money or a career on that counts," the friend explained to him cheerfully.

"But I never..." the actor stammered in a daze and fell silent.

The libel was so absurd that he didn't even know what arguments to use. He wanted to say something more, but at that moment the door slammed and Never rushed into the apartment.

"Get ready!" He called cheerfully. "Vandis is waiting downstairs in a cool convertible with a sliding roof and additional covers for the windows. He has thought about everything."

"He probably always does, he's an Angel, after all," Theo said, getting up and throwing his chessboard into the bag.

Never shook his head.

"I have serious doubts whether he really is one," he said skeptically. "He probably believes it himself, but... He's rather a rare, unusual being, but definitely from this earth. Never mind, let's go. It will be dawn soon."

The car was indeed beautiful - a dark blue Opel with white tires and a black pattern on the hood. Vandis had just finished putting up the folding roof.

"It'll be probably noon before we get to the hospice. We'll be there right for the pickup time," he said. "Get in."

Theo and Gerard settled in the back seat, Never took the seat next to the driver.

"What is Hope like?" he asked when the detective was already driving.

"You'll see," Vandis said. "But don't expect anything nice. Hospice children are usually gloomy, introverted and aggressive, and Hope is no exception to this rule. I visited her as often as I could, but I couldn't make her open up... although people usually like me."

He sighed miserably.

"I'm not going to make her open up," Never said openly. "To be honest, of all the vampires I know, only Fronda likes children, actually he is crazy about them. Others give the impression of being afraid of them, because you can neither suck out nor perpetuate them. Maybe women feel differently, I don't know."

"What if one of you drank a child's blood or gave him his own?" the detective asked after a long moment.

"Giving our blood won't work, hemolysis or agglutination will occur regardless of the compatibility of the blood type and the Rh factor. And as for drinking... the same growth hormone that causes those effects will have similar effects in a careless bloodsucker. It is not worth the risk. If you've read vampire books, don't believe what is written there. 99% of it is total nonsense, for example about vampires attacking animals. I once drank the blood of a cat when I was in a real need and I meowed for a week instead of talking. Contrary to appearances, you can't cheat the nature."

"When one tries to rise above Nature one is liable to fall below it. Sir Arthur Conan Doyle," Theo recited sleepily from his place.

"Better get some sleep, knight," his friend advised. "The sun is already rising."

"Okay," Theo put on his headphones, connected to some small box.

"What is it?" Gerard asked curiously, though his eyes were already heavy too.

"Walkman," answered his friend "A cassette player in a nutshell, you can say, very practical. You slept through its invention."

He leaned against the padded seat back and closed his eyes, listening to Montovani's music flowing from the cassette. The atmosphere in the car favored taking a nap. Additional covers on the windows protected the interior of the car against solar radiation, and the air conditioning kept the interior pleasantly cool.

"Is this your car?" Never asked Vandis.

He shook his head.

"It's Jeannie Meadows' car," he said. "When you want to leave Bluewaters, you can call me and I will come for you.

During your absence I will take care of the girl you entrusted to me, and teach her how to deal with these transformations, but it will take a while, so take your time."

"Don't worry," the Indian reassured him, watching with some interest the road they were following. It was his second nature - he liked to know where he was going and how he could return from there without anyone's help.

"But... how will you explain your photophobia?" the detective asked carefully after a while, not wanting to offend his companion.

"We'll deal with that. You probably can't lie, but we can lie through our teeth and don't even blush," Never smiled with a sneer.

It was indeed so, and although Fronda did not like to lie, when he did it, he was much better at it than his Hindu friend. He had great imagination and his fantasies were very colorful.

Opel stopped in front of a large, stylish building, surrounded by a park.

"Wait here," Vandis got out, leaving his friends in the car.

He was away for quite a long time, and when he returned, a thin and pale girl with a dark expression was trotting by his side, dressed in ragged farmers and a cap, squeezed on her bald head.

Never moved to the driver's seat, making room for her.

"Good luck, Hope," Vandis said, helping the girl take her seat and fasten her seat belt. "Won't you say goodbye to me?"

"Goodbye," the girl snapped shortly, not looking at him.

Never laughed and turned the key in the ignition.

"She's charming," he said. "Take care, man."

"See you later," the detective slammed the Opel door and stepped back. He raised a hand in a farewell gesture, then turned and disappeared between the hospice buildings.

The Indian drove, glancing occasionally at the map pinned to the dashboard. He was the only one of the four who could read maps. Theo had not learned this art, the maps were a mystery to him to the extent that he could try to locate France somewhere in Australia on the globe, and looked for Paris in Czechoslovakia. In spite of this, he never got lost anywhere. Oggy found the right way through her sense of smell and hearing, and Gerard, although theoretically acquainted with maps, was wrong too often to be trusted.

Under these conditions, it was indeed better for Never to become a temporary driver. He drove with a steady hand, carefully following the rules and not paying any attention to the grumpy child sitting next to him. He had no intention of worrying about somebody's sulks, and as he didn't have an overly tender heart, it was easy for him.

"The fact that someone suffers does not give him any right to cause suffering to others," he used to say, when someone's behavior was being justified by illness or difficult experiences.

His behavior proved to be right - as the trip continued, Hope relaxed, and he stopped sensing a hostile distance from her. When they stopped at a gas station, she even ate a small dinner and drank tea, and then she was persuaded to play on a small slot machine, like any normal child her age.

"Are your friends going to sleep all the way?" she asked when Never was counting her points.

"They are tired, let them snooze," he told her. "Don't mind them, they don't play slot machines anyway. If you want to go to the bathroom, then go and I'll pay the bill and refuel the car. You will be home soon, are you happy?"

"On the one hand, yes," said the girl seriously. "It is my home. On the other hand, Bluewaters is sad. Only adults or old people live there, there are no children at all. My mother said that young people are not interested in working in a paper factory, so they leave and that's why the city is dying."

"It's important that you feel good there," said the vampire rather indifferently.

The sun was still high in the sky when they left the bar next to the station. Never winced slightly. He didn't like the sun even though he was almost insensitive to it. He quickly got into the Opel, where he was protected by the tinted windows.

Theo was awake.

"Hello, little bird," he said kindly, seeing Hope. "Nice to meet you. Rajah, is it still far to go?"

"Far," Never told him. "Sleep, Fronda, don't whine."

Theo fell silent, looking at the window behind which the trees and hills were passing. The road meandered through an increasingly wild countryside, among the forests he loved, and although American redwoods did not resemble French beeches or birches, they did cause some familiar dreaminess. Gerard, who had already woken up too, did not speak at all, only looked at Hope, visible in the rearview mirror, with a feeling of severe pain in his heart.

The sight of this child reminded him of Anne-Marie, the beloved daughter who, from the day she appeared in this world, wrapped him around her finger, and from whom he was now separated not only by thousands of miles, but also by the abyss that divides the two worlds. She had now been an adult woman for a long-time, and he remained a vague memory for her. He still couldn't get used to the pain felt at the thought of his children.

Suddenly, Opel jerked as if it hit something big, and Hope screamed.

"Damn, where did this dog come from?" cried Never, jumping to the side of the road.

Gerard followed his example before he could think, and the two of them ran to a huge black furred mongrel with a schnauzer muzzle and pointed ears. He looked slightly bewildered, but unhurt.

"He's not hurt," Never said with relief.

"No collar, probably a stray," Gerard added sympathetically, feeling the mongrel to see if his bones really were in one piece.

He always felt sorry for stray dogs, especially that not all of them could be helped.

"Listen, doesn't the sun burn you?" It was only now that Never realized that his friend was kneeling in the full sun without any consequences. Gerard frowned in surprise, but they didn't have time to think about it, because Hope joined them.

"Poor doggy!" She called out. "All alone in the middle of nowhere. Let's take him with us."

"What will your mom say to that?" the Hindu asked doubtfully.

The girl knelt and embraced the dog's neck.

"She won't say anything," she muttered. "I'm supposed to die after all."

The men exchanged helpless glances behind her.

"Right. This is an argument," Gerard murmured uncertainly.

As if he understood what they were talking about, the dog waved his tail and jumped into the car, straight into the back seat next to Fronda, confused by his sight. Hope slipped behind him, delighted with such company.

"I'll call him Tommy," she said, hugging the dog's shag trustingly.

"That's strange," Gerard grunted, taking his seat next to the driver.

He felt an unpleasant pulsation on the skin, but it was the only effect of being in direct sunlight.

"You must be a marten like me. We didn't check it before, because your predecessors were without exception moths, so I took it for granted that you will be like this, too," Never said quietly, lowering his voice to the frequency not heard by the ordinary people's ears. "Congratulations, this will broaden your freedom of movement."

"Never mind. Let's go. Let's deliver this girl as soon as possible, before she tells us to take an unhappy elephant from some menagerie," Gerard answered equally quietly.

He had some doubts about surprises like this, but he didn't want to argue with Hope. Let her take this dog if she wants it so much, and let her mother worry about what to do next. Either way, she will have the final say here, not them.

For now, the dog was not causing any problems. He sat in the back seat, calm and content, letting Fronda scratch his ears, and occasionally licking Hope's hands. Initially, Gerard wanted to point out that this may cause an infection of the weakened child's body, but upon reflection he decided not to interfere. According to what Vandis said, it didn't matter anyway. Let the child enjoy the presence of the gentle animal while she can.

Soon the travelers saw the town they were heading to, illuminated by the last rays of the setting sun. Bluewaters lay in an artificially created valley, with a dam and a huge factory built next to it on one side, and forests spreading all the way to the horizon on the other. The only access road to it led along a steep slope, artificially leveled on top and asphalted. A little lake gleamed below, probably also artificially created, but somehow fitting the area well.

The town itself was perhaps not that large, but it was laid out widely and thus gave the impression of a certain architectural impetus, as if it was once the intention of the builders to build it larger or to expand it later. Jeannie Meadows' cottage lay a bit out of the way, in a nice garden full of peonies, and Mrs. Meadows waited outside the gate, looking out for her Opel.

Her appearance surprised the friends. A small, plump middle-aged woman, dressed in a pink costume, she had very curly hair, dark skin and clearly negroid features, while Hope was undoubtedly white. At first they even thought that they had the wrong address, but their doubts were dispelled by Hope herself, who jumped out of the car with a joyful shout: "Mom!" and threw her arms around Mrs. Meadows.

The woman gave her a hug, then approached the slightly confused friends and held out her hand to them.

"Call me Jeannie," she said. "Mr. Winger spoke to me about you on the phone, and told me that you would stay in Bluewaters for the time being, to watch over Hope. I am very obliged to you."

The men shook her hand in turn, and Theo additionally put a kiss on it, which confused Mrs. Meadows a little, but flattered her even more.

"Come in, please," she said. "I'll serve dinner soon."

Never grunted in embarrassment.

"Forgive us, Jeannie, but we belong to the Ideological Church," he said apologetically. "Our religion prohibits us from performing any physiological activities, including eating, with others. It also prohibits us from military service and working in certain professions. I hope that it will not bother you."

"No, why? My husband's parents were Amish, so religious matters are not a reason for embarrassment to me," Mrs. Meadows comforted him. "Whose dog is this?"

"We found him along the way, mom," Hope said quickly. "He has no home. Can I keep him? Please say I can..."

Jeannie sighed.

"We'll see, dear," she said evasively. "Eat dinner and go to bed now, it's late. Don't worry, this little guy will also get food, and let him sleep in the shed for now. It is very warm, he won't be cold. Please, come to the living room, I will join you soon."

Friends entered the house and the three of them sat on the sofa in front of the television turned on. On the screen, the president Reagan was just finishing his speech and the advertisement of the sports program was beginning to flash.

"Nice idea with that sect," Gerard praised his friend.

"Sure, but what are we going to eat here?" asked Theo doubtfully.

"Don't bother your pretty head with it," said the Indian ironically. "Who, if not me, always thinks about everything? We have a stock of cans in the Opel's trunk. I will bring it inside when Mrs. Meadows falls asleep. It's enough for three weeks if we are frugal. We have to be careful not to expose ourselves, so no hunting, understood?"

"By all means, but now shut up, because this match is going to be interesting," Theo watched the struggle of two powerfully built boxers with interest, and soon everything else ceased to exist for him.

Gerard, who was not interested in boxing, took a binding with yearly issues of some magazine from the shelf and started looking through it. All of them liked very much this living room, decorated a bit in the wild West style, and to the extent that they could not help feeling home... although they actually had nothing they could honestly call home. It was the aspect of being a vampire that they liked the least, but there was no other way. Over-settled down vampires always finished the same way - with a stake embedded in their heart. Even those who stayed in one area, changed their address as often as possible.

"I could live in a house like that for as long as a hundred years," Never murmured, looking appreciatively around the living room, modestly furnished, with this awfully expensive simplicity that shows good taste and wealth at the same time. Arranged mostly in wood, it had a woven mat of the same color as the rest of the interior on the floor instead of a carpet, the pictures hanging on the walls were in fact wooden carvings, even the TV was enclosed similarly.

"It's really nice here, indeed, but I'm afraid that it doesn't meet the fire safety requirements," Fronda said skeptically, without taking his eyes off the screen.

"Probably impregnated, don't pick on it like that, brave fireman," Never said, making an allusion to his friend's old adventure, when he was the head of the volunteer fire department in Lisle for three months. As one of the few vampires, he was not afraid of the fire, the fear that vampires have in their blood and which often grows to absurd dimensions, and none of them, even the bravest, will walk over the flames for anything in the world. Theo, as was said, was an exception, and not only in this respect.

"Hope is already asleep," said Mrs. Meadows, entering the living room. "She was very tired."

She sat down on the couch next to Fronda. Now that she could let her face rest, it could be seen that she was older than she appeared at first, and very tired of fighting her fate.

"It must be not easy for you, Jeannie," Gerard said, looking at her sympathetically.

He knew from the example of his wife, how exhausting it is to look after someone who is terminally ill, and to put on a brave face at the same time.

Mrs. Meadows looked at him without even trying to smile.

"I'm holding up somehow, because I have no other choice," she said. "My mother urges me to move in with her, in Illinois, but it's a little easier for me here than there, where there are as many people as in the state capital. Hope also loves this place, although she is the only child here... or maybe that's why, I don't know. She's a strange girl."

She folded her dark hands with pink fingernails on her lap and sighed deeply.

"When my husband died, it seemed to me that nothing worse could happen to me," she continued after a moment. "I was at the bottom of despair. And then, when Hope's illness came to light, I was surprised that I could have broken down so badly. I realized that I was crying not for Henry then, but for myself, that I was feeling sorry for myself, forgetting Hope. I am glad that you will stay to help me, because if I had to quit my job, I would end up drowning in a lake under the dam."

"We will stay as long as it takes," Theo promised her, embracing her with compassionate look of his black eyes.

Jeannie sighed miserably.

"It won't take long," she whispered sadly.

"You never know," said Never, who contemplated one of the carved pictures by the wall. "I studied medicine, and although certain circumstances prevented me from obtaining my diploma, I know enough to assure you, that the life in itself is an unsolved mystery. You never know who will die and who will live."

"That's nice of you, but unfortunately, my daughter has no chance. Even a bone marrow transplant didn't help her. I would give my life if it could turn out otherwise," said Mrs. Meadows, but the tone of her voice became a little brighter, as if against all the rational arguments, the Indian's words poured some comfort into her heart. The three men, described to her by Vandis as trusted friends, aroused her sympathy and made the impression as if she had known them for a long time, even though they seemed a bit strange.

"I will put you in the attic," she said. "We used to have a guest room there, but no one has been sleeping there for years, so the mattresses are rolled up."

"We'll lay them out ourselves. We are not very attached to comfort, so we might as well sleep right on the floor," said Gerard warmly. "Please, don't bother with us, Jeannie. Members of our Church try not to bother anybody, they programmatically reject any sybaritism and imposing wills on someone."

"A non-warring Church. That's nice," Jeannie smiled.

She liked her guests more and more. After taking them to the attic, she looked for a moment to the child's room, where Hope slept peacefully, breathing steadily in her sleep, and then went to bed herself.

Never waited until his psycholocation sense told him that their host was already asleep, and then moved the thermo-insulated bags of tinned blood, loaded into the trunk by Winger, to the attic. The dry ice inside the bags kept the right temperature, but the fact that the attic was additionally equipped with a large fridge, turned out to be rather favorable. Thanks to this, their food supply was secured, which was of great importance in this sparsely populated area.

"No hunting in the city," he said, opening one of the bottles. "Possibly somewhere out of town, but let's stick with the cans for as long as possible."

Others agreed with him without words.

*****

Hope was playing in the garden, throwing sticks at a mongrel who jumped around her with his tongue out and squealed happily.

"I see you get along well with this animal," Never said to the girl, stepping out onto the porch.

"This dog is so friendly, that it seems strange that someone just got rid of him like that," said Gerard, swinging on the porch railing, where he was sitting under the cover of the dangling elm branches, reading the newspaper.

"Where's your pretty friend?" Hope asked, stopping.

Despite a relatively small effort, she was panting heavily, and her face, pale as paper, was covered with sweat.

"Theo suffers from ophthalmopathy," Hindus answered her scientifically, rubbing the head of a dog who run happily to him. "His eyes can't stand the sunlight, it's a disease. He goes out only after dusk, or before dawn, unless the sky is fully covered by clouds. Why, you don't like us?"

"Why not, you are not that bad after all," Hope said defiantly.

Tommy's company seemed to be really good for her, she was even smiling, although that smile made unpleasant impression on her emaciated face. Perhaps as a result of illness or the chemotherapy, she developed some psychic abilities, and therefore she could not bear the presence of Vandis, whose pain because of her condition she was empathetic to. Gerard suffered from cancer himself, so he felt understanding rather than pity, and Never as a rule did not feel sorry for anyone.

Only Theo could be a problem, but his mind and psyche were a time compilation that was not available even to a telepath, so he couldn't make a bad impression on Hope. Someone in whom the fourteenth and twentieth centuries fused into unity, had to be a mystery to every possible psychoanalyst.

Hope threw another stick for the dog.

"Bring it, Tommy!" she called, and the mongrel dutifully leaped to carry out this order.

"How are you doing?" Never asked Gerard quietly.

The actor smiled, looking up from his newspaper.

"Not bad," he replied. "Nice to be able to enjoy the day again. Poor Fronda, he is now alone in his photophobia."

"He'll survive it somehow. Fortunately, with all his flaws, Fronda is quite unselfish," Never, as usual, was not going to be tormented by anyone's feelings.

Theo, however, really did not envy them both the daytime walks. It was quite pleasant in the attic, where he spent the days - he could sleep, read or listen to the radio, and even watch TV, because there was a small TV set there. Most of the time, however, he slept, gathering strength for the night activity, and it was a great way to not get bored. At night he went out and spent a nice evening with friends, and when Mrs. Meadows and her daughter were already asleep, he roamed around.

During these trips he hunted a little by the dam, which, as it turned out, was a popular camping site for various hikers who liked to relax close to the nature. The proximity of the factory somehow did not bother them, and none of them was aware of the presence of the vampire prowling between them, though many of them for some reason had a headache the next morning.

Never and Gerard, who looked after Hope and kept her mother company, preferred to sleep at night, so he wandered alone. Also that evening, his friends were too weary to accept the invitation for a walk. Theo didn't blame them. He knew that caring for a sick child could be exhausting. In addition, Never made a point to relieve Jeannie Meadows of household chores, so they really could feel tired. As soon as they fell asleep, he left the house.

The evening was really beautiful, warm and fairly bright, so he walked slowly, his hands in his pockets, enjoying the stroll and not paying much attention to anything.

"You're wandering again, son. You are a night owl," these words came so unexpectedly that he instinctively and rather senselessly jumped aside.

It took him a moment to realize that they had been spoken by a rather harmless looking old man, sitting in a deserted garden surrounding a wooden shanty.

"Are you watching me?" he asked.

The old man took a sip from the flat bottle he was holding.

"Call me Buggles, son," he said. "I don't follow you, I just see Jeannie Meadows's house perfectly from my garden, and since I have nothing to do anymore, I like to watch things. Every night I see you going out on a tramp. I don't need much sleep at my age, but you, such a young man? Care for a drink?"

"Thank you, Mr. Buggles, I don't drink. As for the second matter, I sleep, but during the daytime," Theo had already recovered and decided not to worry. "I suffer from a type of photophobia, an allergy to sunlight."

"It happens," it was clearly difficult to surprise the elderly gentleman. "I see you stay with Jeannie Meadows. Poor woman, she is unlucky in life, though she is so pretty."

Fronda climbed over the jagged fence and sat down next to the old man.

"Do you know her well, Mr. Buggles?" he asked.

The man nodded.

"Since childhood," he replied. "When Henry Meadows came here looking for sensations, Jeannie Delamico was nineteen years old, and a year later they were married. People were saying that she was too young to be a second mother for the little girl, but I thought it would go well. Jeannie has always loved children, and besides, she has a heart of gold. People, of course, were just jealous and dissatisfied that a white journalist marries a Mulatto girl from a small town, the illegitimate daughter of the sheriff and a waitress."

"So Hope is Mrs. Meadows's stepdaughter?" Theo summed up the matter.

"Well, that's how it looks, but don't be fooled. She is a wonderful mother," said the elderly gentleman emphatically. "When Hope got sick, Jeannie had borrowed heavily so she could finance her treatment. The only thing she did not get rid of is the car, because it is actually not hers but her mother's, and the house, because she rents it. But she sold her own apartment, and all the jewelry Henry bought her, and she has more debt than hair on her head. She really loves this little girl."

He took another sip.

"What kind of sensation was Henry Meadows actually looking for in a town like this?" asked Theo after a while.

"Henry was of the same opinion as most metropolitan wise men like him," said Mr. Buggles. "That small towns always hide a secret. He kept asking me questions about what might have happened here, especially since he learned that I had been a sheriff here for thirty years. But apart from one lynch, nothing particularly interesting has ever happened here."

"You had a lynch here?" Fronda asked.

He often went to the movies to watch westerns, and he was very interested in everything that had anything in common with the Wild West.

Mr. Buggles nodded slowly and took a sip.

"Yes, we did," he admitted reluctantly. "Long time ago. I was the sheriff's assistant then. A murder was committed in the city, a young girl was killed. The town's general opinion was that Daryl Sharpclaw, a Metis who lives right outside the town, committed the crime. We arrested him, but the agitated residents did not want to wait for the judge, they broke into the office of the sheriff, Roy Delamico... the one who later became Jeannie's father... and demanded to release the prisoner to them. Maybe if we stood up to them...? Well, but after all, there were only two of us, so maybe Roy was right that he forbade me to interfere in this matter. Either way, six months later it came to light that the actual perpetrator of the crime was someone else, but the lynch leaders were never punished. The state police simply did not find anyone to testify against them. You understand, son, everyone felt more or less guilty, so there was no point to stand out, right? And that's all. Nothing else has ever happened here."

He sipped again.

"This story did not seem interesting to Meadows," he continued after a moment, his voice almost low to a whisper. "But I admit to you, young man, that it poisons my peace to this day, it's rooted in me like every meanness a man does, and can't be drowned out with even a good whiskey."

"You couldn't do much against the whole city," Theo said comfortingly.

The old man shrugged.

"Maybe I could have done little... but more importantly, I didn't even try. You see, at your age you don't understand such things yet, but in my years you already know that it is better to die for what is right than to agree to the wickedness committed in your presence. Lack of self-respect is a real misfortune, it's not worth living with. It is fine if people hate you, if they despise you, but you know you're okay and you have nothing to blame yourself for. But if you despise yourself, and while looking in the mirror every day you see a bastard there..."

Theo got up and put a hand on his shoulder.

"I think you really are a respectable man," he said. "Precisely because these are your feelings. We all have something in our biography that we are ashamed of, but what matters is whether we can draw the right conclusions from it. I think you have done that, sheriff."

Buggles looked at him with a weak smile.

"You're a good boy, son," he said.

The sky above them flashed and a thunder could be heard.

"A dry storm," Buggles explained flatly, seeing Theo startle. "Tomorrow or the day after tomorrow we will have a downpour. At this time of year it's almost the rule."

The sky flashed again.

Fronda decided to return home, because vampires are known for disliking thunderstorms, dry or not, due to the risk of being struck by lightning that is many times greater than in humans. This is the result of a much stronger bioelectrical activity of the vampire's body and its ability to ionize air. He preferred not to risk it. He decided, however, that he would visit Mr. Buggles again. He liked the old drunk somehow, or rather... the man seemed interesting to him.

"You came back early today," Gerard muttered from his mattress.

"There is no one to play with," Theo answered him, then settled himself on his bed and immediately fell asleep with his arm bent under his head.

Unlike him, Gerard couldn't sleep. Thunders outside the window scared the sleep off his eyes, and to make matters worse, the sound of the storm was accompanied by a dog's bleak howling.

Concerned, he got up and walked to the window. It was quite dark outside, but in the short flashes of lightnings, he could easily see the black silhouette of the dog that sat in the middle of the garden and howled with his mouth turned toward the sky. The thought flashed through the actor's head that maybe it would be good to go down and let the animal into the house, and he was about to do it, when the dog, as if he was sensing his thoughts, turned his head and looked towards the attic window.

Gerard felt the blood freeze in his veins, and his neck hair bristle as if alive. Even from this distance he could clearly see that the animal's eyes were burning with a strong red glow, like two carbuncles lit from below, and their expression was full of focused, inhuman, infernally malicious intelligence. He wanted to scream, but he couldn't make a voice out of his tight throat. He couldn't even move, he just looked, gripped by a terrible terror, until the dog looked away indifferently and began to howl again. Then he slumped to the floor, as if he had been freed of the force holding him, and lost consciousness.

That's how his friends found him when they woke up in the morning. After an hour of attempts on their part, the actor finally opened his eyes and looked at them in surprise.

"Did something happen?" he asked, trying to get up.

"What do you mean, did something happen?!" Never burst out angrily, pale as death. "You tell us! We found you unconscious on the floor! You weren't breathing! What the hell happened here?!"

Gerard frowned and shook his head helplessly.

"I don't remember anything," he confessed. "There was a storm... Did I come to the window? I don't know, forgive me. Oh, my head..."

He gripped his temples. He really couldn't remember anything, and it bothered him, because he had the impression that what missed from his memory, was something very important. Unfortunately, everything that roamed around his aching head was a mixture of remembered sounds from which he couldn't pick out anything specific. He did not understand where the sense of danger came from, which appeared unexpectedly and did not leave him.

"You guys didn't hear anything?" he asked with weak hope.

"We were sleeping, you idiot! What were we supposed to hear? You were sleepwalking at night, not us. Sit down, I will examine you," Never took out a stethoscope from his bag and began to listen to his friend's chest.

"Nothing suspicious," he said finally, relieved. "If you remember something, tell us immediately. One doesn't faint for no reason, something must have happened here."

"There was a dry storm yesterday. Maybe it was a lightning?" Fronda asked, looking out the window, where gray clouds were swirling.

"A lightning? Not a chance. There are no characteristic marks. And it would look much worse. It is not a lightning, and whatever it was, there is no trace of it now," said the Indian with some disappointment.

Gerard lowered his shirt.

"I told you I am fine," he muttered.

It wasn't quite true - he felt terrible, though in his mind rather than physically. He was upset and tormented by an indefinite fear, which he could not cope with, especially since he could not locate its source.

"Vandis would probably help you," Never said thoughtfully. "I wonder who he really is?"

"Maybe a mutant?" Fronda asked quite seriously. "There is a whole pile of comic books about people referred to as X Men and..."

"Theo, I'm begging you, don't talk nonsense like this, because I want to puke even without that," Gerard interrupted him with disgust and lay down on his mattress.

Just in case, he lay in bed until the afternoon to get a good rest. Even then, he felt somehow ill. When he finally decided to go downstairs, he discovered that he could hardly walk down the stairs, he was so afraid of them. That was truly alarming. He had never been afraid of heights before, and even if he had, it was unusual to feel dizzy at the top of the stairs. He went downstairs carefully, leaning heavily on the carved handrail, finding that at the same time with an outstanding deterioration of his well-being, his ability to see through the senses sharpened. He saw much more clearly than usual, as if someone had colored the whole world anew just for him.

Maybe that's why, looking at Hope playing with the dog, he suddenly noticed that the girl looks much better than she should. She was lively, too active for a child sentenced to death, he saw it clearly and was amazed at the sudden improvement. He did not know much about cancer, even though he suffered from one himself, but he felt that there was something strange, something unnatural about it.

"Are you feeling well now?" Hope asked, eyeing him in her usual way.

"Not bad," Gerard said cautiously. "And you?"

He sat at a table with newspapers, resting his head against the wall.

"Fine," said the girl briefly.

The dog lay down on its back and waved its paws in the air, demanding caresses. The Frenchman looked at him, frowning slightly, but despite his efforts, he could not recall the events of the last night, nor see anything unusual in this animal, anything that might have caused this strange anxiety in him.

"Hasn't he bitten you yet?" he asked just to say something.

"What an idea," Hope also lay down on the carpet, and embraced the dog's neck.

"What is..." Gerard did not finish, because Never came into the living room.

"You're up, that's good," he said. "Stay with Hope, me and Fronda are going to the city. Something strange is happening here, we want to look into it."

"Something strange always happens wherever they send us," Gerard muttered grimly.

"This time it is serious. I'll explain later. Keep an eye on the girl until we get back," the Hindu said harshly and disappeared behind the door.

"What does it mean that something is always happening wherever they send you?" asked the girl, looking at Gerard curiously.

He scratched his ear thoughtfully.

"This is our fate," he replied. "That's how we earn a living, child, revealing someone else's dark secrets. Here, however, we were just going to rest."

Hope chuckled.

"Mr. Winger has warned me you are pretty weird and I see he was right," she said. "You are like UFO hunters, or those who are looking for chupacabra. You have a similar look in your eyes, all three of you."

"Like what?" the actor did not understand.

"I mean, like haunted," she explained to him.

"There's something to it," he agreed with her. "We're not looking for a UFO or that other one, but we like things that are difficult to explain. And since they are paying us for that, why not take advantage of it?"

"Just like Mr. Winger. He also gets into various puzzles and they pay him for it," the girl got up from the carpet and moved to the couch.

"Not exactly. Vandis solves criminal matters, and we rarely do something that should be the responsibility of the police. Let everyone do their own thing. There's nothing on TV? You could watch something," he suggested to her, feeling that the conversation was going in a dangerous direction. It seemed anyway that Hope was guessing something, but didn't feel like talking about it.

"Not at this hour. Besides, I don't really like television, I prefer cinema, but there have never been any in Bluewaters. When I was in the hospice, sometimes the cinema would come to us, then we would play Star Wars. Everyone wanted to be Princess Leia, but I preferred to play Emperor. He is such a cool, bad character. Lord Vader is also quite good, he just unnecessarily leaves the Dark Side of Power path at the end. It spoils everything."

Gerard had never seen "Star Wars," but he still understood what the girl meant and it surprised him a little. He had never encountered putting things this way before, although from the point of view of his acting experience, he had to admit that dark characters tend to be much more colorful than positive heroes, usually pitifully one-sided. That is why he played the role of Caligula in the theater, the role of drunk doctor in "Reborn" and the role of the cynical seducer Valmont in "Dangerous Liaisons," although all directors saw him rather in positive roles.

Actually, his last two film roles, Oktave Mouret in "Pot Buille" and Ramon Vasquez in "El Pao Fever", were very ambiguous, especially the latter, full of contradictions, the role of a weak man, torn between inner sense of justice, and the possibility of making a career and getting a beloved woman. What would be the next ones?

"Ah, what a pity I'll never stand in front of the camera again!" he exclaimed involuntarily with grief in his voice, thankfully in French.

Hope studied him with maliciously narrowed eyes, as if she understood everything.

"Han Solo is cool," she said after a moment. "He seems to be changing, but it is so only on the surface, one can feel that if necessary, he will throw off the too smooth mask. And Chewie is nice too, a shaggy bear. But Luke is a hopeless jerk and that's it."

"You're probably right, though I have no idea what you're talking about. A negative hero is often more colorful, but one shouldn't be guided by that. Maybe screenwriters these days can no longer create someone who would be good but not boring," said Gerard.

Fronda came to his mind, undeniably positive, yet full of hidden dark secrets, at the same time good and cruel, knightly and romantic, equally inclined to sacrifice for others as to murder in the name of a just cause. The series treated his character with amazing one-sidedness, although he had to admit that the authors managed to avoid infecting their creation with boring moralism.

"Yes. It's not easy to make movies now. You almost must be a wizard for the children not to laugh at the finished work," she said melancholically after a moment of silence.

"That's exaggeration. They just need to think before they start filming," Hope said calmly.

"I will have to watch these Star Wars at the earliest opportunity," the actor sighed, concluding sadly that he had a lot to catch up on.

The dog yawned and jumped out through the low window into the garden.

"Strange. Dogs are generally afraid of the storm, and there are thunders again," Gerard turned on the television.

"Oh, Star Trek!" Hope cried out happily.

The Frenchman sat next to her and watched, but he understood almost nothing from the on-screen action.

Science fiction was never his favorite form of literature or film, and this episode, taken out of context, seemed an incredible silliness to him. He looked with resignation - not wanting to hurt Hope, who was clearly fascinated by this nonsense, and after a while he realized how much it had to cost Fronda to adapt to the changeability of the eras, which after all also required him to go to watch such movies and to concerts of music that was completely incomprehensible to him. After all, for him, the actor from the fifties, this series was almost modern, considering the time distance that separated Fronda from the concert of Elvis Presley or The Who group.

How many such adaptations he had to have experienced before he learned to absorb the right knowledge on a regular basis and to adapt smoothly, without shocks? How did he manage to change like this and still remain himself, the same medieval knight he was when his tissues were fixed by the factor conditioning the transformation? It was almost incomprehensible for Gerard, when he looked at this film, alien to him in both content and form of implementation, although it was made only twenty years after his departure from the world of humans.

Maybe if it wasn't for the insanity that he succumbed to, which caused him to jump over the entire era in time, he could more easily understand what was currently appealing to young minds. During these two decades, when he was wandering in a state of mental eclipse, the world moved forward, but then Fronda was hiding in the forest among the wolves, probably sixty years after his perpetuation, and yet he managed to readapt to human life. What did he feel, when he left the woods to see that everything he was used to, had changed, and the people he knew no longer existed?

What did he think, when the boy he remembered from the village as a callow youngster, stood before him as a decrepit old man and looked at him with dull eyes, while his toothless mouth mumbled: "Sir, you look just like..."

Gerard understood what he felt: boundless loneliness, incomparable to anything. He had to shape his life without anyone's help, because he couldn't even find the Black Lady anymore, who would have helped him. Where did he get his strength from?

"Star Trek" ended, and immediately after the commercial break, the words "Robin Hood, the hooded man" and a handsome dark-haired boy with a bow slung over his shoulder appeared on the screen.

"Michael Praed is great," Hope said appreciatively. "This is the best Robin Hood I've ever seen."

Gerard smiled at her in response. At least that was understandable to him, though the convention was somewhat different from what he was used to. He got so absorbed in the movie, that he didn't even notice that the murmur of the storm grew stronger, and the air became dry, unbearably hot and stuffy. Staring at the screen, he did not even notice when the bright, though cloudy day darkened menacingly, it was only a loud crack, sounding like a shot, that snapped him out of the concentration on the movie.

Hope screamed. The house's doors and shutters closed as if at the behest of some invisible force, and at the same time a storm broke out with a wild force, seemingly endowed with its own personality. Gerard rushed toward the door, but unexpectedly neither the door nor the shutters moved, as if they were closed from the outside with huge bolts.

"What's happening?" Hope exclaimed fearfully.

"I don't know! Maybe it's an earthquake! We have to get out of here!" he replied to her, shouting over the sounds of the element raging outside. "If you know where your mother keeps documents and important stuff, bring it quickly!"

He did not know why he gave the child such an order - he suddenly became certain that there would not be a stone upon another left in this place, and that it was necessary to save whatever they could.

He struggled with the door until unexpectedly someone came to his aid, hitting the lock from the other side with an ax, and banging stubbornly until the door opened. Retired Sheriff Buggles stood on the threshold, wet from head to toe.

"The dam is breaking!" He shouted. "Take the car and get out of here, I am running to warn others!"

Gerard grabbed the keys from the hook on the wall and pulled the girl, who had just returned from her mother's room, clutching a black box and a plastic briefcase, outside in the rain.

Never and Fronda came running from the other side.

"To the post office for Jeannie!" the Hindu shouted commandingly to Gerard, struggling with the roof of the Opel, which jammed as if out of spite, and could not be moved. The rain streams, pouring from the sky, did not make the task easier.

"Hell with the roof, we're going like this!" cried Theo, leaping inside and cringing as another lightning tore the sky apart.

"Where's Tommy?!" Hope shouted desperately.

Nobody answered her. Never managed to start the car and, despite the torrential downpour, drive it out onto the road.

"Where's Tommy?!" repeated the girl, trying to jump out.

Theo held her tight.

"There is no time for that!" he shouted in her ear.

Hope struggled in his strong hands, but the storm drowned out her scream. Arriving at the post office, Never jumped out of the car and returned a moment later, pulling Jeannie Meadows by the hand. The crying woman caught her daughter in her arms. The Indian hurriedly led Opel to the street, aiming for the high road above the lake - the highest point of the area, where they could take refuge.

"What happened?" Jeannie shouted, barely holding Hope, who tried to break free.

"The dam is breaking!" Gerard yelled back to her. "If it collapses, the water will flood the whole valley! We have to get out of here!"

"We have to find Tommy!" Hope screamed desperately.

"There is no time for that! Sometimes people are more important than dogs," Rajah said with conviction, putting all his skills into controlling the car.

Opel was staggering like a drunk on the road that resembled a rushing stream, and the water flooding its interior did not make the things better, either. Never, excellent driver, did not know himself how he finally managed to force the car to climb the slope to this only relatively safe place - the hill under which the lake stretched. The dam visible from a distance, trembled as if it were alive under the crushing waves, and each time the lightning ripped the sky, dark blue from the clouds, they could clearly see the wide cracks through which the rising water was getting through.

"Oh Jesus, Sodom and Gomorrah," Theo whispered, crossing himself automatically.

"I'm going back!" Hope shouted defiantly and, taking advantage of her mother's momentary inattention, broke free from her embrace.

Fronda, who was nearest, despite being fast, did not manage to catch her when she rolled across the frame of the car straight to the lake under the rocks. Jeannie's scream merged into one with another thunderbolt, and at the same time something unbelievable happened: the sliding roof started automatically and the black dome slammed shut over them.

Jeannie hit her hands against the window desperately. Theo, pale like a death, struggled

with the door, but the lock jammed for some reason, as the roof before, and did not give way.

"This is crazy!" howled Gerard, covering his head with his crossed arms.

A storm was raging around them, and the roar of the water bursting from the broken dam invaded the car, not letting them hear their own words. It was a terrible, supernatural experience, in which even their subjective time stood still, because they were not able to figure out how long they were crouched in the car, which was hit by gusts of furious wind, carrying a veil of water.

Jeannie sobbed unstoppably, squeezing the arm of Fronda, who was still struggling to break through the door or push out the window, which was also unexpectedly resistant to his muscular arms. Finally he gave up, embraced the crying woman and froze, giving up all attempts for action. Both his friends had already done it much earlier. They never felt as human as they were now - locked in a storm-torn car, helpless against both the raging element and the forces that unleashed it.

Suddenly Gerard looked up.

"This dog!" He shouted in a changed voice. "I remember now! His eyes... This scoundrel can be anything, but not a dog, you understand me?! He was looking at me last night and I couldn't even move! How could I forget about it?!"

Never grabbed his shoulders and shook him violently.

"What are you talking about?!" he called out.

Gerard fell silent, unable to formulate the thoughts that were swarming in his head. Vandis was enough of a mystery for him, the ghostly animal was already beyond his comprehension, and fear overwhelmed him, probably related to the one felt by Fronda in Stonehenge.

"It doesn't exist!" He shouted hysterically. "There are no ghosts or demons, understand?! There simply is none! The world is knowable! Life is a form of biochemical processes and came out of the ocean, there is no God, there is no underworld or a soul, there is only matter! You understand?! Protein!

Molecules! What I can touch, exists! And if I see something that is not logical, I have hallucinations and I should get help!"

He fell silent because the Hindu gave him such a strong slap on the cheek, that he hit his head against the window, unprepared for this kind of reaction.

"Sorry, kid, it was necessary," Never said coldly. "You start losing it, and this can lead you astray. Control your emotions a bit."

His calm voice worked like a bucket of cold water, even more than the shock of being hit. Gerard fell silent and resigned, curled up in his place.

The storm outside calmed down, and after a moment only the last late raindrops hit the roof. Never pressed the door handle without much faith, and to his surprise, the Opel door opened obediently. The friends got out of the car, still half-stunned by what they experienced, and looked around.

There was no trace of the town in the valley. In the place where Bluewaters was located that morning, now a huge lake rippled, almost black in the still ghostly lighting of the stormy sky.

"Look," Gerard said through his choked throat, pointing with a shaking finger to the rocky shore of the lake below.

The well-known black shape was crawling out of the water. With visible difficulty, the huge mongrel pulled ashore a figure in torn and soaked overalls, as inert as a rag doll.

"Hope..." Jeannie moaned, cuddling up to Fronda, who was embracing her.

The dog released the child's clothes and, bending its mouth over the girl, began to lick her face. Hope shifted and reached with her hand to her head. The animal turned its head and looked at the four people looking at him in silent terror, his eyes glowing red for a moment. Frozen by terrifying fear, the people could have sworn they could hear him laughing with a low, slow laughter. Then the animal got up and ran off in a slow trot towards the nearby forest. They never saw him again.

*****

Theo was returning from a social welfare office in the suburbs of Chicago. He already knew that almost none of the town's inhabitants survived. The breaking of the dam, combined with a violent storm and a hurricane, took everyone by surprise. Oddly enough, the house rented by Jeannie Meadows was saved, the water did not reach it. The rest, along with the people, was gone.

Rescuers sent to the disaster site managed to find the retired sheriff, who hid on the high bank, along with several people. Nobody except them survived. Everyone already found shelter with family or friends. Mr. Buggles was placed in a state shelter as he had neither living relatives nor any personal property. What was in Bluewaters, was completely destroyed, so he couldn't go back there. He also needed care, because what happened had greatly weakened his strength.

"I could actually visit him," thought Theo. "It is cloudy, and it is already six o'clock, so the sun will likely not come out anymore. I will probably make it there before dinner."

He didn't usually think too long when he came up with an idea, no matter how silly, so he didn't think long about it, either. He just stopped a passing taxi and told the driver to take him to the shelter.

Subconsciously, he was expecting a shanty, the way similar places looked like in his time, but it turned out to be, to his relief, a rather nice place, although the building was indeed old and not very well maintained. There were deckchairs and small tables in the garden, ivy wrapped around the building, and curtains hung in the windows. The elderly nurse he met in the hall showed him Mr. Buggles' room, but she asked him not to stay there too long. There were certain rules that had to be followed here.

He went to the indicated room, where the retired sheriff sat by the window and looked indifferently at the garden, chewing on an unlit cigar. His roommate, who looked to be about eighty to one hundred and twenty years old, was dozing on the bed. At the sound of the footsteps, Mr. Buggles turned away from the window and his wrinkled face lit up with a faint smile.

"Is it you, boy? I'm glad you made it too," he said.

"And I am glad that you also came out of it alive and well," Theo answered him cordially. "Unfortunately, not everyone was so lucky. Almost nobody."

The old sheriff nodded.

"I know. And Jeannie and Hope, were they with you? Is everything okay with the girl?" he asked.

"Oh yes," the Frenchman looked out the window, then turned and leaned back on the window sill. "An astonishing case, Sheriff, but... yes."

He fell silent, not knowing how to explain it. When they brought Hope to the hospital, the doctors ordered all the tests, which was understandable given her illness. The results exceeded all expectations. Out of blue, there was a significant and incomprehensible improvement, as if the girl's bone marrow suddenly began to work normally, as in any healthy child. The doctors could not stop wondering and finally decided that it was a belated, positive reaction to the bone marrow transplant.

"Oh, that's wonderful news. Jeannie is probably madly happy," Mr. Buggles sighed slightly, probably regretting that he cannot now visit the daughter of his former superior.

His desperate attempts to help the residents of Bluewaters resulted in the fact that he managed to save several of them, and that was a positive thing. However, he suffered a severe back injury when a flood wave hit him, and he could hardly walk.

"Yes. She now lives with her mother and will start working at the Post Office on Fourth Avenue next week," said Theo. "A sudden improvement in the health of the little girl brought back her will to live, she is a completely different woman now. Hope just despairs for the dog..."

The sheriff looked at him strangely, and Fronda suddenly felt an unpleasant shiver creeping along his spine.

"What dog are you talking about?" asked the old man.

"Well, the dog. The mongrel who came to live with us. Hope often played with him in the garden, you must have seen him," Theo said uncertainly.

Mr. Buggles was still looking at him with the same strange look.

"You didn't have any dogs," he said finally. "I looked at Hope as she played, always alone. I felt sorry that such a nice child has no one to play with..."

Now it was Fronda who was looking at him with round eyes, trying to understand something of what he had just heard, and suddenly he paled so terribly that the sheriff was afraid that his guest would faint. Vampires pale differently from humans, they get chalky white in a second, with gray circles around their eyes, and they look terrifying then.

"Is something wrong, son? Don't take it so seriously, children often come up with imaginary stuff..." the sheriff grabbed his hand. "Take a deep breath."

Theo controlled himself with an effort of will.

"Temporary indisposition," he said soundlessly. "I'll be fine soon, I just need to rest for a moment. Please forgive me."

He sat up, trying to breathe calmly and think coldly, to get rid of the choking agitation. After all, the old drunkard did not deserve to be believed unconditionally, he could have been seeing things that did not happen, or could not see what was obvious, but deep down Fronda felt the same fear that struck him in Stonehenge - fear in the face of the unknown. He was the true child of his time, and he faithfully believed in ghosts, demons and devils, and above all, in the punishment, inflicted by supernatural powers on those who deserved it. Even if he claimed that he had already gotten rid of such superstitions, this was not true.

A nurse looked into the room.

"I'm sorry but you have to leave now," she said. "These are the rules. You can come back tomorrow."

"Yes, thank you, nurse. I'm leaving now," Theo said weakly.

He shook the sheriff's hand and followed the woman into the corridor.

"Has he suffered badly in the flood?" he asked carefully.

"Not really," the nurse answered. "Lumbar spine injury and general exhaustion, that's basically all. Is he your relative?"

"A friend," he murmured briefly.

He still couldn't forget the image that had crystallized in his mind under the influence of Mr. Buggles's words, and the theory he knew he would never be able to test. He hesitated whether he should mention it to his friends. They could laugh at him and not believe a single word, they already had him for an incorrigible fantasist.

"I'll talk to Vandis about it," he finally decided, and the idea seemed quite reasonable to him.

Whoever Vandis was, his knowledge of supernatural phenomena had to be more extensive than theirs, so he could know something about what actually happened in Bluewaters.

After a moment he remembered that even if it was a good plan, there was one obstacle to its realization - that for now, they could locate neither Vandis nor Oggy, left under his care. Nobody answered the telephone number he left them, the apartment was empty, and no one knew where the detective had disappeared.

They couldn't go to the police for obvious reasons. For now, they settled in Vandis's apartment and waited, not very worried yet, because they did not know what exactly his therapy for Oggy was. Never, being a polyglot, looked into the detective's computer, specifically to the file inside it, made in several different languages and thus giving the impression of being encrypted. He wasn't doing well, because in addition, Vandis was using some outdated shorthand system, which obscured the already vague sense of the notes. Gerard wandered around trying to find any trail, but he returned to the apartment almost simultaneously with Fronda.

"So?" he asked, taking a bottle of blood from the fridge.

Theo sat in an armchair, hanging his long legs over one of the armrests, and resting his neck on the other in American way.

"Almost nobody saved," he replied. "Bluewaters has ceased to exist. Fill one for me too. Still no Vandis?"

"No," Gerard set a tall glass in front of him. "I'm starting to worry, you know? Maybe I wouldn't worry so much, after all it's not easy to hurt this angel, if it wasn't for our little girl disappearing with him.

"Oggy is a werewolf, not a kitten, we don't have to worry about her. For decades she was doing well without our care and it was fine," Theo growled.

He wasn't really as calm as he posed to. Oggy meant a lot more to him than he wanted to admit, and he worried about her deep in his knightly heart more than he should have.

"It's not funny," Never raised his head from the flashcards he studied, and looked at them. "I came across some interesting information here. The folders have different dates, but relate to the same case, and the latest note is from a week ago. It seems to be the last thing Vandis Winger was working on before disappearing."

"What is this case?" Gerard asked.

"I haven't translated everything yet," Rajah tapped his pen lightly on the notebook, in which he wrote down what seemed important to him. "It seems, however, that our friend got a job two years ago from desperate parents of a teenager, introduced by her friends to a vampire sect."

"What?!" Theo stared at him, his hand carrying a glass of blood frozen half way to his lips.

"Of course, Vandis corrected this message," Never continued. "In his opinion, this is the Satanist sect. Ultimately, anyone can drink blood, strong nerves are enough for that, you don't have to be a vampire. People, when they get bored, can find various shocking pastimes, and one of them is playing the worshipers of Satan, making animal and human sacrifices, black masses and other stuff like this... The fun becomes dangerous when it gets to murders, in addition, let's not forget that the human psyche is a very delicate instrument, easily twisted in any direction. Vandis has begun working on a group called Pentarog and if I can translate all the information, we will have a point of reference."

"You assume he got Oggy involved?" Gerard asked after a moment.

"It is possible." The Indian nodded and looked at the computer screen again.

"Two years..." Theo looked glumly at the window without finishing his thought.

Gerard understood him without words. Two years is a very long time in the world of ordinary people, and if someone like Vandis could not find a trail for twenty-four months, the situation looked almost hopeless.

They knew his capabilities and commitment, so it was hard to believe that finally finding an anchor point, he did not take advantage of the opportunity. But then where was he? Why did he take Oggy with him, even though he was working alone? So far there were only questions in this case, only the unknown. Gerard already knew that vampires rarely interfere in people's affairs, and they certainly do not work on solving their problems, but now their friend's safety was at stake. He didn't know much about sects, except that one had to stay away from them, but he knew that for the Satanists, catching someone like Vandis could be quite an event. Only how did they do it?

Gerard shook his head in desperation. He was ultimately just an actor, the long died star of the scene and screen, not a commando from a special intervention group. He never even played anyone like that, he had no idea where to start.

Fortunately, his friends had far more experience, so he could rely on them.

"Here are some bearings," Never monologized, looking through more records. "And dates at every location... He worked out these guys very methodically, though without any special results, or maybe he was delaying on purpose? Who knows. Anyway, we have a trail. Me and Fronda will check this information: tonight they are to celebrate a black mass combined with an annual human sacrifice. Fanfan stays in case Vandis returns, and besides, he is not properly prepared for such actions and would only be a drag for us."

He got up from the computer, took the bottle from the table and drank the rest of its contents in one gulp.

"Are you going to push me away from everything forever?" Gerard asked, frowning.

"Not forever. Only until we teach you something," Rajah answered him. "Understand, you are physically weak, badly damaged by illness and you will never be significantly stronger."

"But the perpetuation... your blood... After all, Theo has the strength of a bull."

"Fronda is such a strong man not because he became a vampire and not because he lives so long, but because he had always been strong and he was seasoned to be a knight from early childhood. You will have to rely not on physical strength, but on agility and intelligence, if you want to fight. In my spare time, I will teach you fighting that requires minimal energy, but it must take time. For now, stay here."

"All right," the actor murmured reluctantly.

He could not deny the sense of this reasoning, although he did not like staying in a safe place while his friends would set off on an interesting mission. Deep down, he was simply afraid of losing them again. Years of abandonment now appeared in his dreams as an unbelievable nightmare, and he was afraid of another such ordeal again. However, Never was right - Gerard's fighting skills were basically limited to show fencing and several flashy, but ineffective strikes, learned for the movie. In a direct battle he would be in a downright lost position.

Left alone, he turned on the television and for a long time tried to get interested in the action of the film that was broadcast, but it dealt with matters not only foreign to him, but also completely indifferent. With resignation, he turned off the TV and settled on the couch, closing his eyes.

He was going to sleep until his friends would return, since he couldn't do anything else. He couldn't even try to continue Never's work, for he didn't know as many languages as he did, a shorthand was foreign to him, and computers were a puzzle. They already belonged to a new age in which he was an intruder. Yes, he read the notes Never left, for lack of something better to do. But he understood very little from them and finally gave up.

He napped until noon. Friends were not back yet. It did not worry him too much, for he knew that they could take care of themselves, regardless of the circumstances. Faced with this spare time, he decided to visit Hope. He drank some blood, took a shower and went to the hospital. He could now walk the streets quite freely, no one remembered movie star from the fifties now, and he was safe from intrusive glances. He deluded himself that he was also safe from the Hunters, but he might have been wrong.

Hope was lying in her bed reading a book, but at the sound of the door opening, she raised her eyes and smiled reluctantly.

"Hi," she greeted him. "You are alone?"

"My buddies have something to do," he explained to her. "How are you feeling, ma cherie fille?"

"Not bad. My mother said that the day after tomorrow she would take me home," the girl replied. "Do you know anything about Tommy?"

Gerard got sad. He preferred not to mention this animal, but he could not help that it meant so much to the girl.

"Unfortunately not, but he rather has not drowned, because I saw him running down the road for a moment. I think he returned to his real owner," he said carefully.

Jeannie peered into the room.

"Oh, how nice that you came," she said happily.

The actor apologized to the child and walked out with the woman into the hallway.

"I'm very happy about this sudden improvement," he said. "I couldn't bear the thought that Hope was dying."

"It was a surprise to everyone, but I can't imagine that anything better could happen to me, even if I lived a hundred years," Jeannie said and turned to the plump black woman in a pink costume. "Mom, let me introduce to you Gerard Vadim, my friend. Were it not for him and his companions, I would have died in the flood, together with Hope."

He shook hands with the old lady, who gave him a warm smile.

"A friend in need is a friend indeed. Will you have dinner with us?" she asked.

"Forgive me, I can't, a religion forbids me," he said with some embarrassment. He didn't like to lie. "I'll stay with Hope while you ladies go to eat."

He had to repeat Never's ideas to avoid being exposed. Anyway, he really preferred the company of this child with too penetrating eyes than the women, whose honest gaze made him feel guilty. He felt like a villainous cheater.

"It's good they left," Hope said as he sat down next to her bed. "I wanted to talk to you in private. Grandma and mom could come in at any moment, and like this we have about an hour. Grandma eats slowly. As a child, she choked on something and is still cautious."

"What do you want to talk about?" he asked, smiling at her tenderly. She really reminded him of Anne-Marie, she had a similar look and expression of her lips.

The girl reached under the pillow and took out a film monthly magazine. She opened it on one of the pages marked with a bent corner, and showed him a black and white photo.

"It's you," she said. "Don't try to deny it. And your name is not Vadim, it's Phil. You can tell others a tale that it is a random similarity, but I will not believe you. Your buddies lie through their teeth, but you can't, I know well when you lie. It says here that you died in nineteen fifty-nine."

Gerard took the magazine and looked at the photo.

"Bad shot," he said dryly. "What do you want to know, Hope?"

"To know? I already know. You are a vampire, and so are your friends, too. At some point I understood it, just as you begin to understand letters while learning to write," said the girl calmly. "That's why you stayed young. I guess that's why you didn't die. Tell me one thing: why did you help me? What was in it for you?"

Gerard sighed. He did not foresee such a turn of events, although it surprised him less than one would expect.

"We are not bad," he decided to get things out in the open. "We're really almost normal people, mentally anyway. We know how to love, be afraid and feel compassion like others. Is that so strange? Me and Never are a little unusual, because the sun harms us less than others, but it does not change the facts. What now?"

Hope laughed.

"I like you," she said, putting the magazine under her pillow again. "Especially your buddy with black eyes. He's divinely beautiful. But you are not bad either. Don't worry, I won't say a word to anyone, I know there are those who hunt people like you. The bastards. They are not concerned about the good of humanity, they just envy you. Will you play something with me? I'm bored."

Gerard embraced her spontaneously and kissed her forehead. It was not the first time he came to the conclusion that it was better to be friends with children than with adults, and deep down he regretted that there was no place for them in the world of vampires.

He spent the entire afternoon playing checkers and Parcheesi with the girl, but when he returned to the apartment, his friends were not there yet.

"I guess they'll be back at night," he thought. "I'll eat something, watch the news, and take the opportunity to have a good night's sleep."

He was almost asleep when the door slammed. He jumped to his feet, instinctively searching for a weapon. However, it was not the enemy that rushed into the apartment, but Oggy, shaken, in a torn dress.

"Gerard!" She shouted. "You are back?! Where are the others?"

"They went looking for you," he replied, looking at her in amazement. "What happened?"

The girl sank into one of the chairs.

"Something terrible has happened," she moaned. "Something terrible. Vandis was imprisoned by Satanists whom he followed. His power doesn't work on them. They must really have pact with Satan himself. They locked us in a basement. Vandis managed to free me, though I don't know how, and told me to run away, bring the police, but I can't go to the police station without documents! Where's my card?"

Gerard grabbed her by the shoulders.

"Calm down," he demanded sharply. "No police. Before they decide to do something, it will be too late. Never read on Vandis' computer that the sacrifice was to be made that night, so there is no time to waste. Take me to this place."

The girl nodded.

"You know what to do?" she asked quietly.

"I have no idea," said the actor curtly. "But Rajah and Fronda are probably already there, they just don't know that it is Vandis that is to be sacrificed. And there is no Satan, understand? This is a bunch of youngsters on high and that's it."

"You say that because you haven't seen them. Because you weren't there with me. But since your wish is to get to know the dark powers, I will take you there," Oggy was dead serious.

Apparently what had happened to her and Vandis must have been really scary.

Gerard shook her, irritated.

"There are no dark powers!" He shouted. "There are only people obsessed with the insane idea! Lead me to them, we must warn Rajah and Fronda. I don't know if they found the information about the place of the rituals in Vandis's records, but if so, they may be in trouble. Satanists probably know how to kill vampires."

Oggy quickly changed into a tracksuit, giving up further attempts to convince her friend. The sect guru who imprisoned Vandis had a tremendous gift of persuasion and could scare anyone, so it was not surprising that she too succumbed to his influence and was trembling with fear. Perhaps Theo would be able to calm her down, but he wasn't here, and Gerard remembered at this very wrong time the ghostly dog from Bluewaters, and felt uneasy himself. His whole sensible, materialistic worldview was falling apart, and despite the greatest effort, he was not able to assemble anything sensible from these debris. However, he desperately refused to believe in the devil, it was definitely too much for him.

Oggy led him through the night streets of Chicago all the way outside the city, to a great cemetery in a classic style, overgrown with old trees, and very black at this hour. You had to be a really brave person or have a strong motivation to get in here.

"I didn't become a vampire to be afraid of cemeteries," Gerard thought, straining his eyes to see something and biting his lips to control his nervousness.

Between the tombstones, far in the depths of the necropolis, a light loomed, as if a distant reflection of a fire.

"It's them," the girl whispered, trembling at his side.

Gerard reached into his pocket and clenched his fingers on the handle of the little browning. He brought it cautiously, though he wasn't sure that it would help him. Never always insisted on weapons, but he, a pacifist by nature, did not like weapons and did not handle them well.

They crept closer to the looming flames and froze still. A circle of figures in black hooded cloaks surrounded one of the graves, exceptionally stately, with a monument in the form of a pedestal, on which lay a naked girl with loose hair, and torch flames cast flickering lights on her tattooed skin. A little lower, on a wide marble platform, three expertly gagged men lay tied to a slab, in whom one could easily recognize Vandis, Never and Fronda.

"Satanists torture their victims during black masses and then drink their blood before they kill them," Oggy whispered.

"That's not good. I don't know what the effect of drinking Vandis's blood would be for them, but Rajah and Theo... This poses a threat of the appearance of more mentally twisted vampires," whispered her companion anxiously.

He still couldn't figure out what to do, and in addition, new sect members kept coming.

"Damn, too many of them," he muttered, biting his fingers irritably.

Satanists were slowly chanting some disturbing melody with words he did not understand, but sensed their sinister content. He did not understand how Never and Fronda could have allowed to be caught so stupidly, but he understood how wrong he was in his assessment of the opponents.

Regardless to whom those people performed their ardent acts, they were dangerous and clearly dumbfounded by their ideology. It could not be ruled out that it gave them some real strength. The sects' influence can reach even the highest state structures, just as it was with Freemasonry. In addition, if this group operated unobstructed, they must have had powerful protectors.

A tall man now entered the tombstone and placed a large, golden goblet on the girl's belly.

"Glory be to Azazel!" cried the girl.

"Glory be!" the fellow believers answered her in chorus.

Gerard looked around helplessly and his eyes fell on one of the tombstones, made of already crumbling limestone.

"Help me, Oggy," he whispered, taking a folding knife from his pocket.

He began to scrape the limestone frantically, trying to do it as quietly as possible.

"What do you want to do?" asked the girl in amazement.

"I can't fight like them," he said desperately, without interrupting his work. "But I'm an actor and we have to use it. I can't make it without you."

He took off his shirt and began rubbing his face, chest and arms with the limestone dust. Oggy, finally understanding what he meant, took care of his back.

"Give me that burned piece of wood now," Gerard pointed to one of the tombstones.

He drew circles around his eyes with charred wood, highlighted the ribs and outline of the jaws, and the girl marked the bones of the shoulder blades and the spine on his back.

"I will distract them and you free the boys," he instructed her, handing her the knife.

"Can you scare them?" she asked doubtfully.

"I won't know if I don't try," he said grimly. "Anyway, the most important thing that I keep their attention, that will probably be enough. Remember, you must act quickly. If time runs out, at least tear off Rajah's gag."

Oggy nodded. Made up with limestone dust and charcoal, the actor loomed before her in the dark like a ghostly phantom. She had some doubts as to whether such a view would frighten the people praying to Satan, but one had to try. She crept quietly into the back of the gravestone serving as the altar and waited, clutching the knife handle.

The blasphemous rite continued and Oggy thought sympathetically of Theo. How awful it had to be for him to participate in such a thing, even as a passive spectator or a future sacrifice. He, a practicing Catholic despite his transformation and the passage of time, who strongly believed in what he had been taught to believe centuries ago, had to experience indescribable psychological torture. He always felt everything more intensely than others.

She looked at the Satanists swaying to the chanted words and suddenly understood how they had managed to lure Never and Fronda into a trap. There were few adults in the group, mostly teenagers, and even several children, as she noticed in horror. Theo had his principles and it was hard to imagine him hitting a child. He probably didn't suspect them to be his enemies until it was too late. This age structure of the group allowed, however, to hope that Gerard's plan would not fail.

"It must succeed," she whispered to herself, gripping the knife handle more tightly.

She would feel much more confident in her canine form, but she couldn't take it on now because she needed her hands. She didn't know where and when Gerard would appear, and she squeaked softly in surprise when she saw him behind the guru performing the ceremony. In a flash of understanding, she realized that it was the only logical and safe solution, especially since the guru did not immediately notice that something unusual was happening.

Gerard didn't give anyone time to come to their senses: he simply grabbed the sect's leader by the shoulders and dug his teeth into his neck. He had never obtained food this way before, unless when he was wandering befuddled around the world, but he did it for the first time consciously. He found the bite site almost instinctively and felt an unknown to him shiver as blood spurted from the bitten artery.

He drank greedily for a moment, then threw the bleeding man aside and jumped onto the plate, where the tattooed girl was lying, frozen in terror. He grabbed the goblet and threw it over the heads of the gathered, then he jumped to the ground and moved like a ghost from another world among the sect members, who stepped aside before him. He knew he had time until they would recover from the initial shock, and Oggy had to free their friends during this time. He hoped that none of the Satanists would think of touching him. In that case they would find out that they were dealing with a person of flesh and blood, no more devilish than themselves.

He felt that the members of the sect were in the grips of the superstitious horror, and that horror played in his favor. He knew, however, that when this fear would leave them, both he and his friends would be in a real danger.

The safe moment did not last long: the girl serving as a living altar, apparently more experienced, was first to get over the surprise, turned on her stomach and shouted:

"The prisoners are running away!"

Her words caused the spell cast by Gerard to burst like a soap bubble. The Satanists howled with one voice. The actor turned abruptly, but only managed to see the backs of his friends, disappearing in the distance. A wolf ran after them, getting caught in a tracksuit, and barking desperately. The stress caused by the unusual situation was too strong and poor Oggy did not manage to keep her human form, despite previous training.

"Capture the blasphemer!" The tattooed girl shouted, hopping off the tombstone.

She ran to the guru, lying motionless, and began to examine him, while her fellow believers overpowered the actor, desperately fighting back. Someone brought a rag, wet it under a water tap nearby, and unceremoniously wiped the ghostly makeup off Gerard's body.

"So that's what it is..." he whistled through his teeth. "You'll regret getting in our way, smart ass."

"Darla, what about Washtar?" cried another one, maybe fifteen-year-old boy with a freckled face. "Can he finish the rite?"

"Washtar will not celebrate today's service," replied the tattooed girl. "Maybe he won't do it ever again. Our prisoners escaped, and the interrupted ritual doesn't bode well for the future. We must make at least a propitiation sacrifice, otherwise we will expose ourselves to the wrath of our Lord and his anger would be terrible. I'll run the ceremony myself."

She emerged from the darkness, moving as freely as if she had not noticed her nakedness at all, and approached Gerard, who was held by several pairs of hands. Up close, she seemed older and more demonic, which was largely influenced by an unusual makeup: black-painted lips and eyelids, black triangles on the cheeks. The actor shuddered.

"Tie him to the tree," she instructed her fellow believers.

They obeyed her immediately, thus showing that she was someone no less important than the guru himself. They tied the actor's hands to the branches of a young poplar, growing nearby. Gerard struggled for a moment, but the springy bough was stronger than him, and the cords too solid to break. He didn't understand why his friends had left him like this, but after a while he realized that it wasn't any malice on their part. They simply had never seen a black mass before and, not recognizing him, they could think that it was a part of the rite, and Oggy in the dog form could not explain anything to them.

"I'm all alone," he realized in a panic.

"Heat up the sign!" Darla called imperatively.

One of the Satanists turned on the machine, from which a bluish flame began to go out with a bang. He directed it at the iron he was given, resembling a cattle stamp. Darla intoned a grotesque sounding song in a high-pitched voice. When others joined, she took the stamp from a fellow believer, and approached Gerard.

"To Azazel's glory!" She called out. "Oh, the great prince of darkness, receive this atoning sacrifice from us!"

The actor howled in pain when the hot iron touched his bare torso, leaving a burned pentagram mark on it.

"He's yours, Azazel, he's yours!" Darla shouted triumphantly.

She tossed the iron and returned to the pedestal, reciting something that sounded like a litany with her arms raised high. Now two men armed with leather whips approached Gerard, and the first blows fell on his bare back. The satanists drowned out his scream by singing some scary song. Gerard writhed under painful blows, screaming and sobbing alternately, feeling he was losing his mind and all hope of rescue.

"Enough!" Darla cried finally, and the awful song died down. "He's yours!"

Satanists jumped to Gerard, licking the blood drops from his skin. Some, apparently more dumbfounded, bit into his wounded body as if in sexual ecstasy. He surrendered to them, thinking that there was no longer rescue him, and wishing with all his heart that all this would finally end.

Meanwhile, the refugees, who were already far outside the cemetery, stopped to catch their breath.

"What on earth is it with this girl?" Never asked, pointing to Oggy, who was snarling, barking pleadingly, and obviously trying to turn them around.

"Wait," Vandis knelt down and grabbed the wolf's head.

After a short while, Oggy assumed a human form and, panting heavily, ran to Theo.

"Why did you run away?!" She called in despair. "You left Gerard there!"

"Oh, no," Fronda moaned.

Never took off his shirt and tossed it to the girl.

"Cover yourself," he commanded her. "Now I understand everything. We have to go back there, but I really don't know how to free him. There are too many of them, and we have no weapons. It will be too late before we bring the police."

Vandis straightened up.

"Wait a moment," he said. "We have to use triangulation."

"What? Isn't it a bearing method?" cried Never, feeling he is losing his mind.

"Not only. Come, I have to give you some of my power and explain what you have to do. Listen and don't ask anything because we don't have time," said the detective firmly.

His eyes glistened in the dark with golden-blue light like precious stones, as he lectured his friends on the essence of his plan, and, with the touch of his hand, gave them a stream of energy, burning like nettles. They listened in amazement, wanting to protest against something so crazy, but to their amazement they could not. This strange man could control their will, feelings, even the way of thinking. It was scary to think how much evil he could do if he only wanted to.

They returned to the cemetery, trying not to make noise along the way, which was unnecessary caution, considering the singing of the Satanists, carried throughout the entire cemetery. They hurriedly took up the positions designated by Vandis.

Members of the sect continued to perform their rite under Darla's leadership, which reassured friends - Satanists usually kill their victims only at the end of the ceremony, and this one apparently was not coming to an end yet. Darla was reciting ritual verses, and her fellow believers answered her chorally, swaying to the rhythm of the spoken words.

Vandis unexpectedly appeared by the tattooed girl and put a hand on her bare shoulder. The surprised Satanist fell silent. Never and Theo, spaced by the detective so that they formed the other two vertices of the isosceles triangle, closed their eyes at this sign and focused as much as they could, just like he had previously asked them to.

They immediately sensed what he was talking about - they were jerked with such force that they could barely stand on their feet, as if they were connected to a high voltage transformer. The noise around them fell silent as if cut off with a knife. What Vandis tried to do, was incomprehensible to them, but they trusted him, yielding to a subconscious impulse. They were helpless themselves in the face of what was happening, unable to stand up to the opponent that outnumbered them. However, what they felt now was so unpleasant, that when the force finally ceased, they greeted it with a groan of relief, and staggered, opening their eyes.

The scenery around them apparently did not change: they were still in the cemetery, lit by dozens of torches placed on the graves, but the atmosphere of terror was gone. The Satanists took the hoods off their heads and looked around in amazement, a few younger ones began to cry, a thin voice called for mother hysterically.

Vandis stepped off the pedestal, leading Darla by the hand, and covered her with one of the abandoned coats.

"Calm down," he said in a steady, calm voice. "You are free. Return to your families and don't believe the people who persuade you to do evil any more. If you want to meet, you can do it during the day and not at the cemetery."

The sect members got rid of their ceremonial coats one by one, hurriedly, as if in shame, and went away into the night. Those who were older, took care of the younger ones protectively. Soon the cemetery was almost empty.

Vandis looked at Darla and put his hand on her forehead.

"I feel the good in you," he said gently. "Develop and nurture it, and it will bring you happiness. Go in peace."

The girl wrapped her coat tighter and walked away, looking back every few steps, as if she was afraid of some trick. Vandis looked sadly at her.

"Poor, lost soul," he whispered so softly that Never barely heard him.

Theo and Oggy, who had just arrived, cut the rope that restrained their friend's arms and held him as he slumped to the ground.

"He is in a state of total hysteria," Fronda reported anxiously, watching the wounds on Gerard's body by the glow of the torch, and looking at his mad eyes.

Vandis turned his inscrutable gaze towards him.

"I'm sorry," he said softly. "I can't help him anymore."

"What's wrong with you?" Never grabbed him and carefully placed him on the ground.

The concerned friends gathered around the detective, even Gerard immediately forgot about the hell that had happened to him, and bent his pale face over him.

"Vandis, what's wrong with you?" Oggy cried out tearfully.

He smiled weakly.

"Nothing," he replied. "I'm dying, that's all."

"No, it is not possible! How come? You? And nothing can be done about it?" Theo looked at Never for help, but he shrugged helplessly.

"Nothing," Vandis said calmly. "But you don't need to worry about that. You forget that I'm not human like you. Your lives are tragically short, so all your efforts are directed towards prolonging your existence. We live in indefinite time, so our goal is not life but death. That's what we want, what we envy you. How wonderful it must be to always be aware that it is so easy to stop suffering, achieve peace and silence... This is not given to us. I have exhausted my possibilities all the way to the bottom, absorbing and neutralizing evil in the amount that has accumulated here, and this is killing me."

"Nooo..." Oggy wailed, covering her face with her hands.

Vandis touched her shoulder with his fingers.

"You didn't understand?" He whispered gently. "It's the best thing that could happen to me. I'm dying. Finally. After so many centuries, millennia. Can there be anything more wonderful? Finally, I will reach a state that is basically only available to people, a state that every one of us longs for and desires. For you, fleeting insects of eternity, this may indeed be incomprehensible, but take my word for it, I'm more happy than I've ever been before. You are afraid of death, it appears to you as a skeleton with a scythe, but for us it has the form of a gently smiling sister of mercy, whose touch brings relief and is sweet as a dream after a hard day."

"We will miss you, Angel Without Wings," Gerard whispered sadly, leaning his head helplessly against Fronda's shoulder.

Vandis smiled at him.

"Will you believe that you are the first and only friends I had?" He said with an effort. "I've achieved much more than any of my kinsmen and when I think about it, I don't regret anything."

"Why exactly does it have to be this way?" Theo was supporting Vandis's head with both hands, and therefore he was unable to wipe the tears flowing down his cheeks. He cried for the first time since Gerard, and even Never, knew him.

"I won't be able to explain it to you," Vandis looked away from him and sighed slightly. "I'm leaving. Goodbye."

His voice died, his body went limp in the arms supporting it, and got still, stiffening in one position.

*****

"Don't move away from me. I know it hurts," Never treated Gerard's wounds with some bad smelling ointment, burning like fire. "It will help you. It will stop hurting soon, you have to endure a little longer. Unfortunately, opiates don't work on vampires the same way as on humans. This is interesting, but although we are susceptible to most anesthetics to the same extent as people, analgesics do not affect us at al. I could give you ether by inhalation, but I prefer this way. The pain will stop and you will be conscious."

"Really?" Gerard asked through clenched teeth.

"Well, at least that would follow from my theory," answered the Indian. "They made real mess with you. Fortunately, it wasn't anyone of us, because it would cause a tragedy. Your blood is not active yet and it cannot perpetuate anybody, so it doesn't matter that some crazies have licked it. These scars will heal quickly, but the pentagram on your chest will unfortunately remain for some time."

Gerard buried his face in his hands.

"Terrible," he groaned.

"Don't whine, kid," said Theo comfortingly. "You are not alone in your misery. Look."

He pulled off his shirt and showed him his left arm. The convex, irregularly shaped scar did not differ much in color from the skin, but it was still visible and perfectly felt under the fingers.

"You too?" the actor looked at his friend in disbelief. He nodded.

"I was disgraced in public, without the consideration for what I experienced before," he replied. "I was accused of treason and as it was not proven during the trial that I was acting deliberately, and because my young age aroused compassion (I was barely nineteen), I was only sentenced to flogging, stigmatization and banishment. This word basically only meant that I had no access to Paris area. The thing is, I was innocent and in my naivety I thought that if I did not admit anything during the interview, they would believe me. I was tortured for two days before being brought before the royal court."

"They didn't believe you?" Oggy asked sympathetically.

"No," he confirmed. "King John was in captivity at the time, and his son did not want to make a mistake in releasing the guilty, so he convicted me, although the evidence was weak. The next day I was tied up naked to the pillory, whipped without mercy and stigmatized, and then the people chased me away with stones outside Paris, as it was customary."

"That's terrible!" Gerard called out. "Why were you treated so cruelly?"

Theo shrugged.

"I have already said, that was the custom," he explained. "It was called 'consecrating out of the city' and everyone took part in it willingly, because it seemed to people that they were acting fairly and having a lot of fun at this. Besides, don't forget, Fanfan, they took me for a traitor who gave the secret plans to the English. Most of the Parisian population were of the opinion that the dauphin was too kind to me anyway, because he should have me quartered or skinned. He probably would have done it, but he had doubts, and it worked in my favor. Later the case was cleared, and I even had the opportunity to return to Paris in the glory of the hero, but before then... Humiliation was worse than pain, just think, in those days the stigmatization of a noble-born knight was tantamount to trampling him in the mud, and then this whipping... I didn't want to live when it happened and I begged the quack friend for some fast-acting poison. He had mercy on me and prepared some decoction for me, which could poison ten people, according to his words. However, I survived, although I have to admit to you that I was sick like never before in my life and on top of that, got a reprimand from the priest."

"I think they didn't mention it in the TV show," Never said.

"Sure. This story was totally non attractive for media," Theo shrugged and buttoned his shirt.

Gerard touched the pentagram on his chest and hissed in pain. It was depressing to know that he would wear it on his skin, perhaps for the rest of his life. To make things worse, he had always been against tattooing, and ultimately such a stigma is not much different from a tattoo.

"But how come Vandis's forces ran out so suddenly?" Oggy asked after a moment from her corner.

The friends still lived in the detective's apartment, benefiting from the fact that he had paid the rent for six months in advance. They wanted to take some rest before continuing their journey. They could do it, because another order from Octavio, to be picked up with the password at the main post office, was not there yet.

"Maybe the triangulation method he used turned out to be too heavy for him? It seems to me that it requires three specimens of the same species as Vandis, and without having two others on hand, he poured his power on us and this did him in," Never said after some consideration. "On the other hand, though, Vandis was supposedly a legend already during the Roman Empire, which means that he had to be incredibly resistant to destruction. Maybe the loss of wings weakened his regenerative abilities?"

"We have no indication that he ever had them," Theo remarked. "We don't even know who he really was. Even I don't really believe that he was a real Angel."

He sank into thoughts. He got to like Vandis, no matter who he was. It didn't matter, after all.

"What shall we tell Jeannie Meadows when she asks us about him? What will we say when anybody at all asks us?" Gerard noticed with relief that the pain in his battered body was indeed a bit duller and weaker.

"We won't say anything. In general, we will disappear from here as soon as you recover. I don't want police on my back," Never said.

He was really fed up not only with Chicago but with all of America. He knew from the news that an exsanguinated man of undetermined identity had been found in the cemetery. And he didn't even want to guess why nothing was said about finding Vandis's body. Once, even quite recently, he would gladly investigate this matter himself, but now he preferred to stay away from it. Compared to things the existence of which they had recently discovered, their own existence was something most mundane in the world.

He looked at his friends with brotherly tenderness. They have already changed the subject of the conversation.

"The movie unnecessarily idealizes the Middle Ages," Theo explained to Oggy, and Gerard listened to it with interest. "Those were terrible times, I say this from personal experience. The filth, stench and poverty. I also don't understand how the writers can see anything romantic in hiding in the woods. You get nephritis from sleeping on the bare ground, there is nowhere to wash, especially in winter. Hunger is common regardless of the season of the year. In winter, you go crazy with boredom, you get rheumatism from the wind rushing through your hideout. In the spring there's nothing left to eat and your belly is sucked up to your spine. And in summer and autumn, all kinds of vermin eat you alive. What is romantic about it? I survived all this and I guarantee you that the life of the so-called forest knight is terribly down to earth."

"You didn't find any pleasure in it?" Gerard was surprised.

"When you are young, you get used to everything," his friend replied enigmatically. "Besides, did I know anything else? Only from the perspective of the twentieth century can I see how terrible it all was."

Never approached him.

"Did you really have to kill your sister?" he asked in a seemingly indifferent voice.

He thought about this revelation for a long time, and he couldn't quite imagine it. He belonged to a different era already.

Theo gave him a hard look.

"What was I supposed to do?" He replied aggressively. "Give Odette to the rapes of angry soldiers? She was just under twelve years old. It was a universally recognized procedure then: if the knight could not defend the honor of the lady entrusted to him against defilement, he had to kill her. Death is pure."

"You're talking rubbish as if you were stoned," Gerard muttered with an involuntary shiver.

"No, it really was like this, I read about it somewhere," Never rubbed his mouth with the back of his hand. "Let's not jump into judging things too fast. Fronda did not mention all this to us, and he was right, for us the life in his epoch is completely incomprehensible. I shouldn't have brought it up again. Let's forget the past and live only with what the present brings us, otherwise we will all go crazy."

"Are you saying we're normal?" Oggy asked wryly.

She walked over to Fronda and hugged his side, embracing his arm with her hands. He kissed her absentmindedly on the cheek.

"You know what? I will go to the main post office, maybe there is already something there," Never said after a moment and ran out of the apartment with relief.

After all the revelations he heard, he wanted to walk a bit and cool down. Fronda was sometimes an embarrassing company even for him, and his confessions could be shocking, so he tried not to provoke them. His own experience in India was pretty nasty, but what his friend was saying sometimes, bristled the hair on his head. It was a miracle that he remained relatively stable mentally.

He wandered the streets for a while, then headed to the post office, where he received, to his surprise, an elongated blue envelope. It certainly wasn't there that morning when he was asking the clerk for the news for the password "Seville". He wasn't really happy about it, but on the other hand he had to admit that the next order could prove to be salutary - far too much had happened here lately, and they needed a change.

"I hope the new task will require us to leave this schizophrenic country," he thought as he opened the envelope.

Even without the encryption key he could read the message, which turned out to be completely satisfactory. Satisfied, he returned to the apartment, where everyone was preparing to go to bed.

"Sleep well, my monsters," he said, waving the envelope. "Octavio demands from us to come to Spain, as soon as possible. We are coming back to Europe."

"Perfect. I already missed the Old World," grunted Gerard, straightening his arms with involuntary grimace of his lips. "Here it is definitely too witchy, noisy and ruthless. I don't like America, I've never liked it."

Never looked at Fronda, who was sitting on the couch, leaning against the wall and mechanically scratching the dog, holding a big head on his lap, behind the ears.

"Don't ask me for my opinion, you all know it anyway," he said sleepily.

"It's decided then. Everyone goes to bed. Tomorrow at dusk we are moving to Europe," the Indian tossed the envelope on the table and went to take a shower before bed.

"It all ended better than I thought," he muttered to himself, rinsing the dust and fatigue of recent days off his swarthy skin. "I just don't know where this choking sadness comes from."

There was a bit of hypocrisy in those words because in fact he knew well what was wrong with him. He never thought that he would become so attached to someone he had seen only a few times, and with whom he had absolutely nothing in common. Vandis, however, was indeed an extraordinary being, different in every inch, and made people have warm feelings for him, even against their will. Now that he was gone, it was not only Never who felt that the world became poorer and more sad. Vandis's body was not found, but everyone who knew him, knew he was dead, and it is not exactly clear how and why they took this awareness as something natural.

No one wondered how the message got to them, because there was no mention of it in the press or on television, the police took no steps, and yet they knew. Everyone knew. Jeannie Meadows sat all night on the balcony of her mother's house, smoking one cigarette after another.

Hope cried into the pillow until she got tired and fell asleep.

The juvenile drug addict, whom he had recently found on the orders of her parents, called her father from the rehab and apologized to him for all the trouble.

The countless others, often thousands and tens of thousands of miles from Chicago, woke up, paused their work or play, stopped on the road with a sudden sense of irreparable loss, realizing after a moment what had happened.

Rajah tried to suppress in himself the feelings he was not used to, but it was a hopeless fight. He had not learned how to deal with such circumstances. True, neither he nor any of his many friends had ever come across anyone like Vandis over the centuries, at most they had heard stories about them starting with "I heard that...".

Similar stories spread among humans, but the vampires, despite their otherness, or maybe thanks to it, kept a sober look at the world, and it would take something truly unusual to amaze them. The strangest one among their company was Shadow, but everyone was used to his inexplicability, and no one thought about it anymore. Ghosts, demons, ghouls, all this shunned the "children of the night," and Never did not remember any of his kin ever come across such a thing. A ghoul dog would be an exception - if you believed in him. Because there was no tangible evidence.

Rajah, however, did not believe that all events related to this animal could not be logically explained. Only Vandis eluded all the rules he knew.

"The law of a series," he said to himself as he left the bathroom. "Nothing happened for ages, and now all kind of weird things almost at the same time. I wonder what else awaits us."

"I wouldn't be so curious in your place. For now, what has happened is enough for me," Gerard muttered from under the blanket.

"Me too," Theo agreed sleepily. "It's good that we're coming back to Europe. It is somehow more normal there, after all, although I do not think that supernatural events are reserved for America."

"There is nothing supernatural in this world," Oggy said firmly.

"Look who is saying this?" Never laughed without joy.

He wondered if Vandis had managed to teach her enough control over her wolf nature, but he decided not to ask. It could not be improved anymore anyway. He patted the girl, curled up next to Fronda, on the neck, as if patting a dog.

"Let's sleep now," he said. "We need to regenerate after everything that happened to us here."

He lay down on his mattress and closed his eyes. As usual, he fell asleep without trouble. He just didn't know why that night, instead of the abstract pictures usual for him, like a Salvatore Dali painting, he dreamed of a fairly ordinary town and a fairly ordinary seasonal worker living in a hut off the beaten track. He had long hair, clearly Indian features, and would not have attracted anyone's attention were it not for the red flash in his eyes when he looked at Never's face. And a mysterious smirk, half malicious and half infinitely sad.

TO BE CONTINUED......

www.ingramcontent.com/pod-product-compliance
Lightning Source LLC
Chambersburg PA
CBHW020838020726
47497CB00005B/1148